I0551862

THE ZENITH'S SPY

DAMEON COX

Lezen Publishing

The Zenith's Spy

Lezen Publishing, LLC.

This book is a work of fiction. Names, characters, locations
and events are either a product of
the author's imagination, fictitious or used fictitiously. Any
resemblance to any event,
locale or person, living or dead, is purely coincidental.

Original Cover Concept: Kästle Olson
Map Illustrations: Kästle Olson

Manufactured in the United States of America
Library of Congress Control Number: 2014941156
Lezen Publishing, LLC, Phoenix, AZ
ISBN 978-0-9960063-0-9

In loving memory of
Lillie Mae Cox
always devoted, always supportive

Dedicated to
Raul R Whyte
a true friend

THE ZENITH SERIES MAPS

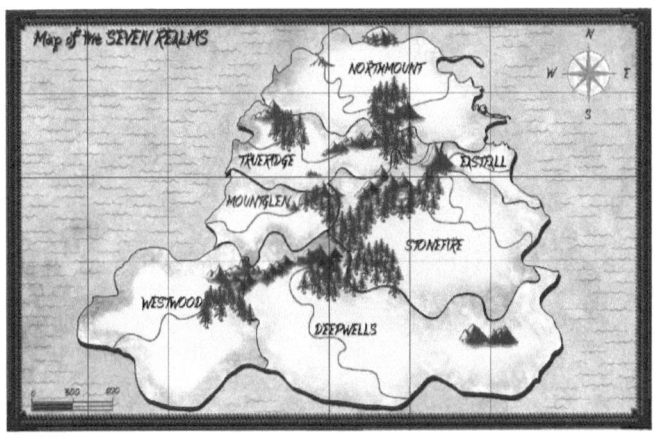

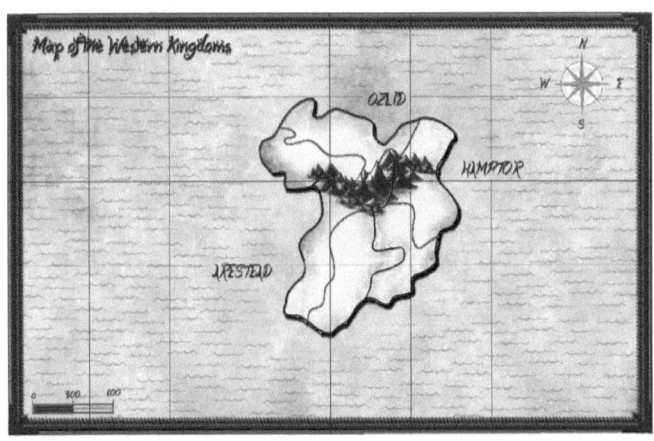

PART ONE

1

ZACK Stand rode up the mountainside with the bandit band of nearly four hundred led by Gaston, waiting for the Guard to spring their trap. The road had a sheer, half-mile drop off on the west, and thick deep evergreen woods on the east. Chill winds buffeted the men. The lack of traffic left the ground rocky and in poor condition, with dead trees littering the way in several places.

He wondered when the Guard would make its move. *My message must have gotten through . . . I hope!* He prayed for a good outcome, it was too late to do much else. They rounded a bend in the road, and Zack saw a wide, barren field to the east.

"AMBUSH!" The scout galloped back toward the bandit horde, fear radiating from him. Sharp bugle blasts underscored the warning. Guardsmen galloped out from both ends, north and south of their position, closing in on their enemy. Polished boots over royal blue trousers, gleaming swords drawn from a black baldric over a red tunic made an impressive sight.

Startled men cursed. The drop off forced the bandits onto the open field. Some looked for avenues of escape. The thick forest would slow them to a crawl, leaving them an easy target for men following on foot. Others scrambled into hurried defensive formations.

A flash of steel drew Zack's attention to Gaston, the bandit chief. "You bastards, fight the Guard or fight me! Form a square, damn it!" he shouted, cutting down one

1

of his men who tried to flee. With threats and curses, his lieutenants forced others toward the battleground.

At last, Zack thought. Galloping to the far end of the field with the others, he turned to estimate the attacking Guard force. His heart sank. *Damn, they're no more than two hundred; they're outnumbered two to one. Where are the reinforcements? We planned for this contingency. Will they remember? I don't want to slice up my own men!*

Looking for a plausible foe, Zack rode into bloody chaos. Screams from horses and men filled the air. A guardsman met Zack's charge and attacked with a full-on sword stroke. The steel-on-steel clash radiated up his arm.

A Guard officer forced his way between them, and ordered the guardsman away. A nod of recognition eased Zack's turmoil. They sparred back and forth while edging their horses out of the melee's confusion. Spellbinder, a well-trained warhorse, did not recognize the potentially fatal game Zack was playing; he pushed forward in full attack. Selected guardsmen alternated their assault against Zack. These kinds of battles rarely lasted more than a quarter-hour, but the constant battle blows without follow through and pulling his sword strokes began to tire him more than a real encounter and his joints began to ache. Charge, clash, engage, break off and re-engage, for show not death, left his mind as stressed as his body.

The latest guardsman Zack sparred against faced away from the main fighting when a bandit charged at the other man's unprotected back. Zack signaled Spellbinder with a knee; the gelding pushed the guardsman's mount to the side. Zack's sword missed the guardsman by inches and pierced the bandit's throat. Blood splattered against Zack's face and shirt. The bandit dropped his reins and his horse pitched him from his saddle, galloping off. The bandit's foot, caught in its stirrup, dragging the body over rocky ground, battering it into a bloody mess.

That little action could get me killed if anyone saw it happen. Will this ever end? Zack thought.

As if responding to Zack's question, the bugler blasted the signal to regroup. Guardsmen galloped toward the road to the south, killing several more men on the way. No one followed. Zack observed many bloodied bandits and several guardsmen on the blood-soaked ground. He saw several dozen more criminals herded together under guard. *Gaston has lost many; his men are untrained for this kind of fight. Even outnumbered, the Guard did well.*

Gaston signaled his remaining men, and they galloped north. A mile up the road, he ordered two men to lag back and insure the Guard did not follow them into the mountains; if guardsmen did follow, Gaston ordered them to ride forward to warn him. Zack hid his pleasure at the anger on the bandit leader's face.

Zack rode near the front of the column, close to Gaston's lieutenants, looking for harbingers of detection. He found none, but knew Gaston's men would report after they reached their base. If enough men had noticed his less-than-deadly actions, he might be accused of being a traitor.

Memories of Gaston's barbarism haunted him. Accusing two men of betraying him, the bandit leader had tortured them for three days, cutting off various body parts and forced pieces down their throats until they were barely conscious. Finally, he'd ordered their legs tied to different horses and had them pulled apart over agonizing minutes, a slow, gory death. *If he discovers my treachery, my death will surpass anything I saw.* Memories of his wife and daughter replaced those of ripped, mangled bodies. *I can endure anything except not to see them again. Will I get out of here alive?* Apprehension tingled through him as he searched for signs of discovery.

Gaston had never told him the exact location of the camp, and the mountains surrounding it included too many dells and small valleys to search effectively. Zack had had no recourse but to continue on with them, and once he'd found the location, escape.

3

Dark shadows covered the encampment's cleared area when they limped in. Those men that collected food from the cook's tent ate little. The survivors snapped at their companions as they spread out to their campsites in small groups. Little conversation flowed across smoky fires. Zack joined two men at the fire near his belongings. He ate silently and listened.

"Damn, I never saw anything like it. They cut us to pieces. I saw Brack's arm fly over my head. I can still hear his screams."

"Gaston was a fool to attack them. We should've run and fought them on our ground."

"It wouldn't make any difference—those Guard bastards know how to fight. I think we lost close to two hundred. Gaston must be pissed. The damn caravan had best be worth it."

Zack pushed their words from his mind as he rubbed protective oil on his sword blade while staring into the fire. Reflections from the flames leapt along the glistening metal and calmed his nerves, but not his nervousness. His body still ached from the day's fighting. One recurring thought plagued him: *Will I get out of here alive?*

He realized the bandit's losses would curtail their activities along the trading routes and that brought a brief smile hidden by the cowl pulled low across his forehead. The larger goal of the band's complete capture remained elusive if the Guard couldn't find the encampment. Zack had spent months planting the information that five large caravans would combine for safety. Gaston's men rarely formed into one group; the five-caravans-into-one story had tempted him to bring his scattered forces together in the hope of carrying out a huge strike. The Guardsmen must capture them before they split apart again. *If the reinforcements had arrived in time, I would be enjoying ale with Guard officers instead of worrying about accusations. This last mission before retiring from fieldwork has had one complication after another.* Zack's thoughts drifted to his wife and daughter.

He longed for their touch and embrace.

Romar, Gaston's second in command and favorite, swaggered up to the fire. His approach broke Zack's concentration and wiped away his smile. The man's flattened nose and scars across his left cheek and right eye to his forehead destroyed any vestige of handsomeness he might have had. Arrogance hung over everything he did. He took the last open spot across from Zack and sat there, motionless. His unflinching black eyes stared at the Guard spy through gray smoke. The cowl hid Zack's eyes as he glared back at his foe. Romar slammed his fist into the palm of his hand after a few moments, rose, and stomped away.

Zack watched the man's broad back disappear into darkness. He remembered their brief encounter after a robbery three years ago and Romar's getaway. He had been on the periphery at that time, but Romar might still have seen him. The thought knotted his stomach and he rose and left the fire a minute later. *He hasn't recognized me yet; but if he makes the connection, all seven hells will break loose, and escape will be near impossible.*

Broken clouds shielded the moon as Zack disappeared under the boughs of darkened trees and began working his way around the encampment's perimeter. Twigs and jagged rocks bit into him as he crawled the last few feet to Gaston's tent.

Lamps inside the tent projected shadows on the outer canvas in a strange, synchronized dance as two men talked. The ominous shadows matched Zack's apprehension; the heated conversation fed the fire in his gut.

"Gaston, the Guard captured or killed half your men."

"I fail to see any connection to Delan."

"I tell you, it's him. I don't remember his name, but it's not 'Delan.' The dirty bastard nearly caught me."

Impatience emphasized Gaston's words. "Romar, if I suspected everyone that used an alias, I wouldn't get any sleep. Most of the men here don't use their real names."

After a slight pause, Romar's tone became more determined. "I was watching him in the battle today. Did you see him wound or kill a guardsman? I didn't. Why are you always on his side?" Zack grimaced at his words.

Gaston's exasperated tone sounded a warning. "Because he's smart and deadly, and his ideas on raiding this caravan are damn good. I need men like him; he's skilled, quick and with his muscles, not many would challenge him even with weapons. He's a bit crazy to wear red, but he hasn't made me suspicious. You make a serious charge. What proof do you have? A detachment of guardsmen intercepted us on some kind of exercise. They would've sent larger numbers if they'd planned an attack. We won, and they retreated. Bad luck to lose so many, but that happens. Besides, how and when could Delan have let the Guard know our plans?"

Romar's anger exploded. "There's something wrong about him!"

"Romar, he knows nothing of my future plans. I'll keep him in the dark until we investigate. Will that satisfy you? If he is a part of the Guard, we'll make his death one my men will remember."

Romar's shadow jerked with his nod and diminished to nothing as its owner left the tent. Gaston's shadow grew large, then small as he paced inside. Zack rose and hid behind a large oak closer to the tent, pulling his cloak tightly around him while he waited.

Within moments, Gaston emerged and continued pacing near where Zack leaned against the tree. Infrequent moonlight through the towering trees accentuated the bandit leader's angular frame as he looked around. Cunning eyes held force over a hooked nose above slim lips prone to a cruel smile. The dim light deepened angry lines etched in his face as he looked around. *He's too damn edgy,* Zack thought.

Gaston stopped in mid-step, then rushed back inside

his tent. Zack's anxiety increased when the bandit leader reappeared wearing a red shirt and slipped into the forest. *Now what's he up to?*

His training took hold; taking action eased Zack's nervousness as he followed the other man away from the encampment. Gaston traveled along a meager trail for two hundred yards before he stopped at a clearing's edge deep in the woods. A banked fire produced little light. A well-made lean-to was behind the fire and off to the right side a rickety, poorly-made one seemed to barely stay upright. *Brun's horse must be back at the camp,* Zack thought. He recognized Gaston's father, Brun, who had disappeared after the battle. The onerous little man with a scraggly beard fed small sticks into the flames. His squat stature contrasted with his son's tall frame. *Too bad they didn't catch the whoreson,* Zack thought. Brun stood, knife in hand, when one of Gaston's steps snapped a twig.

Frozen in place, Zack watched until clouds hid the moon; the darkness allowed him to creep within earshot. He pulled his cloak closer; his hand warmed his sword's hilt. He breathed slowly; his racing heart galloped on. Even in the chilly night, sweat beaded on his brow. He saw a leg in blue trousers and a polished boot partially covered in blood and mud sticking outside the unstable lean-to.

After a quick look at the captured guardsman's badly made lean-to, Brun hobbled over to his son. Gaston spoke without greeting. "Did any of my men find the bastard?"

"No. I gagged him. He roused once. His wound's infected and he has a fever. He won't last long. There are no orders on him, but I found a letter. His name is Kurt Shell."

Zack stiffened; Kurt was one of the officers he'd sparred against earlier in the day. A rescue was not in his plans, but he would not leave the man to die. *Damn complications will get me killed; too much depends on what happens tonight. Obstacles on impediments, be damned.*

The old man frowned at his son. "Why are you dressed in red? You said it drew too much attention and you would wear it only at parties."

"Delan says he wears red for the same reason I won't. Fighters focus their attack on the first thing that demands their attention. He said he wanted to fight the best and strongest. I thought him a fool that would soon die. Perhaps he wanted to spar instead of fight. Romar believes Delan is working for the Guard. I intend to find out."

Zack forgot his stomach pain; his anxiety sharpening his concentration, a trait he used to its fullest. He instantly decided to rescue Kurt and escape. *I need to capture Gaston and his father if I can. Gaston has too much information the Guard needs, and the rest of the bandits would scatter.* Purposefulness counteracted his fears and concerns: he became even more alert, his face set in determination. As his resolve firmed, his face relaxed and he began to plan.

A shower started; Zack welcomed its distractions. He watched Kurt lying in dense cover, partially hidden by the crumbling lean-to. Bending low, he prayed the rain and cloud cover held as he worked closer to the still body.

Gaston approached the guardsman within ten feet of where Zack hid. Gaston bent under the lean-to's protection, knelt beside Kurt, removed the gag, and shook his shoulder. He poured water over the wounded man's pale lips. "Kurt, can you hear me? It's me; I've come to get you away." Zack could barely hear his words over the rain.

Kurt squinted at the dark shape hovering above him. Faint flickers of dying firelight illuminated bright red cloth. He fought to speak. "Zack ... is it really you? Thank ... thank the Light's Source ..."

Gaston nodded and dribbled more water into the officer's mouth.

8

"We got . . . we got your signal too late," Kurt continued. "We couldn't raise the reinforcements in . . . in time. Let me see . . . if I can stand." He reached a hand out to the nebulous shape for help.

Gaston pushed him back down. "Not now, I have to make arrangements." Kurt settled once again and closed his eyes as Gaston joined his father by the rain-decimated fire.

The bandit leader's angry words reached Zack. "All this trouble to keep him away from the men, and now he'll be lucky to make it through the night." A wry smile crossed the bandit's face for an instant. "He did give me information, though. The name of a traitor is worth much." Gaston chuckled, "The Guard'll pay almost as much for a dead man as they will a live one, and I'll have two bodies to bargain with. They'll need to put one together from small pieces, though." An evil smile Zack had not seen before played across Gaston's lips as he turned from his father and disappeared into the forest.

Barely breathing, Zack stood motionless, considering a stratagem. *Gaston is sure to rouse Romar and others to find me. I must get horses and return here before they make their move. The trail circled to the east; if I can cut across it, I might reach camp ahead of him. First, I need to silence this old fool. If I can knock him out without him shouting, I won't have to kill him. It would be easier if they had left Brun's horse here.* Drawing a throwing knife, he started creeping toward Brun. The warmed steel in Zack's hand felt comfortable, familiar.

Brun turned, his eyes opening wide, raising cupped hands beside his mouth to call out. Zack's hand twitched; his thrown blade sliced through the old man's neck before he could call for help. Trotting to the twitching body, he removed the knife and cleaned it on the dying man's shirt as rainwater carried bright blood in small rivulets to soak into the ground. *Damn all the seven hells! Gaston will come after me with a vengeance—his reputation and control over his men demands it. Sorry, old bastard; you should've let me knock you unconscious. Your reflexes were good, but not good enough.*

Grabbing Kurt under his arms, Zack hauled him closer to the small fire pit, setting him under its better-constructed lean-to. The officer's young face was pale in the firelight, his light blue eyes and red hair dark against his pallor. His prowess in battle belied his image; he had amazed Zack during the fighting. *Seven hells, how many more delays before I can get us away?* It took several precious seconds for Kurt to recognize Zack and understand him. "I have to dress your wound."

The filthy bandage and the chest wound's appearance, showing the red, angry signs of early infection, made Zack grimace. Kurt gritted his teeth while he cleaned it, then pulled a packet of Feverfew from inside his cloak and cut a section of his shirt to hold it in place. Kurt moaned when he applied it. The rain had stopped by the time Zack finished. He built a new fire with dry wood from the lean-to's covered stack. He also found food and a waterskin under the shelter. "Kurt, you must eat and drink, you'll need the strength. Gaston roused you earlier. He knows I'm a spy. We're leaving as soon as I return with horses." Kurt nodded and took the food.

Zack cut straight across the wooded terrain to the main bandit encampment. Lights danced in Gaston's tent a hundred yards away. Men moved toward Zack's campsite. *I have little time.*

Dark skies helped him reach the picket line without incident. Ten feet from the horses, he crept up behind a snoring guard and snapped his neck. Zack approached Spellbinder and scratched him behind the ear. The large gelding woke and eyed his master with interest. Zack untied him and moved him out from the line. Choosing Gaston's prized black gelding for Kurt, he tied both horses' leads to a tree limb and saddled them in record time.

Zack saw Gaston and his men had reached his

campsite and were searching for him. Zack grabbed the picket line's main rope and cut it with one swipe. He snapped the rope hard; startled horses pulled at their leads. His yells rushed them toward sleeping men. Zack led Spellbinder into the shadows, mounted him and set out at a trot; Gaston's big black did not fight his lead. He followed the picket line, freeing and shooing horses as he went. They panicked, galloping toward bewildered men and clusters of tents. Gaston and his men rushed to gather the scattered horses as Zack found the trail back to Kurt.

Kurt was propped up on his late captor's saddlepacks when Zack returned to the small clearing. He was chewing something, and took a last swallow of water. The food, water and herbs had helped; he looked stronger. It took two tries to get Kurt seated on Gaston's gelding and tied in place. Zack swore at the pain the exertion caused the officer. Remounting Spellbinder, he eased the horses into the forest. The sounds of men crashing through the forest and loud voices slowed him a dozen yards away from the clearing.

Romar's angry voice broke the forest's solitude. "I knew he was a traitor! I'll kill the bastard for you."

Gaston's bellow interrupted Romar. "Damn! He's killed my Da! You kill him and it's worth five golds. Make him die slow!"

Spellbinder, urged into a trot, slipped between trees while Zack prayed neither horse found a hole. He could see blood soaking Kurt's bandage, and prayed his wound would not worsen on the ride. Keeping a close watch on the officer and a closer lookout for Gaston, he urged Spellbinder onward.

A mile passed before he burst from the trees onto the north road, just a few miles south of the nearest Guard post. The trip took longer than Zack thought it should, and his concern for Kurt grew with each stride. Predawn light washed out the road's hues when he spotted the fort's gates.

Exhausted, Zack didn't relax until guardsmen carried Kurt to the healer's rooms. Zack saw Kurt's luck held: the healer held a graystone, channeling its power into his patient. Kurt's pain-twisted face relaxed as the magic's influence took hold and stopped his bleeding.

Reassured that he was in good hands, Zack headed to the post commander's office; Commander Scott rushed out to greet him. His presence of command enhanced a square face that focused on Zack's every move.

"It is a pleasure to see you, Zack." Commander Scott grasped Zack's forearm with genuine warmth. He turned serious when Zack did not return his smile. "I knew it must be complications from Gaston's bunch when they told me you were here. If it's trouble, we're ready for them. Three detachments of troops arrived last night."

Zack spent the better part of two hours reporting the night's events, the bandit's plans, their actions over the past several weeks, and pinpointed the area where he thought Gaston would go next. Scott listened, and the questions he asked proved pointed and astute. At the end, he thanked Zack and offered him a bed in the officers' barracks.

Men poured from quarters to bugle calls as Zack trudged to the bathhouse. Four detachments of men rode out as he found the bed assigned him and fell into it. He was fast asleep as the last guardsman cleared the gates.

* * *

A familiar dream caused Zack's grin: His wife, smiling as she held out her arms in greeting. He rushed to her and swept her up in his embrace. Her face faded as a hand shook him awake.

When his eyes focused, he saw Commander Scott looking down on him. Zack regretted the dream's demise. The commander spoke quietly, "Good and bad news: Kurt will survive. The healers say you got him here just in time. The bandits left in a hurry and their trail led to the area you predicted. We captured them without much trouble. They laid down their weapons when they saw we had them surrounded. The bad news is that Gaston and Romar escaped. I've sent messages to the other outposts to watch for them."

Zack waved Scott away, who left in obvious good humor. He pulled the blanket over his head; happy that Kurt would live, but that did not counter his anger about Gaston and Romar's escape. *Five golds will set a man up for life in a good-sized business. Romar won't give up searching for me.* His last thoughts slowed as sleep pulled at him again. *This is my last assignment in the field. We will capture them if they come near the Spires and once I'm there, I don't plan to leave. Someone else can track Gaston and Romar down. I've a wife and daughter back home.*

He did not recapture the dream.

* * *

TWO weeks later, Zack stood beside his horse, watching his wife work in the garden. Her luxurious, long, black hair contrasted with his white-blond mane. Her gaze mirrored Zack's clear, deep blue eyes. Her features, soft and beautiful, flowered in full contrast with his strength and massive physique.

Jewel, his three-year-old daughter played nearby. She had inherited Zack's blond hair and her mother's looks. They didn't know who had given her mischievous black eyes. Zack's thoughts filled with pride and love: *Both of them are so beautiful. How could I ever think I would miss fieldwork when I have them here?*

Judith looked up as Zack walked toward her, a huge smile on his face. She dropped her implements and rushed into his arms. "Zack, oh my darling, you're back. I've missed you so much. Are you all right? Are you hurt?"

"No love, I'm fine." He felt her breath quicken; the

glimmer of tears danced in the corners of her eyes. His often-occurring dream played in his memory again; he smiled as he swung her around, covering her face with kisses.

He felt a familiar wholesomeness. *Thanks to Light's Source, they're fine. I love them more than life.* His heart soared, warmth flooded him; he held her close, feeling her heart beat against his chest. He felt complete for the first time since he had left her. The depth of his love for her—for both of them—made him dizzy. He stopped his spin, set her down and kissed her passionately, which was readily returned.

Jewel's high-pitched voice yelled, "Da! Da! Da is home!"

Judith snuggled against his cheek. "Are you actually home for good?"

Zack chuckled at his wife's exuberance. "Yes my love, I'm home and don't plan to leave anytime soon." Their ensuing kiss was long and ardent.

With Jewel in one arm and Judith at his side, they walked into the house. He had been away with Gaston's bandits for ten weeks, including the aftermath of reports and before that, several other trips to plant the false information. Their home looked the same on the surface, but he soon noticed little improvements as they settled in the parlor: a new cloth over a small table and her finished painting on the wall. The loving emotions that surged through him left him humble and a little giddy.

He sat in their comfortable main room as his two ladies regaled him with tales of what had happened in their neighborhood while he had been away. Jewel played at his feet; Judith sat on his lap. He was content and unabashed joy filled him. Judith's demeanor promised a blissful night filled with pleasure.

Judith's coy smile intrigued him. "Darling, we need to put Jewel down for her nap." Her hand caressed his inner thigh.

I pray she sleeps long and deep. Zack's smile deepened before he kissed Judith on her neck; her response promised bliss.

2

ZACK finished his inspection of Carson's work on his house. "You did well. The paint is smooth and the trim even." He handed over the payment, the other man's grin widening as he pocketed the coins.

Judith came from the backyard. "It looks good. Zack, would you purchase some of those honey cakes Jewel likes at the Spires tomorrow?" she asked.

Carson's voice contained a tinge of awe. "You work at the Spires? I would climb one of them to work there. Could . . . could you help me talk to someone that might need a good worker?"

Zack considered the request. *I like him. He arrives on time and does what he promises. Besides good work, he also has a sense of humor. He spent a good bit of his own time making toys for Jewel.* "I'll see what I can do."

"May Light's Source bless you, Zack." After much ado over Zack's kindness, Carson left, acting like a child who had just received one of the toys he made.

Judith smiled up at Zack. "That's nice of you."

Zack shrugged. "He does good work and the Spires looks for good men. And yes, I'll get the honey cakes."

* * *

THIS *place feels of power beyond its physical boundaries.* Zack looked in wonder at one of the three slender, rock spires that soared upward over seven hundred feet, its surface slick as well-made steel. The spire's placement formed an equilateral triangle with its two identical brothers; the distance of a mile between each of them did not vary an inch. A row of massive, twelve-story buildings connected

16

the spires that formed the base of the triangle. They housed the Zenith Lord's seat of power, his residence, the Seven Realms' central government, and five thousand guardsmen.

The inner walls surrounded the spires. He rode through guarded, fortified gates toward the outer battlements a mile away, making a much larger triangle; they enclosed buildings that housed fifteen thousand more guardsmen, along with barracks, visitor's stables, forges, and many, many shops licensed to service the needs of the Spires' inhabitants.

Traveling through the inner and outer walls had become familiar in the year since Zack's departure from fieldwork, when he'd joined the central planning staff. He enjoyed his assignments in operational planning, but missed a spy's action. Those longings diminished, however, when he saw his wife and daughter.

He wove Spellbinder through the constant flow of carts, wagons, riders and passersby going to and from the Spires until he entered the outskirts of Stonefire, a city of over four million people. Zack had arranged the interview Carson wanted, which had earned the man a place on a list of new men for consideration. He would still have to wait months for his name to reach the top of the list, but it was a start.

In the meantime, Carson showered Zack and his family with attention and did small jobs as compensation for Zack's efforts on his behalf. Always pleasant, he doted on Jewel and brought her more toys. They soon enjoyed a firm friendship, and Carson came often to their home.

The scope of the man's knowledge amazed Zack. He was well educated and conducted himself with a certain refinement that belied his handyman status. For all his strength, light-gray eyes, black hair, and strong features, he never mentioned a family or love interest. Every time Zack had probed for information on his background,

17

Carson had fallen into a deep melancholy. After this happened a couple of times, Zack hadn't tried to bring up his past again. He had checked the Spire's reports, however, but found nothing for "Carson Phylip."

Would Judith understand my stopping at an inn if I weren't meeting Carson? I don't think so. Spellbinder turned into the inn, Zack's usual haunt, without guidance, making him chuckle.

Carson sat near the door. He rose and slapped Zack on the back, his face one big smile.

"What are you so happy about?" Zack asked.

"I've landed a big job two miles northwest of here, one that will see me through until the Spires sends for me," Carson replied. "They want me to rebuild an entire house. I need to contract some work out; it's too much for me alone. Will you to take a look at what's entailed and see if you know some men that might fit the job? I've mostly worked alone and I don't know that many men I can trust."

I know several retired guardsmen whom are fit and might want something like this. Some of them helped me over the years. It's time to help them back. "When do you need me to look at it?" Carson looked sheepish and Zack recognized his expression. "Tonight?"

Carson smiled and nodded. "It's only two miles away and we still have the light."

Zack could not help grinning at the other man's eagerness. "Alright, but we won't have time for ale."

* * *

THE northwest road off a well-traveled main road was unfamiliar to Zack. The pleasant evening and Carson's running banter shortened the ride. The handyman turned into a lane that led to a house set back among trees and in much need of repair.

They tied the horses to a crooked hitching post at the side of a set of rickety wooden stairs. Zack wrinkled his nose. "There's a lot of mold and mildew in here. Sure it wouldn't be easier to knock the whole thing down and rebuild?"

"It's better upstairs, but I think most of the walls need to be replaced." Carson took great care to show Zack the entire lower level, and then led him upstairs. "Now, this is the room you must see."

As Zack entered the large room; he felt a sharp pain on the back of his head, followed by darkness.

*　*　*

TWO men looked slightly out of focus when Zack regained consciousness. He made out two gold coins as they dropped into Carson's open palm. Zack recognized Romar's familiar face when he turned toward him. Zack felt more disoriented. Carson smiled at Zack, his voice flat. "It's nothing personal, Zack. Gold is gold."

The expression on Carson's face ranged from surprise to pain and back to surprise before he fell to the floor. A pool of blood spread under his chest and crept slowly outward as Romar pulled his sword from his body. The bandit's smile showed his satisfaction. "The fool thought I'd actually pay him two golds to bring you here."

Romar walked toward Zack, the smile in place. He picked up blood-streaked coins and slid them into his money pouch. Zack twisted his head in time to avert most of the impact from a vicious kick. He saw flares of light and fell back, unconsciousness approaching. His last thought hurt more than his head. *Will I see Judith and Jewel again?*

*　*　*

ZACK's awareness swam toward clarity from muddy depths; with it came new, incomprehensible pain.

Harsh laughter rushed in on him. It took time for his eyes to focus through desperate tears of frustration. He saw white clouds and the tops of trees in morning's light through a huge hole in the roof. He caught glimpses of spaces in the walls where windows had once kept the wind at bay.

The agonizing pain came into sharp focus. Cold winds flayed his naked body; contrasting warmth ran slowly down his arms as blood oozed from ropes that gnawed into his flesh with every uncontrolled shiver. Arms spread wide; he dangled in cold air tied with ropes hung from hooks in beams under the remaining ceiling. His feet, similarly tied with ropes from hooks in the floor spread his legs painfully apart making efforts to ease the tension on his body fail. Fiery pain, down his chest, side and back contrasted with the dull, cold ache from his wrists, arms and shoulders.

Romar's arrogant voice dripped with satisfaction. "I see you're awake. Ready for more fun? It's only day two. I haven't really begun, my boy. Gaston wants me to make it last a long time before we find your pretty wife."

Ropes jerked as muscles flailed helplessly at the mention of his family.

"Now, now, don't strain yourself. We'll see that the bitch is well tended to, like the broodmare she is. Gaston and I will take her many times before we kill her. On the other hand, perhaps we'll keep her for the men. No, I think not. She'll just have to make do with our attention for a few days. I doubt your daughter will last long, though. Most likely we'll rip her apart."

Swollen throat muscles tried to scream at Romar without effect. The sadistic bandit buried his fist in Zack's midsection, followed by a roundhouse punch to the head. Beaten flesh slumped; unconsciousness reigned.

* * *

MID-AFTERNOON sun struck Zack in his eyes as he clawed back to reality. Romar stood before him with a strange, metal implement he caressed lovingly. "Ah, you're awake again. You are a strong one. How nice."

He waved sharp, hooked steel claws at Zack. "Do you like my new toy? I had it made especially for you. It's my pet bear claw. Let's see how well it works."

Romar's face filled with glee as he sunk the razor-sharp points into the flesh above Zack's left breast. He used his weight to pull it down to waist level and around to the back.

Thankfully, Zack passed out when the claw passed his breast. New pain from his left side flooded over him when he roused next. Shaking off the excruciating memories, he tried to bring his head up to a normal position. He felt his hair, tied in the rear, pull tight on his scalp; it restricted his lines of sight and left him looking upward. He barely glimpsed his bloody wrists. Ragged, hysterical laughter sounded again; it took him several moments to identify it as his own. Darkness caressed him back into unconsciousness.

* * *

SHOCK impaled him. Zack's senses snapped agonizingly clear. Pain erupted through him as cold water dripped from his convulsing, naked body. Fresh agony tore at his mangled wrists with each quiver. Gaston's voice floated to him, dreamlike, after an eternity of torment.

"I have a surprise for you, Delan . . . or should I say Zack?"

Pain, dry mouth, and the angle of Zack's head destroyed any hope of an answer. He wanted to scream at Gaston, and the small sound that died in his throat left him feeling inadequate. Acrid smells of burning flesh preceded more pain than he ever thought possible, producing the full-throated scream his injuries had denied him seconds before. He jerked in uncontrolled torment. Acid ate deep into his mangled body. After what seemed like an eternity, blessed darkness regained its prominence.

* * *

ZACK woke lying next to something cold and wet. The cold thing felt warmer than his shivering, broken body. Soreness racked every joint and muscle. His groin ached, and he remembered a sadistic kick. His memory slowly returned with the increased awareness of pain. *Was it only one kick?* He could barely move. Dried crusts of blood broke apart, and his wounds oozed substances he did not want to ponder.

My arms and legs are free. He forced them to move, even though every inch brought new suffering. He identified the cold thing behind him as Carson's body, the wetness as semi-dried blood; its crust broke apart at his touch; his hand slid in viscous, clotted fluid.

The effort to find the dead man's belt seemed to take hours. *Romar could come back at any minute*, he thought. He found the smooth, bone hilt of a razor-sharp dagger he'd shown Carson how to hide behind his belt for protection. Forcing his numb fingers around it, he drew it with his right hand and hid it next to his body. *Do I have the strength?* He wanted to laugh; a small gurgle came from his restricted throat. *If I don't, I'm dead.*

A door slammed, followed by the fading sounds of a horse trotting away. *Have they left me?* Footsteps coming up the stairs answered his question. The door swung toward him.

Through swollen, slitted eyes, Zack glimpsed a sloshing bucket dangling below Romar's hand. Feigning unconsciousness, he readied himself for the onslaught of freezing water, trying not to react. His body involuntarily disobeyed him, and quivered as icy needles cascaded over him.

Warm hands grabbed his shoulders. The pain from his left shoulder and side forced a scream from his raw throat. Romar's smirking face leaned forward as Zack's eyes opened. *I must make this work . . . only get one chance . . . damn, I'm . . . so tired.* Zack slowly pulled his arm out from under his side. With the last of his energy, he thrust it upward, shoving the blade into his torturer's throat.

Clutching at the dagger, Romar fell forward. His head crashed on the floor, shoving the blade through the bottom of his jaw into his brain. He did not twitch. His body rested in a heap of splayed limbs.

Inch by inch, Zack crawled out of the room. He eased down the stairs on his buttocks, one step at a time. Finding food and water on the main level, he forced it down.

His clothing lay in a heap near the kitchen door. He barely got his pants on. He did not find his boots or shirt. He did not look very hard. His cloak was crumpled on the floor by the front door; he stumbled onto the porch, pulling it around him.

Spellbinder grazed at the end of the yard in near darkness. Zack forced a whistle through dry lips. The horse lifted his head, eyed him, and then walked over. Zack's muscles burned with pain, his body protesting every single movement required to mount the horse from the porch. "Home," Zack whispered.

He leaned forward against Spellbinder's neck as the horse set out, blood seeping into his mane. His thoughts seemed improbable, and their clarity surprised him. *Judith and Jewel! Are they safe?* His thoughts danced once more. *That blood is going to be difficult to remove once it dries. How long has it been, hours, days?* His eyes closed.

When he opened them, Spellbinder stood next to his porch at home. The sunlight was just breaking on the horizon. He stifled a scream while sliding to the safety of solid wood. Barefoot, he stumbled toward the door; his foreboding soaring to new levels when he found it ajar. His pain was forgotten, and he forced his battered, protesting muscles to take him to the second floor, where he entered their bedroom.

His anguished scream must have unnerved passersby.

* * *

A man rushed toward the guardsman. He stopped to catch his breath, pointing down the road. "I've never heard anyone yell like that! It came from the house on the corner."

"That's Zack Stand's home!" The guardsman kicked his horse into a trot until he reached the house, then dismounted and walked inside.

He found Zack unconscious in a bloody heap at the end of the bed. A lady lay naked atop it; a thick stake had been shoved between her legs and up into her abdomen. Her viscera hung from a cut in her mid section. A little girl's bruised and lifeless body lay across the room, her crotch bloody.

The experienced guardsman turned away and vomited.

3

HIGH Healer Tobias Sternwood held a small, gray stone between his large hands. Zack felt eerie movements within him as the healer's mind worked inside his body. *After a year of treatment, it's no longer an ordeal, just odd.*

Perspiration formed on the healer's heavy brow when he came out of the near trance state his efforts required. There were few healers with the ability to wield the graystone's power and Tobias Sternwood was arguably the best in the Seven Realms. *How must it feel to channel power through stones?*

"Zack, I wish everyone in my care responded like you." The healer motioned him to stand. His face held a strange detachment as his fingers lightly traced his scars from the front of his shoulder, down and around his waist, then rising up to the center of his back. The healer's soft touch hid a power and ability that Zack found difficult to comprehend. Tobias nodded approvingly and told Zack to dress.

A rare smile played at the edge of his mouth, a departure from his serious mien. "The exercises the Zenith Lord ordered have done wonders over the past six months. I'm just sorry you weren't able to start them during the first half-year, but that time was needed simply for your basic physical recovery. I appreciate your devotion to the regimen I prescribed. Your muscles are strong, and with today's treatment, you are functionally sound. You have no further need of my skills, young man."

Relief filled Zack's response. "It is I who should offer you and the Zenith Lord my appreciation. I have no doubt that without your help, I would be much worse off than simply saddled with hideous scars—" Zack stopped speaking at Tobias' raised hand.

"I have told you before that you perceive the scars as much worse than others seeing them. They'll fade in time, but you will always have some evidence of your ordeal. I implore you, do not dwell on these relatively minor imperfections left after so much injury. Your face is free of scars. You are a strong man. Don't ever let their presence make you think less of yourself." Tobias patted him on the arm, and then left the room.

Zack stood before the mirror fastening his shirt; its reflection made him shiver. He smothered a response for only a moment. *How can he not see the horror I've become? I'm truly ugly. It has been a year, and the scars are the same as when we started. I am as strong as I was before. My reflexes are as good or better. Does that make up for a grotesque appearance? What kind of woman will want me?* He wanted to smash the mirror, but turned and pounded his fist into the stone wall instead.

Zack pulled on his trousers and boots while remembering the past year. Tobias' treatments that had repaired his ripped muscles caused much pain in the beginning, but tapered off to minor twinges over the last months. The first exercises to rebuild his strength had made him grit his teeth to choke off his screams. Now, he would miss their pleasant burn, and he vowed to continue them.

The door opened, breaking his train of thought. Zack smiled as Michael Gaz entered the room.

The spymaster's small wiry frame belied his deadliness; Zack pitied any foe that angered him. His soft, brown hair and eyes, along with a pleasant, unassuming face, disguised his considerable skills. His demeanor, countenance, and soft voice lulled any unknowing person into false impressions. Those who worked for the spymaster called him Gaz at his request.

Zack considered him his only friend now, and

welcomed his visit. He knew the spymaster was responsible for his excellent care and continued pay and benefits while he'd healed. Gaz had personally arranged for Judith and Jewel's cremation ceremonies and taken care of the many details of his shattered life for the first six months of his recovery. The spymaster had proved his friendship many times; he was the only person toward whom Zack felt any personal emotions. *When one feels nothing, friendship can be an awesome thing.* His fleeting thought produced a smile.

Gaz looked up into Zack's eyes. "High Healer Sternwood stated that you may return to work if you wish. If you do not, the Zenith Lord has authorized me to pension you from his service. The pension and the property we bought over the past years will afford you a comfortable life."

Zack's voice rang with impatience and a tinge of bitterness. "Gaz, say nothing more. We've repeatedly discussed this. I want to return to fieldwork. I want to catch Gaston, and I want to put every murdering bandit I can find in a dungeon or kill him." He pulled his cloak on, and then his shoulders relaxed. "I'm sorry. The idea of retirement leaves me cold. I want to work."

"Well, let's see if we can accommodate you."

4

Four Years Later

ZACK's head hurt. His searching arm stretched across cold, coarse bedclothes. "Why am I alone?" he whispered. "Damn. She promised . . ." A low moan escaped him while he tried to focus on the water clock in the dim light.

With the help of a low burning lamp, he found his clothes neatly folded on a chair across the room. Zack scowled at the bedpost his arm caught and he grimaced when his ankle sent a footstool flying as he stumbled across the room to the washstand. The bell pull resisted a frustrated yank that further annoyed him.

He upended the basin at arm's length above his head; cold water splashed over him. Droplets flung from his nude body caught vivid lights from the fireplace and the many-colored glass panels of the glowing lampshade. Icy shivers surged over him and threw more coruscating brilliant worlds of color into soaring arcs. Those that fell into the fireplace hissed their death on glowing embers.

Anger rose when he considered his choice of a companion for the evening and night—well, at least part of the night—celebrating his thirtieth birthday. Clear perceptions formed through his recollection's muddled haze. He remembered a beautiful smile, charming voice and pleasing touches. He sneered at his next thought. *I should have known.*

The downstairs common room's familiar noises verified the time. His purse lay on top of his clothes. Leather slid against leather to reveal more coins than there should have been after a night of merrymaking.

Zack's muddled thoughts left him confused. *I must have gotten drunk . . . I certainly don't remember much of the evening. Perhaps that's why I woke alone.*

Sounds from screeching door hinges tore through his skull. His head continued to throb as he stumbled toward the door.

"Master Stand, is there something you need?"

Zack recognized the voice of the innkeeper's youngest son before he completed the turn. *Damn. Why did it have to be Tad?* He found Tad a good lad, and quite reliable during the months at a time he stayed at the inn. Zack sloshed about to face the door and watched the color drain from the boy's face.

Tad's expression froze as he stared at the long, jagged scars for the first time. His round blue eyes narrowed as he took in Zack's large, taut muscles stretched over his big frame; he viewed the scars again with grim fascination etched into his face.

Zack waved him into the room. "It's all right, I'm sure you've seen a nude man before." He knew his nudity wasn't causing the reaction. Zack sighed. "I need a hot bath with fresh water. I'll pay for the extra work during your busy time. I'm sorry to do this to you, but the time got away from me and I must be away. It's important." Zack tried not to show the increased throbbing in his head his speech produced.

Tad's voice remained steady. "Master Stand, you have always been a good guest and my father favors your custom, there will be no extra charge. I'll have Rob and Jes bring the tub up and I'll start the water heating."

Tad hesitated, and then continued. "You didn't cause trouble last night." He hurried on before Zack could question him. "My father and I know your habits, and we never saw you drunk. The woman with you must have given you something. She and two men tried to get you into the street. My Da stopped them with a few guardsmen from the common room. The men dropped you and they ran. Da and a Guard captain put you to bed." Still staring at his chest, Tad backed from the room and closed the door.

Zack knew the boy's reaction well; he'd caught the same expressions from most people who saw him without a shirt. Their reaction to his scars, much inflated in his perception, left him cold. *I wish he hadn't seen them, but they grow up fast working at an inn.* His thought registered briefly, and then joined many like it, forgotten and locked away in the recesses of memory.

Familiar noises refocused him. The tall tubs used for baths rolled into the room, pushed by Rob and Jes. The tub's circular shape fit through the doorways, but required one of the innkeeper's boys to stay in attendance to help the bather in and out. Tad, Rob and Jes had readied the tub and water sooner than Zack imagined possible. He bathed, shaved and dressed in his best time. *I might make it on time,* he concluded.

* * *

ONE did not wish to be late for an appointment with Master Michael Gaz, but Zack found himself in that exact unfortunate position, to his dismay. His friendship with Gaz increased his desire for perfection, and being late fell into a category he did not allow. He hurried along the prescribed route to meet his superior and damned the bitch's treatment of him. He fumed until the coach's sounds alerted him of its presence.

Street lamps did not abound in this area, and any available light flared from behind the black coach that stopped a few paces in front of him, when the driver nodded, once. Zack waited for the coach's door to open, and then hurried to get in. It rolled on before he could completely close the door.

Zack watched while Gaz' brief glance took in his appearance and demeanor. The voice that issued from the slim, wiry, man held all the nuance of a raised eyebrow. "I trust you found her worth it?"

Zack replied with force. "Hardly."

Gaz smiled enigmatically, and then took a serious tone. "I have an assignment for you—if, that is, you can keep your pants on long enough to complete it." Zack groaned and did not catch the other' man's sly, fleeting smile. "I want you to penetrate Ozlid and discover all you can about its government and people."

Zack sat up straighter. "Being late is one thing, but do I deserve that?"

Gaz gave no evidence that he'd heard the question. "We need to know our neighbors. They're not that far off our coast, and we know nothing of Ozlid, or how it manufactured its grasp on Hamptor and Arestead, only that they are using water as a death-hold—" Zack hated it when Gaz listed things he already knew. "—nor how they manipulate the kingdoms, nor much about their rulers."

Zack slowly shook his head.

Gaz went on. "The kingdoms have always been isolationist. Nonetheless, the Seven Realms may want to quietly open diplomatic relations with Hamptor and Arestead. We must know how Ozlid will view our overtures, and what ramifications it might have on the adjoining kingdoms before we proceed. We certainly don't want to increase Arestead and Hamptor's troubles."

Gaz' façade broke, and Zack saw worry in his face for an instant. *There's more to this than he's telling; he's too concerned.*

Cool air flowed through the coach's barely open windows but did not quench the heat in Zack's response. "Gaz, be reasonable. Not many have gone beyond Ozlid's borders, and the ones that returned reported nothing good about the experience. It's a suicide mission. You want me to go farther into Ozlid than anyone has traveled before and learn about its *government?* We don't even know the name of their ruler." Zack knew exactly what Gaz meant: A profile of every man with major power and how he used it; the sheaf of papers Gaz held out would leave no doubt of his assignment's requirements.

Gaz held up his hand, and Zack slumped. "There is a way and I'm sure you will find it. You have no time limit, but try to return within six months. That should give you three months within Ozlid's borders and sufficient travel time. If anyone can uncover the information, you can. I alerted the commander at Elizabethville to help you in any way she can."

Gaz shoulders relaxed and his voice softened. "I have a dire premonition about the need for this assignment. We buried Zenith Lord Richard the last time I experienced this kind of fear. Zack, this is important. Hamptor and Arestead are at their breaking points. Their resources dwindle every year, and their kings seem powerless. Their population numbers are at a standstill. There is an evil in Ozlid that may soon occupy the whole island subcontinent."

Gaz' raised hand stopped Zack's frustrated comment before it could be voiced. "The Seven Realms are many times the three kingdoms' size, but that precludes nothing. Evil, Zack, horrific evil, travels by many means. We must know more. We must know if the evil in Ozlid is the same that we fought two millennia ago and if so, how strong it has grown. We must know if another war is imminent."

A cold chill crept up Zack's spine. He leaned forward to protest again, then collapsed against the black seat cushions, lost in thought. *He has made his decision and nothing I say will change it. I hope they mention the honor of receiving this assignment at my cremation ceremony. 'Yes, Zack Stand. I remember the name, a spy sent off on a suicide mission over a war scare.' A new war. The last Great War resulted in the deaths of over seventy-five million people and the Seven Realms' near destruction. What will be left of our civilization if Gaz is right?*

Zack no longer felt the coach rumble across potholes the driver could not avoid, and Gaz did not intrude on his thoughts. *The complete destruction of a society and a people ravaged for all time. Gaz is seldom wrong, his feelings based on hard evidence. Perhaps the time is near. A new war—may the Light's Source protect us all.*

Zack's expression took on a far-away look, and then he got a gleam in his eye. Gaz' body movements told him he had noticed. "I will pass by Quince's inn on the way to Elizabethville. I want to stop and see what I find, and if I find he is still buying and selling stolen property as we suspect, I want a free hand to act."

Gaz did not answer. He nodded once after a long moment.

5

ZACK tied down the last of his belongings for the innkeeper, Darwin, to store in the locked area of his cellar.

All I own fits into three medium-sized chests. The remains of his household brought painful memories to the surface; he buried them and pushed the images of his murdered wife and daughter deep into locked chests within him. Ideas to examine each of those memories lay suppressed. His anger at those that could have saved his family on hearing their cries and did nothing had escalated to encompass most of humankind. Concepts and feelings about humanity stowed angrily and rapidly away with little notice of the process. *I won't be like those that ignored my family!* The thought felt strange.

Zack took up his saddlepacks and left the rooms after one look around. He locked the door without regret. Downstairs, he gave the key to Darwin with the money for the chest's storage for a year.

Zack paid for twice the time he planned to be away. Darwin's clear puzzlement of his journeys over the past five years remained unspoken, and Zack mentally thanked the innkeeper for that. He remembered an overheard comment from a Guard's officer to Darwin that had caused Zack to chuckle at the time: "Taciturn neatly fits Zack. He never explains his whereabouts or deeds, and it does no good to ask."

Zack knew several of the Zenith Lord's guardsmen that visited the inn's common room, mostly officers. Many assignments included the Guard's support, and word of his exploits garnered him respect. His steadfast refusal of offers to buy him ale, wine, or a meal drew Darwin's obvious dismay, but the guardsmen never took offense.

Zack said farewell and walked toward the inn's stable yard with a purposeful stride. Spellbinder, saddled and ready for him, pranced impatiently. The desert-dune colored gelding swung expressive eyes to his master. He wondered how Spellbinder might show his displeasure when they approached the ship. From his reactions, memories of previous voyages were definitely not among Spellbinder's best.

The realities of his craft had dispelled danger's thrill long ago; the excitement of a new mission remained, however. Zack's heart greedily captured it with one reservation. Gaz said he had a premonition about this mission. *I do, too, one of finality.* Try as he might, Zack could not shake the feeling.

Horse and master developed a ground-eating rotation of gaits that spared both of them from exhaustion. Zack planned their stops for the maximum rest in the shortest time and the best accommodations available. The three-week trip to Elizabethville might take sixteen to seventeen days by rising early and riding until after sunset. He looked forward to the stop Gaz had reluctantly agreed to. Any thought of Quince brought Zack's ire to the surface.

* * *

DARK shadows encroached on the road when Spellbinder trotted over a rise. Zack saw the village and breathed a sigh of relief. "I could've sworn it was closer than this." His mount dipped his head and nickered, making Zack chuckle. "You too, huh?"

The Bristled Boar Inn brought back memories. *A rough crowd frequents it. Quince caters to bandits. Maybe I'll get lucky and find a few.* He remembered the groom, the unvoiced reason he'd insisted on returning, and wondered if he still lived. Zack nudged Spellbinder into the inn's yard.

The groom was still there, looking worn and tired. His undernourished body increased Zack's anger. Dirty blond hair lay matted against his head. Large brown eyes, a pug nose, and full lips should have been alive and animated at his age. He was not. He looked up into Zack's face, and a faint expression of recognition briefly crossed his face.

Zack dismounted and led Spellbinder into the stable; the surprised boy followed. Zack pointed to an empty stall in the middle of five on the left side that would provide warmth from chill winds.

The boy nodded, and the two of them removed tack and saddle. Zack found curry brushes in a pail and tossed one to the boy. Spellbinder showed his enjoyment of dual applications with nudges to his benefactors. They finished at the same time. Zack fished in his pouch and looked at the boy, softly speaking for the first time. "Do they still make you pay for your food?"

The boy lowered his head. He looked unsure, and a moment passed before he nodded. "I'm not supposed to tell. Please sir, don't tell Master Quince."

Old Quince is still alive. How does he survive with his clientele? Perhaps I can put him out of business this time. Zack shook his head at the boy's worried, drawn expression. He pulled a half-silver coin from his pouch and held it out.

"Oh, sir, no, I cannot take it." The boy looked up at Zack's questioning gaze. "They'll accuse me of stealing if I have a coin worth so much, and take it away."

Yes, Quince is definitely alive, Zack thought, watching the boy's eyes follow his hand as he put the silver back. Fishing around in his pouch, he withdrew several newly minted coppers. The boy's face brightened when the shiny metal fell into his hand.

"Thank you, sir, thank you very much. My name is Dale, and I remember you from a year ago. I will take good care of your horse."

Zack waved away Dale's words. "Will you be here

early tomorrow?" Dale nodded. "Get something to eat tonight." The boy nodded again and smiled. *How often does he smile? Bastards.* "Dale, I work for the Zenith Lord." Dale's grin disappeared and his eyes widened. "Quince is a bad man. I promise I will make sure you are cared for if anything should happen to him while I'm here. Not a word to anyone about this, you promise?"

Dale recovered quickly, and the exuberance of his bobbing head nearly made Zack laugh. He felt secure in the boy's hatred for his master.

Zack entered the inn with his saddlepacks over his shoulder. Still early for Quince's regulars, he surveyed the four men in the common room. Two men spoke quietly at a table near the fireplace, glanced at him, and then turned back to continue their conversation. They had the look of merchants, and Zack rightly assumed they would leave early. One snored, facing the far wall, on a table near the rear door.

Quince looked up from behind the bar and frowned while Zack approached. Hard, swinish eyes full of hatred glared at him. Pockmarks covered Quince's face; a large, bulbous nose and fleshy lips set in determination did not move as Zack reached the bar.

"Quince, I want room four if it still has the lock and bar on the inside. I want lastmeal and some ale. I do not want to hear you utter anything but 'Yes, sir.' Does that bother you?"

"Zack Stand—" Zack's hand dropped to his sword's hilt while Quince's frown deepened, "No, uh, yes . . . sir." Quince reached under the bar, brought up a stout brass key, and dropped it in Zack's outstretched hand. Zack left for the upstairs room.

He lit the room's lamp with the one from the hall. The only room that featured a good lock had not changed its drab and dirty status. Zack inspected the bedclothes for vermin and found none, to his surprise. *Quince must've hired a new housekeeper.*

He looked around the room with its one small window high up on the wall. Its bars cast shadows across the raised pallet that served as a bed. A cloud of dust motes flew when he dropped his saddlepacks on the pallet. Zack waved his hand in front of his face and shook his head. His close inspection of the lock satisfied him that it properly functioned. The stout oak bar added the protection he wanted when in the room. The lock's bolt slid home with a solid click when he left for the common room and a questionable lastmeal.

Zack found a table in the corner and sat facing the room. Quince and the sleeping man had left. A haggard-looking serving maid opened the kitchen door and looked at Zack with little interest. Zack saw Dale on the floor, his back against the wall, wolfing down food from a steaming bowl. The boy looked up at him with a worried smile.

The barmaid zigzagged through the tables to Zack. Dark circles made her eyes seem more sunken than the contour of her face suggested. Lank, mousey brown hair shifted on her shoulders. She had been pretty at some time in the past. She stood with one hand on her hip and gesticulated with her other in quick, jerky movements as she spoke. "Mutton stew or chicken with herbs is two coppers, there is no wine, and the better ale is a copper per mug." Her tired voice matched her eyes.

Zack set three coppers on the table's corner. He examined a half-silver he turned about in his fingers and looked up into the serving maid's eyes.

Her interest flared briefly, and then dissolved into sullen disdain.

"Not what you think," Zack spoke softly. "Watch my back?"

Interest returned to her half-closed eyes that examined Zack and settled on his sword athwart his lap. She nodded once, and Zack flipped the silver coin that she caught and it disappeared inside her long skirt. "My name is Opal."

She returned moments later with an overflowing trencher of steaming stew, brown bread, and a mug of ale. The stew's flavor and meatiness surprise Zack. He settled down to enjoy his lastmeal.

Opal put her hand on her hip. She whispered, "Quince hates you. What did you do to him?"

"I've always thought he was a crook. I couldn't find the evidence to call in the Guard, but I had him run out of two towns. He took offense at that."

She walked away, smiling.

Zack looked up from his empty trencher when Quince returned. He glanced in Zack's direction, and a slight smile appeared before he hurried to the kitchen. Moments later, Opal returned to Zack's table with a mug of ale he had not ordered.

She leaned forward with a cloth only slightly cleaner than the table she wiped. Her whispered words breathed into Zack's face smelled of infection. "Trouble. He sent for three men." The hate generated in her tone justified Zack's trust.

"Get Dale and you away," he whispered back.

Opal started. Zack could not read the expression that flashed across her face. She left the full mug and hurried to the kitchen with the empty trencher and mug.

Zack saw no sign of Quince or Dale when the kitchen door opened. He leaned forward and slid two knives from his boot into his sleeves. Zack settled into the corner and balanced on the rough-hewn chairs' back two legs; its joints creaked. He sensed danger when three men entered the common room. Their eyes searched the room, and they tensed around the shoulders as he returned their glares. *Three of them, Quince must hate or fear me more than I realized to spend that kind of coin.*

The largest man's voice boomed across the room. "I'm Larson, and these are Rukert and Narce. Is Zack Stand here?"

Larson reminded Zack of a bull, but with half the brain. Two deep scars went from cheekbone to jaw on his left side beside a flattened nose. Rukert followed, and looked like a smaller version of his leader. Narce was another matter: quick, darting eyes and a stance that suggested training and determination over a small, thin frame. The idea that their names should impress him produced a smile.

Quince appeared on cue from the kitchen, smiled, and pointed in Zack's direction. "Why, Larson, that's Master Stand in the corner." The innkeeper's outstretched arm trembled slightly.

Larson did not bother to put much emotion in his accusation. "You raped my sister." The three new arrivals drew their swords and started in Zack's direction.

Zack stood before they reached the room's middle. "No, no, you got it wrong. My horse had his way with her. However, you shouldn't be upset. He did your mother first."

Larson stopped in his tracks so quickly, Narce ran into Larson and Rukert into Narce. Upstaged shock, followed by anger, settled on Larson's flushed face. Zack chuckled loudly.

Zack's three attackers moved toward him again. His arm streaked out in a blur of speed; his knife lodged in Rukert's greasy throat. Blood gushed out, spattering Larson's head and shoulders and onto the floor in front of him. Rukert gurgled and sunk to the floor.

The small, wiry one reminds me of Gaz. I pray to the Light's Source that his training is less. Zack threw the full mug of ale at Larson's feet.

Blood mixed with ale caused Larson's next step to fly out from under him. He crashed to the floor. The startled expression on his face changed to anger. He struggled to rise and fell again with loud expletives. He surged up.

Narce leapfrogged over a table while Zack drew his sword. The wiry, little man moved with precision; two tables remained between Zack and him. Narce held his sword like he knew how to use it.

Dale's high voice screamed from overhead beams. "Duck!"

Zack dropped as Quince's thrown mug glanced off his shoulder and crashed into the wall behind him. He came up in time to block Narce's double-handed overhead sword stroke. Zack's fist followed, jarring Narce off the floor onto the table behind.

Zack's follow-through to Narce's neck was stopped halfway by Larson's sword. Zack spun, lowered his sword and worked his way to the table's other side. Larson fell forward, overbalanced by the sudden release of resistance. Zack's sword continued across Larson's abdomen and produced a line of blood.

Zack's second knife dropped into his hand, and he buried it in Larson's chest under the sixth rib on the left side. A small, sucking sound escaped when he withdrew it. Larson dropped backwards, rendering a table into firewood. The look of surprise and pain on his face remained as the light in his eyes died.

Movement on his right caught Zack's eye, and he jerked backward as Narce's sword flashed in front of him. Zack leapt aside, putting another table between him and Narce.

A startled scream caused Zack and Narce to look in its direction. Quince's anger-twisted face rushed toward them with knives in both hands raised for attack. Zack held no illusion as to which man he sought.

Quince stopped midway across the room when the contents of a bucket loaded to the brim with fresh horse dung and urine fell on his head. His dung-streaked eyes rolled upward, his mouth sputtered as the hurled bucket followed its contents and crashed against his head. He wavered, and then fell to the floor. Dale's gleeful laughter rang from overhead.

Zack's chuckle joined Dale's shrill pitch. It stopped

short with Narce's exasperated roar of anger. The swordsman's wide swing brought his body closer to Zack as Dale screamed from above. Zack took his only opening. His fist, still holding his sword, crashed into Narce's face. Narce staggered backward and fell; his eyes went wide as Zack's knife plunged into his chest. He did not move.

Zack looked at Quince's face, streaked with horse filth, as he staggered back up. A chair appeared from nowhere behind him, crashing down on his head with the sick sound of split bone and broken wood. Opal's slight frame shook with emotion as the innkeeper crumpled to the floor. Zack regarded the frail looking woman's strength when he saw gray tissue mixed with bloody gore leak from Quince's skull. Opal collapsed, sobbing.

A rotund woman emerged from the kitchen with a frying pan raised for defense. She possessed a kind, round face and her cleanliness contrasted sharply with the rest of the inn. Her premature gray hair, bound into a no-nonsense bun, sparked an air of authority matched by her countenance. Dale followed on her heels. Her eyes searched among the bodies until her gaze fell on Quince. Her face relaxed into a broad smile. She dropped the pan and went to Opal, gently helped her stand and held her until her sobs quieted.

Zack retrieved his boot knives before the cook, who introduced herself as Effie, shooed him out.

* * *

ZACK slept well, albeit still dressed and with his sword at his side on the bed. The next morning, he rose and pulled on his boots. The closed inn sounded quiet. Vaguely remembering noises from below during the night, he quietly left his room and checked the hall before descending to the common room.

The heavyset cook beamed a smile at him when he entered. Silver and gold coins on the table in front of her caught Zack's attention. The room, thoroughly cleaned, showed no signs of bodies or gore any more. Effie bubbled with excitement as he walked across the common room to her table. "Master Stand, I believe these coins should compensate you for your trouble last night.

Zack counted six half-golds and a small pile of silvers. He chuckled. *I never believed Quince would pay so much,* he thought.

"Effie, what do Opal, Dale and you plan to do now?" He perched on a table across from her and watched while she deliberated his question, changed her expression to a serious mien, then slowly shook her head.

"I will give you the names of several men you can hire for a while to keep the usual customers out and discourage their return," Zack stated softly. "You will have more than enough to pay them and put the inn to rights. Reopen it with a new name and a new face."

Effie's stuttered incoherently words.

Zack continued with a smile. "I will sanction these actions with the Guard and the Zenith Lord's ministers if you agree to accept Opal and Dale as equal partners and see to Dale's education."

Effie still did not speak, but sputtered. It did not matter; her joyful smile provided her answer.

Zack refused the feelings of achievement and pleasure that struggled to rise in him. He started to return to his room to collect his belongings when a voice stopped him.

"Closed, what is this stupidity?"

Zack reached the window just in time to see a man walk up the hill and out of town. Effie followed Zack's motions and joined him at the window. "Who is that man?"

"That's Danford, one of Quince's regulars. He lives in the house on the hill just outside of town."

"I should return in an hour or two. Ask Dale to have my horse ready to saddle." Zack slipped out the door before Effie could answer. Walls closed on him from the village's other inn and the cooperage across the road. Sparse pines allowed a view of the hill from the back of the inn. Danford disappeared into the barn behind a two-story house. Strange sounds drew Zack to a pit halfway up the hill. His twitching nose identified its nature before he reached it: the village's midden dump. Bypassing it, the rest of the way to the barn offered no encumbrances. Shadows allowed him to accustom his eyes at the entrance to the barn. Danford used a pitchfork to distribute hay to two horses and two cows. Zack eased into the barn. His low voice carried a dire warning. "Greetings, Gaston."

The pitchfork came around in a smooth motion and flew at Zack; its tines sunk into the barn door inches from his face. He pulled the quivering handle free and positioned it as a weapon while he ran toward Gaston. Metal screeched against metal as Gaston drew his sword from where it hung on a post. The blade sunk between iron tines. Zack twisted the handle, and the pitchfork and sword flew over his head. Knives appeared in his hands as if by magic. Gaston swung his scabbard and hit Zack above his right ear. The move left the bandit's right arm exposed; Zack cut a long slash from shoulder to elbow. Gaston recoiled and brought his knee up toward Zack's crotch. A quick turn and the knife tore into Gaston's flesh again; his thigh's blood spread across sand-colored thews.

I thought I would enjoy butchering this piece of filth. I don't. Enough of this! Zack spun around and pulled Gaston's arms behind him. He kicked his feet out from under him and Gaston fell in a heap, his arms pulled high. A hard-heeled boot between his shoulders pressed the man's twisting body until both arms dislocated; his screams stopped when the same hard-heeled boot kicked him unconscious. Moments later, Gaston lay naked on the floor with a soiled cloth stuffed into his mouth, his ankles and useless wrists tied.

* * *

WATER splashed over Gaston's head as the empty bucket hit the floor. Shallow cuts oozed blood in the knife's wake down his back, buttocks, and legs. Zack flipped him over on his back. Muffled screams escaped from the gag as Gaston's weight crashed down on his shoulders and arms. Zack methodically continued his cutting across Gaston's chest, stomach, and the top of his legs. He poised the knife's point over hairy testicles. *No, he's not worth it.*

A cloak hung near the door. More muffled screams caused the tethered animal's additional agitation when Zack rolled the bloody body into the cloak and hefted it over his shoulder. Zack walked leisurely to the midden pit; there he half-threw, half-rolled Gaston into the filth hole. The pit's noises subsided when he drew close; movement had completely ceased. Zack threw Gaston's cloak over the body and waited. Movement resumed!

Zack waited until Gaston's muted screams floated up. Movement under the cloak continued to a fevered pitch. Several of the rats scurried from beneath the cloak with strips of flesh in their mouths. The screams had stopped, but not the frenzied movement as Zack turned and walked back to the house.

The barn did not yield up what Zack was searching for. He found many bottles of the Seven Realms' finest brandy. He loaded a cart from the barn with them; most would go to the inn's bar, the remainder would go into his saddlepacks. The cart's wheel caught in a crosswise rut mostly covered by straw in a corner of the barn. Zack cleared the straw away from the trap door. Well-oiled hinges moved soundlessly. Gaston's treasure trove lay within, packed in securely tied burlap sacks. *The reward from this will ease my retirement, if I live that long.*

45

* * *

GASTON's best horse stood loaded with his gold and jewels. Zack hitched the cart to him and led him to the inn. Dale looked confused when Zack arrived at the stable.

"Dale, take the horse out of his traces and unload the cart into the inn's storeroom. Leave the horse loaded. Ask Effie to fetch the village elder and tell her I'll need pen and ink." Zack's solemn countenance confused the boy. Zack left for his room without speaking further.

Morning light from the high window spilled across the cot as Zack searched in his saddlepacks and found a folded parchment. Thoughts flooded his mind as he placed it aside. *I thought I would feel something besides pleasure from ridding the world of scum when I killed Gaston. I thought his death would displace the emptiness inside. It didn't. Are Effie and Opal like the rest of the world that would stand by when a tortured woman screams? I think it best to continue my visits to Dale from time to time.*

A light knock on the door, followed by Effie's pleasant voice, brought him out of his deliberations. "Master Stand, Alfred Rouse, the village elder, is here." Zack clutched the parchment and followed Effie to the common room.

Alfred's balding head shone in the light from several lamps. Effie made the introductions and stood back.

"Master Stand, on behalf of the village, we want to thank you for disposing of Quince and his thugs."

Oh, Zack though, *the Guard would have acted long ago if the village had ever complained. I wonder how much Quince paid out to keep the elders quiet.* "Master Elder, I'm an agent of the Zenith Lord, who owns the house on the northern hill as you come into the village?"

"Danford . . . Danford Dewest. Has he done something wrong?"

"He has, but he won't anymore. I killed him. His

46

property now belongs to the Zenith Lord. As village elder, you will post this order on the door's house and insure no one enters the property. The animals in the barn must be cared for until the Guard arrives to collect them." Zack unrolled the parchment, filled in several blanks with Effie's pen, made sure the ink dried and handed it to the elder. Alfred looked at the parchment as if a coiling viper might bite him; he took it, gingerly. "I will make a full report to the Guard. If anything is missing, you'll be held responsible." Zack retreated toward his room. "Tell Dale to saddle my horse."

Zack rode out a half hour later, leading Gaston's horse. He found pleasure only in Dale's smile.

Twenty miles south of the village, Zack spotted the tower of the Guard station across a small valley. He hoped the stop would not slow him more than a few hours.

6

THE highest tower at Elizabethville's garrison formed a black silhouette that rose straight up, a watchtower of strength; the halo that flared at its peak from the setting sun provided symbolic justice. Zack breathed a sigh of relief, and Spellbinder whuffed and threw his head upward. They had made excellent time, and needed a well-deserved rest. Zack looked out over Elizabethville's seaside from the hill above the city. No ship's masts in the harbor reached for the blue sky.

Zack visualized the two ships that made the trip from the Hamptorian port, Hagan's End. They continued in service, old and in need of repair. Zack refused to sail on the oldest for fear of drowning. The exchange rate between Hamptor and the Seven Realms made it near impossible for a Hamptorian captain to afford any but the most needed work. He nudged Spellbinder forward.

Spellbinder eased into the Silver Tankard's stable yard, and Zack saw to his care. The stable had all the necessities and much more. His horse would be quite happy.

Zack liked the inn's cleanliness and its administration. He knew the innkeeper, Franc Horn, when he served on active duty. Most who saw him knew at once that he had served in the Guard. His bearing carried a military stance into retirement, his clothing clean and crisp, his manner direct but polite. He walked with a slight limp gained from an encounter with bandits that added to his statue rather than diminish it. He had a pleasant face and dark brown hair streaked with gray, a smile that welcomed guests, and a look that could freeze troublemakers and drunks. He ran the inn and provided a safe place for Gaz's agents when needed. Zack looked for his contact that played the part of the inn's most disreputable guest and found him absent.

Franc brought a mug of his best ale to Zack when he sat at a quiet corner table. The innkeeper's baritone voice sounded cheerful. "The first is always free for you, my friend. It's been a while, business or pleasure?"

Zack took the proffered mug and gulped a goodly part before answering. "I've come from Stonefire in thirty-one days and I'm tired. And, alas, it is business and I'll be on my way to . . ." Zack waited until the approaching serving maid took his order for lastmeal and left, ". . . Hamptor."

Franc leaned forward and spoke softly. "You will have time to rest. Captain Briggs won't return for a few days. He put out for Hagan's End yesterday."

Zack smiled in resignation. "Then I'll have another mug of your fine ale." The two men gave each other a mock salute, and Zack found peace and quiet for a few moments.

Halfway through the second mug, Calbris sauntered toward him with a mug of ale sloshing with his drunken steps. The man's act never ceased to amaze him; honed to the point that Zack could not tell if he remained sober and on duty or drunk and at his ease. Zack shrugged off that thought for another. *Calbris is always on duty.*

"Want ya buy . . . want to buy an old guardsman a drink?"

Zack appreciated the act, but wished Calbris would leave off some of his illusion's finer points, the stench reeking from his clothes and body for one.

He fell into the seat opposite him and Zack muttered, "Damn. Calbris, do you never bathe?"

The other man easily reverted to normal, crisp speech. "Every night, my fine spy. It took two years to become used to my fragrance, and after all that effort you want me give it up?" Zack sighed and shook his head.

"What brings you through my area of the Seven Realms?" Calbris slurred his words to perfection, wavered a bit, spilt a little ale on the table and grinned at Zack's apparent displeasure as it ran toward his lap. "Hey, I have to get rid of this stuff any way I can. You don't want the town drunk to be drunk, do you?"

Zack chuckled. "I'm on my way to Ozlid. Can you tell me what's happening over there?"

All levity left Calbris. "About midnight, in your room. I'll have someone with me. Will you use the name Delan?" Zack nodded and Calbris rose, almost falling over. "Cheap bas'ard, won't even buy . . . buy me a drink."

Zack watched while Calbris wove his way around tables and across the common room by a route only a drunk would understand and out the door. It occurred to him that most people wouldn't notice his strength under his illusion. Smells of mutton and vegetables seasoned with herbs and mint replaced Calbris' stink and provided welcomed relief. Zack enjoyed the fare, and then ambled toward his room to doze until midnight.

* * *

THE light tap on the door brought Zack instantly awake. Calbris and a stranger silently entered and waited until Zack barred the door before sitting. The man with Calbris mostly looked at his hands but stared, unblinking, at Zack when he raised his eyes. Nondescript and neatly dressed, he clashed with colorful, smelly, and dirty Calbris.

"Delan, this is Mosstell." Zack and Mosstell gripped forearms firmly for a second.

Mosstell wasted no time. He spoke so softly that Zack had to lean forward to make out his words. "All seven hells have broken free over there. Ozlid offered Arestead and Hamptor a huge sum in gold and free water for a year to the kingdom that can give them information about a black stone. One must describe the stone and its location or produce it. I tortured four Ozlid men to death to get the stone's true description." Thin lips produced a barely-formed, brief smile. Mosstell's statement concerning his captive's deaths sounded as dead as the men he had killed.

Calbris merely nodded at Zack's questioning expression.

Mosstell continued in the same near-whisper, as if his deeds comprised everyday affairs. "Every person that can is scampering to find any information about the stone. One night a drunk bragged he knew all about the stone. A man tried to beat the information from him before he could leave the tavern, and killed him. Then, the rest of the customers killed the murderer for destroying Hamptor's chance to get the reward. There are many more stories in the same vein, enough that some must be true. I advise you to play dumb with regards to any stone." Mosstell leaned back from whisper range.

Zack started when Mosstell spoke in a normal voice. "That is all I know about it. I'll go now." He hurriedly grasped forearms with Zack and Calbris as they stood. Zack let Mosstell quietly slip out the door and barred it again.

The two men eased back into their chairs. Zack spoke in a normal tone. "Is he always so social?"

Calbris chuckled. "He's a little peculiar; nonetheless, his information is the best available. I believe he did torture those men to death to get the stone's description. The interesting part is the damn thing is the exact description of a stone that High Lord Mountglen wears. In fact, he never takes it off, or so states the woman who gave me the information. She's been accurate and reliable in the past."

Moreover, well paid, I'm sure, Zack thought.

"She rarely sees Mountglen any more, however. He has someone he uses most of the time after that business with his wife's death.

"The stone is about the size of the end of a man's thumb and the dullest, blackest, thing you ever saw. You remember the old stories our mothers told of the Dark Stone, and how they threatened small ones who misbehaved with all sorts of ills coming from it?"

Zack chuckled and nodded.

"Well, the stone Mountglen wears could well be the one. It seems to pull in the surrounding light. Mountglen may be the High Lord of this realm, but he thinks nothing of bringing a man to ruin through ruthless business affairs." Calbris' expression implied the same low opinion of Mountglen that Zack held.

The spy continued, disregarding Zack's detached look. "I don't know much more. Ozlid still has Arestead and Hamptor by the throat over water. The kings can do nothing to salvage the situation and have not tried since their most recent attempt failed a century ago. The people are virtual slaves to Ozlid, and there seems no way out for them." Zack reflected the disgust in Calbris' tone.

"Do you trust Mosstell's report?"

Calbris nodded. "Oh, he's not one of ours. Our orders still prohibit torture, thankfully. He's from Arestead. He comes here to buy steel. As I said, I've tested his information and always found it true. Ozlid has some hold over him that he won't discuss. Ozlid's military uses a form of torture we can only imagine. Mosstell makes the instruments they use: finely barbed steel pins inserted into the victim and scraped across bone. The victim usually passes out quickly from pain, if they're lucky. From what I've heard, many are not."

Calbris' ghost of a smile lasted a few seconds. "Every time Mosstell hears of an Aresteadian or Hamptorian being hurt or killed by Ozlid, he uses the instruments he makes on one of the lower echelon officers who are his customers. They will eventually catch him, and he acknowledges the danger. But until they do, he has the ear—and sometimes a few other parts—of the men the two kingdoms hate."

Zack felt a chill work up his spine as Calbris continued. "He shows up here once in a while to keep me informed. I got him out of a tight place near Ozlid's border several years ago, before I became Elizabethville's town drunk. He thinks that Ozlid will invade someday and take over the kingdoms. I doubt it. They have it all without the trouble and expense of running two additional kingdoms and fighting insurrections."

Zack and Calbris talked about more pleasant subjects for a while, catching up on gossip and the elite's doings. The young Zenith Lord Jarod Greatstone and Zenith Lady Maress expected their first child. That comprised the best news from Stonefire since their wedding two years ago. The premature death of the young Zenith's father had hastened him to the dais of the Seven Realms long before normal.

Calbris promised to pass along any new information he might discover, and to notify Gaz when Zack sailed. After he took his leave. Zack waited with anticipation.

A light tap a few minutes after Calbris' departure brought a smile to his face. Debra, one of the inn's serving maids, entered silently and Zack closed the door. He swept her into an embrace, and their kiss lasted long with passion and remembrances.

Zack considered her pretty. She seemed content with him, and had never once stared at his scars. Zack gathered himself greatly privileged; the talk in the common room named her "unattainable." *What does she see in me?* He no longer questioned that their time together—or his time with any woman—still left him feeling empty, the pleasure he received purely physical except with her.

Zack denied his handsomeness, although women's actions and the truth contradicted his perception. His scars produced a profound false perception that ate at his self-image and constantly fed his distrust. Zack saw his scars whenever he looked in a mirror, dressed or not. His chest, abdomen, and back, all restored beyond their former strength and contour, looked hideously deformed to him. The scars had faded, and his hardened, muscled abdomen further distracted from their appearance. The faint scars' length and obvious vicious nature caused people's reaction, not the barely noticeable scars. He remained in superb shape, powerfully built with rippling muscles in perfect proportion through constant exercise.

She never seems to notice my scars. She always makes me feel happy, and she does little things for me that's not part of her job. I feel something with her I don't with other women. She is so beautiful, and she says I'm her favorite and she thinks I'm handsome. I don't pay for her time. Why would she lie to me?

Debra pushed a strand of blond hair from his face and his thoughts fled from his mind.

Will blond hair and blue eyes be a problem in Ozlid? The question was forgotten as Debra's bare arms pulled him down beside her. Consideration of Ozlid and his assignment did not arise the rest of the night. He slept late and woke alone, much refreshed.

Zack enjoyed his firstmeal, and then made his way to the garrison commander's office to pay his respects. She saw him immediately.

"Zack Stand, it's been a long time, before that terrible business with Gaston."

"You—you know about that?" He tried not to show the shock he felt.

"I had an assignment at the Spires, and your file had been misplaced into a group I studied. I realized it belonged somewhere else and took it to Gaz. He ordered me to never tell anyone. I never have, and I never will. Now, how can I help you?"

Zack started not to speak and leave, but thought better about it. He had talked to only Gaz and High Healer Sternwood about his torture. *I think she means it when she says she'll never speak of it.* "I have a mission across the sea. I

54

don't know what I'll encounter while there. I may need assistance when I return."

"I'll be honored to do what I can. I'll be retiring in a few weeks, but I'll be sure to impress your importance on my successor."

They chatted for a few minutes about the goings on in Starfire before Zack wished her well on her planned retirement in a few weeks. Then, he found the resident priest of the Seven Realms' religious order to send a message. The priest worked for Gaz with his order's blessing.

Zack watched the priest perform his special talent. Intense concentration and effort caused sweat along his brow. He captured his messenger's thoughts through the channeled power of his graystone, in this case, a red-tail hawk. The priest imprinted a message to Michael Gaz reporting Zack's arrival at Elizabethville, adding the bird's destination and released the bird to fly to the Spires for another priest to interpret the message and pass it on.

Finished with his requirements and suppressing the irritation of waiting on Captain Briggs, Zack set out to see the changes Elizabethville had experienced since his last visit.

* * *

DEBRA's long black hair spread across the pillows behind her. Moist, deep brown eyes and the smile on her pretty face, flush from their lovemaking, painted her satisfaction. A delicate sigh came in the form of a small gasp. "I'll miss you." The words matched a gentle caress that mirrored the desire they had enjoyed moments before.

"I'm not gone yet," Zack whispered.

"You will be soon. Captain Briggs' ship will reach port tomorrow afternoon, and you will sail on the evening tide."

Zack felt surprise at her anguish-laced words. "Now,

how could you possibly know that?" He flipped on his side, intertwined his legs with hers, lightly stroked the outside of her leg, and followed the curve of her body to her waist. He kissed her full on the lips.

She pushed him away, slipped from the tangled bedclothes, and padded across the room to dress. She answered quietly, hesitantly. "You know how. I told you about it. I see things. They usually come true."

With his back against the headboard, Zack watched her dress. She spun around faster than normal, breaking Zack's concern. The hem of her dress rose nearly to her knees; he laughed.

"Zack, be careful on this trip."

She scurried out before he could rise from the bed. He called after her once, with no response. Zack tried not to let her words disturb his pursuit of sleep; gradually, he relaxed and nodded off, only to wake with a start, his nerves still jangled by Debra's warning. Sleep found him in the wee hours. He woke later than normal, and felt as if he had not slept at all.

Zack came late to the common room and looked for Debra in vain. He did not inquire after her. Memories of her expression and timorous warning consumed him; he hardly knew when he finished his firstmeal and came to himself tapping his spoon against an empty wooden bowl. *Could she be right?*

Preoccupied by her warning, Zack shambled to the stables, saddled Spellbinder, and rode toward the northeastern hills. Spellbinder expressed his pleasure for the exercise by prancing and fought to run. Zack gave him his head, and the horse galloped along for a few hundred yards. Then Zack slowed their pace, and enjoyed a few hours riding over rolling hills.

Spellbinder trotted to the crest of the hill outside Elizabethville in the early afternoon. Zack reined him to a halt and stared out to sea. He pulled his spyglass' smooth brass cylinder from within a full saddlepack and used it to gaze at a dot far out at sea.

Captain Briggs' sails held a unique flair. For all the ship's drab state caused by the lack of proper maintenance, her sails lifted spirits and displayed the captain's measure with their colors: the outer jib, deep sky blue; the inner jib, bright yellow; and the forestaysail, bright red.

Questions swam in Zack's mind. *How could she have known . . . and what of her warning?* Zack nudged his knees against Spellbinder's side and let him amble back toward the inn. He wanted to speak to Debra before he left, to try and get some answers from her.

It was not to be.

7

UPON opening the door to his room, Zack discovered Calbris packing his belongings into an open saddlepack, with various things of interest spread across the bed. Zack felt little surprise at finding the other spy there, although his activities raised an eyebrow. He stood next to the bed and surveyed the new items.

Calbris slyly remarked, "I took a few liberties. I didn't know when you might return, and Briggs may leave on the evening tide. He rarely stays in port overnight."

Zack's annoyance at not finding Debra left him despondent, and the partial confirmation of her prediction perplexed him.

Calbris walked to the bed, breaking Zack's train of thought. He tossed a supple, dark brown leather cloak over Zack's shoulders. "The leather is most subtle, waterproof, and reversible. Notice the knotted leather woven at the clasp. Pull it."

Zack adjusted the cloak as it fell over him. "Well, first of all, it's nice to see you, too." Calbris made a small, undecipherable noise. Zack found the clasp. His finger muscles twitched with effort; the leather knot broke away and a stiff leather strip slid free. Zack's hands stretched the garrote wide with a *snap*. He looked at Calbris' smiling face. "Clever."

Calbris' reply sounded like a teacher with a recalcitrant student. "The garrote is simple to thread back into the cloak. The leather thongs are worked with wire and are very strong."

Zack watched Calbris slide the garrote back home, and then push hard on the clasp until he heard a *click*. With a frown, he continued in a matter-of-fact tone. "Gaz said he had people working on the click." Zack smiled. Calbris did not.

More items on the bed drew Zack's interest. He ran his fingers over a deadly set of six throwing knives, their hilts wrapped with leather worked into discerning beauty. Highly polished steel glistened in the sunlight as he drew one; his fingers twirled the blade with perfect balance.

Calbris beamed. "I thought you might like those. The cloak has four sheaths sewn in across the shoulders and two in the front."

Calbris continued his instructions, making Zack feel he was attending a class at the Academy. "As I mentioned earlier, the cloak is reversible. Its inside is lighter colored, with variations that will be useful to hide you in different terrains. The leather's pattern has the knife's sheathing worked into it. A lappet adds further protection and secures them. There is another clasp on the reverse with the same surprises and another lappet. Notice the small knobs along the cloak's hem. The hem is weighted but those are not the weights. You may pull them off. Each one contains enough concentrated venom to kill a warhorse. They're crushable, and the whole mess becomes clear, odorless and tasteless in liquid."

Zack slid the bright, perfectly balanced steel blades into their hidden homes. His expression accurately projected his rising concern. *How many more surprising things lie in store?*

"Try not to get upset, Zack." Calbris backed away, hands raised and looking like he dreaded the next lesson.

"Spellbinder is being fitted to a new saddle." His raised hand cut off Zack's remark. "It has a pommel that twists apart. The powder inside is fine and fans out rather well. It will blind someone for several minutes if it hits their eyes, and a small amount thrown into a fire will produce a remarkable flash of light." Underneath the stirrup leathers is an awl-like piece of steel screwed into a flattened steel crosspiece that gives enough support for an effective stabbing tool. Both ends of each stirrup break away and allow access to two more stabbing weapons. A leather flap protects Spellbinder. The cantle houses two throwing knives like the ones here." Calbris paused for a breath before continuing. "What do you think of the riding crop?" The crop's beautiful spirals of bright yellow, blue and white feathers down its length were more in keeping with a woman's tool.

"It's a little fancy for me." He picked it up, gingerly, not sure, if it might bite. Calbris took it from him.

"I know. It's the feathers, right?" Zack nodded. "Both ends twist off. The feathered pieces are darts that pull away. Insert one into the end of the crop and blow at your target. I understand that it takes a little practice, but they can be quite deadly up to ten paces away. They are loaded with poison. There are several empty darts in your saddlepack to use for practice."

Zack's apprehension increased.

Calbris held up a small cylinder of shiny brass. "I know you have a spyglass. Exchange it for this one that's much smaller and twice as powerful." He shook his head. "Damned if I know how they did it."

Zack hardly believed a spyglass the size of his second finger held greater visual power than one that stretched to a forearm's length. He peered through the window and started. He saw solid blue canvas from Briggs' outer jib like he was standing on the dock next to the ship. "I like it."

Zack turned back around to see Calbris holding a boot, stronger and much sturdier than his. "Each heel contains herbs you will recognize. It takes a strong twist to the right to open them. You won't have to worry about trailing their contents behind you if you turn on your heel."

A light tap on the door interrupted them; the looks on their faces showed quite different emotions: Zack's sparked with the hope it might be Debra, and Calbris' face darkened with what Zack judged as annoyance. Zack cracked the door to find Franc's son with his hand raised to knock again. His face fell.

"Master Stand, sir, Captain Briggs says he will be leaving on the evening tide, and your passage is welcome for the same fare as last time." The lad pulled in a deep lungful of air. His white teeth gleamed from regular use of teeth twigs, and his eyes sparkled when Zack placed two new coppers in his hand.

Zack closed the door and barred it again, his thoughts reflecting his growing concern. *How many lethal devices will I have, and why does Gaz feel their need? I use six knives and a sword; four knives are out of sight. A heavily armed man creates problems. It's hard to finesse when you clink with every step. At least they hid most of it . . . perhaps it's for the best.*

Calbris continued as if the interruption had not happened. "One more thing, and I'll leave you to sort it out and finish packing." Calbris picked up a burgundy-colored belt and held it out to Zack. "Quite simple, the device on the buckle twists to the right and a short knife will slide out. If you pull on the buckle's tongue, another garrote emerges. Any questions?" He sat on the bed, looking pleased.

Zack swept his arm wide to encompass the weapons of death around him. "Why all this? Am I merely to spy on Ozlid or conquer it?"

Calbris shrugged. "I assume that Gaz believes you may need them. He has worked on these devices for some time. Perhaps he wants you to see how well they function. They arrived shortly after you left this morning. I have been figuring out the instructions for the tools of our trade. They are in your saddlepack. You need to destroy them as soon as you become familiar with them."

Zack snorted. "Hang the tools of our trade. I'll feel like a walking armory. You know what happens if I'm caught with this many arms. My captors will think the worst and throw me in a cell, or worse. This mission is to gather information. Do you know something that I don't?"

Calbris smiled and said in his best-drunken slur, "I just follow orders, old friend." He changed to sober speech. "Gaz didn't pass on any more information. I just think he wanted you to have every advantage. Now, I must go and you have little time. Oh, one more thing, there are twenty gold coins in the leather pouch. That gold will be worth several times its value in Hamptor. I do not have the foggiest notion why Gaz provided you a fortune. Perhaps you should simply try buying Ozlid, and we all might rest easier."

They said their farewells, and Zack watched the befuddled drunk wander off down the hall.

He took all the time he dared to arrange and pack his deadly gifts. The few personal items left over, he pushed on top of a nearly full saddlepack and strapped it shut. He paid his bill and collected Spellbinder. Fine tooling graced the new saddle, and the leathers used came from the best hides he'd ever seen. Zack shook his head. *This saddle is more likely to draw thieves rather than be any additional use in my traveling armory. Oh well, I can handle thieves.*

Zack bought oats and grain at the stable, adding the bags to Spellbinder's increasing burden. He made his last stop for travel gear. Hamptor's main roads had provided enough inns for the traveler on his previous three trips, at least for the distance inland he had traveled, perhaps half the distance to Ozlid's border. He might not need the additional gear, but being prepared made him feel better. *Sleeping in the open can get cold and uncomfortable.*

Zack caught sight of Debra's worried face in the crowd as he nudged Spellbinder toward the ocean. She clutched the small crystal stone she wore around her neck. A tear slid down her cheek as she turned and disappeared into an alley too narrow for Spellbinder to enter. With too little time for him to follow on foot, he continued toward colorful sails.

8

SPELLBINDER reared at the sight of the ship, his displeasure obvious. Zack didn't blame him. Locked up in a dark hole on a rolling ship for close to two days was something he didn't think much of either.

Great bundles of raw cotton filled most of the hold, but an aisle had been created that opened onto an area large enough for three horses. Spellbinder navigated the ramp with disdain manifested in every movement. Zack did his best to settle him. The Captain had ordered straw brought aboard and a makeshift stall fastened to the main mast. It met Spellbinder's needs.

Zack noticed freshly done oakum and thought: *Briggs must do well to afford this kind of maintenance on his ship. If they had dry docks at Hagan's End, no doubt Briggs would keep his ship in top shape. The difference in our gold's value must wear sorely on Hamptorians. The trade from here is small, but we buy some goods from Hamptor and Arestead. It's strange their kings won't support the captains' ships. I wonder if funds there are so scarce the kings can't afford the help or just won't do it. Are they that shortsighted?*

Zack tried to imagine the ship's center. His conclusion pleased him. *Spellbinder's placement on the orlop deck, amidships, might prove advantageous. He will have less movement this far down, and the surrounding cotton might deaden the noise that spooked him before. Perhaps he will grow to like ships.* Zack's chuckle brought Spellbinder's glare on him.

Laden with saddle and saddlepacks, Zack reached the top of the ladder to the main deck. He felt the ship roll forward rather than rocking. "Captain Briggs is in a hurry," he muttered.

He stowed his gear and left his claustrophobic cabin to watch their departure from the main deck's larboard side. They had barely cleared port when the main and fore sails caught the wind and hurried the ship into the prevailing current. Zack watched Elizabethville fade from view when First Mate Bronson arrived to lead him to the Captain's cabin beneath the poop deck.

Zack passed between the first mate's cabin on the larboard side and his cabin used for the odd passenger on the starboard side, along a narrow passageway leading from the main deck to the Captain's cabin, stretched across the stern. Briggs sat behind a large desk positioned in the center of the room. He had changed little since Zack's last encounter with him, standing slightly over six feet tall, with a balding half-head of brown and gray hair. Hard, brown eyes could change in an instant to an impish twinkle that Zack surmised his crew never saw. A short, pug nose hovered over full lips. He carried a large, beefy frame that held little fat. "Come, come, Delan. Have a seat and some food with me."

Briggs' joviality made Zack smile. He knew him to be a tough captain, and the crew probably never saw levity from him while at sea. On previous trips, Zack had stayed out of his way when on deck and had noticed he projected a particular sternness when the situation called for it. He seemed fair to his crew.

"Thank you, Captain. I'm honored."

Briggs snorted, "None of that. You know me well enough. I want to hear the gossip surrounding High Lord Mountglen, his realm, the other realms, and some intelligent conversation. I usually find none on a voyage. How is the precious gems business?"

Zack smiled. *I have no idea what gave him the impression I deal in jewels. It's a good pretense; though, not one I would have picked. My knowledge on the subject is better than most I suppose from studying at the mines for a mission. Does he think I'm an adventurer? He hasn't come out and asked, except that one time.*

How did he put it? Ah yes, 'why leave the Seven Realms, where life's struggles are lighter?'

The meal concluded as Zack ran out of choice tidbits of gossip. Briggs had given him much consideration during their meal, and did not hide it well. He gave the distinct notion of an impending explosion if not allowed to speak about whatever was bothering him. Finally, Zack simply asked, "What has happened in Hamptor?" With that opening—*more like harpooning,* he thought—the Captain sallied forth.

"What do you know about stones?"

Zack caught the usage of the word "stones," not jewels or a particular jewel; he let it go unnoticed in his answer. "What kind of jewel?"

"No, not a—well, I guess it could be . . . no. It's said to be a black stone." Briggs sounded flustered, and fell silent shaking his head.

Zack spoke with the casual assuredness of an expert. "There is a chalcedonic stone that's often dyed a black color, and there is hematite, that is a black crystal. Are those what you mean?" Briggs did not see the sly smile that briefly played across his face.

"No, I'm sorry, my friend. Let me start from the beginning. You know the situation between Ozlid and her neighbors—of course you do. What am I saying?" Briggs took a deep breath and started over. "Ozlid is looking for a black stone." He went on to describe much the same information Mosstell and Calbris provided, except for the stone's physical description, and ended with a warning. "Delan, many a common room brawl has ended in death over this accursed stone. Some of my fellow citizens think it's a way Ozlid tortures us, and it doesn't even exist. I don't know what to think, just that you should be careful." Briggs leaned into his chair, took a long draught of ale and said no more on the subject.

* * *

ZACK spent a great deal of time with Spellbinder: rubbing him down, feeding him, keeping his area clean, and talking to him. The horse behaved more calmly than on previous trips, and Zack hoped he would eventually overcome his fear of seas and ships. He brushed the animal's sand-colored coat that did not need brushing. Spellbinder's soft nudges signaled his enjoyment, and it provided Zack something to do. He did not hear the crewman pad in on bare feet.

"You sure take good care of that horse."

Zack started, glad that Spellbinder stood between them. Zack walked around his horse to face the crewman standing ten feet away, holding implements to muck out Spellbinder's stall in one hand. Zack's internal alarms rang: *Briggs sends someone else down a few times a day for that duty, but I finished it myself less than an hour ago, and this crewman watched me on deck.*

Zack kept his voice calm and his manner casual. "He enjoys it, and it helps keep him distracted from the rolling seas."

"Uh, Master Stand, do you know anything about a . . . uh . . . a black stone? We would sure be glad if you could tell us about it."

Zack watched the crewman retreat a step when their eyes met. *He's probably not supposed to be here, and Briggs would have his balls if he knew of it.*

"Who is 'we'?" Zack noticed the crewman kept one arm from sight. Zack leaned down on the pretense of checking Spellbinder's perfectly sound ankles and slid a boot knife up his sleeve.

"Oh . . . uh, just me and some of the crew. We, uh, figured you might know of it. You make these trips and well, you know, you come from Jewel and all, we figured you might even have a black stone yourself. I mean, you do trade in jewels."

Zack rose suddenly, and the crewman retreated again. "What I trade in is no concern of yours or the crew. Now move aside, I'm going topside."

The crewman backed up until his shoulders came against the cotton bale's corner that formed the beginning of the aisle. His arm whipped around in front of him, his hand clutched a gaff. Barbed hooks glistened in the light from the only lamp. His snarling words sounded desperate. "We know you got it, or if not you got just as good as. A shame that the horse there killed you, and I'll make it look that way."

Zack wasn't too concerned as he considered the man. *He's big enough to be a danger, but he's scared. He may know how to brawl, but from how he's holding that gaff, he's never used it as a weapon. He wants me down here, or he would have attacked before.* "I just have one question."

"Uh . . . what?" The crewman faltered.

Zack's voice softened. "Why should I not kill you now rather than wait?"

The crewman started, then came at him, bright metal swinging in an arc toward Zack's face. At the last moment, Zack simply stepped aside, pressing against the wall of cotton bales. The crewman followed through, diving headlong to where he had stood at the beginning of his charge. The lack of resistance from not hitting his target left him off balance. Zack brought the blunt end of his knife down on the crewman's head. He collapsed to the floor, unconscious. Zack made sure he wasn't in danger from Spellbinder's hooves.

He found a length of coiled rope used for lashing cotton bales in place and cut off two strips. He left the crewman gagged and bundled like the cotton bales, then headed to the ladder leading topside. Dark clouds moved swiftly overhead.

He peered over the hold's coaming. Three unarmed men held the struggling first mate on the main deck against the outer wall of his cabin and the captain stood on the poop deck with a sword that he held competently. Much more competent than the two crewmen on the main deck brandishing gaffs and knives up the ladder.

Drawing a knife, Zack stepped back down into the hold, and pitched his voice aft and loud. "Well, Captain Briggs, how many of these men should I kill, and how many do you need alive to crew this ship?" The sounds of wind, waves, and creaking planks filled several seconds that followed.

The captain's voice sounded strong and confident. "Oh, if it comes to it, you and I can take her in. We're not that far from port, and I consider you a good candidate for seamanship."

In the confusion, yelling, and a cloud that darkened the quarter moon, Zack slipped over the coaming and knelt behind the rolled bull rope for the main mast. The shadows maintained his favor as he peered aft. The captain stood his ground, alone on the poop deck. Zack chose the best time with the shadows, the ship's roll, and the movements of the men, picking one of the three crewmen pressed against the housing wall and holding First Mate Bronson.

A gasp came from the two men on the mate's right side; the crewman on his left made only a gurgling noise. Zack's knife in his throat kept him from making any other sounds. Zack turned his attention away. *The crewman below is out of action for a while. One is dead. That leaves a man for each boot knife and the captain's sword.*

Zack bided his time until another obliging cloud blocked the moon. He looked over his cover. The situation remained much the same: Two men struggled to contain Bronson while two more kept their backs to Zack and continued threatening the Captain. Zack chose the one doing all the bravado yelling below the captain. "Captain, I've wanted to slit your innards from the moment I got on the ship." The knife caught him between the shoulder blades and he dropped face first to the deck without making any more annoying threats.

His crewmate spun and ran in Zack's direction. Zack lay flat on the deck and blessed the darkness. The crewman stopped on the bull rope's other side and searched everywhere but behind the coiled rope. Zack struck out and sliced through the mutineer's hamstring. The crewman fell to the deck, his screams adding to the confusion. Zack grinned. *In times like these, I love confusion.*

Zack watched the Captain ease down the ladder to the main deck and engaged one of his first mate's remaining captors by sword. The unarmed crewman made the mistake of throwing a punch, and the captain ran him through with practiced ease.

Zack ran aft to assist as the first mate reversed the hold on his remaining captor and lifted him quite satisfactorily over the rail, clearly not needing Zack's services. The crewman caught the rail; a large wave swung him away from the hull and his grasp failed. Zack did not hear the splash when the crewman dropped from sight.

Zack watched as another attacker crept from the shadows, jabbed toward him with a knife and ran forward. He got even with the foremast when a dense thud sounded. Cackling laughter ushered from the cook's near toothless grin while he held his iron frying pan high over his head. "They forget the old ones." He cackled again and disappeared into the ship's lower portions toward the galley, swinging his pan.

Bronson and Zack hauled the still unconscious crewman from the hold, bound hand and foot and laid him out beside the hamstrung crewman that looked nearly in shock. Zack tied his hands in from of him, with no need to tie his feet.

Predawn light gave way to a glorious sunrise. Rays of light split white clouds, in sharp contrast to the gore on deck. Zack retrieved his weapons from the various bodies, cleaned them, and slid them into his boots as the Captain approached. "I guess I owe you my life and my ship, Master Stand."

"You owe me nothing, Captain. My presence probably started this mess in the first place. They thought I possessed or knew something about the black stone you mentioned."

"No, they're mutineers no matter what the cause. The dead already have their reward, and the living will be branded and shunned the rest of their lives if I don't decide to hang them." Briggs slowly shook his head. "They're not my normal crew, the cook and Bronson are the only two aboard from my regulars. Now I know what kept my men from reporting for this trip. Speed was important, and I found this bunch waiting at the harbormaster's office." The Captain and Zack looked over at the newly conscious crewman struggling with his bonds, banging his heels on the deck in frustration, and chuckled. "I should have known better than sail with an unknown crew. No, this episode started before you came aboard. My cargo is for a friend that may lose his business if he doesn't get it in time. I think, therein lies the true motive behind our dead and bound friend's actions. You would have just been a bonus for them."

Noise from above drew Zack's attention. The first mate brought in the topgallant as the captain said, "We will go in with the mainsail alone. There is land."

Zack's eyes followed the direction of the captain's pointing arm, surprised that land lay so close. He could make out the port city of Hagan's End.

"Well, Master Stand, you'll be a hero when word gets out. I doubt you will have to pay for a mug of ale for a month."

"If you don't mind, Captain, I'd prefer that you leave my name out of this episode."

The captain shook his head. "As you wish, but I reserve the right to feast you."

"That you may, Captain, that you may."

* * *

ZACK found the Blue Sail Inn still provided excellent service and accommodations. The captain provided a true feast for his lastmeal in a private dining room. Briggs looked jubilant. Zack kept his feelings hidden. He noticed that the captain drank little of the fine wine he had ordered, and Zack followed suit. *For once,* he thought, *I don't have to feign a drunkard.* The mutiny did not enter the conversation until the serving maid had delivered dessert and left the room. "What fate did you decide for the mutineers?"

Briggs looked up from his plate of sweet pastry with a twinkle in his eye. He cleared his throat before answering. "I decided to hang them. Captain Pinch of the *Gallant Sea* and the local army commander persuaded me to hold off until the commander could talk with the scum. I received word hours ago that Derson, the one the cook knocked colder than ice, confessed when told that he might have his hamstring cut like his mate and branded. As I'd suspected, my friend's competitor planned the attempt. Their orders were to heave us overboard and deliver the cotton to a cove up the coast, after which the ship would be painted and renamed at Wellsport's dry docks in your realm of Deepwells. They must have been crazy—I wouldn't attempt to sail that distance with my ship in her condition for ten times the payment.

"The three of them met the magistrate this afternoon. They confessed within an hour. I learned they didn't twitch overly much when the rope jerked." Briggs sat back, as if the telling of the mutineer's demise pleased him as much as the meal. "Now, my friend, tell me of your purpose in Hamptor, and mayhap I can help you in your endeavors."

Zack considered for a moment. *Briggs may be loyal to me, but caution must prevail.* "Captain, I may have to leave

Hamptor in a hurry during one of these trips. I would like to think that I could count on your help if such a need arises. I'm not a thief, or lawbreaker of any kind, but at times I have enemies, much like your friend, and it's often wise to be quickly away." Zack took a sip of his wine, never breaking eye contact with the captain.

Briggs considered but a moment before answering. "You have my promise, my friend. It's a small thing for so great a service you have given me. Is there nothing else?"

"Only that we strive to become friends, Captain," Zack answered

Briggs started to answer as quickly, and then paused, his face growing somber. "Aye, I have few friends, and I'd be honored to count you as one." Neither man spoke for a moment then the serving maid tapped on the door and entered. The conversation resumed on a lighter note and an hour later when they parted, the grasp of their forearms and their countenance suggested the foundation of a firm friendship. Zack felt satisfaction as he made his way to his room.

Zack found his bill paid the next morning. A note and a list of inns that Briggs serviced with imported goods. Zack read the note with interest and could not help smiling.

> *The bearer of this note is Master Delan Stand. He provided me a great service, without which I would have lost my ship and you would have lost my services for all time. Please offer Master Stand whatever he may require on my behalf.*
>
> *With respects,*
>
> *Crawford Briggs, Captain*

The innkeepers needed Briggs, and his note would carry weight. Zack looked across the wide Seawall Street and found no ship in harbor. A beautiful day with few clouds greeted him. *Might the day portend a better land trip than the sea provided?*

9

ZACK's map and notes made on previous trips included several inns on Briggs' list. He set the same ground-eating pace he used on his way to Elizabethville. The last of winter had evaporated into the first pleasant days of spring. A land that should have been budding with life stood bare with dead grass and trees. The lack of water hurt the people and the land of Hamptor and Arestead. Bristling anger returned when he saw the dismal landscape had deteriorated from his last visit two years before.

Zack's thoughts jarred him. *Death-holds come in many varieties. Tyrants express ruthlessness in many ways. Tyranny of this magnitude is incomprehensible in its scope, and manifests great evil. The Dark's Source directs acts of this kind.* He could think of no greater evil than that committed by Ozlid's rulers. Shock settled over him as Gaz's fears took on elements of prophecy. Zack's hope for better conditions faded. He rode on, trying to put his anger aside. *I don't have the leeway for anger or its lover, mistakes.*

Zack believed Spellbinder covered distance as rapidly as any horse could, and felt his progress that day proved it. Slight breezes swung the inn's sign, the first name on Briggs' list, as he passed it in early afternoon; the last rays of sunset flickered on the inn's sign, the second name on the list, that evening: Running Bull. The stable yard's cleanliness and well-tended stable provided a good sign to an experienced traveler.

Light hazel eyes widened when the groom saw Zack's sword, and became wider still at his closer inspection of Spellbinder and his saddle's workmanship. Zack judged

74

the boy to be near his Age-of-Man, time and smiled at the stable boy's attention. The boy's surprised look continued when Zack followed him into the stable and set about removing Spellbinder's tack and saddle.

"He's a fine horse, no?" The boy nodded emphatically. "Such a horse gives his all to his master, and it's a loyalty that must be repaid."

Zack brushed Spellbinder on one side while the boy helped on the opposite side. Spellbinder enjoyed the dual applications for his comfort, and showed it with nudges to his pleasure givers, as he often did, that brought a smile to the boy. Zack added a handful each of oats and grain to Spellbinder's feed tray. Bewilderment continued on the boy's face when Zack piled the two pairs of saddlepacks atop the saddle and hefted the load to his shoulder. The boy looked on approvingly while Zack adjusted his load and headed for the inn's entrance.

Lanky limbs started toward Zack when he stepped into the common room. "Master Ballrand?" Zack spoke while resting his burden on the table nearest the entrance as he looked around. The clean inn showed the great pains taken to vent the smoke from the room, leaving almost pleasant air behind.

"I'm Master Ballrand."

The voice sounded cold to Zack for an innkeeper of an obviously well run establishment. Zack knew the Hamptorian dialect well, and pronounced it with little foreign inflection. He wondered what caused his unease: *Perhaps he caught my accent and it caused his wariness, or is it a stranger knowing his name?* Pulling Briggs' note from his tunic, he handed it to his host.

Ballrand read the note twice before returning it. "Captain Briggs provides a valuable service for us and has been fair in his dealings. He has not asked a favor before; I will provide what help I can. I have a fine room that's available and a good cook. I believe you will be happy with the service I provide. You must tell the Captain that

75

it's no more than I would do for any traveler. I cannot promise anything more until I hear your requests."

Zack's dismay at the man's stiffness forced a frown. "I wish for a quiet room, food and good care for my horse and I expect to pay your usual rate. No more requests than those."

The innkeeper looked contrite. "Forgive my tone, Master Stand. I realize that you must have ridden fast to arrive here from Hagan's End in one day. The innkeepers along this road have been warned about strangers arriving alone or in a pair, and few people carry swords." Ballrand's eyes fell to Zack's sword hilt. "They call the innkeeper by name, and later rob and kill him or one of his guests. They have not operated this far south, yet. Still, I think we innkeepers are all jumpy. I have two cousins who are coming to help me in case of trouble. Most of the innkeepers are getting help. I recognize Captain Briggs' hand, and you're more than welcome."

Zack followed the lanky innkeeper upstairs to a room at the hallway's end. The stout iron key unlocked the door, and as Master Ballrand pushed the door open, Zack had a pleasant surprise. Pale yellow walls caught the light from the fire in interesting hues. Two windows on the sides of the fireplace were guarded by stout iron bars on the outside and framed by dark brown draperies hung from ceiling to floor. Two plush chairs covered in green, the color of dark forest moss, were set at angles to the fireplace; a small table and wood chair placed against the wall opposite the bed and a washstand beside the bed completed the room's furnishings. Dark oak planks formed the wood moldings and furniture stained the same color as the highly polished floor. The imposing bed contained four posters but no draperies. A feather mattress covered in crisp, white bedclothes with warm blankets to soothe him. A feather blanket of good quality, matching the drapery's deep brown color, would be warm on the coldest nights. The washstand held a pitcher of water, basin, and mug.

The large room and bed looked comfortable, especially the bed. *What will Gaz think of my taking such quarters?* His usual accommodations comprised a common sleeping room with several snoring men on pallets spread too close together while he projected the look of an unimportant traveler. The memory of gold hidden in his saddlepacks stopped such questions as being pertinent, and he grinned at the conclusions it brought: *Baths. Not having to look for smelly, common wash areas that are rarely available, not having to go days without a decent cleansing. I could get used to traveling like this.*

Zack placed his burden on the bed's far side, hidden from the door and walked to Ballrand, who held out the key.

"I have the only other key locked away. I suggest you eat early. The inn will fill quickly this time of night. We have some wine that's not very good, and cost more than I think it's worth to boot. However, the ale is excellent. You have clean bedclothes with no vermin. The cost is a half-silver and three coppers more if you require a bath. The tub and water will be brought to the room." Zack reached into his purse and brought out a silver coin for the room and bath. Ballrand looked surprised when he felt the weight. "Where did you get this?"

"Why?" Zack anticipated the question. Calbris did not have Hamptorian silvers to exchange before Zack left Elizabethville.

"The weight is different than we're used to." Ballrand took a silver coin from his pouch and weighed them side by side, hand to hand. "Your one silver is the weight of three of ours. I have not seen silver minted like this in a long time. Where did you get them?"

"I'm from the Seven Realms, the land you call Jewel."

Surprise caused the man to look up sharply. "Few of your countrymen ever travel here. I have scales downstairs, and can exchange your silvers if you like.

That's something I can do without charge, and honor Captain Briggs' request. I suggest you bathe after your lastmeal."

Zack nodded at the suggestion and followed him out. Ballrand locked the door, handed him the key, and led him to the common room. The food and ale matched Ballrand's description and Zack ate with satisfaction. He noticed Ballrand's look of approval when he refused a third mug of ale and left an empty trencher that had contained a healthy portion.

He made his way to his room and had hardly stuck the key in the lock when a voice asked, "Would you like your bath, now, sir?"

The lad he'd met in the stable yard stood behind him with three older boys whose heights formed evenly spaced steps. Zack nodded and smiled when the four youngsters sprinted down the rear stairway. Minutes later, the four lads hefted a large tub into the room with little noise except for a few groans. Zack had stripped to his trousers by the time the first of the brothers brought a bucket of hot water to dump in the tub. He eased into the steaming tub when it reached the half-full mark. Three buckets later, the water filled the tub three quarters full and Zack told the boys he had enough. He enjoyed the water, watching road dirt and grime color it. Happy thoughts filled him. *This is the only real pleasure a trip like this offers, and I plan to make the most of it.*

The boys left, except the youngest, who brought over a bar of soap and a stack of large drying cloth. He flushed. "My name is Tym. They chose me to stay and see to your needs." His flushed cheeks darkened a shade while he busily folded drying cloths.

"Oh? Did you win or lose?"

"I won." His face colored nearly scarlet when he realized what his eagerness implied. He bowed his head, nearly touching his chin to his chest. "I wanted to talk to you."

"Well then, perhaps you should start."

Tym's face slowly reached a natural shade when he found Zack not upset at his request. "Da said you came from Jewel. That's what I want to do when I'm grown."

"What?"

"Oh, I mean travel. It must be wondrous to see different lands, and be on the road all the time." Zack tried not to snort laughter in the boy's face, and barely contained himself. "I want to have a fine steed and see many lands."

A steed, yet, Zack thought. "And how do you expect to earn your way?"

"Well..." Tym hesitated, "...I'll..." another hesitation, "...do what you do." Tym seemed pleased with his logic. "You must make much silver, and maybe gold. What... uh...what do you do?"

Zack couldn't hold his chuckle in any longer. Fortunately, it didn't seem to disturb the boy who smiled at him, his wide eyes filled with hero worship.

"It's not safe on the roads, sometimes. Did you not see my scars?"

Tym became solemn. "Yes, Master Stand, I did. Did it hurt much?"

"It hurt a great deal at the time, and for a long time afterwards. I'm lucky I didn't lose the use of my arm, or worse." Zack did not explain what might have been worse, and Tym did not ask.

Zack stood, water cascading down. His body did not bind with great, bulging muscles; the water streamed over toned, large muscles that few men had built. Tym looked on approvingly when he handed Zack the drying cloth as he stepped from the tub.

Tym opened the door, and his brothers filed in with buckets to fill. After emptying the water, the boys were grappling with the tub when Zack told them to wait. He fished out four coppers and gave one to each of them. They looked startled and thanked him profusely. Zack waved them away, thinking the coppers must be heavier, too. The oldest hurried away with his day's clothing for cleaning overnight. He chuckled and locked the door when the last of the struggling boys cleared the tub from the doorway.

Zack went over the last few instructions for his "Walking Armory," and then threw them into the fireplace. Flames curled the paper to blackness, and then to white ash. He was glad to see the last of them.

Zack spread the drying cloth in front of the fire to dry. Darts flew from across the room at the board he'd found on the road and had placed it in the chair. Satisfied with his advancing skill after an hour's practice, he packed the darts and "riding crop" away and sat on the bed, nude. Surveying the plush room around him, he hoped his luck in finding such accommodations during the rest of his trip might hold.

Zack retrieved his mintstick and cleaned his teeth. The sturdy twigs came from a hardy plant that grew throughout the Seven Realms. He'd worn out three small twigs to nothing on his first trip to Hamptor before he returned to the Seven Realms. Not finding them available and never heard of there left him dismayed. Resigned, he used the white, pasty, and unpleasant-tasting substance the Hamptorians used for the last part of his trip and found it much less effective. He jealously guarded his hoard of mintsticks and did not mention their existence to anyone.

He started to clean his boots, yawned, thought better of it and settled into the feather bed's distinct comfort with his back to the fire the boys had built up before they had left. He fell asleep within minutes without any consideration of the morrow.

* * *

ZACK woke at his usual time, a few minutes before dawn. He heard noises from below, signifying the inn's staff at work. Dressing quickly, he left for the common room after locking the door. He found it empty and went to the same out-of-the way table he'd used the night before. He had hardly sat down when a serving maid brought him a mug of steaming, spiced mead. Shortly thereafter, a trencher of eggs and a slab of ham appeared with thick slices of dark bread.

She looked at him with an appraising eye. "Are you staying over?"

With his mouth full of ham, Zack shook his head.

"Pity, that." She swirled her skirts gracefully away and left him choking, the mead helped him swallow. His tearing eyes caught approaching boots, and he looked up to see Master Ballrand chuckle while approaching his table. He sat across from him, grinning. He had Zack's freshly laundered clothes, neatly folded, that he set on the bench.

"She likes to tease, but runs if someone responds. I trust you had a pleasant night?"

"I did at that, Master Innkeeper."

Ballrand smiled at the complement. "I must thank you for not encouraging Tym in his wanderlust."

"He seems a good boy, and traveling the roads for a living is a hard life. He will do much better to follow in his father's way."

Ballrand's smile grew. "I'll be sure to tell him your words. I have weighed your silver piece and it's almost exactly what I guessed. Your silver is a hair over three times the pieces we have here. I can exchange ten of yours for thirty of mine if you wish." Zack counted out ten silvers and handed them over for an answer. "I'll return, shortly." Ballrand hurried away while Zack continued his meal.

The innkeeper reappeared as Zack swallowed the last bite of his firstmeal and handed him a handful of silver. Zack slid it into his pouch and tied it to the belt inside his tunic. "You didn't count it."

Zack's deep blue eyes pierced the innkeeper. "You would have said nothing on the subject if you meant to be dishonest. I trust you, the weight felt right, and I will return this way." *Hopefully,* he thought.

Zack's smile took the sting from his words; still Ballrand looked at him with respect. Innkeepers needed a finely honed sense of judgment regarding their guests if they wished to run a quality establishment and stay in business. Ballrand's inn ranked one of the best he'd ever stayed at.

Four men clamored down the front stairway and made for a table, discussing the weather. Ballrand rose. "A cold snap hit us last night. I fear that one more winter storm will blow this way. A heavy cloak is advisable." He glanced over his shoulder at the men and lowered his voice. "Plead ignorance if asked about a black stone. I broke up two fights in the last month, and my local clientele are usually mild in nature. I don't allow a rowdy bunch to have reign over my business. Travel well, and stop in again if you come this way." Ballrand extended his arm and Zack grasped it for a few seconds before he hurried off to take care of his guests.

Zack returned to his room and collected his things, slightly surprised that knives didn't fall on the floor when he shook out his cloak, even though he carefully held it from the top.

Tym led Spellbinder from his stall when Zack emerged from the rear stairway leading to the stable. He saddled Spellbinder, making sure the saddle's extra components lay smooth against his coat, and tied the saddlepacks behind the cantle. Holding out a closed fist to Tym, he dropped a copper into his outstretched palm.

"Master Stand, Da says your silver is heavier than ours,

and so are your coppers. Are you—are you sure?" The boy looked longingly at the bright metal in his hand before his questioning hazel eyes peeked upward to meet Zack's smile.

"You're a good lad, Tym, and honest like your Da. Consider what I said last night. The road is not what you think. The copper is yours." Tym smiled brightly and his face contained the same hero worship Zack saw the previous night.

The boy's countenance became solemn while Zack mounted. "Fare well, Master Stand."

Zack waved without looking back he nudged Spellbinder into a trot while passing the stable yard's gate.

10

THE next several days passed without incident. The inns Zack visited lacked Ballrand's quality, but they suited well enough. He exchanged more of his silver and coppers when the opportunity presented itself, until he calculated he had sufficient Hamptorian coin to last throughout his journey. The countryside and the inns' clientele became rougher as he traveled farther north. He lost count of the fights begun over arguments concerning a black stone.

He made a habit of talking with each innkeeper and reaching an understanding that he wanted a private room and a quiet stay. His success in finding available rooms came from knowing the distance between the inns on his map and timing his arrivals accordingly. His only problem was that he would soon run out of map, and the inn he visited the night before was near the end of Brigg's list. The luck of the road would be all he would have in another few days. He nudged Spellbinder into an easier pace.

* * *

ZACK heard horses galloping toward him from behind and guided Spellbinder to the side of the road. He glanced behind him to see who punished their horses so far from an inn. He saw two men, memorizing their faces. Spellbinder shied away from the closing horses as the nearest man struck at Zack with a short lash woven onto the end of a riding crop. The handle, sharpened to a sparkling point, barely missed his head. He gave chase, but did not follow when they left the road and headed into unfamiliar countryside. Suppressing his anger, Zack resumed his journey north.

The long days northward from Hagan's End and the attack brought recollection of young Tym's wanderlust and desire for stories of his travels. Zack laughed, the lad might have found the idea of a deadly attack an adventure. How could Tym imagine long hours in the saddle, running sweat that chafed in summer, dust clouds eating at his eyes, mud in spring and fall that slowed and tired man and beast, cold numbing him in winter and cold camps that might lessen his discovery by those he looked for or those looking for him, unsavory inns with unsavory clientele that meant restless nights caused by the villainy found in various forms in the villages, towns, and sometimes in the country? He shook his head and hummed a tuneless melody while Spellbinder settled and the normal creaking of leather and small clinks of metal lulled him.

Zack and Spellbinder needed a rest. The past several days of uncomfortable weather irked him. The last two inns provided no bathing facilities, and that combined with one night under the stars had left him more than uncomfortable with road dirt and sweat. He planned to stay in the next village for two days. The black stone's mystery incurred more interest and trouble the closer he got to Ozlid's border.

Smoky common rooms did not help ease a man's day, and on his first night at the next inn three fights swirled around him at various times. Zack followed his usual procedure of informing the innkeeper of his preferences and in every case it visually eased the innkeeper's fears. He also consistently searched for the most out-of-the-way table available. The fights surprised him. The small well-kept village didn't seem the type to allow the brawling.

That precaution did him no good the next night. The fight overflowed to where he sat. Zack saw the blow coming. He rolled backward and crouched low, guarding himself. Most fights he'd witnessed over the black stone did not involve weapons, and it surprised him when a blur of steel passed through the space he had just vacated. The swordsman's unarmed opponent blocked deadly thrusts and slashes as best he could with a chair. The defender looked good with his hands, but blocking a sword with unarmored flesh would produce severed parts while fighting with fists garnered only bruises and perhaps a broken nose or two.

His automatic defenses came alive. Ten seconds later, the attacker, now pinned against a wall with Zack's sword at his throat, looked amazed that Zack also held his sword. His fighting spirit cooled rapidly.

"Master Stand," the innkeeper's voice sounded with a touch of awe, "this fight's cause is a girl, and I believe the one you have there wants his opponent's humiliation, not his blood."

"Bring the unarmed one to your private room." Zack's voice brooked no argument, and his piercing eyes conquered the young swordsman as much as his sword had done. Gleaming steel nudged the unarmed swordsman's throat, who cautiously stepped to the side until he reached the door, and then stepped into the small room.

"Sit." The swordsman sat.

The innkeeper weighed a good hundred pounds more than the defender of the fight that he bodily hustled him to the table on tiptoes; he did not resist.

Zack pointed his sword to the opposite seat from the swordsman. "Sit." The young man sat. His voice took on a normal tone. "Good innkeeper, I believe you have guests to tend to, and I would appreciate it if you closed the door behind you." The innkeeper complied with a wry smile.

"Gentlemen, I'm too old to play nursemaid. It's an annoyance at any age, but it makes one cranky the older one gets." The swordsman started to speak. Zack's sword at his throat stopped him before he uttered the first sound. The sound died in his throat at about the spot where the sword's point pricked his skin. "What is your name, swordsman?"

"Jace Bellmore, uh, sir."

"And yours?" the sword blurred again and pricked the defender's neck.

"Michael Restwood, sir." He had not even blinked when the sword found his throat. The barest hint of red showed on both men's throats. Zack needed no threats to insure their good behavior, nor did he offer any.

"Michael, you're taller and stronger than your opponent." Zack turned his attention to Jace. "Is that why you went after him with a sword?"

"No. I brought the sword on a lark, and my temper flared when I saw Michael. I would have attacked him unarmed, too." Pride rang in the room.

Zack ran through a quick and complicated form using two swords that left both young men looking awestruck. "Do either of you doubt that I could deliver an extremely long and painful death to each of you at the same time? Are either of you murderers?"

"No." They answered together. Zack realized Jace's answer held a little more indignation than Michael's, but not much.

"Jace, do you realize that if I hadn't rolled out of the way, you would have cut me with what might have been a deadly blow?" Zack continued before the young man could answer; not that either of them looked as if they wanted to say much of anything. "And, if my temper had flared at your unprovoked attack, do you doubt that you might be dead?" Again, Zack continued before either answered. "Do you believe that the lady in question would be disposed to think kindly of you if you murdered Michael? Is she cold-blooded? Have you ever felt the blade of a sword pierce a man's body, and watched while his life ebbed away? Or, are you the kind of man that these things matter little to you?"

Jace's eye slowly rose to Zack's questioning face after a moment's silence. His voice softened and he looked subdued. "No, sir."

"I'm assuming that both of you have known each other for some time. Jace, tell me Michael's good qualities."

"What?" Jace blurted. Zack's sword flashed so fast it became a streak of silver light until the point gently nudged Jace's neck. Zack's skill and control must have begun to sink into the youth's consciousness, finally and his expression implied he might keep it in the forefront of his thoughts.

"Well ... uh ... Michael runs his Da's farm, and does a lot of the work himself. We attended the same classes the village gives. He knows how to read, write and do numbers as well as I. He's honest." The sword pulled away from Jace's neck. This time, no mark remained behind.

"Michael, tell me Jace's good qualities."

Michael had the good sense to start speaking without an outburst. "He helps his father, the village cooper. He's good at it, and some even say he exceeds his father in skill. And ..." Michael's voice dropped in tone slightly, "... and he's honest."

Zack's next question contained more than a little skepticism. "Would you like to expand on that honesty bit?"

"Well, he never told me how he felt about Emily, and she never mentioned him. I first heard he sought me a week ago, and didn't know why until tonight. I have been seeing her for over a year. What right has he to try and come between us?"

"You have been seeing her a year." Jace's incredulous voice softened. "I have been seeing her over a year." Both young men looked daunted while the truth sunk in, and Zack let out a peal of laughter.

"Gentlemen, the young lady in question would

certainly be upset to see you fight. She would have pitted you against each other much sooner if her purpose runs to such petty involvements." Both young men's countenance said they did not like that statement, but they kept their mouths shut. "She will make up her mind when she feels the time is right, and she will let you know when that is. You will soon learn that it is the woman that controls these things much more than us poor fools that they make of us. You boys—" Both young men clearly did not like the term, but neither voiced an objection. "—are not enemies, you're rivals. Can you see that she would be upset if she knew you fought over her to the point that one of you bled, or died?"

Michael and Jace sheepishly frowned. "Fighting over a woman is lunacy," Zack continued, "You don't want a woman that enjoys such things. She would probably cause your death at some point. Do either of you want such a woman?"

Heads shook slowly.

"I suggest that you continue your affairs until the lady has chosen. I also suggest that each of you tell her you know that she's seeing you both. Might there be a third young man?"

Zack spent considerable energy to keep his laughter silent from the looks on the boys' faces. "Now, to more serious matters. Jace, you could have killed me out there. I believe that I'm due something in recompense for that, and I'll tell you what I want. You will live and work with Michael on his farm for seven days. In addition, I want you to host him for an equal amount of time in your father's business. It's not easy to get away from a farm as it is a cooperage, so it might stretch out for a while. I want you both to discover a way to make the other's life easier in your respective occupations. I'll be through here again, and I'll want to see what the two of you have learned and how it helped you. I'll be sorely disappointed if there has been no accomplishment on your parts, and I may take my disappointment out on your parts if that's the case. Now grasp forearms on your honor, and I think the rest of the night you might discuss the nature of how to run a farm and how to make a barrel."

The young men smiled slowly at first, ending in a flourish of laughter. "Michael, I became a fool and I apologize most heartily." They walked together toward the door, joking with one another, when Zack's voice stopped them.

"Jace, remember well, you may have been lying dead on the common room floor if another man had sat where I did." Jace looked at him and Zack watched the color drain from his face. He tossed the young man's forgotten sword, and Jace caught it without mishap. He sheathed his weapon at the same time Zack's sword hit home and they recognized the quality of the sword and scabbard for the first time. Their eyes widened and they left the room talking about things other than their occupations.

The common room fell silent when the boys stepped out. They looked at each other, and then the room before they both folded up in laughter. Many in the room joined them.

Zack sat at a table in a dark corner that hadn't been available before the fight. *Perhaps it's for the best,* he thought. The slashed bodies of his wife and young daughter flashed before his eyes, and the pain he kept deep within him sunk its claws into his spirit. *Will I ever trust again? Are these people worth my life? No. I do this for the Seven Realms, my Zenith Lord and Gaz.*

A mug of ale appeared almost magically in front of him, jarring Zack from his contemplation. The burly innkeeper smiled. "This is on my custom, Master Stand. Jace there is a hothead, but he cools like one of his Da's stays thrust from the forge into water. You did the village a fair service tonight, and I thank you for that."

Kell, the innkeeper, grew hesitant, and Zack motioned for him to sit. "Master Stand, there have been eight killings that I know about over that hellish black stone Ozlid seeks. Men—and a few women—have gone mad trying to find it, doing things no sane person would do. Do you see any way to keep the turmoil away from here?"

Zack hesitated a moment. "You are a big man. Are there more of your size?"

"Boys!" Kell bellowed. The kitchen door flew open and identical twins, well over six feet tall and heavily muscled, looked about the common room until their eyes fell on their sire. They quickly walked over to him. "Master Stand, these are my sons, Derk and Kerk." The boys each gave Zack a short bow and eased into the two remaining seats at the small table that had felt large enough until their arrival.

Zack took in their countenance as Kell continued. "They say they get their muscles from hauling barrels of ale about and not drinking it." He chuckled and patted his more rotund middle. "Perhaps I should learn from my sons." He chuckled again.

Zack looked over the boys again. "Well met, lads." He grasped forearms with both feeling steely muscles larger than his, but the twins held respect in their faces, too. "Your Da asked if I know of a way to stop the fights over the black stone. I have one suggestion, well two, actually. I gather that the villagers here can read, from what I heard earlier?"

Kell's answer came filled with pride. "I'm on the village's council, like my Da before me. We've kept a teacher of words and numbers for as long as I can remember. We teach the lads—and girls—when they're young. We're a prosperous village, and believe it's due in no small part to our learning these skills. Not many villages do as we have done, and neither do they prosper as we have."

Zack smiled, genuinely. "I suggest that you put up a sign, the size of one of your boys declaring: No black stone exists in your inn, no conversation concerning such a stone will be tolerated, those persons ignoring this rule will be expelled hastily and found outside on their buttocks, or words to that effect."

Zack's companions chuckled.

"Place it near the entrance, where it won't be missed when one enters. My second suggestion is that the lads check for weapons when a guest enters and hold them if they find any. Return them when the guest leaves, and place another sign to that effect outside so that there is no misunderstanding. Beside those suggestions, I can see nothing else you can do. I have found that if you take away the reason for a fight and the means to fight, there will be few, if any fights."

Zack regarded the twins and the thought of them bearing down on him on a dark night caused a shiver along his spine. "I suspect that these great, hulking mountains of muscle you sired—" Both boys smiled at that, "—are of a gentle nature overall, and won't cause much harm to guests that choose to ignore your requirements." Zack's voice softened; "You must be on guard if you adopt these suggestions. I believe you will find that most of your guests will enjoy a respite from the subject, but there may be a few that strenuously object."

Kell's nod and serious mien showed equally in the lads' demeanor. "We will give it a try. Guests may enter with a weapon as long as they take it to their room and leave it there until they quit the inn, and the villagers don't usually carry weapons anyhow. It may work out, and is certainly worth a try. I thank you again for your counsel, Master Stand. Will you take another mug?"

"No, master innkeeper, I'll take my leave. I have no great love for ale, and I must be on my way early in the morning."

Kell talked with his sons while working their way around guests toward the bar. Zack vanished up the stairs to his room.

* * *

ZACK arrived first in the common room the next morning, and left the inn before the other guests arrived. Derk and Kerk worked behind the stable, fashioning planks of wood into a surface for two large signs. *Who knows,* he thought, *it might work.*

Gray clouds promised rain. Zack spun his cloak over his shoulders. It fulfilled its outward use, sheltering him from the morning's cold winds. It kept him warm, and he found the waterproofing the finest he had ever experienced when a brief but fierce storm had hit a few days ago. Zack noticed Kell hurry toward him as he mounted Spellbinder.

The innkeeper told of two murderers and thieves that had barely escaped after killing a merchant three days ago. Their description matched the men Zack encountered on the road, one of which carried a deadly riding crop. Zack found no problem remembering them. "The men you describe attacked me while on the road coming here. Perhaps you should let the other innkeepers in the area know."

"I will do that. Thank you for everything, Master Stand. I hope to have your custom again, soon."

"I hope so as well."

As Zack rode out, he did not see the puzzled look on Kell's face.

11

ZACK chose a small inn two days later that impressed him with its cleanliness. The meaty stew, prepared with herbs and seasonings the way he liked it, rapidly disappeared. After cleaning his bowl, he leaned into the shadows to chew the dark bread that came with his lastmeal, sated and relaxed. *The food, ah the food, better by far than many larger inns I have stopped at on my journeys,* he thought.

Rays of fading sunlight shredded through trees to make patterns across his table, tinted orange by the window glass. Dust motes reflected the strange color, and floated on soft eddies in the air. Zack looked forward to a peaceful night.

The door opened, allowing a brief breeze of fresh air to reach his table and swirl the lazy dust motes into a fury. The innkeeper crossed the room to greet mother and daughter. His smile looked genuine and warm.

"Doris, how was the day?" The man's voice boomed across the common room. "Hello Rachel." The small girl smiled and flushed at the attention.

"It went well." Doris' pleasant voice carried a hint of fatigue. She handed the innkeeper an empty bag made from coarse material and several voucher notes. "I got a better price than we planned." She held out her hand containing another voucher.

The innkeeper waved the last one away. "I quoted you a fair price, the gain is yours if you did better. Don't worry if it's ever less than we expect. I'll not question it. I know I can trust you. Now, I have some chilled juice in the cellar, and you need a rest before going on. I'll be

94

back in a moment."

Doris and Rachel took a seat away from the door. They received their chilled juice moments later and relaxed. "Mother did well at the market." Rachel's shrill voice carried throughout the common room. The innkeeper smiled at the child while Doris quieted her.

Zack admired Doris from his dark corner. He found her attractive in a strong, no-nonsense way. He questioned the absence of a man. Visualizations of his wife and daughter's death washed through him as they did with decreasing, but still persistent, regularity. Anger flared, and then died.

Doris reflected a pleasing attitude, and the child's behavior heralded a good upbringing. The child and mother's obvious fatigue from a long day of travel and the probable stress from haggling over prices had not dampened their spirit. Rachel quieted without fuss and chatted with her mother.

Zack's attention returned to its usual alertness when two men emerged from the darkness across the room and left through the rear door. He recognized them when the outside light illuminated their faces for a brief second. The riding crop hanging from the taller man's belt confirmed his identification.

He saw them again through the front window a few minutes later as they inspected Doris' wagon and the direction it came from. The riding crop looked more like an affectation than a deadly weapon. They mounted horses and rode out.

A few minutes passed before Doris and Rachel finished chatting with the innkeeper and left. They climbed aboard the wagon and started out at a much slower pace in the same direction the two men had traveled.

Normally Zack didn't get involved in local troubles, and avoided notoriety whenever possible, but this trip had been the exception. He took offense when someone tried to kill him, however, and knew if the riding crop had connected with his skull, he might be dead or badly wounded. The possibility of the same thing happening to Doris and her child that had happened to his wife and daughter, without help from neighbors or passersby, lurked just below the surface of his anger.

The innkeeper came to Zack's table. "Is there something else I can get for you?"

"No; I'm fine. I couldn't help overhearing the girl's conversation. Does the lady run a farm?"

"Yes, her husband died some time ago, and she took over its operation. It's a small lot a couple of miles off the north road, but she learned a great deal, and does better than some larger farms run by men."

"That's good to hear."

As the innkeeper walked back to the bar, he rushed upstairs. Zack's room looked undisturbed. He did not know if the thieves might have rummaged through the sleeping rooms. The lock on the doors might be easily forced. A quick test of his saddlepack's weight reassured him; he buckled on his sword, locked the door behind him, and went down the rear stairs to the stable.

The groom readied Spellbinder when Zack opened the stable door and hurriedly brought him out after noticing his impatience, muttering, "Seems everyone's in a hurry today." The boy's mood lightened when Zack gave him a few copper coins.

It did not take long to catch up with the wagon and Zack nodded to Doris and Rachel when he passed them. Rachel waved, and Zack rode on into the gathering darkness. A mile farther along the road he jerked his head to the right at the sound of a horse's whicker.

Tall hardwoods interspersed with pines filtered the remaining light from the setting sun and partially concealed the horses while they pulled at their leads to reach new grass. The trees and waning light rendered them hard to see and Zack's cloak worked well to do the same for him.

Zack walked Spellbinder to the sequestered animals, seeing no sign of their riders. He reached below each animal's stirrups and pulled the cinch to free their leathers. Then, leading Spellbinder, he disappeared into the forest. He kept the road in sight and followed it from inside the forest's covering branches. Voices drifted to him a hundred paces further on. He stepped silently and cautiously until he was sure they were between him and the road. He stopped, dropped Spellbinder's reins, and then eased quietly toward the voices.

The wagon swung around a bend into view. The men rushed from their concealment and approached the wagon from behind. One grabbed the horse's tack while the taller man pointed his sword at Doris before she could react.

"I hear your market day went well this trip." The largest man's shrill voice grated on Zack's nerves.

The horse reared and protested the different signals from Doris and the man holding his reins, but soon obeyed the one closest to him. "Now, I want your purse and it makes no difference how I get it," the man continued. Doris snapped the reins, and the horse reared again.

Zack found the irony pleasing when he blew the dart from his riding crop. Shoulders jerked upward, then the body relaxed completely, and the dead murderer hit the ground. The taller man pulled hard on the reins and brandished his sword. He might have questioned what had happened to his partner, but he did not lose control of the horse. Zack could not get a good line of fire at the constantly moving man, and whistled. Spellbinder crashed through the woods and Zack mounted him on the run.

Disbelief showed on the murderer's face while Zack charged him. Bright steel arced through the air and left the murder's sword arm hanging by broken bone and useless muscle. The man fell to the ground, watching his life's blood gush out. Pain washed over him and he screamed.

"Get your daughter away! Now!" Zack yelled while rounding on the screaming thief.

The horse and wagon lurched forward, racing up the road before Doris got the horse under control. Rachel's startled cries faded when the wagon turned another bend in the road.

Searing pain spread across Zack's left arm from the thief's weakly thrown dagger. Warm, viscous blood flowed down his arm. He knew the shallow wound had severed a vein or an artery, or both to cause that amount of blood. He felt faint as more blood gushed from his arm. The crop dangled below the biceps for a moment before falling to the ground. Zack brought Spellbinder to bear on his attacker, and his sword came down on the man's shoulder with a snap of bone. The murderer screamed in anguish and frustration while he tried to arrest the blood spurting from his shoulder.

Zack pulled at the sleeve of his shirt to make a tourniquet, but failed. Too much blood flowed from the wound. He guided Spellbinder toward the road, and saw the murderer trying to sit up. He looked quizzically at his arm while shock settled over him. He pitched forward and rolled with his arm caught under his body. Muscle and skin pulled from his stump and the arm remained a few feet from the rest of him. He shrieked once more, and then rolled onto his back, silent.

12

ZACK woke in a room so bright it hurt to look around. Several minutes passed before he could focus in the bright midmorning sunlight. Light blue curtains covered half of one window. The bedframe, a chest against the wall under the window and a washstand and chair next to the bed were all painted to match the blue curtains. Freshly whitewashed walls reflected the light and increased the dull throbbing in his head.

He lay on a comfortable bed, and his newly bandaged arm did not ache. His boots were on the floor beside the chair, and his ripped and bloodstained shirt lay over the back. The thought formed slowly. *Hells to the Dark One, I liked that shirt.*

A glass of water was on the bedside table, and he drained it. Then he gingerly loosened the bandage to get a look at his injury. The cut on his arm did not look serious. The worm-like stitches and blue-black bruises made it seem worse than it really was. Familiar smells of healing herbs laced the air, and the close stitches in his arm looked professional. He wrapped the bandage in place with little discomfort as the door opened and Doris looked in on him with a smile. Moments later, she brought in a steaming bowl of meaty stew, offered a few words of greeting, and then allowed him to eat and rest in private.

She returned after he finished eating, and they chatted for a while.

"I'm sure you saved the life of my daughter and me," she said. "I want to do what I can to ease your healing."

Zack smiled. "And you may have well done the same

99

for me. I think we are even."

"No Delan, I want to help. I got you into the wagon and brought you here. You have a smart horse; he followed us. Early this morning, I found the murderers' horses. They're in my stable, too. I took the bodies to town and gave them to the innkeeper. He will see to the cremation. Their vouchers and coins will pay for all that." Doris gave an impish smile. "It also paid your account with a good bit left over. The horses and the rest of their coins belong to you. I gathered your belongings and brought them here, they're under the bed. We only opened your clothes bag, and your things are drying on the line."

"You've done a great many things in a short time. I don't know how to thank you."

"There is no need. You look tired. I'll let you rest." She left the room, closing the door behind her.

Later in the day, Zack and Doris argued until she agreed to take half the purse and keep one horse for her trouble. A second horse might be of great benefit on her small farm; if not, its sale would produce welcome income.

He admired her spirit and determination. Soft, brown hair attractively framed her face. Her dark brown eyes had sparkled while they had argued over the purse and horses. She carried herself with a natural grace that long hours of work on a farm had not diminished. Her honest directness might have put off some men, but not Zack.

The next day, she sounded exasperated. "Zack, I think you are leaving too soon. Please reconsider."

He smiled at her stern mien. "Well, I might be persuaded for a favor." He cocked his head to the side and waited.

Doris sounded hesitant and looked sterner. "What kind of favor?"

Zack chuckled. "I would like you to keep a leather pouch safe for me, nothing more."

Zack found no fault with her previous insistence the next morning; he felt much stronger after another night's rest. He bathed at the washstand, then shaved using the items he carried in his saddlepacks. *When might I next have such a luxury?*

After dressing, he walked to the barn to check on Spellbinder. He talked quietly to the gelding while brushing a tangle of dried blood from Spellbinder's mane, for which he received a soft nicker as a reward.

Zack opted to take the better of the thiefs' horses rather than argue any longer with Doris. His instincts said not to take Spellbinder into Ozlid, and he'd learned long ago to trust them, no matter how much he hated the idea. Doris and Rachel seemed genuinely glad that he needed to return for Spellbinder and the pouch. Rachel promised to exercise Spellbinder regularly with a huge smile for so small a face.

Doris expressed her apprehension at Zack's plans to travel beyond the border into Ozlid when he asked for the closest route. He did not elaborate on why he was going, and she did not ask.

Rachel stood beside her mother, waving until the trotting gelding had disappeared from view. The little girl sighed. "Mama, he's pretty."

"Handsome, dear."

"Yes mama, that, too."

* * *

ZACK felt good to be on his way again. A faint feeling of accomplishment stirred at the back of his awareness, and after a few seconds he dismissed it when it would not surface.

The weather could not be more agreeable. Cool spring breezes replaced the cold wind from a few days before, and made him feel alive and energetic. Doris had supplied him well for the one-day ride to Ozlid's border. Zack's foreboding feelings surfaced and caused a frown. *If the*

Dark's Source minions resided in Ozlid, how strong are they? Will they know I'm a spy? If so, I hope Doris eventually opens my pouch and uses the gold for her and Rachel's good.

13

THE road's congestion, five miles before the border caused by four merging roads, slowed all progress. Wagonloads of supplies rumbled alongside individuals both mounted and on foot. The main road met with several small lanes about a mile from the border, leading to an open-air market larger than any Zack had seen that stretched beyond sight.

The road continued on to a forbidding stone fortress; its stark lines increased its dark aura. Zack rode directly to a few soldiers standing together. Black uniforms and boots without emblems or ornamentation of any kind gave them a menacing appearance that, no doubt, had figured in its design.

The group's largest and strongest eyed him with contempt. "What in blazes do you want?"

"I have heard that you look for a black stone."

The man's cruel smile set his countenance while his men drew their swords and surrounded Zack. The man who spoke took his horse's reins and led him toward the fortress. Swords pointed up at him without command. The guards smirked. A man came toward them wearing the same plain uniform, except with a black cape and a blue stripe running across his tunic. The large man stopped abruptly, and his body snapped to position when they arrived within speaking distance.

"My Master, I bring you this fool who states he knows of the black stone."

"Put your weapons away." His voice projected force, but he sounded bored. "You, on the horse, dismount and follow me."

Zack did so. The guard's hasty search yielded his weapons—the obvious ones—and missed those hidden. He wore his cloak with its surprises and his boots contained his cache of knives.

Zack followed the man into the fortress. The building's inside matched the sparse bleakness of their uniforms. They entered into a small room, and the man directed him to a chair. Zack sat down while the man removed his cape and looked at him with disinterest.

"You are the fourth one today. The other three knew nothing of the black stone. They're out there."

Zack craned his head to look through the tall window where the man pointed. The first three sets of ten large crossbeams driven into the ground supported barely recognizable, naked men. He could not tell if any skin remained on the upper portion of their bodies. Blood drained into pools; mixed with the dirt below, it had changed to a dark, unnatural color. Their heads hung against the raw muscles of their chest. The rigidity of death had come and gone, leaving its unique stillness; in contrast, the attending flies flew rapidly between them.

Zack looked into eyes that still reflected boredom. "You have a particularly distinct way of getting one's attention. What do you need to know to persuade you that I know what I'm talking about?"

"Describe this black stone."

"It's not large, about the size of the end part of my thumb. There is no shine to it. It's said to be the blackest thing you will ever see."

The interrogator's attitude changed dramatically. His eyes remained cold, but now they searched Zack with interest.

"You know where this stone is?"

"No and I have never seen it, but I know where it should be."

"And, where is that?"

"Around a man's neck."

The man jerked as if prodded with a spear. "What is your name?"

"Delan Stand."

"Come with me. If you lie, may the spirits of your ancestors protect you." Zack followed his interrogator down the corridor and up three flights of stairs. The room they entered contained, rugs, padded chairs, a doorway leading to an inner office, and a heavily muscled giant of a man guarding the door.

The man pointed to a chair. "Sit there and don't leave."

Zack looked at the living mountain that followed them into the room. "I don't think I want to try." The guard's expression left the impression that he would welcome any attempt.

The man disappeared into the inner office. A few minutes later, he appeared in the doorway and waved Zack inside. After Zack entered the room, the man left, closing the door behind him.

The plush inner office contrasted sharply with the accommodations Zack had previously experienced. A broad-shouldered man stood looking out the window.

He spoke with a casual tone. "Have you seen the three men I'm looking at below?"

"Yes."

"I have one question for you. If you answer it correctly, you will live. If you answer it incorrectly, you will join those three below."

The man turned to face Zack, and a startled expression passed over his face for a brief second. Their eyes locked. The scar from a deep gash ran from his right eye to his jaw, pulling the muscles into a grim countenance. He had once had a handsome face. "You may sit down if you like."

Zack remained standing. It seemed to please his host.

"My name is Durton, my title is Master of the Gold. The man that brought you to me is Karel, he has a habit of anonymity. The fool thinks it makes him intimidating.

"You came from the direction of Hamptor, but you don't have the look or sound of that land. I have also never seen a cloak as beautifully made as yours, and I know it didn't come from Hamptor or Arestead. Unfortunately, I don't believe that Hamptor or Arestead have the life left in them to produce such fine workmanship." A tinge of sadness mingled in Durton's statements. "Delan Stand, where is your home?"

"I come from the central southern lands of the Seven Realms that you call Jewel, across your eastern sea. I have been in these lands for about two months."

"How did you hear of the black stone?"

"Practically everyone I spoke with wanted to know if I'd ever heard of it. Some stories were wild tales, while others sounded more like what must be the truth. It took me a while to make the connection between the stone I remembered and the one they described."

"Well, Delan Stand, on this question your life depends. How long has the Stone been known to exist?"

"It's at least two millennia old, from the stories I learned. We don't have a history of it before that time. It disappeared, and was thought to be lost. I only heard about the stone one other time after my childhood. A man in the realm of Mountglen described it." Zack tried to relax without success.

Durton's sigh held his attention. "You will live, at least a while longer." His voice became reflective. "You will go on a five-day journey to meet the Master of Masters. You will be the first man not born in Ozlid to have that distinction in many years." Durton lightly stroked the scar along his cheek for a brief second. "Tell the Master of Masters that Durton sends his regards."

Zack's sigh of relief brought a smile to Durton's lips, but his eyes held a warning and he heard sadness in his voice. "There will be guards with you. They will have orders to hunt you down and kill you—or worse—if you try to escape. The guards traveling with you are expert in torture, and they rather enjoy it." Disgust radiated from Durton's expression. "Currat will lead your party. The trip can be dangerous. We will return your weapons, but Currat's men will take you apart at the slightest provocation. They'll have orders not to kill you, but you might wish they had when they get through with you. I advise resisting any impulses to see more of our land than the trip will provide." Durton sounded resigned to actions he did not like. Then, he smiled. "You might find Currat interesting, however." Zack wondered about his strange remark.

"The guard outside will take you to get something to eat. Delan Stand of the Seven Realms, I hope to see you on your return trip." Durton did not sound very assured that such a meeting might ever take place.

14

THE journey started much like Zack had imagined, with one exception that answered the question raised by Durton's strange remark. Currat's resemblance to Zack truly amazed him. The closeness of their physical appearance left him more than a little shaken. They might have passed for identical twins except for coloring: Zack's blond hair and crisp blue eyes contrasted with Currat's black hair and nearly black eyes. Neither one commented on it.

They counted eight in all: Currat led, followed by two men riding abreast, then Zack, followed by four men. The last pair led two packhorses. The attitude from the group that had met Zack at the fortress changed dramatically under Currat's leadership. Currat, cut from the same pattern as Durton, brooked no misconduct. He acted professionally, and Zack appreciated that.

Great stands of oak and elm towered above them, blocking the sun at times. The hardwoods gradually thinned as they traveled on, and pine trees took their place. The trail easily accommodated two horses abreast. Zack found resting areas placed at regular intervals consisting of small camps with a fire pit and a permanent latrine that allowed them to stay on the trail longer and conserve energy.

The mountain's majesty, not unlike those found in the Seven Realms, stirred Zack's memories. The forest, trails, and campsites all looked well managed. That surprised him for a reason he could not quite determine. The image of the three men flayed to death rose unbidden in his mind; he felt the incongruity of that and the peaceful forest while a chill crept along his spine.

Larger rest areas appeared at locations to correspond with the end of a day's journey. Zack received a tent to set up on the first night, and it became his each night. Three of the men took shifts standing guard duty alternating with the other three the next night. His guards did not ask him to do any work other than maintaining his tent and no bonds confined him at night. They watched him constantly, however. They brought him food at firstmeal and lastmeal, with utensils on a wooden trencher. They reclaimed and cleaned them when he had finished. Midmeal consisted of hard bread and cheese that they ate while they rode. The first night, a blast of cold air sped down the mountain.

Currat furtively looked at Zack from time to time when he thought Zack did not see him. Zack did the same. Their conversation had been practically nonexistent since the trip's first day.

One night, Zack woke and pulled his cloak closer to him. Thunderous hooves raced at full gallop on the trail a few yards from their encampment, heading toward the fortress. Zack could not imagine someone galloping a horse at night on a trail in almost complete darkness. The waning moon's light barely filtered through the forest canopy. He eased the tent flap open a sliver. An unconcerned guard sat on his haunches at the small fire's other side, fully awake. Zack despised the guard's disregard of the equestrian. *Perhaps I dreamed it.*

The guards said little to him for the journey's first three days, and maintained their constant surveillance that Zack ignored. He saw smoke from campfires on several occasions and twice saw small encampments of people looking dirty, thin and hard-pressed for the necessities of life. They scowled at him as he rode by. His guards took no notice.

Currat spoke in an educated and civilized manner that became more evident in contrast to the guards' boorish behavior. More than one incongruity crossed Zack's deliberations. Currat all but ignored him when the guards were close by.

Early on the morning of the fourth day, while the men broke down the camp, Zack pulled a knife from his boot and lunged at Currat, knocking him backward to the ground. The guards drew their swords, ready to end a life, when Currat waved them off.

Zack stood before him with the severed head of a viper in his hand, drops of venom still dripping from its deadly fangs. He held out his free hand to Currat, who still lay on the ground. Currat hesitated a few seconds, and then took the proffered hand.

One of the guards retrieved the knife from the ground and wiped it clean on the grass. He looked at Currat expectantly. Currat's expression remained grim; he nodded once. The guard flipped the knife in the air, caught it by the blade, and handed it to Zack.

Zack noticed considerable talking among the guards while they rode higher into the mountains. Neither Currat nor the guards said anything to him about the incident. Currat brought Zack bread and cheese when they stopped—for the first time—to share their midmeal. He also gave him a cup of wine poured from a skin he kept in his saddlepacks. Currat called the guards and Zack together when they finished their meals.

"Delan Stand, you saved my life. It's the custom of our people that when such a deed happens, we are bond by that deed in life. In effect, it means that if the time should ever come, I will sacrifice my life for yours. This tradition survives in the army, but not in the general population. You acted bravely on my behalf, and you have my thanks and my pledge." Currat offered his outstretched arm, and Zack grasped his forearm.

The rest of the journey went without incident, and Zack found himself having interesting conversations about the cultures of their two lands and how they differed while he rode beside Currat. Zack did not mention the Zenith Lord nor how the government functioned and neither did the officer mention the Master of Masters. The guards remained distant, and spoke in whispers away from them. Currat ignored their actions as Zack had. He held no illusion that the guards would take great delight in killing him in moments and without hesitation if he stepped out of line, no matter what Currat said.

They passed several larger encampments that showed signs of permanency, peopled with sullen inhabitants. They made no move to approach the travelers and turned away, but not before showing their displeasure.

In the middle of the fifth day, they rode through a mountain pass and emerged high above rolling hills. A palace in the middle of a valley, far away, covered many acres, or even miles. Zack thought no building larger than the Spires existed anywhere in the world, until now.

Groups of cottages, villages, and towns spread in every direction. It became clear why Ozlid needed produce and materials from their neighbors: they had no room for farms of any kind. Villages radiated outward from towns that in turn radiated around cities, with the palace in the middle of it all. Small vegetable gardens grew around and on top of nearly every building. The population of Ozlid filled its fixed borders to overcrowding, and the need for additional farms meant a waiting disaster.

Currat slowed until he came even with Zack. "Impressive, is it not?"

"It's much more than impressive." Three wide and swiftly flowing rivers formed the palace's moat. That alone jarred Zack's conceptions. *How could there be such an upwelling of water to supply three rivers?* The shimmering light reflecting off the water gave the impression that the palace floated in stillness on turbulent seas. He realized the pressure it must require to feed three rivers and it astounded him; he again questioned its source. One river flowed north; the other two ran southeast and southwest. The closest river flowed to the southeast into the solid rock of a mountain.

Currat saw the surprised look on Zack's face. "All three rivers go underground at the mountain range's edge. We know where they emerge, but not the route they take. The water is our greatest resource, and is the only thing we have to barter for our needs." Zack said nothing, and the conversation died for over a mile.

He began to see people: alone or in groups, working and at leisure. The contrariety of the two types of Ozlidians Zack saw seemed immense. Small, impecunious encampments of huts sat sullen and bereft on the opposite side of a mountain from a civilized organization that may have come close to the Seven Realms' prosperity. Currat had given Zack much information through normal conversation while he had maintained a passive role for the most part. He made his first overt statement. "The people and villages we passed on the way here seemed much different than what I see before us now."

Currat pitched his voice for Zack's ears alone. "The people of Ozlid who live outside our valleys are convicted of crimes. We have only two punishments here, one is death, the other is banishment to the land outside the valleys and rolling hills that is the real Ozlid. It's cruel to some; however, we have few crimes committed in Ozlid. A person found guilty and sentenced to banishment goes with his family outside the mountain ranges that protect our rolling hills. A few rejoin our society for services to the kingdom. We remain isolated for safety."

Zack's voice remained neutral. "I have not found nor heard of lands with the same laws."

"We barter for raw materials and many more supplies with our water. I'm aware of how others perceived us in Arestead and Hamptor. Our people have no idea of what our neighbors think of them." Currat twisted slightly in his saddle, and Zack saw a warning written plainly on his face.

The way to the palace held no surprises; the people they passed paid little heed to them. Zack could see wagons of supplies making their way into the valley between broader passes with wide roads. The trail they'd traveled could not support such heavy loads on its bed or its width.

The bridge over the moat to the palace looked like a normal bridge from a distance. It proved not the case when they came closer. Its span covered at least a mile. The water rushing around the palace looked more like a vast area of churning rapids. The outer waters slowed to match the river's flow Zack had seen in Hamptor. Water filled the rivers' heads at sharp, unnatural right angles with no visible corrosive effects; confined to a lesser space, it surged toward the mountains with a force and speed that rivaled the inner waters next to the palace.

The large complement of guards posted at each end of the bridge looked for the slightest sign of trouble. The palace itself loomed three levels above ground. The Spires surpassed its size several times over on closer inspection, an observation Zack did not comment on.

They made their way across the amazing bridge. Zack saw no possible way the slender underpinnings could hold the graceful bridge's weight against the tremendous forces of water. Unseen powers obviously strengthened the structure. Currat's written orders drew close examination before the guards allowed them on the bridge, and Zack got a careful inspection. No one tried to take his weapons. The same procedure awaited them at the bridge's other end, with the same results. Currat gave orders to his men that they seemed to dislike. Muttering, they led their horses and the pack animals away.

Currat ordered Zack to follow him. They rode in the opposite direction that Currat's men took and after approximately a hundred yards, they veered onto a ramp descending under the palace. Zack felt his skin crawl at the idea of the immeasurable amount of water pressure held at bay by only a few yards of dirt and stone.

The well-lit and remarkably clean ramp curved to the right and ended at the largest stable area Zack had ever seen. His amazement continued at the lack of usual smells; horse sweat tinged with a slight whiff of their dung, barely infused the air. The odor of so many steeds in an enclosed space should have been overwhelming, and rather hard on one's stomach. His ears gave him his first clue, and then he saw torrents of fast-moving water racing along channels behind each line of stalls that carried the dung away. Grooms brushed a pair of horses at the end of each row.

Currat received two pale yellow tokens with numbers on them from a bored attendant and handed one to Zack. They rode along rows of stalls until they found a row that matched the color and numbers on the tokens. A groom seemingly appeared from thin air and took the reins of both mounts. Currat's tired and somewhat resigned voice cut Zack's questions off before he could ask any. "Take your saddlepacks and come with me." Zack looked again at the rushing water behind the stalls. The officer said, "We know only that the water carrying the dung and piss does not contaminate the rivers, but not where it goes." Once again, a warning expression crossed his face.

They climbed an open, circular stairway into the palace proper. Zack could see one set of stairs at the end of every tenth row of stables, and knew that if he had brought Spellbinder here, he might never have found him again. Once again, his instincts had served him well.

Friendliness had not seemed a trait the people of Ozlid enjoyed, and Zack kept his surprise hidden when he received an invitation to eat with Currat and his friends. He followed the other man through a maze of corridors up to the second floor. They passed all manner of people: Men and women who looked like they held some sort of official position walked purposefully; others, alone or in groups, walked more leisurely; and families, at times with more than one generation, strolled together. The amount of well-behaved children scampering along the lighted corridors surprised Zack the most. The considerable traffic did not crowd a space wide enough to allow ten men to walk easily abreast. Everyone he saw dressed as one might expect in a palace, and acted polite while they carried out their duties or walked at their ease. Currat strode purposely, turning corners when he reached them without a look at the numbers inscribed on the walls. It came to Zack suddenly; *Currat grew up here.*

Currat stopped along a corridor free of heavy traffic, approached a door set five feet into the wall and inserted a key into a lock. His hand twisted to the right; the lock opened with a satisfying *click*. The door swung open at the midpoint of a wall ten feet thick and revealed, not the cell Zack expected, but a lavish, two-room suite.

Currat followed Zack inside, then closed and locked the door behind him. He looked at Zack with a wry smile. "Yes, a prisoner, but not so bad a cell, yeah?" His smile faded. "Delan, you need to stay here unless you leave with me. Your description has been given to the guards." Currat saw the surprise in his face. "Oh yes, we passed many guards that you didn't see, but they saw you. You will be safe with me. Alone, you won't make it out of the corridor outside. Did you notice the wall's thickness when we entered?" Zack nodded. "They're not ten feet thick for architectural purposes. Eight feet of space lies behind every corridor wall, manned with guards watching through kill holes that are quite cleverly hidden."

Currat paced about in a small circle, agitated. His concern did not show in his even voice. "I watched you on the trip here. You are a man used to traveling, and a man who can live well in the forest with little more than his skills. I believe that you're an honest man. You are in great danger. I'll do what I can to lead you from harm's way. I'll not ask you to trust me; you have no other choice." He said the last with a tinge of sadness.

Currat pointed through the lounging and reception room to the bedroom beyond. "There is a bath off the bedroom that has something I'll wager you have never seen." Zack looked where Currat pointed. "There are two small knobs over a tub. One brings cold water and the other brings hot." Zack stared at Currat with an unbelieving look in his eye. "You will see. Enjoy yourself. I'll be through there." He pointed to the door to an adjoining suite. "It's my suite when I'm here. The door will be locked, but I'll hear you if you knock." Currat left Zack standing in the middle of the room and walked to the door, exposing fatigue Zack had not seen before. He opened it with another key, entered, and closed and locked the door behind him.

The tub covered the size of a small pool, built with large slabs of highly polished marble. Zack found the two knobs on the rear wall with a statue of a dolphin between them. *Well, that's simple.* He twisted the red knob and water gushed from the dolphin's mouth into the pool. Zack felt the water and found it barely warm. *So much for hot water.*

He surveyed the rest of the room. Two basins lay in what looked like a small table on the far wall with the same red and blue knobs above each of them. Steam billowed upward when Zack looked back to the dolphin. He quickly twisted the blue knob and soon adjusted the water to what he calculated might be the right temperature when the pool filled. The tub, as Currat called it, measured uniformly four feet deep, five feet across, and ten feet long. Water roiled in from the marble dolphin's large mouth. Zack looked on in astonishment while the water level quickly rose. He twisted the knobs the opposite way when the water reached six inches from the pool's top and the great, gushing fount diminished to a trickle, and then stopped completely.

He stripped off his clothes and eased into the steaming water. Muscles relaxed as his body became accustomed to the heat. Soft sponges lay beside a small bucket of white paste that Zack found to be soap. Neatly folded, white drying cloths lay next to the bucket. Five days of travel dirt, sweat, and the smell of campfire smoke dissolved into the water. He floated in bliss with his arms along the marble's side in a sea of warmth, and felt the tension from the last week drain away.

He lathered his body from soaped sponges with a crisp, clean smell he liked, and soon his body radiated the scent. He washed his hair last, dunking his soapy head below the water. Something poked the calf of his right leg when he stood. It looked like a lever pointing downward. Zack grabbed it and it easily moved upward. Gurgling water sounded from beneath his feet and he soon saw a whirlpool form in the tub's middle while the water swiftly drained away. The pool's floor proved not as flat as he supposed. Water flowed toward the pool's center and he finally saw a depression about a foot across. He stood, dumbfounded when the last of the water disappeared. The lever moved easily downward; Zack watched as a circle of marble rose and seamlessly filled the hole. Soft, thick cotton cloths pulled the remaining water from his body.

Naked, he walked into the bedroom and scrounged in his saddlepack until he found the small, exceedingly sharp, knife he used for shaving. Thick rugs he had not felt through his heavy boots caressed his feet. He returned to the table against the wall containing the small basins and filled one with hot water. Soap from a small pot between the two basins lathered his face and he gave himself the most enjoyable shave of his life.

Zack heard Currat calling him, and went out to his reception room with the soft cotton cloth wrapped around him to find Currat similarly washed and shaved, dressed in fresh pants. He padded to meet Zack and handed him a fine set of trousers and matching shirt in dark blue wormcloth.

"These are mine, and I'm sure you will have no trouble with the size. I don't think we could be anymore alike. He held them out, and Zack took the clothing. Currat's callused fingers traced the scar a few inches down Zack's chest. "That looks like it hurt, a lot." His voice remained sad and quiet.

Surprise flooded Zack, but he felt no anger at this relative stranger's—*or perhaps 'captor' might be a better definition*—touch what he felt the most personal part of his anatomy. Perhaps it was the amazing likeness between them or his respect for Currat, but he did not mind the other man's touch.

Currat pulled his hand away. "I should not have done that. Forgive me." Zack's left arm, still draped with the borrowed clothing, relaxed. He grasped Currat's right forearm, the mark of friendship and greeting, something you did not do with an enemy. Currat looked as their hands closed, comfortably firm, and slowly raised his eyes to meet Zack's gaze. The pain he saw in the man's face urged him to cry out. He remained silent, and they pulled their arms apart. Zack watched while Currat silently reversed himself and disappeared into his rooms. He did not lock the door.

Zack found a clean privatecloth and dressed. He could not relinquish the thought that while he may be a prisoner, Currat shared his status, albeit under different parameters. He cleaned his boots as best he could from supplies in his saddlepack and slid them on, hardly noticing his actions. Fully dressed, his image in the mirror reflected a man he had not seen in a long time. He once wore fine clothes, but had found no use for them over the last five years. The clothing shimmered over his muscled frame and it pleased him.

Zack's knuckles rapped lightly on the door between the two suites. "Come in, Zack." The door led him into a suite of five rooms much larger and more lavish than his quarters.

He looked around and whistled. "They must pay you much better than they do us in the Seven Realms."

"Things are not always what they seem. Let's find some food. I think I could eat a horse."

Zack suppressed the tired retort. He followed a rejuvenated Currat, who again walked with purpose, strength and no sign of the emotional pain Zack had seen a few minutes ago. Currat locked his door and led Zack off through the overwhelming maze of corridors. *I could wander around in here for days.*

He soon gave up any idea of memorizing the corridors; it would be hopeless without a map. He walked along beside his guide. *How does Currat possibly remember the way with the numerous changes in direction and intersections?* Then he caught him looking swiftly at the molding on the corridor's base. Zack noticed the color; it changed, slightly graduating while they walked. The intersecting corridors displayed different colored molding; colors that one might not have noticed changing except in slight shading until, after passing several corridors, he saw a different color. It was an elegant system. Zack felt sure that once he found the key he could walk where he wished with the same confidence Currat possessed. He pitied any colorblind person living in the palace.

Only a number gave significance to the door they entered. Everyone in the room was dressed in uniforms, with the insignia of their officer's rank emblazoned on their breast by bars of color. Zack and Currat's clothes stood out like the red center of a target amongst the dark uniforms. He hoped the analogy was incorrect as he followed Currat through the room. His guide answered nods and waves while Zack received more than one startled look; he selected a table for four with two officers wearing the blue mark across their chest.

Zack, when introduced only as *Delan*, did not take

offense. The officers he met, Danyl and Ryman, did not seem surprised by the omission either. To his eyes, they looked healthy and fit. They maintained looseness and spontaneity in their behavior that he hadn't seen in the officers at the border. These men and the others in the room might all have been members of the Zenith's Guard.

Both the men they joined looked surprised, but Ryman spoke first. "Currat, I didn't know you had a brother."

Currat's tone remained light, conversational. "We keep him away from the palace. He's colorblind, and is forever getting lost in the ladies wing."

"Ha." Ryman snorted. "Then he takes after you. Delan, you will have to show us your way to what we all desire. There has always been the rumor that there is a secret way into the palace. I believed they started it to give us something to contemplate during our off-hours, not that we have much time for it. Seriously, do you know of a secret way in?"

Currat glanced at him with a rueful chuckle. "The way—at least the way he told me—lies through our dear Spercine's chambers. I'm sure he'll tell us if we pester him enough."

All signs of humor disappeared from Danyl and Ryman's faces. Ryman spoke in a soft whisper while looking around the room and even the air above them. "Currat, you should not even say that as a joke. You never know when . . ." His voice trailed off. The two men's somber mien startled Zack.

Zack picked up Currat's subterfuge and tried not to smile while his countenance took on a solemn display. "I told you never mention that. I don't think I, or we, would enjoy the consequences."

Currat grinned. "Sorry. Tell the Master of Masters that they told you . . ." He pointed to his two friends, ". . . if you're ever questioned about it."

The color drained from both Danyl's and Ryman's

faces. Currat started to grin first, and soon progressed to a hearty laugh. Zack picked up on the cue, and chuckled along with him. It took a moment before the two young officers regained their composure and color. They smiled first and soon after were laughing with their companions.

Danyl spoke softly when the laughter died down. "Still Currat, you should not joke about such things. You have been out in the wilds too long. It has become dangerous to even mention her name. People will do anything to garner favor with her, and several have tried by repeating conversations they should not have. The results leave fatalities to the one involved and his or her family."

Ryman cut in. "We don't know that to be true, Danyl. They disappear, but that doesn't necessarily mean they're dead." His voice, softer than his friend's, held little conviction.

Currat waved his hand. "Peace. I didn't understand that things had progressed so far here. Neither of us will discuss her again." The conversation returned to normal subjects of duties and work schedules by the time Zack and Currat received trenchers of hot food and mugs of cool wine. Danyl and Ryman finished their meals and left to return to their duties.

"Who is she?" Zack whispered, feeling no need to explain whom he meant.

Currat answered in the same whisper. "I wanted you to see their reaction before you meet her."

"The ruler of Ozlid is a woman?" Zack asked.

"No, but she's extremely powerful." Currat changed the subject and they resumed talking in a normal voice. Zack listened carefully while he explained the color keys to the corridor's maze.

"It's artfully done." Zack groaned at his unintended pun as Currat slowly shook his head. "When do you think I'll meet your Master of Masters?"

"He's not my Master of Masters," Currat hissed and quickly banished the distaste he projected.

Zack let the remark pass, and changed the conversation to the structure of Ozlid's society.

"Seriously, how does a person that's colorblind manage the maze?" he asked as they returned to Currat's rooms.

"I explained about the numbers at the corridor's intersections." Zack nodded. "You can navigate by the numbers, alone. It's much more difficult, however and you must be cognizant of where you started and how many sections you have passed through." They chatted about the palace's construction and design until they reached their destination. They left and did not speak while walking back to their rooms.

Currat unlocked the door and Zack followed him in. The other man locked the door behind him and held his finger to his lips. Motioning for Zack to follow him, Currat led him into his bedroom. He closed the door behind them and sighed in relief. He waved Zack to a plush chair while he sat on the bed.

"I'm going to tell you a fact that would cause my death if it's divulged to the wrong people. Unfortunately, that includes all but a handful of men and women."

Zack's attention peaked. "Currat, I'll not put you at risk for helping me. I'm sure I wouldn't have experienced the hospitality you've shown me if we hadn't had such a narrow escape with a certain viper."

He watched while Currat eased his boots off and crossed his legs on the bed, appearing to be so deep in contemplation that Zack questioned if he knew what he was doing. Currat put his hands to his face and, after a moment, ran them through his hair and placed them on his knees. He appeared to have made a major decision, but one he still questioned. "This room is what we call a 'dead room'."

Zack did not like that particular choice of words, but rationalized that if immediate danger threatened, they probably would not kill him in Currat's bedroom.

"The Master of Masters has some method of hearing what is said in all but a few rooms. Over the years, we have been able to identify these 'dead rooms' and make use of them." Currat waited for a moment before proceeding. "Delan, will you tell me about Jewel?"

Zack relaxed. "We don't call it Jewel. That name became attached to us because of the minerals and precious stones we sometimes trade, although, not often any more. We call ourselves the Seven Realms. Two millennia ago, a war raged that nearly destroyed our civilization and much knowledge. The land's decimation, along with famine and disease, took a great toll on its people's life, both during the war and for many years afterwards. We fought against the powers of evil and came unbelievingly close to defeat. Our leader became the first Zenith Lord and his six commanders the High Lords, with the continent divided into Seven Realms. The realms are ruled hereditarily by the descendants of those first seven men and women."

Zack saw the surprise on Currat's face. "A woman commanded the second largest force. Women have ruled her realm many times, as have some others ruled their realms, although not as frequently. The consorts retain their names and usually act as advisors, but not always. One consort, a wealthy merchant, devoted his married life in philanthropic ventures for his wife's realm. Also, I have heard there is a branch of our High Desert People that have women warriors that are quite deadly."

Currat's interest grew.

"The Zenith Lord rules the realm of Stonefire. He oversees our armies and the judicial system, manages trade, acts as an arbitrator in rare disputes between the realms, and is overlord to all. The realms have been at peace since the war. Oh, there've been squabbles between lords and High Lords, but our army—referred to as the Zenith's Guard—and the Zenith Lord steps in to settle the disputes before anyone goes too far. Each realm has their forces too, but these are small and provide more of a policing effort for their realm. The Zenith and the High Lords have men that earned favor by deeds, and act as lords over districts of land. We're a prosperous country, and are self-sufficient for the most part. We have little need to trade with our neighbors, and most of what we sell is surplus goods for gold or the few things we don't produce internally, such as some spices. Our gemstones are rarely equaled, and much desired by our neighbors."

"How big is the Seven Realms?" Currat asked.

"The country is approximately thirty-five hundred miles across and twenty-five hundred miles from north to south."

Currat's awed manner amused Zack, but he did not show it. "A thousand years ago, we sent ambassadors to Ozlid, Hamptor, and Arestead. Your young kingdoms didn't receive us well. We have not made overtures since then." He leaned back in his chair.

Currat's eyes shone bright and alert. "What is your capacity in the Seven Realms?" Zack hesitated. The other man continued in cold terms. "Your description is known by the bridge guards, you won't have the correct papers to get a horse, and you will be killed if found without me. You are a prisoner, albeit a pampered one now. It's my desire to get you away from here alive. I don't give an oath lightly and in truth, I like and respect you. I have trusted you with information that could get me killed. You must trust me, or you will not leave here alive." Currat breathed deeply, let the air out slowly and waited patiently.

Zack possessed an excellent ability to judge one's character, a skill he honed to a razor's fineness over the years. He might have been dead many times over if he had not developed that facility. He did not like disclosing his true mission to anyone who did not have a need to know his purpose and the reason for his actions. He searched Currat's face and peered deeply into his eyes.

Currat did not flinch away from his stare. Zack made a decision that he considered near the import of the one Currat made earlier. He kept his voice low.

"Let me say only that I gather information and perform other activities to help my Zenith Lord."

Currat's body sagged while tension drained from him. Zack could not evaluate the heavy stresses he functioned under until he had totally relaxed. He questioned that, for a moment, Currat might even keel over.

Currat composed himself with some effort. "We are ruled by an evil that's over three hundred years old." He waited for Zack to consider his words carefully. "His name is Wathdure, but it means death to call him by that name without his permission, which is rarely given."

He took a breath and continued. "Three hundred and four years ago, Wathdure appeared among us. He was little more than an oddity at first, dressed in normal clothes for the time, and appeared to be a regular looking man, although it's said that his features contained a male beauty to a degree no one had ever experienced before." Currat organized his thoughts before he continued.

"No one dares oppose Wathdure's authority. We're internally self-governing for the most part, but his word is law. It can be, and often is, deadly. He holds most of those he meets in his sway. They seem to find him perfectly normal and a generous and kind ruler. If you dare comment on his strangeness or age, they look at you as if you're insane. We don't know how he does it or why some of us are excluded from his control."

Currat settled into the telling of Ozlid's history. "There are a few families that are not influenced by him. He believes he purged them a few years after he took power, but enough of us survived to inner-marry without problems, and we have kept the truth alive. We dare not involve others. They would be compelled to tell of our existence, and the result is death for both parties."

Zack leaned forward with interest. "The palace is a

dangerous place for you. There are many among us indoctrinated with hatred for strangers, so there may be an attempt on your life, and that's another reason why I must stay near you. I'm as entangled in these circumstances as you are. I'll be killed if you don't survive to meet Wathdure." Currat sighed and spread his hands out. "There is a real danger to your Seven Realms if Wathdure is part of the evil your ancestors confronted."

Shock at Currat's words jolted Zack's mind. The one concept he desperately tried not to dwell upon confronted him. *It's not only true; it's highly probable.* He did not want to broach the subject again until he sorted out what his own actions should be. "When will I meet Wathdure?"

"We don't know. He rarely makes personal appearances any more, and we have found, by chance, that he is not physically here for days, or even weeks."

They talked long into the night. The more each heard, the more it became clear that Zack must get Currat's information about Ozlid to the Seven Realms.

When Zack finally went to bed, he lay in lavish luxury, staring at a ceiling made of white marble like the walls and floor. He did not think he would sleep. A small fountain built into the wall opposite the bed sang delicately with the chorus of falling water, and he closed his eyes. The needs of his body manifested their influence in the form of sleep without his cooperation.

15

TWO days passed without incident, and Zack felt that he might become accustomed to the style the palace offered. Unfortunately, he felt evil growing stronger while each hour passed. At first, he thought his feelings were just a part of his stress and fatigue. That changed as persistent unease seeped around him. He asked if Currat felt the same, and knew the answer by his countenance before he could speak. Currat hosted all conversations regarding the true nature of the Master of Masters, Spercine, and his kingdom in the *dead room*. It was an island of hope and despair.

They ventured out for meals and some brisk walks to get exercise. The rest of the time, they performed exercise routines in their rooms, usually together. Zack found them perfectly matched in their abilities as in their appearance, likes, and dislikes. They never discussed the uncanny similarities between them that questioned and amazed them. Zack realized late one night that he felt kinship toward Currat, a feeling lost for all but Gaz over the past five years. Zack felt a spark pass between them on the few times they physically touched. He was sure Currat had felt it, too. Neither of them spoke of it.

* * *

ONE afternoon, Zack walked beside Currat along the seemingly endless corridors. People spoke softly, not wanting their words to bounce off the hard marble around them.

Heads suddenly turned when cries and shouts reached them from two intersections ahead. Instantly alert, Zack

127

and Currat stopped aside the corridor's wall, its cool marble hardly felt. Currat steered Zack toward the intersection they had just passed. Guards stood to the left passageway. They walked briskly into the side corridor to the right. People ran toward the commotion, leaving them standing alone within seconds. Zack whispered, "Diversion." in Currat's ear. They centered themselves in the corridor and walked forward. Sound startled them when a door twenty feet ahead flew open and hit the wall.

No doubt existed about the man's sanity who leapt into the corridor yards away. Crazed, wild eyes stared at them. He alternately pressed his hands from his forehead to his chest in agonized motions between bouts of brandishing a knife in their direction in short, stabbing motions.

His voice remained soft, the man's torment raked over Zack and Currat. "You . . . you brought strangers into the land, into the palace. The Master of Masters—" the words held reverence and awe, "—does not want strangers in our land, and to bring him into the palace is blasphemy. I'll kill him, and then you, Currat!" He lunged in their direction.

The fool's ravings gave them his plan of attack, but one in his condition usually generated greater strength than normal. They did not wear swords in the palace, and Currat hadn't wanted to draw attention by going against tradition.

Zack sidestepped the lunging man and ducked under the knife jabbed in his direction. His attacker swung around amazingly fast and grabbed Currat, pushing him against the wall. *So much for plans of attack.*

Currat, overbalanced, struggled to stay on his feet and fight the raving maniac off while Zack ripped the tongue of his belt buckle loose and the garrote flew from his belt.

Currat saw a blur fall between him and his attacker. Then, he found freedom. He saw the man's, feet slipping on the floor. Zack's sharp whisper exploded in the silence around them. "Do I kill him?" Currat grimaced and hesitated before nodding.

The hyoid bone's lesser and greater cornu snapped and ripped through the struggling man's windpipe. Zack unwound the garrote and let the unwanted weight slip to the floor. Bright blood pooled from the man's mouth onto the white marble beside the head that stared at them with the madness they saw moments before, gone. Silent and useless muscles produced nothing to help the dying man find air.

Zack pulled Currat to his feet and they walked quickly to the next intersection and darted down another corridor without regard to numbers or molding colors. Currat took his bearings at the next intersection, and they reached his rooms within minutes. The time seemed like hours to Zack.

Currat looked on in amazement while Zack retrieved the garrote from his tunic and threaded it back into his belt. "Do you have more surprises on you?"

"Possibly," Zack smiled. "Do you have any more madmen running free?" Currat could not help but laugh and shrugged. "I wonder," Zack mused, "what happened to the men in the walls?" Neither of them ventured a guess nor discussed it further in or out of Currat's bedroom.

Currat sat with his boots off and cross-legged on his bed, his usual place for discussions. "Wathdure has always discouraged people from outside Ozlid from visiting our lands. Some have taken that attitude to a fanatic level. Several here would gladly kill you because they believe it would gain them favor in Wathdure's eyes. I don't think he would care, but Spercine would certainly enjoy the murder." They talked on lighter subjects for two hours, and then began their exercises.

* * *

THE next day, Currat arranged for Danyl and Ryman to

join them when they ventured outside their rooms. Zack assumed that the two officers belonged to those special families Currat had mentioned, but he did not ask. If their new companions knew why Currat had asked for their involvement, they did not comment on it. The four men carried on a light banter that mirrored lighter times.

Zack felt surprise when no mention of the maniac's death surfaced; so much control placed on the population caused a shudder along his spine. *I can think of no way they did not see the dead body; even if guards immediately carried it away, someone must know of the incident and its aftermath.* Another day passed, and still there came no outcry of murder. Zack understood the helplessness Currat must have felt.

The following day, they returned to the small officer's mess they had visited on Zack's first day at the palace. Danyl and Ryman joined them at a table for four. The conversation remained neutral, unrestrained, and on subjects far from recent events. They received no undue attention.

Zack felt like more than a guest, and among good companions for the first time in years, although he held no illusions about his status. No one mentioned his upcoming audience with the Master of Masters. He eventually concluded that Danyl and Ryman were in the dark; no one could keep up such a pretense of normalcy and know the dire circumstances Currat and he foresaw.

A distinguished man in a white tunic with a broad black stripe across his chest entered the room. Over two hundred men silenced their conversations and sat still. Currat stood and faced him from across the room. The man said, "Continue," and then made his way with quiet dignity to where Currat remained standing.

The rest of the men continued with their meals and conversations and ignored his passing. Zack questioned for the hundredth time if any in the room knew what lay beneath the surface of their congenial surroundings. He felt uneasy as the man quickly took in his countenance before turning his full attention to Currat.

Currat briefly bowed. "Master of the Black Duval, I salute you. My life is at your command."

Duval answered, "Master of the Blue Currat, I'm honored to see you again."

Duval focused his attention on Zack, who rose to grasp the proffered forearm. The arm beneath the sleeve felt muscular and firm, despite Duval's stark, white hair. "Currat will see that you're allowed to bathe and dress appropriately to meet the Master of Masters in two hours." Duval nodded to Currat and retraced his steps out of the room.

After quickly finishing their meal, Currat led Zack to a large room with a sunken pool in its center that made the pool in his suite seem insignificant. Zack's surprise at finding Danyl and Ryman already swimming in the water did not show. The whispers of steam coming off the water looked inviting. Currat stripped off his clothes and dove into the pool without any preliminary discussion. Zack followed Currat's lead and plunged naked into the warm water. He stood and the water came level with his heart. A gentle current flowed through the pool. Currat swam to the poolside and dipped a sponge into a bucket. He threw it to Zack, and then got one for himself. Zack found the sponge loaded with a different soap than the one he used. It had a pleasant, woody scent he liked.

Two orderlies appeared with thick strips of cotton woven into drying cloths when they left the pool area. Currat motioned Zack to follow him into an adjoining room that Danyl and Ryman had disappeared into moments before. Modesty did not to play a major role in Currat's culture. No one looked twice when a nude man walked through the room. Currat dropped his towel and went to a rack of uniforms. Danyl and Ryman dressed rapidly to return to duty. *What conventions hold in mixed company?*

An orderly approached Zack and removed the cloths wrapped around him without speaking or acting in any way that his actions might be unwelcome or out of the ordinary. He produced a knotted cord and measured Zack's waist, arms, and shoulders. Zack's apprehension surfaced when he kneeled down to measure the length of his leg. The orderly continued, Currat laughed at his uneasiness, and Zack's face flamed red.

The orderly left and returned shortly with a beautiful suit of clothes. Zack hardly recognized his boots. The orderlies had cleaned and polished them while he'd bathed in the pool. He found a new privatecloth similar to the ones he used and started to dress. The suit, made from fine, dark green wormcloth, came with an equally elegant white shirt. Zack followed Currat to a mirror against the wall, where he selected a comb and handed it to Zack.

Currat looked at Zack in the mirror while he combed out the tangles in his hair. "Be careful, my friend, or this may be the suit of clothes used for your cremation. The Master of Masters won't tolerate any levity in your responses. Don't be mistaken; you may still die today. Master of the Black, Duval is a friend. You should follow his lead. I can give you no further advice." Zack nodded once, his smile lacked any humor. He stared at Currat in the large mirror.

Currat's amusement plainly showed. "You noticed it, too?"

Zack nodded, chuckling at the understatement. "Me and anyone else that has seen us together; we could be twins from the neck down and, if not for the color of our hair and eyes, the neck up." Their muscular broad shoulders and powerful legs stated quite firmly that they could handle most men singularly and certainly as a team. Muscles defined by hours of exercise rippled under the fine wormcloth while they groomed themselves. Currat's dark hair shimmered nearly black; Zack's light blond hair approached a shining white. Neither man grew body hair except for their private parts, which seemed as identical as the rest of them. The blue of Zack's eyes contrasted with Currat's black eyes. Their faces formed, rugged and handsome, around strength. They finished grooming without speaking further.

Currat led Zack through corridors he had not traveled before, down to the first level finally arriving before two massive doors. Each door's normal-sized width rose, three levels, carved in a relief pattern of a giant waterfall. A guard stood at the center of each door, and Duval waited nearby.

The three men met away from the guard's hearing, where Duval quietly said, "I understand you're bonded to my son. I'll do what I can to guide you along the right path. It's extremely important that you don't speak until they ask a direct question. Pay no attention to anything that might happen in the room that does not directly concern you. Do not show surprise at anything you see or hear."

Zack looked at Currat. "Your father?" He merely smiled and retraced his steps toward his rooms. Duval concentrated a moment. "Our culture primarily uses first names. Our family names, known to few and found only on official documents, are private. I understand that's not the case in many lands, including Hamptor and Arestead."

Zack nodded, and the two men waited in silence for nearly an hour. The waiting produced torturous effects on his nervous system.

16

A barely audible gong sounded through the heavy doors, causing Zack and Duval to jerk their heads in that direction. The two guards smartly stood to the side and pulled the doors open. Zack followed Duval into an audience chamber. The room, occupied by at least fifty people, could have held ten times that number. A dull, black throne inlaid with gold in a scroll design sat on a platform three steps above the main floor at the room's opposite end.

Zack could not believe his eyes; the person sitting on the throne possessed beauty to a degree he never imagined. She was dressed in a long, tight-fitting, white gown. A black train rested lightly across her shoulders, and fanned out for several yards behind the throne. Her long, wavy, black hair cascaded over her shoulders. *How does that low-cut gown stay on over those breasts? Spercine?*

A conversation continued between a group of men and women standing near the throne. No one had paid any attention to their entrance. Duval led Zack to the room's right side, away from the others. They stood there, waiting for nearly an hour as ministers that stood close to the throne pronounced quick decisions to petitions from those in front of them.

Spercine finally said her first words since they entered the room and cut off the debate before her as if responding to a signal. "I recognize Master of the Black, Duval." The crowd separated and created a path from where they stood that led directly to the throne. Duval did not hesitate and walked toward Spercine with Zack staying close behind. They stopped near a circular line formed in the stone flooring's pattern with the throne at its center.

Duval did not bow or kneel. "I, Master of the Black, Duval, have the honor to be recognized by the Mistress of Masters, Spercine. How may I be of service?"

"You may introduce the stranger to our lands."

"I present to Ozlid, Delan Stand."

"Delan Stand, you are no longer a stranger to us. You are welcome in our lands." Her voice flowed like honey, slow and sweet; her eyes confirmed that the honey contained poison.

Zack tried his best to show no emotion. "I'm unfamiliar with your customs. Please know that it is not my intent if I should say or do anything that offends you. I wish you and your people joy and happiness for all time."

The woman's cold, raven-black eyes pierced Zack's body from head to toe. "You sound more like a diplomat than an adventurer. Your admittance of ignorance is noted. This audience is closed."

The room's occupants started filing out without obeisance or any show of protocol one might expect. No one spoke. Zack followed their lead, and started after the last man. Duval's hand grasped his arm in a vise-like grip that belied his age and countenance. Zack turned around and found Spercine's eyes probing him as if he might be food for a light meal.

"Guards, bring chairs and privacy."

From behind dark blue draperies at the room's rear, two guards stepped out from behind the throne. Zack strained to keep his mouth from dropping open and did not quite believe his eyes; the men measured well over six and a half feet tall with huge, muscular bodies; they wore tight black leather trousers and sandals. Their bare upper bodies glistened with oil, and hammered gold cuffs circled their wrists. Their braided blond hair fell to the small of their back; the identical twins matched each other in every respect, and their motions synchronized as one. They met a few feet behind Zack and Duval as they pulled the heavy draperies in a circle around them. Zack saw a small gold bar that pierced through the flesh behind each nipple. He had never experienced such a thing and questioned if it hurt all the time or just when someone breathed on it. A thick gold ring hung an inch below their pierced lobes. An outline of the same size ring lay positioned to show through the leather at their crotch. Zack decided he did not want to know what it pierced, and a shiver flew up his spine.

Four guards with the same general build and costume followed the blondes. The first two carried plush chairs and set them beside Zack and Duval. The last two carried an ornate chair with precious gems embedded in the gold overlay. These men, whose hair glimmered as black as Spercine's, looked enough alike to be brothers, and functioned in practiced precision. The men's submissiveness housed in bodies of brute strength set a perfect counterpoint to Spercine's overwhelming lasciviousness, softly flowing with every movement that held true power. Sex fairly dripped from the ceiling while the guards circled their mistress in a voluptuous and complex mating ritual designed and performed in trained symmetry.

They set the gold chair next to the platform facing Zack and Duval. The two blonds walked to the throne, gently lifted Spercine, and set her in the gold chair while the remaining two guards rearranged her train. Her hands rested on the guard's bodies as lovers might touch in private throughout the entire time of the transfer. Her laughter rang clear as a bell through the room, reminding Zack of a carefree schoolgirl.

The completely obscene and perverted performance, displaying the power to defy the normal governmental and judicial procedures, protocol, and respect, disgusted Zack. Duval seemingly accepted the defiled blazonry with resignation that Zack surmised came to one used to daily distaste.

Duval leaned close to him. "Kneel when the Master of Masters arrives."

The room grew dark while the six guards positioned themselves close enough to the woman so that she could still touch them if she liked. She hooked a finger under the blonde guard's waistband on her right and pulled him closer to her; she disengaged her finger and lay her head against his side, easing her arm along the inside of his leg from the rear. The guard showed no surprise; indeed, his only reaction revealed a rather prodigious manhood that pressed its ring harder against black leather trousers.

Zack looked through the slight gap in the draperies behind him. The entire room grew darker by every beat of his heart. Spercine's faintly visible white gown formed a ghostly figure in the gloom; he could see a vague outline of the guard's golden cuffs. They too, disappeared within a few heartbeats. The darkness around him began to feel oppressive; more than oppressive, it oozed evil incarnate. He held his hand in front of him and could not see it. He heard no footsteps. He remained standing.

The light change began so slowly that Zack considered it his imagination. Gradually, he realized that a dark figure now sat on the throne. The light continued to brighten, until it rivaled a sunny summer day. The air felt moist and dead like a catacomb, albeit, a bright catacomb.

The features of the figure on the throne lay hidden under a heavy black robe; his head hid within the deep, oval fold of its cowl. Duval knelt at once, and Zack followed his example.

A voice, as dead as the air around them, said, "Rise."

Duval sat in the chair behind him and Zack followed his example.

Spercine sat, not moving a muscle, facing forward with a demure smile on her face. The guards stood at position; they stared straight ahead.

The dead voice asked, "You know of the Dark Stone?"

It marked the first time Zack heard the stone Wathdure wanted referred to by its name used in the Seven Realms. It did nothing to alleviate the overwhelming feeling of death and evil washing over him; rather, it confirmed it. Zack repeated the information about the stone as he had before.

"Do you know the man who wears the Dark Stone?"

"My Lord, at the time I heard the story a man named Eric Mountglen wore it. I don't know who wears it now. I assume he still has it."

"I am not a lord. In this kingdom, they call me the Master of Masters. You may call me Wathdure." Spercine's face registered shock for a brief moment, and then regained its demure mask. "And what is the news from Mountglen? It has been a long time since I visited there."

Zack thought, *I really don't need any more confirmation, and you scare the Seven Hells out of me. How long since your last visit indeed, two millennia, perhaps?* He answered while hiding all trace of his emotions. "The land is at peace and prospers."

Wathdure's black-gloved hands emerged from the long sleeves of his robe. He slowly tapped his index fingers together. "Your information has been of value to me. I do not search for that stone. I know of that one. How may I repay you for your kindness?"

"Surely, you are a better judge than I. I have been away from my homeland for too long. I wish to be on my way back there."

Wathdure reached inside his robe and produced a large pouch. He held it out to the throne's side closest to Spercine. She stood, reached over, and took the pouch. Her fluid movements matched the honey in her speech. Gliding seductively over to Zack, she handed him the pouch. Her long nails raked across his wrist and bit into his skin. A momentary jealousy of her guards rose while he watched her amazingly fluid body move back to her chair, but for only a moment.

"I am sure Duval can find a comfortable room for you to stay as long as you wish," Wathdure said. "Currat will guide you to the border when you are ready."

Duval started to rise, but settled back into the chair at the sound of Zack's voice. "I have a message from Durton. He sends his regards."

Wathdure's gloved hands gripped the throne's arms for a mere heartbeat. Then he relaxed. An evil laugh filled the room. The room became dark in another heartbeat. In the space of a breath, normal light returned. Wathdure had disappeared; his laugh slowly faded after him. Spercine and her guards left the room without notice or regard to its occupants. She walked much quicker than before, displaying the same liquid articulations Zack found so seductive. Her right arm encircled one blond guard's waist while her left hand played with the other blond's buttocks.

Zack and Duval slipped through the draperies, with his guide setting a pace that approached a run. Zack followed him through the maze of corridors and people until he finally stopped at a familiar door. He pulled a chain holding a key from beneath his tunic and over his head. Nervously fumbling at the door, he opened it and yanked Zack inside. Duval dropped the key while trying to lock the door. Zack reached down, retrieved it, and locked the door. Duval collapsed into a plush chair in Currat's bedroom. He looked up as Zack held the key and chain out to him.

"Give the key to Currat. I'm getting too old for this; you must listen carefully." His words came in gasps. "Did Spercine touch you when she gave you the gold?" Zack nodded and watched Duval go pale when he showed him the scratch on his right wrist. "Quickly, get out of your clothes."

Zack's old clothes lay on the table. He looked at Duval, surprised. "Quickly, I said, I'm trying to save your life!"

Zack stripped to his privatecloth and reached for his trousers. Duval's tone emphasized his frustration. "Everything, or do you want to die because of modesty?"

Zack took off the privatecloth. Duval's voice calmed. "Come over here by the light of the window." Zack hesitated again. "For the love of the Creator, I'm not a lover of men. We'll both be dead if you don't hurry."

Zack had not quite stopped walking to the window before the other man started a thorough inspection of his body at his head.

"Just my wrist." Zack said, trying to make sense of Duval's bizarre behavior.

Duval lifted the arm Zack used to receive the pouch. He searched his fingers, wrist, and on up the arm. He spent some time meticulously searching the few hairs under his arm. His hands lightly skimmed over Zack's side and chest, hardly noticing the scars. "It's good that you have little body hair."

Little? Zack thought, *I have no body hair except my head and my private parts, which I just as soon you leave alone.* "Perhaps it will help if you told me what you're looking for."

"I'll show you when I find it." Duval's hands went to Zack's pubic hair while he knelt on the floor. "Spread your legs to the side."

Great Light's Source, why me? Zack complied with more than a little reluctance. Duval peered at the left side of Zack's scrotum; his eyes searched inches away from Zack's crotch. Duval seemed not to notice the close proximity to another man's private parts; his voice became excited. "Here it is."

Zack's mind filled with acerbic thoughts. *Yes. It has been there all my life. Moreover, if you're quite through, leave it alone.* He said nothing. Duval produced a small wooden

140

stick with a barbed point.

"Listen carefully, get the pouch Wathdure gave you and open it wide. Once it's open, hold it in the palms of your hands and be quick." Zack retrieved the pouch that Duval had placed on the table next to the window and returned to Duval's kneeling body. "This will sting."

Zack gritted his teeth when he felt more than what he called a sting. He followed Duval's instructions and held the open pouch toward him. He nearly dropped it when he saw what Duval had impaled on the stick. Curled tightly around the end; it measured at least two inches long, the width of a thin reed, and definitely alive. Duval dropped it; still squirming on the stick into the pouch, he then pulled the strings and tightly closed it.

Duval went to a chest by the window, took a cloth sack out of it, and held it open. "Put the pouch in here, then the clothes you just took off. Try not to let anything touch me while you're doing it."

Zack followed the instructions. Nothing touched Duval's hands. Duval pulled the sack's drawstrings tight when the last item fell into the sack, opened the window and threw the sack in the moat below. He collapsed into the chair and wiped sweat from his brow. He absentmindedly looked at Zack standing by the window. Zack's expression did not express joy.

"I'm sorry. I'll replace the gold, and I know you have questions." He pointed toward a small table with a basin and urn of water next to a chest. "Clean your wound; it should not bleed much. Fortunately, we got it before it anchored. There is a uniform in that chest by you. Put it on and I'll try to explain." Zack bent to do as Duval ordered, again.

"The creature I pulled from you is what we call a deathworm. We know no other name for it. They grow at amazing speed once they taste the smallest bit of blood, and that is the reason Spercine scratched you. They search out a point of entry, and that action is quite puzzling. It enters the body without you feeling it, grows rapidly once inside, and will eventually kill you. It's a painful death. There seem to be several different types. Some enter as yours did, or by the underarms or crotch. Others enter through the chest and attack the heart. A third kind enters at the neck and attacks the brain. The type you received is the worst. It eats the intestines over a period of days and produces a long, agonizing death."

Zack felt goosebumps forming across his body, and not from the chill in the room.

"I'll report that a deathworm attacked your heart and killed you. It's the fastest and will coincide with the time I threw your belongings into the moat. Wathdure can feel the worm's presence, and can track them at will, but the cold water will kill it on contact. There might have been more deathworms in the pouch or on your clothes. We hope Wathdure will believe that the time you entered this room approximated the time of your death. The bag I threw in the moat will eliminate any trace of you or the deathworms he can detect. At least, that's what we believe."

Hoping Duval wasn't guessing, Zack finished dressing.

"The uniform is one Wathdure's messengers wear, and is part of an escape plan. The black stripe across my white tunic is one of rank, as are the stripes of different colors on the military uniforms. The white tunic denotes me as an administrator. The black uniforms are for the army. You will wear the same black cape with a cowl and head mask covering all but your eyes that only messengers wear. If all goes well, Currat will have you on your way tonight."

Duval's words slowed, and Zack watched as his body relaxed. *The last few hours seemed more of an ordeal for him than me. The stress in his life must be unbelievable.*

"I'll leave you for a while. You will need many more things to survive the trip. You must have seen your weapons in the chest. Conceal them beneath the cloak.

The messengers carry few weapons. Be ready to kill anyone who comes in other than Currat or me." Duval listened at the outer door for a few minutes. He tripped the lock and disappeared.

Zack waited until he heard Duval walk away and locked the door. He picked up a plush chair and carried it to the wall next to the door. Retrieving his sword from the chest, he drew it from its scabbard, then sat down next to the door, hoping he held the advantage if it should open. Zack slowly shook his head. *I hope I don't need an advantage. Worms that crawl under your clothes to find their own little paradise, rooms blocked from Wathdure's recognition, will anyone believe this? I'm not sure I believe it.*

Zack remained in the chair with the sword athwart his lap. He thought of Currat. The warmth of friendship he had forgotten over years filled him with a shocking newness. He bathed in the reawakened feelings.

He repeated all he learned in a practiced protocol that insured he would be able to recall everything he'd discovered, thinking of and reinforcing each minute detail since he'd entered the rolling hills of Ozlid. Nearly two hours later, a key turned in the lock, pulling him from his memorization routines. Zack stood instantly, his sword ready.

The door opened no more than a foot. Zack recognized Currat's voice, "It is Currant and Duval." He kept his sword ready until both men entered the room and locked the door. Currat set a large sack on the floor. He sidestepped Zack and carried the plush chair to the corner of his bedroom where the other two chairs provided a seating arrangement for them.

Duval looked fatigued, his face pale. Still, he spoke first. "Currat has told me what you told him since your arrival."

Both men relaxed and took a deep breath. Duval continued, "What I'll tell you in brief is explained in detail in a message we shall give to you for your Zenith Lord.

Most of it you already know." Zack's surprise showed without garnering comment as Duval continued Wathdure's history.

"Gradually, Wathdure's power grew. He influenced our ruling class, and they eventually elevated him to the level of minister. Not long afterward, he gained the same influence over the army. He did this in three years. The army slaughtered the entire ruling class, over one hundred and eighty people, in one night of horror, and installed Wathdure as our sole ruler.

"One hundred years later, Spercine appeared."

Zack's mouth dropped. "She's two hundred and four years old. Great Light's Source, how long do you live here?"

Duval answered, "We live what we believe to be a normal life span of sixty-odd years. Neither Wathdure nor Spercine have aged in my lifetime. Wathdure began to change around the time Spercine arrived, from what I can deduce from the few true records we have. They describe him as an extremely handsome man and that hasn't changed, it only improved. There is one reference stating that his skin turned black as the darkest ebony. Now, his public appearances are rare, and no part of his skin shows. No one in my lifetime has ever seen his face. Could you see anything beneath his cowl?"

Zack shook his head in answer and disbelief. *Three hundred and four years . . .*

"I wish we could say the same of Spercine. We know little of her. She attends the social and state functions in place of Wathdure. She's blatant in her use of men, as you may have surmised. The men around her that she calls 'her guards' are nothing more than her slaves in and out of bed. She selects them when they are first able to produce their seed. She taunts it as a great honor, and pays their families well for as long as they live. The men are equally cared for, but she does have favorites. She gives them enough gold for a lifetime, and sends them on their way when she tires of one, unless he displeased her, then death or worse awaits. She has no power to change the orders of our ministers, but misses little, and reports everything to Wathdure."

Zack noticed Duval's manner: *His fatigue grows, and he still looks ill. I know he possesses physical strength that many men his age might envy, but his burden is heavy, and the constant fear of discovery must erode his spirit, not to mention his nerves.*

Currat picked up the conversation when Duval slumped into his chair. "Two hundred years ago, Wathdure ordered the moat around the palace built. Natural springs and the melt-off from the high mountains surrounding us provided our water until then. Water sprang from under the palace on the day they finished the moat and the last bridge reached completion. It quickly filled the moat and raced around the palace exactly as you saw it. The rivers of Arestead and Hamptor dried up in a matter of days. Wathdure sent messages to both lands proposing that Ozlid supply their water at an extravagant price.

"Our army dug the riverbeds from the moat to within a few feet from the mountain's edge while the kings debated. They started at the moat's end on Wathdure's orders. Not one drop of water flowing around the moat went into those riverbeds until they completed them at the mountain's edge." Currat eased over and sat cross-legged on the bed before continuing. "It created quite a stir." He groaned at the pun.

"He has been careful to keep Arestead and Hamptor's production of crops at a minimum so they cannot prosper. That also keeps them under his control."

Zack sat waiting, saying nothing as he tried to categorize the additional points Currat hadn't mention during the last weeks. The omissions did not anger him; he may well have done the same in their place.

Currat started again, slowly. "I assume you heard the misfortunes of Hamptor about one hundred years ago.

The water ceased to flow in their riverbed the day they sent their ultimatum refusing to pay. People came from all of Ozlid to see water flow pass an empty riverbed some thirty yards deep and as many wide. Our records say the same interest and amazement captured the people during the excavation. It did much more than to provide a spectacle for the people's amusement—it cemented Wathdure's power once and for all. I'm sure he enjoyed the Hamptorian's suffering." Currat looked at Zack with a frustrated and helpless expression. "It's almost as if he bides his time, waiting for something to happen. We don't know what he is waiting for."

Zack sat on the chest, his feeling of dread at hearing Wathdure's evil growing stronger. Duval continued. "Recently, the black stone he searches for has generated much activity. Do you know anymore about it than you told Wathdure?"

Zack cleared his throat and spoke with the same careful tone Currat had used. "I heard stories of the Great Stones of Power used in our war two millennia ago. Most people today think them a myth. The Great Stones didn't include a Dark Stone, but there are stories about one used by the forces of evil. The kind of children's stories told to make them behave. I never gave credence to them after my Age-of-Man time. Several months ago, a retainer of High Lord Mountglen's became talkative and well paid by a colleague of mine; he related the story that I told Wathdure today. I told the truth as I know it, and held nothing back."

Currat said in a near whisper. "That is probably why you didn't die in the audience chamber. He may not know that Spercine gave you the deathworm, but he certainly would not care, and possibly may have rewarded her. I don't think you will make it outside the rolling hills alive without our help."

Zack's voice remained calm and even. "We have always believed only three kingdoms reigned here. Who does the river to the north benefit?"

Duval sighed. "You have hit on the biggest mystery in Ozlid. The island's northern end still gets its water from springs and runoff from the mountains. The one pass through the mountain range in the north is heavily guarded. We have heard of soldiers going through the pass from curiosity, but none returned. Our histories tell us that there is little there to warrant the effort. The land is poor for crops, and not worth the trouble of traversing the mountains to claim it for the few months it is free from ice. The river ultimately flows below that mountain range like the others."

Zack looked at the messenger's cloak. "I think my cloak will pass for this with the dark side out."

Currat looked at him curiously. "It's a beautiful cloak. Is there another reason?"

"None, except that it holds a few surprises."

Currat's eyes went to Zack's belt. "By all means, keep it. We will need all the help we can get."

Duval cleared his throat and started again. "Our rolling hills are misleading from the way my son brought you in. The palace is at the southern end. The rolling hills are over a hundred miles long, and jut westward at the northern end. In places, the land is nearly two hundred miles across. We have a population of over five million people. That's twice the population of Arestead and Hamptor combined. How large is Stonefire?"

Zack answered without hesitation. "The realm is approximately the three kingdom's combined size, as best I can tell. Stonefire is one of the Seven Realms. It's not the largest."

Duval considered this for a moment. "We have always been told that your lands harbored no aggression internally, or to the lands across the seas. There are many of us who believe Wathdure is evil incarnate and may have grand designs on other lands." Duval shifted in his chair, worrying at its arm with his fingers before continuing.

"Lately, Wathdure has been sending supplies to a certain point in the northern pass. The area is bare when the soldiers take the next day's shipment. The supplies are only for the manufacture of weapons and uniforms. He sends no food." Duval's disgusted look matched his son's expression.

"He certainly controls Ozlid, and for the most part Arestead and Hamptor as well. He has no need for so many weapons here. Your Seven Realms are the closest lands he does not control. We don't possess ships for transport. Nevertheless, where else could his avarice lead him? He already has what wealth of Arestead and Hamptor he could extract from them."

Duval's voice became stronger. "I have detailed everything I told you in the packet I mentioned. You must get it to your Zenith Lord. Add this: if the people of Ozlid learn of Wathdure's true nature, they will rebel, and they will lose."

Duval bowed his head and spoke in a softer tone. "I must go to make sure everything is ready for tonight. Currat will stay with you until dark. I'll not see you again. May the Creator see you safely home."

Zack and Duval grasped arms. Zack said, "I don't know how to thank you for your help." Duval's moist eyes and pained expression left him with the impression the older man felt thanks should be flowing in the opposite direction.

Duval shook his head and left. Zack felt as drained as Duval looked. *Does he possess the strength to continue through the night?*

17

ZACK didn't care for the uniform's wormcloth hood, but it didn't restrict his vision or breathing, and his cloak's dark side would blend well in the dimly lit corridors. He threw the cloak over his shoulders and pulled its cowl over his head.

Currat smiled in approval. "Messengers are on these floors at times, but no matter what happens, don't speak. They seem to be mute. You should not have a problem. Most people completely ignore the messengers as if they're not even there. I believe it's more of Wathdure fooling with their heads. Follow me and stay a few steps behind."

Zack reversed the cloak to the lighter side, removed the hood and gathered the cloak tight around him to cover the uniform from guards peering at him through their hidden kill holes. He watched while Currat listened and then unlocked the door, following him out when he signaled. Zack quickly reversed the procedure when they stopped at a turn in a blind corridor's intersection. They walked rapidly through the maze of corridors. The few people they met scurried to get out of the messenger's way and kept their eyes adverted; they paid little attention to Currat.

They descended one level, and Zack's nose could sense the stable's odors. Rounding a corner, Currat froze. Two guards stood at the stable entrance. Zack saw Currat backing away and preceded him. Currat stopped when he knew they could safely speak. "They're not supposed to be here."

Zack whispered in Currat's ear, then staggered around

the corner, falling against the wall and slid to the floor. The other man followed when he heard him fall. "Guards, quick!" The two guards raced toward them. Currat pointed back the way they had come. "Two men tried to take this messenger's pouch. GO!" The guards raced up the hall and to the floor above.

Zack rose and entered the stable, and Currat started for the officer's stable on the opposite side of the palace. Riding a messenger's horse in common clothes would draw immediate attention, and probably arrows. A groom went quickly to a stall and returned with a large black stallion as soon as Zack entered. Messengers filed into the stable area as if on cue. Zack waited until the first mounted and followed his lead as he left the stable. They rode at full gallop by the time they reached the bridge. Three more riders followed behind Zack. The guards stood well clear of the stallion's path. One messenger separated from the group and started north. Suddenly, Zack knew who galloped through dark nights at a fool's speed. He slowed the big stallion to let the three trailing messengers slowly pass him, and then matched their pace.

The horse's speed amazed Zack. They raced over narrow mountain trails that dropped off thousands of feet on his left side. He didn't look but once, and then gave the horse its head. Zack followed the messengers' lead until they merged with a slightly wider trail he recognized as the path he had traveled to enter the rolling hills. The big stallion did not try to catch up with his brothers or their strange riders, and Zack relaxed on the reins. Soon, the horses ahead rode beyond hearing range, continuing at full gallop.

Zack pulled on the reins to slow his horse once they went through the pass. The heart of a normal horse might well burst from running that distance at full gallop. He stroked his mount's neck and received a soft nicker for his effort. Zack saw the landmark of a curious rock formation just in time, even at the slower pace; he stopped about twenty yards off the main trail.

He tied the horse, and then tried to stroke his neck again to calm the big animal. He shied away and reared, and Zack realized the horse was terror struck. He led him upwind, tethered him again, and he calmed after a few moments. *I'll have to wait quite a while for Currat to catch up with me.*

He approached the stallion after an hour had passed, and was able to stroke him. The terror had left his eyes, but his uneasy nature remained. Suddenly, the horse reared, terror returning to his eyes.

Zack felt someone watching him. He swung around and found a messenger staring at him from his horse about ten yards away. The messenger charged as best he could in the wooded area. Zack rolled away, and on the next charge, he flipped into the air, his feet hitting the rider in the shoulder, knocking him to the ground. The rider leaped up before Zack could react and rushed at him with amazing alacrity, drawing a knife from beneath his cloak as he shrugged it off his shoulders.

He lunged at Zack with all his weight. Zack sidestepped and tripped him as he went by. The messenger rolled back onto his feet in less time than it took Zack to draw his knife. He lunged again. Zack easily dodged him, too easily. He saw black eyes staring at him in the moonlight. The messenger fought with speed and determination, but little skill.

He swung his blade in a wide arc on his next charge while Zack easily sidestepped him again and rolled away. Before Zack could stand, he felt the messenger's full weight land on top of him. The black eyes focused directly on Zack's chest as he tried to bring his knife down into his target. Zack shoved with all his strength and rolled out from under, twisting his attacker's arm and forcing him onto his back. Then he rolled and plunged his knife into the prone attacker's neck with all his strength.

An unnatural shriek pierced the night. A satisfying crunch sounded when he felt the knife sever the spinal column. Zack's surprise registered instantly; normal body tissue should have made a near decapitation impossible with such a short blade.

Zack watched to be sure of the man's death. Everything about the fight and the messenger felt wrong. He realized that a man who fought that fast and with such purpose should not have been that easy to kill, unless he had never fought before. The body had not moved; the fluids spilling onto the ground looked strange, and Zack nearly gagged from the stench. He approached the black, still form and saw black eyes staring into eternity as the nearly severed head oozed gore unlike anything he'd ever seen.

The smell of rotten flesh and putrid fluids almost made him lose his stomach once more, gagging him through the hood. He covered his mouth and nose with one hand, reached down, and pulled the messenger's hood off. Zack jumped backward and nearly fell. He approached again with care, eyes wide.

The creature's stark, white skin covered his face quite literally; there remained only a line where a mouth should have been. The blunt end of the nose dented into the face without nares. Zack picked up its knife; he chose to leave his where it protruded half in tissue and half in the ground. A cold breeze took most of the stench away. Zack took the stallion farther upwind to wait. The docile animal offered no resistance. The creature's horse stood some twenty yards away, nibbling at the few blades of grass there. Zack walked to his horse's twin and led him without trouble. Neither horse showed the fear or anxiety that had previously consumed them.

Another hour passed before Zack heard the sound of a horse coming from Ozlid. He bent down and slipped away from the horses to hide in dark shadows. Currat stood less than three feet away when he whispered his name.

Currat jumped at the sound. When Zack stood, he leaned back as a sword flashed at his throat in the blink of an eye. He pulled his hood off, and the sword dropped away. Currat sank to his knees and looked as white as the thing Zack had killed.

Zack knelt in front of him. "I didn't mean to scare you, my friend. What is wrong? Are you hurt?"

"My father is dead, as are several others in our group. I escaped by using one of the old passes most people have forgotten. Then, I rode hard when I came onto the main trail."

"Are you certain about your father?"

Currat lowered his head and his words came in an agonized whisper. "There is no doubt. I saw him take an arrow in the eye and a sword through the chest. He fell into the moat. He planned to kill himself if he received wounds or they discovered his involvement. The others tried to make it over the bridge, and the guards used them for target practice. None of them reached the halfway mark. Danyl and Ryman are dead, too." The sadness in his voice nearly overwhelmed Zack.

"I didn't do a thing." Despair and guilt sounded plain in Currat's words as he knelt on the ground. "I didn't do a thing but sit in the shadows and watch. I didn't do a thing." He lowered his head into his hands.

Zack grasped his shoulders. "Currat, look at me." Slowly his eyes came up to stare at the man for whom his father and friends died. "You did the only thing you could do. Your father and friends died for us to get away and fight Wathdure in a different arena and on another day. Your death would negate their sacrifice. You did the right thing. You couldn't have done anything else without throwing your life away. You are alive, and will fight another day."

Currat's face looked as if he tried to take in everything Zack had said and found it difficult. He stood and sheathed his sword in its scabbard after a few moments. "I didn't have much time to think on the way here, looking for landmarks that I hadn't seen in years. But you are right—I *will* fight another day." Currat looked around. "What is that horrible smell?"

"I had hoped you could tell me that. A messenger returned after I got here. I didn't see or hear him or his horse approach. It was eerie. We fought, not that I would call it much of a fight. He didn't move like a fighter—he was fast, but untrained. The main thing seemed to be a lack of coordination with weapons. I pulled his hood off and he's like nothing I ever saw before. Come, he's over here."

The stench had become almost bearable. Both men strode upwind for clean air more than once. Currat looked down at the creature while it rapidly disintegrated. He pulled his knife and slit the creature's tunic and shirt. Currat spread the clothing with his knife and a stick. He jerked up and walked away to vomit.

Zack caught up with him afterwards. "What did you see?"

Currat expressed incomprehension at every level. "I know . . . knew him. We went through training together. He missed his marks for officer training, but he made sergeant in a short time. He remained bitter about not getting another chance for officer training, and his attitude reflected it. They reassigned him to the northern pass for patrol duty, and he numbered among the ones that went through the pass and never returned. He has a birthmark over his right breast in the shape of a crescent moon. The basic features are his; the birthmark confirms it. However, before he became that—thing—he was once human. Great Creator, what has Wathdure done?"

The distant sound of hooves pulled their attention to the main trail. They crouched in dark shadows. The moonlight allowed enough light to see another messenger at full gallop pass by.

"Would you like to bet that message has something to do with the two of us?" Zack said. "I didn't hear your missing sergeant come up on me. I think we had best be very quiet for a few minutes."

The horse's hoofbeats over hard ground receded, and soon disappeared. A few apprehensive minutes passed before Zack spoke. "You will have a better chance in this uniform. Not many people saw me at the fortress. The hood and cowl may give you an edge. Besides, I'll feel better with my sword, and the messengers don't carry one. Now we know why." They jumped at every sound during the hasty exchange.

Currat pulled saddlepacks from his horse and checked the supplies Duval had given him for the trip. They would use Currat's mare as a packhorse and ride the big blacks. He also insisted Zack take a large pouch of gold his father sent with him.

Zack felt the shoulders of his cloak and found the knives' reassuring light pressure across his shoulders after he mounted. Currat took the unsoiled cloak the dead messenger had discarded that still carried a strange scent. He tried not to think what caused it.

The horses seemed normal enough on the trail. Zack rode beside Currat when space permitted. "Have you noticed the horse's speed and endurance when the messengers are riding them? No horse could stand that pace for a tenth the distance we have already traveled and why stallions; why not use geldings?"

"I never considered it. I guess because none of us ever rode any distance with them. I saw them ride into the fortress many times at full gallop. We believed they did it to put on a show at the end of their ride, after resting."

Zack considered for a moment before speaking. "My horse began to tire badly before I pulled off the main trail, so it must be something the messengers do or their contact with the horses that keeps them going. If those creatures somehow keep the horses fresh and they ride at full gallop without stopping, they will be at the fortress in a day. They will be waiting for us and will have had plenty of time to plan for our arrival. You have been most hospitable to me. I think it's time you enjoyed the Seven Realms' hospitality now."

Currat looked introspective. "These are my people and my home. I cannot leave. Most of my people are good, and know nothing of Wathdure's evil."

Zack's response reflected the same thoughtfulness. "How are they, or you, going to stop Wathdure from doing what he wants? He has full command of the army. If you're able to reach them with your story and they believe you, will they fight a man that held the waters from a riverbed?"

They rode on for a minute before Zack continued, "Wathdure asked about something from my lands, the Dark Stone. He used the name "Dark Stone," not black stone. I have a feeling that your problems are somehow going to become our problems. You might as well fight there, if that's the case. Too many will chase you for the reward of reinstatement to society once your description is circulated, you will be captured. Your father impressed me with his intelligence and his courage. What would he have wanted you to do?"

Currat did not speak for several minutes. His voice came strong and filled with determination when he spoke. "There is an evil in my land. I must find a way to fight it, or my father's death will mean nothing. I fear you're right about my safety, however. I'll be killed if I return to the rolling hills, and that will become only a matter of time if I stay here."

His voice held conviction. "We must plan carefully. There will be patrols out day and night to look for us. They will continue until we're found, alive or dead. I have led those patrols before. The army won't give up until they have a body to give Wathdure." Zack nodded.

"The best place to cross is midway between the

fortress you came through when you entered, and the next one to the west. They send patrols from all three strongholds twice a day; there are a few flaws in their scouting methods. The fortress' patrols rotate every four hours. The west fortress starts first, and then the mid-fortress, and the eastern fortress last. They each send the same amount of men, giving the mid-fortress twice the ground to cover. Their justification is the land. The midland is much easier to patrol, and has mostly open terrain and flat country before they reach the mountain's sheer cliffs. Both rivers come above ground about a mile before the border, and are the point at which the patrols limit their search to the south. The current is too strong to cross. The river's bank west of Hamptor is dense with trees, groundcover, and gullies. It's dangerous, especially in the dark. Falls and large game kill men, mostly at night. There are bears and large cats, and the ground is full of holes from burrowing animals. Most patrols tend to avoid much of that area, especially after dark."

Currat's voice had grown in strength and determination. Zack knew he warmed to the idea of leaving Ozlid. Zack wondered if either of them would see the rolling hills again.

"Another flaw is the officer sent with the patrol is usually a tan-stripe. They're our lowest ranked officer, and have the least experience. Some sergeants are lax, and will let the men get away with cursory searches in the difficult areas, and the tan-stripe knows no better."

Zack was heartened to hear this, glad to know that they suffered some weak links.

"The army looks at the duty as a waste of time. The men from Hamptor and Arestead will kill us if we go over the border, and the ones they chase will be killed or captured if they stay on this side of the rolling hills." Zack looked unsure.

Currat explained further. "Our speech patterns and accent are quite different, as I'm sure you know. Arestead and Hamptor remain in close contact and intermarry. Our isolation has produced many differences in our language. Across the border, I would be dead within an hour after speaking my first word."

Zack's voice grew serious again. "I think your commanders may think the same way you do. They know your history with the army, and may figure you'll do exactly as you propose. Does the army ever chase anyone over the border?"

"Occasionally, but it's usually just one person chasing someone for committing a crime, stealing vouchers or striking a guard. Most of the time we leave them alone after a good run unless it's for stealing vouchers, then it becomes much more serious. Stealing is punishable by death in Ozlid. We have very few thieves. But, if one of them runs, they're still in our territory. The border is actually about a mile south of the trading centers and the fortresses. Why do you ask?"

Zack took a moment to think before continuing. "Is there a way for you to chase me over the border near the fortress? I saw a stand of trees near the market's far end, and I think it's dense in there. Do they ever search there when they send out patrols, and how long will it take for the men on duty to send someone after us?"

Currat's answer came immediately. "No, but the border guard goes through there every two hours. There is one place they don't search—a chasm on the fort's mountainous side. They will see us if we ride, but it's deep enough for us to lead the horses through and remain out of sight. It's considered too dangerous to patrol. The trail is narrow, with a steep drop-off of a hundred yards or so. A couple years ago, I was curious about the chasm and hiked the trail. We can approach without detection, and a hill hides our egress on the Hamptor side. The patrols tend to limit their search when they grow close to the low hills. The sides are difficult to climb."

Zack began to see a ray of hope.

Currat's voice mirrored the same hope. "We stand a good chance of getting across the border if we get that far. I've never heard of anyone else going down into the chasm, and I didn't brag about it. It's dangerous, but not as bad as it looks from the top. It's also unlikely we'll meet anyone living that close to the mountains. If we do, they wouldn't have heard about us this soon."

The trail narrowed. Zack let Currat pull ahead until it widened again, enabling him to drop back along side. He said nothing for several moments, and then picked up the conversation where it left off. "I can see only one drawback. Once we're in the chasm, if someone does think of it, we're doomed. There'd be no going back. One of us will have to fight however many came in front or behind us. I don't know the land nearly as well as you do. If you feel that's our best chance, I'll take your advice."

Currat nodded. "I do think it's the best of the alternatives. They'll increase the border guard in size and frequency. The army becomes highly upset when one of its officers gets in trouble. My death would be long and painful if they catch us. Yours will probably not be quite as long, but certainly just as painful."

Zack smiled. "That's what I find one of your most interesting and enduring traits, Currat. Visualizing your thoughts are always so uplifting. By the way, my real name is Zack Stand."

Currat eyed Zack. "Somehow I don't think Wathdure would care that you that lied about your name before he has you killed."

They both chuckled, and kept headed east, toward the mountain's looming blackness.

18

PREDAWN light marked their stopping point. After securing the horses on long leads to graze, they dug into the provision bags to take inventory. They found plenty of dried meat, cheese, and travel bread, two bags of grains and oats for the horses, and another bag containing changes of clothes. Too many clothes; Zack's travel bag included two extra changes that he recognized as Currat's clothing, and Currat found the same in his. They looked at each other at the same time. "He planned for me to go with you," Currat whispered, startling Zack. "He knew he wasn't going to survive."

Zack said nothing, having pondered the same idea, and come to the same conclusion.

Lastmeal, which they ate at the normal time for firstmeal, went down rapidly. The horses devoured their portions of grain and oats and then grazed a while longer. Their campsite bordered a fast-moving stream. The horses, like the men, drank a little before their meal and more afterwards. They did not even discuss a fire. Golden rays of sunlight filtering through the trees seemed unnaturally bright in the crisp air. Zack climbed the highest tree near the campsite and left Currat looking pleased. He stayed in the utmost branches for nearly half an hour. Currat began to wonder what stayed his interest when he finally saw signs of Zack's descent.

Zack's voice, a bit winded and scratchy, panted with exertion. "Two fires visible. One is a mile almost due south, the second is east of it another mile."

They decided to travel slowly at night, along the smaller trails. Currat mentioned the foothills would be better traveling farther eastward. Zack stated the obvious. "I think we should ride east another few miles." With a sigh, Currat started breaking the camp they had just made.

Zack had disappeared when Currat looked up from packing the saddlepacks. He listened carefully, hearing the normal sounds of a forest coming alive at the start of a new day. He looked up the tree to see if perhaps Zack had climbed it for another look around, but saw nothing. Currat lugged the packs over to the packhorse. She did not look pleased. "Just a little while longer, then you can sleep." He stroked her neck and patted her above her muzzle. She continued to look unhappy. Currat knew how she felt and tied her well. The stallions showed little interest. Later, when Currat saddled them and tightened the last leathers, a moving tree branch caught his eye.

Currat watched while Zack backed into camp from the way they had come, completely obliterating their trail. No sign of their presence remained, and he looked amazed. Zack looked around the campsite for anything Currat or he might have missed. Finding nothing, he mounted and broke a trail leading due east. After an hour of careful riding, boulders jutted into the sky before them that formed a screen.

Zack inspected it, and motioned Currat to follow him around the natural barrier. Giant stones formed a circle, with a passageway through the center wide enough for the horses. Water spilled from one boulder into a well-worn basin of stone. The overflow formed the beginnings of a stream, and then disappeared into the ground. The outer stones blocked strong winds, and the sun inside the circle warmed them. Zack stopped and dismounted, walking around the rough circle that spiraled in toward the center. Currat held the animals at the entrance and waited until Zack returned, pointing to a spot on the far side. "There's a formation that will be excellent for tying the horses."

Zack closely examined the ground underneath an

overhang. "Three campsites in the open are several months old, and one here is no more than two weeks old, with many more beneath it. This is a well-known place. How do the exiles feel about the army?" Zack squinted up at Currat from where he sat on his haunches.

He answered immediately. "They hate and fear us. After all, we keep them out of our cities while we keep others out of our lands. The last time they killed one of us ..." He cocked his head. "It has been two years since they killed anyone in the army. Wathdure ordered us to kill everyone within ten miles of the incident; seventy-three men, women, and children tortured and slaughtered. Thankfully, I resided at the palace during that time. Some of the men that traveled with us to the palace enjoyed themselves immensely. Border duty comprises two types of men: cruel bastards that enjoy needless torture and killing, and those that despise giving the orders for it. We would soon find ourselves at the formers' not so tender mercies, if we didn't give the right orders. The rest of the officers at the border just don't care one way or another." Disgust oozed from Currat.

Zack began to appreciate another facet of Wathdure's evil. He explored further while Currat settled the horses. Handholds chipped into the stone augmented a natural path up the side of a boulder.

A lookout point at the top of the tallest boulder, combined with an easy climb to reach it, provided the best view. It too, showed signs of frequent use. Several initials chiseled into the rock showed age from rounded edges. Zack found flint and steel wrapped in oilskin hidden in a natural hollow, and weighed it down with a good-sized rock. No sign, above or below, indicated a cache of dry wood. Whoever signaled from the rock hauled their burnable material with them. Charred markings, found in a naturally formed indention in the rock, verified its recent use. Zack lay flat on the boulder, covered by his cloak, and peered out in all directions. He could easily see the cooking and warming fires of several encampments to the south, and a few to the north. He identified the campsites he saw earlier from the tree, and they still concerned him the most. He signaled Currat, pointed at him while miming a sleeping figure, then pointed to himself and the boulder where he lay, shading his eyes and looking around.

Correctly assuming that Zack was taking the first watch, Currat rolled up in his cloak, using his saddle for a pillow. As an afterthought, Currat pulled the messenger's hood over his head. He fell asleep within a few minutes.

Zack looked down on the sleeping form of a new friend. *No. Not just a friend, he has proven to be more than that.* He continued his assessment while he searched the area for signs of two-legged life. *He lost his father and best friends because of me. No. That's not right. He lost them to the evil that ruled them and the evil that destroyed the Seven Realms two millennia ago. I lost my wife and daughter to evil deeds. Are they one and the same? Have I blamed mankind instead of the evil infesting some men? I trust Currat, son of Duval. I have trusted no one in five years other than Michael Gaz. Have I been foolish? The deceit that led me away from my family came from a supposed friend.*

Zack looked down again on the sleeping figure of a man so much like himself it scared him and searched his feelings. *I do trust him and I feel more than simple friendship. Perhaps a partner, perhaps the two of us, together, will be more effective in the coming fight than either of us alone.* His head jerked up at the thought. *I have just taken for granted that there will soon be another war forged against the Seven Realms.* He relaxed until his next thought jarred him. *I love Currat as deeply as any brother.* He continued his vigilance while his thoughts repeatedly returned to the repulsive thought of war. Other feelings lay buried too deep to consider the possibility of someone caring for him in any way simply because he existed and had developed into a man that could be valued.

Zack heard and saw unusual occurrences several times during the day; limbs swaying in the opposite way the wind was blowing, a twig or small branch breaking, but no one ventured to their hiding place, and his spyglass revealed nothing further from the ordinary. The occurrences may or may not have been natural. He slid toward the center, slightly down from the boulder's crest, when he saw three men standing directly below him, looking much like the exiles he saw on the way to the palace. Wind and the rock's surface funneled their words to him and Zack heard them as clearly as if he was standing only a few feet away.

The stocky man spoke, "I tell you, I saw one of those damn messengers with a man in plain dress. You saw how their trail disappeared and reappeared farther on. Nothing human could have masked their tracks that way."

Nice complement, Zack thought.

The thinner of the three men answered, "I still believe those bastards carry the armies pay. How else could they get it? Supply trains come every three months and they must get their pay more often than that. I never saw a messenger stop and I never saw one in the company of another man. They're traveling at night and that means they're asleep. I tell you there is gold in those boulders waiting to be gathered and I say we do the gathering."

Zack tossed a pebble on Currat's right arm. He sat up immediately, looking around and then up to see Zack holding up three fingers, and then pointing to the entrance. Currat, pulled his cloak tightly around him and stood behind a stone formation that formed a blind to the entrance. Zack nodded his approval, then seemingly disappeared into the rocks. Currat stood as still as possible.

The men quietly crept into the entranceway, stopping when they didn't see a man or messenger in the circle. Zack watched from the rock's shadows. His cloak concealed him well. The thief who had done all the talking entered last, lagging behind the rest, which didn't surprise him. They frowned at the seemingly empty compound and the absence of bodies stretched out on the ground. Nervousness crackled through them, giving way to spooked expressions and hasty looks around. Zack and Currat maintained clear sight of one another. Zack repeatedly mimed instructions to Currat until he nodded his understanding.

Zack tossed a pebble in a high arc that came down behind the last man. He gasped and the three of them looked around and at the top of the boulder. Currat stepped out into plain view; the messenger's hood and cloak pulled tightly around him, and pitched an anguished moan at the three men's backs. They all jumped. The color drained from their face when they turned to see Currat standing quietly near the circle's center. The talkative one spun around and ran without looking back. Unfortunately, the two remaining men pulled their swords and slowly began circling the still figure in front of them.

Currat played it his way now, sure that Zack knew how to respond. Their goal to scare the thieves off would have been better than the less appealing choice of killing them that would eventually raise an alarm in the countryside. He let the cloak fall loosely around him and slowly raised his arm to point to the circle's entrance. He knew the messengers greatly frightened them.

But fate, not always kind, sent the first man slowly spiraling in toward Currat while his cohort started the opposite way. Currat suddenly pointed to the nearest man and a second later, a knife entered his neck and protruded from the opposite side. As he fell, the second man straightened and stared in bewilderment, closely followed by fear. He started to step away and stopped abruptly, staring down at the knife in his chest; his death came before he hit the ground with the look of surprise still on his face. Currat scampered up the boulders and peered over the edge.

Zack cursed silently until he noticed the crouching figure directly below him, on his knees with his head in his hands, and slightly shacking. Currat saw the silvery reflection of Zack's knife spin through the air and split the first cervical vertebrae and the cord it normally protected.

Zack checked the surrounding countryside before easing down the boulders and joined Currat standing over the bodies he had laid side by side under the overhang. The horses, aroused again and clearly unhappy, pranced nervously at the extent of their tethers.

They dragged the bodies outside the enclosure, and let them roll into a hollow a few yards away from the entrance. Currat fetched the third body while Zack cleaned his retrieved knives. Currat rolled the third man over his dead companions and brought back the third knife before retracing his route. Currat scouted the forest for a moment before returning to Zack. His knives cleaned and replaced inside his cloak made Currat frown. "How many of those knives do you have?"

Zack chuckled. "Oh, a dozen or so." Actually, he carried ten knives, two garrotes and a sword, not counting the poison. "We need to keep moving. It won't take long for the scavengers to come for dinner."

They led the horses past the blood and bodies and a few yards farther on. Zack did his disappearing trick with the physical evidence made by Currat, himself, and the horses, both in the enclosure and for a hundred yards or so beyond, up into the foothills. Their attacker's signs he left in place. Those who came looking would have a rather spooky dilemma to solve; perhaps scaring them to the point that they wouldn't disclose what they had found to the army. There would be no signs of anyone but the dead and those who found them. With any luck, they would ascertain that the army might not believe the butchering had been done by someone who left no tracks, and that would give the army enough of an excuse to start torturing people at random, best to simply not reveal what they had found to anyone.

* * *

ZACK scouted ahead, and found a dell that showed no human signs. He lay curled up with his head on his saddle and watched as Currat caught up to him. He tied the horses next to Zack's and found a place to keep watch while Zack relaxed.

"Zack . . . it seems strange calling you that name, but I think it fits you better than Delan." Currat matched Zack's smile and continued. "I've never . . . killed anyone. I don't know how it will affect me." The smiles disappeared.

"I don't think it affects any two men in exactly the same way," Zack said. "It rocked me the first time. I gradually understood that the men I kill are evil. It doesn't make the act enjoyable, but bearable.

Currat merely nodded.

* * *

DARKNESS and the change in the air woke Zack. He saw Currat cooking over a well-banked, small fire. The dry wood he used produced little smoke, and he had rigged a wet blanket to tent the fire. The bit of smoke that escaped would go unnoticed, and one needed to be standing close to the fire to see it. Zack smiled; known in his circles as having the stealth of a cat, he recognized Currat's skill and covertness that had not awakened him. The stew Currat served a few minutes later held the taste for a starving man. Anything would taste like ambrosia from the gods that he didn't believe in, and that brought a question forth. "Currat, does Ozlid have a religion?"

Surprise passed across his face for a moment, "Secretly, yes, we do. The population forgot that and the royal family dying in one night. Those of us that escaped

Wathdure's influence still believe, with few exceptions, in a Creator. We sometimes question how a creator could allow the destruction caused by a being like Wathdure. Still, the faith that's there is a benevolent power larger than we are, and thrives in hidden places throughout Ozlid. How is it in the Seven Realms?"

Zack put his empty bowl aside. "In the war I told you about, we fought against an evil that we call the Dark's Source. We call the benevolent power the Light's Source. I have never conceptualized that they might be combined, and there is a strangeness there I wouldn't care to discuss with one of our priests. They get a little testy at times." His chuckle brought a smile to Currat's face while he refilled Zack's bowl with stew.

* * *

THEY headed south, following the upper foothills until dawn, and did not encounter signs of anything remotely resembling another human. The rocky areas they came upon remained free of scree and shale. The horses traveled in the dark at their own pace and seemed to be in as much of a hurry as their masters. At approximately half the speed they had made when traveling in the opposite direction, Zack reasoned out the trip's logistics to the Spires. *We will have time enough,* he thought, *especially if Wathdure has been sitting in Ozlid for three hundred and four years, he might not think to look elsewhere. But then, the way things happen in the world, and considering who is chasing us, a faster pace might be called for.* That meant traveling in the daylight, and would require a sharp eye and attention to every sound, not a decision he liked. *Well, I don't like many things,* he thought, clearing his throat. Currat twisted in his saddle with a questioning look. Zack spoke his conclusions and Currat agreed. They planned to stop around midnight and start again at first light.

They spent the following day resting in a secluded dale they found at midmorning. A nearby stream allowed them the privilege of cleaning themselves and their clothes. They lay nude in the grass while the unusually warm sun dried them. Zack made snares and caught several rabbits that afternoon, and another while the sun disappeared behind the mountains. They hurried to cook their lastmeal before nightfall. The breezes from the east conveniently carried the smoke from their small fire away from prying eyes. They finished packing and slept until the last afterglow of daylight disappeared.

19

TWO nights later, Zack woke with all his senses screaming. He stilled his racing pulse and calmed his breathing to the usual, slow rhythm of sleep. Something seriously wrong raised the fine hairs on his neck like tiny snakes slithering around in the undergrowth. Complete blackness covered his left eye, shaded by his cloak's hood. Darkness sharpened into distinguishable shapes as his right eye became accustomed to the dark. Currat crouched a few feet away, preparing a banked pit for the fire.

Moving shadows caused him to blink; there were sounds of others far off in the forest. The giant trees hid all but a few darting flashes of movement, creeping silently closer. *They're good—too good for soldiers on patrol.*

He flicked a pebble that landed next to Currat's hand. The other man hesitated, then rose, stretching, and walked to the saddlepacks lying next to Zack. He kneeled close to Zack's head, close enough to hear his whisper.

"Many men are closing on us." Currat did not look up. "We won't have time to saddle the horses and collect our things before they rush us. I judge it to be an hour or so before dawn. They're not sure of us or they would have taken us already. I have a plan. Act normally and make some stew."

Currat glanced up at the stars shining above in the clear sky and nodded. "I'll cook up the last of the rabbits we snared yesterday and the boar we caught three days ago. All the meat is cleaned and salted. It shouldn't take long to get the stew smelling good."

"Use our spices to make it as fragrant as possible."

A half hour passed before Currat again went to the saddlepacks. "Why are they waiting?"

"Probably trying to determine if we're in the army. I'm sure they don't want a repeat of the last time one of their number killed one."

Shortly afterward, their uninvited guests approached from downwind of their campsite. "Don't eat any stew after I pass my hand over your bowl. You won't live to swallow it," Zack said.

Currat choked a bit at the mental picture he produced.

Zack waited until the stew's smell floated in the right direction, then rose up, stretching. He ambled toward the fire, counted the signs of five men and figured there must be twice that many he didn't see. Their dark clothes–not the army's black uniforms–melted into their surroundings. He saw the glint of two swords. *They may be silent, but at least some of them are not too bright.*

Zack sat cross-legged beside Currat and took the proffered bowl of steaming stew. They ate rapidly and he refilled the bowls. Currat didn't see what Zack dropped in the bowl or the steaming pot. He followed Zack's lead in stirring the bowl with his wooden spoon, and watched while Zack stirred the simmering pot. Several small pods, recently attached to the hem of his cloak, released no signs as they dissolved and permeated the food.

Zack rose and faced downwind. He didn't shout, still, he pitched his voice to carry into the forest. "Will you share our stew?" Zack heard a sword slide home in its scabbard.

More than a minute passed before a man stepped from behind a tree some ten yards away. "You are kind to a lone traveler."

Zack smiled. *We'll play your game,* he thought. "We have plenty, my friend tends to overcook."

Zack watched the man rapidly empty the bowl, and hoped he hadn't misjudged the ingredients he'd added. The man identified himself as Dalward between bites.

171

Zack noticed Currat's brief hint of recognition.

Dalward leaned over, set the bowl on the ground, and came up drawing his sword. Currat found the blade's point at his throat. Dalward whistled loudly, and four other men rushed the campsite with drawn weapons. Thin lips curled into a cruel smile. "Don't be vexed, I'll have had the stew anyhow."

The men took Zack and Currat's swords and belt knives, missing Zack's hidden weapons. "Tie them." His men obeyed without speaking, and Zack noticed no one spoke amongst them and thought it strange until a few men, grouped together, whispered and furtively looked at their leader. *They don't trust him.* Zack thought.

They forced Zack and Currat to sit on the ground with their hands tied in front of them; another mistake, Zack noted. He twisted the device on his belt buckle, a small knife shot into his hand without notice, and he sliced through the ropes on the underside of his wrist. He hid the dangling ends in the folds of his cloak and passed the knife to Currat, who followed his lead.

Dalward and his men focused on the remaining nine men making their way toward their leader. "Ration what's left." he called when his men flanked the fire. Zack watched while the men found their bowls in their backpacks and took a good spoonful of stew. The last man received a half portion and looked disgruntled.

Zack smiled. Much more poison simmered in the pot than in the bowl he'd given to Dalward. *How long will it take and what will be the results?*

He didn't have to wait long. The man with the last half portion started to sit back against a tree and died when his shoulders met the trunk. His face hung limply forward. A companion looked at the dead man and started to cry an alarm. He toppled over before any sound emerged from paralyzed throat muscles. That brought some attention.

Dalward looked at the two dead men while another

nearly fell on top of him. He rose up in a rage; his face flushed in anger. Zack smiled, thinking how much faster Dalward's rage would carry death throughout his system. He charged Zack and Currat's position with his sword held high. Zack rose as the ropes fell from his wrists. He didn't know if it was the poison or his knife slicing through the bandit's throat that killed him. They seemed to have hit at the same time. When he looked around, all of Dalward's men lay motionless.

Currat rose and spoke with a wry smile. "I think I'll continue cooking, Zack. You seem to go a little heavy on the spices."

"Well I got it half-right. I should have put more in the bowl I gave Dalward."

They went through their attacker's packs salvaging what they could. Finding gold and a few small gems surprised Zack. He considered how Dalward had probably amassed his wealth, and his surprise turned to disgust. They backtracked and found horses about three hundred yards west.

One man slept next to a picket line of twenty-one horses with large packs piled next to them. Zack pressed the tip of his sword on the bridge of the sleeping man's nose. Eyes opened wide and then crossed; they slowly slid to a normal position as his gaze followed the glittering steel to the hilt, up Zack's arm and blinked when they met Zack's piercing blue eyes staring at him. Zack motioned him up and retreated backward a step. The man's knife flashed in the morning light when he rose and lunged at Zack. Currat watched and saw nothing but a blur when Zack's sword sliced open the man's throat. "What is this thing you have about throats?" he asked.

Zack shrugged. "It's easier to clean your blade without the muscle and gore from the lower body."

"You knew Dalward's name. Who was he?" Zack asked as they searched through the larger packs.

"We received a few reports of him from the outcast

families," Currat replied. "He attracted murderers and thieves. Supposedly, there are many more of them hiding out here, somewhere." He waved at the forest in general. "He pillaged the families for food and anything of value. He allowed his men to rape the women. They said Dalward preferred the attention of young men, like several of his followers." Currat groaned while moving a heavy pack.

"He would rarely kill his victims, returning later in overwhelming numbers to do it all again. He probably wouldn't have killed us until he found the messenger's uniform, and we couldn't convince him that we killed one and kept the uniform. I think that few, if any, saw what the messenger's hoods hid, certainly not anyone outside the palace. I have never heard of one that went missing. Most people out here didn't warrant a messenger's attention. The few that did disappeared." Currat saw the puzzled look on Zack's face. "Remember; minor offenses, or the imagination of some army officer, or a personal enemy, caused more than a few exiles; I regret to say. Wathdure sent a messenger to kill anyone who might have been proved innocent." They resumed their search in a more solemn mood.

Currat found a chest the size of a small cask of wine in the bottom of the largest pack. The small lock opened easily, and his eyes widened when he opened it. Gold coins shimmered among precious and semiprecious gems. "Evidently, some of those convicted escaped with more than the clothes on their backs," Zack said. Currat nodded and closed the chest. "We may have need of that later. Leave the rest of this stuff to those that find it, and let's be on our way, rapidly." Currat grinned, and his actions agreed wholeheartedly with Zack's last word.

They rode out from their campsite in less than an hour to the horses' immense pleasure. They seemed to object to the dead bodies as much as the men did. "Do you have many buzzards up here?"

"No, they prefer the warmer climes. We have the usual raptors, but not buzzards. I do see where you're coming from, though. We're leaving somewhat of an obvious trail."

"Not necessarily, we have the foothills between us and the main patrol areas. Eighteen men can draw a lot of buzzards."

"I don't think I want to know how you came about such knowledge." Currat's words carried a hint of awe.

Zack pretended not to notice. "They will ignore raptors more so than buzzards, if you had any. I think the route we're following is still the best one."

The rest of that day's travel proved particularly difficult. Natural hazards came every few hundred yards, and they ended up stopping in the late afternoon. They camped in a hollow—more so than a valley—between two hills. Zack climbed the hill to the south and returned smiling as Currat finished the lastmeal preparations. "What made you so happy?"

"From what I can see, we'll have easier riding tomorrow. There is a narrow plain of grasslands running between the hills for as far as I could see."

"You're right. I forgot that we're that far east of the forests. I never saw the plain. Mountains are at the end, and will force us to the west. We should come out about three or four miles north of the fortress." Currat also smiled as he packed away the cooking utensils.

Lastmeal done, Zack took the first watch. He noticed that Currat slept untroubled by the terror he'd experienced the previous nights on their journey south. *Perhaps some pain from losing his father and friends has receded,* Zack thought. He hoped so, for Currat's sake, and he slept well.

20

BARE, hard ground, packed down by runoffs and a mere inch or two of top soil above a rock base, formed a good riding trail between the foothills and the grasslands. Scree occasionally slowed them down, but they easily avoided the worst of it, and made excellent time the next two days. Taller hills squeezed the grasslands to a narrow point, and a rather large mountain stopped their southward progress. Their trek westward, plagued by steep hills, lack of good water, and bandits, made Zack understood why none of Ozlid's army troops posted on the border bothered to come this direction. Their heavy cloaks served them—and part of the horseflesh under them—well against the thornier vines. Several places required them to lead the horses and climb rocky hills that cut into their hands and legs, with the same obstacles on the opposite side going down. Dangers from exhaustion at the day's end, as well as the fortress towers visible over the last hill and sounds of nearby men, made them both edgy. Zack felt happy to be near the end of their journey, no matter the increased danger.

* * *

LYING atop a hill, they looked at the fortress and watched the soldiers' routines as Currat explained their actions. Zack mournfully admitted that the men carried out their duties efficiently and skillfully. He also noticed that the crossbeams now held five bodies. Currat tried not to look at them without much success. His anger rose to the point that Zack gently urged him back down to their camp. They decided to rest the next day. The horses

176

seemed to like the idea, too.

Late afternoon approached, and they set out on the trip's final leg. Their discussions centered on how it might end in freedom, with a chance to fight again, or in death.

Zack felt an additional burden pressing on him. *The Seven Realms will suffer if I don't get this information to the Spires. I must warn the Zenith that we need to prepare for war.* He did not want to think about another great war between the powers of good and evil. Although, there did not seem to be another alternative and indeed, he could think of none.

They started their trip heading northwestward for four miles, through gullies and ravines. Rounding a boulder half the height of a large tree, they faced the last of the heavy forest before the border. The trees thinned until bare land lay for a hundred yards before the fortress and market area. The journey's next part became frustrating and tiring. Zack and Currat hugged dark shadows and prayed to remain hidden. The patrols did exactly as Currat said, reversing direction before getting close to the mountains. They stopped farther and farther away the closer they got to the fortress.

The trail began so gradually they hardly noticed it. Then, within a short distance, the ground to the left of the ledge dropped some twenty yards. Although the trail was barely wide enough for the big stallions, it caused them no problems, as they were used to the trails through the passes. The packhorse viewed the trail quite differently, however, and stubbornly refused the ledge. They backed the animals to the trail's beginning and placed Currat's mare at the end.

Zack insisted on leading. He felt they had a better chance against any opposition if he faced and fought Currat's former men, although he did not voice that opinion. Well along the trail, clouds obscured the little light that shined down from above. Zack could feel the horse's nervousness transmitted through his reins, reflecting his own uneasiness. He felt the chasm's right wall and kept as close to it as possible. The ledge's width became his main concern and worry.

Gradually, they began to hear noises from the fortress. Zack started when the hour's call sounded from the fortress wall directly above, and the lead horse shied away from the wall. His front left hoof landed on the trail's edge, causing scree to fall far below them. Zack noticed it took a long time to hit the chasm floor. Taking a deep breath, he urged the big stallion forward with soft, encouraging words.

They continued at a steady pace, and within a half-hour, the fort's sounds, screened by rock walls, disappeared. They reached the trail's end as the moonlight slipped through the clouds. He could make out the trail's characteristics better, and the pounding in his chest began to subside.

"What have we here, two rats coming up from the garbage heap?"

Zack stopped dead in his tracks, his horse nudging him in the back. He saw a large, dark form standing about ten yards in front of him, and he knew that voice. Zack smiled. The other man had given his position away too soon. He heard a *thud* from behind and below him. He jumped off the trail, and nearly landed on Currat about ten feet below.

He barely heard Currat's whisper. "It's the sergeant you met the first day. He tries to finesse to the left with his sword, but only leaves himself open."

Zack drew his sword with his right hand and a long knife in his left hand. He also heard Currat's sword clearing its scabbard. They knelt down, and Zack kept Currat from moving forward. The horses continued down the trail toward human sounds.

"Sergeant, it's only a few horses."

"Shut up, you fool. They're probably behind them, and now they know there's more than one of us here."

Currat whispered in Zack's ear. "The sergeant is a

178

bully and enjoys torturing. He does, or oversees, most of the torture at the fortress. He's not a good fighter, and probably brought several men with him."

The issuing of orders kept the sergeant too busy to hear Currat or Zack or anything else. Zack and Currat stayed low and close to the wall, taking advantage of the darkness. Their eyes, still acclimated to the night, picked out the best path. Zack whispered, "I see eight. I'm going to change the odds a bit. Let me have the sergeant when the time comes."

Zack reached inside his cloak to the wormcloth-lined pocket holding his riding crop. He removed the ends and let them hang free on their strings. Inserting a dart, he selected the first dark outline he found. The man went down without making a sound. The next man Zack shot cried out, but the sound suddenly stopped.

The sergeant's panic at seeing two of his men suddenly drop dead unnerved him. He usually gave out torture, pain and death and was not used to being on the receiving end of those things. His men huddled together, and Zack shot another dart into the middle of them. The sergeant and his men crouched down, denying Zack a clear shot. He capped the riding crop and returned it to its pocket. Zack and Currat started forward, keeping pace with the mare a few feet above them.

Zack's head paused a foot below the trail when he saw the sergeant's large, dark form sidestep to the left directly in front of him about six feet away. Zack let out a loud shriek and charged the dark form with his sword in one hand and knife in the other. The sergeant's unpleasant shock changed to fear, and he swung his sword wildly. Zack parried the blade and drove his knife into the bellowing sergeant's gut. He twisted his own blade in the wound, allowing the sergeant's entrails to spill out onto the ground. Zack pulled his knife free while the sergeant fell to his knees and made a soft gurgling sound and then fell over and stilled.

Currat charged two men. Zack jumped up on the trail and went for the two dark shadows crouching in front of him. He caught one and stabbed his knife between the man's ribs after sidestepping his lunge. He looked over his shoulder and saw that Currat had dispatched one man and was fighting another. He sprinted to the last man and slipped on some gravel. He hit the ground hard and rolled away when a dark shape came at him. The man hit and rolled off the trail after Zack.

The sword in his attacker's hand pointed at Zack's chest. Zack's own sword lashed out and caught the man's arm. He yelled and dove for Zack's knees. Zack fell backwards and felt the air forced from his lungs. The soldier fell forward onto him; his sword hand hit the ground and shoved the point into Zack's side.

Zack's wound felt like molten steel had been poured into him, and his left hip hurt almost as bad. He tried to jerk his feet free. His opponent rose up with knife in hand to fall onto Zack again. A sluicing sound that Zack knew well froze the man for a second; then, when Zack thrust with his legs, his opponent fell backwards, pushing Zack's long knife the rest of the way through his chest.

He felt the strange sensation of rising without effort as Currat and—Durton?—eased him onto his back before darkness overcame him.

* * *

ZACK didn't know which hurt worse, his head or his side or his hip. He opened his eyes to the faint predawn light. His eyes began to focus on Currat and Durton's faces looking down at him with concern. Zack saw some of Durton's sternness soften. He could only think of one thing to say. "I gave your message to Wathdure. He didn't like it." Durton smiled.

They tore his shirtsleeve off and used it to bandage his side. Zack whispered instructions in Currat's ear and heard the heel of his right boot snap open. He selected a pack of herbs. Currat held pressure on the wound while Durton moistened a cloth and formed a poultice with the herbs. Zack couldn't help moaning when they applied pressure to the wound as they tied the poultice in place.

Durton said, "It's a bad wound, but the bleeding has stopped for now. It will probably start again when you stand. Currat said you have a place to go and will be looked after. I don't want to know where this place is or even what direction it is in, but if it's too far away, you may not make it there alive."

Zack started at the dry, scratchy feeling in his throat when he tried to speak. "I'll make it. I have little choice." He tried to smile. "Currat, remember your promise. You must get that information to the Zenith. I'll send a message, too. One of us has to get through to the Spires. Tell Durton about the messengers." The sudden burst of words exhausted him and he slumped inward.

"I already know. That's why I helped you. Wathdure has held my family hostage because I discovered one without a hood, or anything else for that matter. I simply took a wrong direction and found myself in their quarters. There is something you may not know from what Currat told me; their genitalia are missing, and that area is formed over like their noses."

Zack and Currat winced.

"I nearly escaped without being discovered," Durton continued. "Wathdure still does not know for sure that I saw anything. My father is an administrator, like Currat's father. Mother and Father's orders to reside at the palace made the point quite clear to me. He will kill them if I step out of line."

"Like my father used to be. He died during our escape from the palace," Currat said.

Durton's face showed his sadness. He took hold of Currat's shoulder for a moment. "There are clothes, food, and vouchers in the saddlepacks. Transfer them over, and I'll be gone. I suggest you do the same. I don't know how much bragging our good sergeant did about his plans. Zack, you removed a foul man from Ozlid when you killed him, and have performed a good service in that act alone, even if nothing else comes of your efforts. May the Creator look over you both." Durton mounted his horse, threw the saddlepacks to Currat, and rode off.

Durton's prophecy fell false on one point: Zack's wound did not start bleeding when he stood, but it did when he mounted the mare. He knew her gentler ride might save his life. Currat changed into typical Hamptor-styled clothes and packed the rest of his things in the saddlepacks. He kept his knives and a sword that Durton had brought strapped to his side. He checked Zack every minute or two during the whole exchange.

Currat unsaddled the remaining stallion and slapped it on its hindquarters. The stallion ran at a gallop into Hamptor, not looking back once at his homeland. Currat said, "Smart horse." He mounted and led Zack's mare off at an easy pace.

Zack called to him. Currat let the mare come even with him. Zack said, "You must go on to Hagan's End, like we planned. I'll follow as soon as I can. I'll only slow you down now. Durton is correct. We don't know if the sergeant told anyone he came out here."

Currat started to protest, but then said, "I know there's nothing I can say that'll change your mind. "I'll wait at Hagan's End for a month. The sea captain you told me about will know where I'm staying. I checked the saddlepacks, there are enough vouchers in there for me to stay a year and buy the ship. Get to Hagan's End, and I'll get both of us to your Spires. I'll put some gold and jewels in your pack." He reached over and checked Zack's wound. It had stopped bleeding.

Zack's voice sounded more confident than he felt. "No need. I have the gold your father sent with me, and if I don't make it to the farm it won't matter. Fare well, and always use the note I gave you." Zack pulled his horse away from Currat and started out at an easy pace.

He traveled over an hour, and felt surprise that half the fortress had not overtaken him. His head became dizzy and his sight blurred as the mare kept walking forward. He soon felt nothing.

21

IN one of his decreasing lucid moments, Zack found a copse and made camp for the night. The next morning, he pulled the mare to him by her long tether and stroked her neck. "I'm sorry you had to sleep saddled, old girl. I just couldn't manage that." His perceptions felt sharper, but his wound throbbed with each heartbeat.

Leaning forward to grab his boot sent fresh pain soaring through him. The boot's heel gave him a little trouble, but snapped open when he had almost decided to give up. He pulled the tightly wrapped packets of herbs out for inspection: Some he swallowed, some he made into a fresh poultice and changed his bandage, and some he returned to their hiding place. Searing pain jolted him when he pulled the old bandage free and placed the new one against the wound. He twisted his leg sharply, and the heel closed with a resounding *snap*.

Gritting his teeth, he mounted the mare, trying not to pass out from the pain. Zack felt the warmth of new blood oozing down his left side, but it ceased after a few minutes, when the herbs started to do their work. He had torn the rest of his left sleeve off to form a new bandage for future use; he was glad he didn't need it that soon.

His vision blurred again and he let his horse make her own way. He vaguely became aware of moving faster when his head fell forward against her mane.

* * *

HE came to consciousness in the middle of a circle of men. "I think he's awake," someone said.

Nice words to hear. At least, I'm still alive enough to wake.

184

The man who spoke knelt beside him. "Who did this to you?"

It was harder to speak than Zack imagined. ". . . Ozlid," he finally managed the word after two tries of raspy slurring. He saw the man's face fill with hatred.

"Who are you?"

"Delan . . . Delan Stand," those words came a little easier. *Perhaps those awful tasting herbs actually did something,* he concluded.

"What? What did he say?" a different voice asked.

"Delan Stand," the hard-faced man said.

"Why, that's the man I told you about, the one that saved the woman and her daughter. He's the one that killed those murderers that plagued us for so long." Zack drifted into comforting darkness where pain fled as the new voice started telling the story of Doris and Rachel's rescue.

He rose back to consciousness three times during the journey. The last time he actually realized that he was resting on soft blankets in the bed of a wagon, and it didn't hurt if he lay very still. Voices droned on several feet away and the wagon didn't move. Unrecognizable sounds continued until the wagon lurched forward with a start that hurt, and he welcomed the darkness closing back in around him.

The next time he woke, he felt the rare comfort of a soft bed. He began to perceive light from dark, and nearby sounds became clear. His surroundings seemed familiar, but his memory failed him. He heard a voice he remembered.

"Master Stand? Mama, Mama, his eyes are open! Oh Master Stand, can you see me? Can you see me? Mama, come quick; he's awake!"

His eyes began to focus clearly, and memory of the room returned. He felt Rachel's warm hand pat him gently on the cheek. The child's diffidence had evaporated, and Zack smiled at her excitement.

Doris and a stranger came into the room. He had a large frame and a ruddy complexion, and though his face remained somber, his nearly black eyes held mirth and intelligence. His beard, neatly trimmed, was dark brown with streaks of white, and struck Zack as incongruous. He wore his hair in a long braid without the white found in his beard. His worn clothes had a crisp, clean smell. The man raised Zack's head with calloused hands that smelled of loam and held a cup to his lips. The warm broth tasted of bitter herbs; the liquid soothed his throat.

"Master Stand, this is Roland," Doris said. "He's the healer in our region. A trading party brought you here three days ago, and you have been unconscious except for a brief moment yesterday. A trader knew our village, and recognized your name. Can you understand what I'm saying?"

Zack tried to sit up, but felt his weight fall onto Roland's arm. The man pulled him gently forward, and Doris placed pillows behind his shoulders and head. He became aware of a dull pain on his left side. His bare chest felt warm, and his hand lightly touched a fresh bandage over his wound. Zack lay nude under crisp bedclothes; he felt clean and the light smell of soap lingered on him. *Well, Ozlid has a casual modesty. Perhaps Hamptor does, too.*

Roland said, "You ladies leave us alone for a while." Rachel giggled and smiled at Zack as the door closed. He took a mug and gave Zack several sips of water. The first drinks of which took effort to swallow.

Roland pulled a chair close to Zack's bed and sat where Zack could see him without moving his head. "Do you understand my words?"

Zack nodded slightly. "You are a strong man and I believe you will heal," Roland said. "Your strength and character carried you through. Death often claims lesser men. I judged you had ridden for a long time from the condition of your wound, but frankly, I have no idea how

186

you survived mounting the horse, or how you even got as far as you did. The wound is clean, and I don't see any sign of infection, which is a wonder. It will be several weeks, maybe months, before you will be well enough to leave on your own. Your hip is not broken or fractured, but I believe the bone has a deep bruise. When you're able to stand, use a cane for extra support." Roland's countenance held a quiet confidence that Zack recognized.

"Doris told us the things you did for Rachel and her. We will do whatever we can to help you get home when you're well enough to travel. Until then, you must rest and take the potions I'll leave for you. I'll be here to see you daily for the next week or two." Roland's voice became stern in the way healers do. "You are not to get up for any reason until we agree you may try to rise. Your wound is deep, but you would already be dead if death threatened." Roland ended with a sly smile on his face.

Zack tried to speak. His throat hurt, and the croaking sounds he uttered made no sense. He made the sign of writing on the palm of his hand. Roland left the room and returned with a board and a piece of charcoal. He placed them where Zack could manage them without disturbing his wound.

Zack understood and spoke the language of Hamptor and knew their written language, but had not the energy to write. He took the board, charcoal and wrote the word "message" followed by an arrow pointing to wavy lines. He handed the board back to Roland with concern and some pain showing on his face.

Roland took the board and studied it for a moment. "How important is it?"

Zack took the board and scratched one line through his writing; he pointed to the board, then to himself, and then at Roland. His weak voice slightly garbled the single word, however, Roland's reaction showed he had no problem understanding, "Death." Roland took the board and charcoal and left the room. Several minutes passed before he returned.

"The supplies you need will be brought here this afternoon. There is a sailor in the village that speaks and writes your home dialect. He will come and write down what you say."

Zack shook his head. He pointed to himself and made the sign of writing on his palm.

"As you wish, but you must not let yourself become too tired. I have given Doris instructions on what she must do to help you. Do like we say and you will heal rapidly. Otherwise, you may still die."

Zack was asleep before Roland left the room.

PART TWO

22

CURRAT worried: *I should never have let him go off by himself. What were we thinking? His wound is bad; I let him ride off as if he suffered only a scratch.*

He followed the map Zack had made several nights ago with notes to the innkeepers along the way. The small writing case from Zack's saddlepacks delighted him; his small and pleasing hand was easy to read. The other man's memory had astounded him until he saw the larger map from which he worked. Zack had explained that the map's newest section did not match the older part's scale. Marks between the inn's names denoted how fast he should travel between destinations to arrive in time for the best rooms. The map's reverse contained notes of what occurred during his visit at each inn and the innkeeper's name, his family, and anything else of value. The role they decided Currat should play made him uncomfortable, but it did make sense. He was to play a mute.

The notes Zack supplied explained that he could hear and make some sounds. They asked each innkeeper to provide a private room for him, and have his meals served there as well. It proved the best scheme they could think of at the time, and Currat had not conceived of anything better since he saw Zack ride off alone.

Damn, he thought, *why in all the hells was I so monumentally stupid to leave him alone?* He had grown closer to Zack in the short time they traveled together than anyone he could remember. He had saved Currat's life on three occasions, comforted him on the lost of his family and friends, and helped him get those things in a perspective that allowed him to accept the sacrifices they had made. Zack became a constant wonder to him; his many skills and quick thinking outmatched anyone he knew, and, he liked him. *No*, he though, *I love him as a brother.*

Currat could not help feeling at risk. His accent meant his death if he forgot and spoke more than a word or two. He realized even that might be too much. Perhaps he should endeavor not to say anything at all. That idea sounded better, but harder to implement the more he considered it. The Hamptorians he met would never believe his tale of a ruler with preternatural powers and necromantic messengers. He conjectured that the whole business bordered on insanity, at times.

Nevertheless, it's Wathdure's insanity, and I don't want to cross his path if I can help it. How could I expect a Hamptorian to respond differently, especially with their rightfully gained prejudices? They might think me mad as a loon, but a dead loon is still dead. No, my silence on this trip means my life, and is worth more than all the gold and jewels Zack demanded I keep. Does he have more of his own funds, as he said? I suppose, the gold father sent him will suffice. And Dalward's treasure horde allows for bribes if the need arises. Currat fought to put his thoughts and memories on the living and his current dilemma with partial success.

He found the first inn, and hesitantly presented the innkeeper with the correct note. The innkeeper called his wife to read it. "Oh, the poor man," she said and then read the part he could hear and blushed at her remark.

They settled him in one of two private rooms and brought him his lastmeal piping hot. The innkeeper yelled, "Put the tray outside the door when you are finished!" Currat jerked and questioned why he yelled. *The note states I'm mute, not deaf. If everyone treats me like that, I will not notice when someone yells by the time I reach Hagan's End.*

Currat had never visited an inn before. Their scarcity in Ozlid, coupled with no real need, left him curious. His father had put him in the army's training program when his age first allowed it. His private tutors had taught swordsmanship and formal education. His father provided expert advice on many subjects, but not inns. The room's size matched one of his closets in the palace. Still, its cleanliness and the comfortable bed counted for much, and he rated it higher than his army quarters. The private rooms situated away from the common room's noise suited him well. The door had a key, but the heavy bar on the inside provided additional security. He inspected the window, and saw no way one could enter without making quite a disturbance.

A large washstand stood in the corner, with a bucket of clean water on the floor, and a pitcher of water and mug on the top. He bathed, and used the curious little twig Zack gave him for cleaning his teeth. He found they worked better than the foul-tasting mixture used back in Ozlid, and he liked the mint taste. He pulled the small mirror that Zack had told him cost a fortune in Hamptor or Arestead, and inspected the results. His full mouth of teeth sparkled white. The reflected image of his teeth and lips reminded him again of how much Zack and he physically resembled one another. He realized they also expressed many of the same ethics and principles.

He slid between coarse bedclothes still feeling guilty at leaving his friend—perhaps the best friend he might ever have—hurt and alone. Mental and physical exhaustion finally plunged him into a troubled sleep.

The following days repeated the routine of that first day. He became accustomed to the reactions of innkeepers as he traveled south, and improved his disguise of a mute. His worrisome nights, however, did not improve.

23

MANY miles away from where Currat tossed in his sleep, Gusbarb, recruited by Wathdure years before, set up in his bed with a jerk as an inky-black substance formed in his room.

Not sure if it a man or demon, he really did not care; he, or it, paid him well for his information on the commerce he observed, the status of Hamptor's small army, and the rumors that spread throughout the land. He tried to hold his fear and failed, again. He wanted to resist the mental messages that so completely filled his consciousness. They scared him more than the dark manifestation did.

"I seek two men." The images of Zack and Currat flashed before him, seared into his memory. *"Look well for them."* Five silver pieces appeared with an audible *pop* and fell on his bed. *"You will receive five weight of gold if you find one or both of them alive. You will receive nothing if they're dead. A man will come within a few days for your report. He will call you by name, and introduce himself as a visitor from the dark."*

The form faded to nothingness while Gusbarb squirmed in his filthy bedclothes. On the first visitation, he had concluded it a nightmare until the pieces of silver he found proved to be real. He had soiled his bedclothes then, too. He cursed, pulling the filthy linens from his bed, taking a moment to rescue the silver, and then wiped his buttocks with the bedclothes. He wadded the foul mess up and placed it outside his hut. *Tomorrow, I might use a silver coin to buy the best bedclothes I can find.* It still took him a long time to go back to sleep. The images of Zack and

Currat kept reappearing with frightening clarity. He finally fell into a troubled doze.

The next morning he bathed—not something he did often—put on clean clothes, something even more rare, and left his hut smiling. One gold weight equaled a thousand pieces of silver, and he could not imagine five times that amount. It represented a sum big enough to buy a large inn or some other sort of business. It did not occur to him that he would squander it away as he had his father's leavings, and the funds from the sale of his property. His remembered that lesson well, but his character had not.

He made his way to the village inn at first light, causing the innkeeper to look twice at him with surprise. Gusbarb rarely appeared in bright daylight sober. He described the two men's likeness whose images formed with crystal clarity. "They're friends I'm expecting."

"Gusbarb, you don't have any friends. But, to answer your question, no, I have not seen anyone like you described." The innkeeper stepped away to finish preparing for his guest's firstmeal.

Gusbarb ambled to the main road and climbed the large oak on the village outskirts. A small, wiry man with tight, curly brown hair and the face of a rodent, he seemed to be a new species inhabiting the tree, but for his size. The tree's original furry residents disliked his presence and chattered at him. Gusbarb took great pleasure at tossing acorns at them. He missed repeatedly, and finally gave up.

Despised and nearly run out of the village on two occasions, he garnered the opposite of his father's high regard. Some believed he killed the old man. He had, although his rationalizations precluded the idea. He had ignored his father's needs while he lay ill, and he soon died. Gusbarb's unpleasant character caused further dislike from the villagers. *Will someone try to chase me away from my vantage point?* He crawled to the higher branches, shaking out of fear of falling. Gold coins danced in his head, and he grabbed the tree, scratching his hands and forearms on the rough bark.

24

WHEN Zack awoke, a tray, holding writing instruments, an inkwell, and several sheets of parchment, along with a small bell, rested on the small table beside his bed. It took more effort than he imagined ringing it.

Doris entered almost at once with a mug of steaming liquid. "You are to drink all of this before you start to write. Roland said it would give you strength. I'll get Pavel from the village if you find it too difficult." She tried to voice her words with the same firmness the healer used, but the deep concern in her tone belied her sternness.

She set on the bed's edge as he drank the liquid. "I think I can actually talk now." The first part of his sentence squeaked out, but the last part sounded more like his normal speech. They both grinned. Doris set a pillow on his lap and set the writing tray on top. She watched while he began to write and then left, quietly closing the door.

She's as nice and smells as clean as I remember. How does she run this farm and manage to keep Rachel and her so well, too? She and Rachel's clean clothing, rarely seen at the end of a day on a farm, amazed him; whenever he saw her, the white apron she wore somehow remained spotless. Zack shook his head in admiration and bent to his task.

"Master Michael Gaz, the Spires..." memories flooded to recognition. He remembered leaving this same room to go north to Ozlid weeks ago. He had lost all track of time; *it must have been at least three weeks ago, probably longer, when the trek inside Ozlid started and four days before that when I met Doris and Rachel.*

Sleep tugged at him after he wrote the first few

sentences. Carefully putting the stopper into the inkbottle, he let the writing board slide to his side. He slept for a while and woke again, feeling better. The herbs Roland used equaled those in the Seven Realms in potency.

He repositioned the tray on his lap and started again. Writing and then sleeping became a routine, and he accomplished more than he had thought possible on the first day. The following days brought rapid improvement in his health, and a strong desire to be on his way as soon as possible.

One afternoon, Zack looked up from his work when Doris entered the room. "Are you still writing?"

"I have just finished for today." She looked with admiration at the neat, small words flowing across the pages. "It is not only that, but I feel much stronger. I think I'll try to get up when Roland next visits. You and Rachel have been most kind to me. I might have died without your help." He had expressed his gratitude at least three times in their recent conversations.

"If you remember, you saved Rachel and me from a death much worse than that you might have suffered."

You have no idea how wrong you are, and I do not intend to tell you, Zack thought.

Her face became grave and she handed Zack a slip of parchment with a brief message on it. He had expected it to come at any time. An Ozlidian raiding party of a hundred men was searching the countryside for him.

Zack folded the many sheets of parchment that comprised his report to Gaz into a packet and slipped it into a leather pouch. "Doris, remember the pack I gave you to keep for me?" She nodded. "Please get it for me now."

"It will take a few minutes; I buried it."

She went out the door before she could see the approving smile on his face. A few minutes later, she returned with his leather pouch, still wrapped in its oilskin. She put a cloth over his pillow to catch the remaining pieces of dirt and started to leave again.

"No, stay."

She stopped and sat on the chair by the door. Zack untied the oilskin's bindings and looked at the knot holding the pouch's large flap. He could see the short hair he had placed in the knot's middle when he last tied it closed; it had not been disturbed. The ease with which his fingers undid the knot surprised him. *Perhaps Roland's herbs and potions did more than I believed.* Pulling the smaller pouch from the larger, he motioned Doris closer. She sat on the bedside at his knees. Zack reached into the small pouch, counted out three coins and transferred them to the palm of his hand. He pulled his fist from the pouch and held it toward Doris.

She put her hand out without hesitation, but with a look of curiosity. Zack set the three heavy, gold coins into her palm. Her eyes widened. "Great Creator . . ." she gasped. The coins represented more money than she could make in ten lifetimes, and probably Rachel's, too. For a moment, Zack feared she might faint. She tried to form words, but nothing came out except a tiny squeak.

"Doris, that gold is yours and Rachel's, for I'm going to ask a lot from you in the coming days. You are to leave this place and go to Hagan's End, and I prefer, on to my own lands. There you will be able to live in safety." He continued slowly. "I have put you in danger. There is going to be much trouble here, and you will not be safe. They will kill you and Rachel if they find me here or learn that you cared for me. The three of us must get away as soon as possible. It has been seven days since I arrived. I expect they will be here tomorrow or the next day at the latest." Zack's difficulty expressing his feelings irked him. "Doris, I—I have wronged you. You must leave your home and friends because of me. I . . . I'm sorry."

Doris put her hand on his. "Zack, you have given us our lives, and more gold than I ever dreamed of owning.

I'll miss some things and some people here, that's true. I might want to stay if my husband still lived, but probably not with an opportunity like this for us. He would have treated you the same as I did. Now, the farm has painful memories, and I don't have the time to give Rachel the teaching she needs." Her beaming smile played across her lips. "We will be fine."

Zack's uneasiness at what he was going to require of her nagged at him. "I want you to go into the village and hire a carriage or large coach as soon as you can. I should have already sent you if I had any brains. I trust someone in the village has a carriage, or better yet, a coach?"

"No one in the village has either, but Master Donce has a coach and horses. His home is about an hour's ride away. He makes a big show of using it to go to the village meetings and into the southern cities. He won't likely let us use it." Her face still looked surprised.

Zack removed another gold coin from the pouch. "Not even for this?" He held the coin out. Doris' smile told the answer. "Ride there as quick as you can to buy the coach and horses. Tell his driver that he can have the coach and horses after he delivers us to Hagan's End—if you think he can be trusted, that is. If not, offer him gold. Get a driver and that coach here as soon as possible, whatever it takes. Send Rachel into the village to a place of safety until we can collect her. Go now and hurry."

"But, but . . . your wound."

"I'd rather die trying to escape than be caught by Ozlid's men. Death would most likely be quite tiresome at their hands. In fact, it might be days upon days of torture. Now go, as fast as you can." Within minutes, Zack saw Doris outside through the room's small window. She sat on the mare, with Rachel holding on tightly behind her. She rode toward the village as if the Dark's Source chased after her. *Perhaps it is.*

Zack's eyes snapped open at the sound of the door opening. His breath eased out slowly while his hand grasped the long knife under the bedclothes. The door to his room opened slowly, and Roland's head peeked cautiously around it. He held the door wide and motioned with his hand. Ten men crowded in behind him. Zack slowly eased his hand with the knife toward the bedclothes' edge.

"We have come to watch over you until Doris can return. No one from Ozlid has ever come this far in decades. We're armed, and we'll protect you." Roland's words garnered nods from his companions.

Zack let out a long breath. "You have my thanks. They will be in force if, or I should say, when they come. I'm sure they will be here soon. I appreciate your courage but you won't have a chance, they'll slaughter you in minutes. It's best if you leave now, and tell no one you ever saw me. Whatever you do, do not let them find out someone from your village harbored me."

A large young man pushed his way to the front. "I'm Ursel. You don't understand. Ancestors of every man in this room died at the hands of Ozlid soldiers. The debt of their lives passes from generation to generation. Now, it's our duty to kill them as best we can, and we do it for us. We all know how you saved Doris and Rachel's lives. I do know that we'll fight them, and if we kill only one on our soil, it will ease the debt by that much blood. I suspect we'll kill many more than one."

General agreement from all the men swept the room. Ursel's face remained hard-set, his eyes showing little emotion. Zack questioned what pain he had suffered to set his countenance to such a stern manner. His voice held firm, but Zack sensed a lack of confidence in the towering young man.

Zack started to speak. Roland's voice took on an edge of command that surprised him. "Save your strength."

The healer stepped forward, a sack in his hand. "Here are all the medicines you will need for a month. I didn't have time to pack the doses individually. Doris will have to use the packs she has as a guide. It should not be too difficult for her. Many stops on the way will provide supplies for brewing. They can be drunk cold or hot once they have been brewed." He smiled, "Some actually taste better hot, if you can believe they could taste better at all." He set the sack on the side table

Zack nodded. "Thank you, for everything. I need to speak with Ursel a moment, and then I'll rest." Roland slowly nodded, and the men filed out. Ursel stood over Zack with a stern look of determination.

"You must get my words to your king." Ursel's eyes grew wide and surprise marked his features. He knelt on one knee, bringing his face closer. Zack continued in a slow, calm voice. "The general population of Ozlid is twice that of Hamptor and Arestead combined. They know nothing of what Ozlid's ruler did to your country a hundred years ago. An evil rules them that is unknown here, but well known in my lands. We defeated it two millennia ago. We must crush that evil. The people you know living in the hills that lead to their mountain passes are outcasts, sent there for supposed crimes they committed. They send their families with them.

"One of Ozlid's highest-ranking administrators helped me escape, and lost his life for it. His son is an officer in the army. He and other officers saved my life. Many risked their lives for me and they are still at risk, several died." At that, Ursel growled deep in his throat.

"I'm entrusting this information to you to deliver to your king. I learned there are a few that know the truth in Ozlid. They keep the ones that know the real inner-workings of the country under strict control. The people believe the trading done with Hamptor and Arestead is an equitable agreement. They have never seen the border; they have heard lies for hundreds of years. Your hatred is understandable for what Ozlid did to your ancestors. But, the vast majority of Ozlidians know nothing of it, including much of the army, from what I saw."

Zack could not read the mixture of emotions he saw crossing Ursel's face. His head spun and he closed his eyes.

* * *

HE opened his eyes and felt movement. Six men held the mattress and carried it through the house to the waiting coach. The open coach door would not accommodate it. The floor space, stacked with Doris' things to the height of the seat, made a flat, level surface with Rachel's narrow mattress on top, taking up half the compartment's width. They held Zack even with the mattress inside the coach, and two men from inside the coach slid him across to what would be his home for the next several days.

Even with the women's belongings inside, the coach still provided ample space for its three passengers. Zack's weapons lay wedged between the seat and the coach's side within easy reach. He placed the one in his hand into its empty scabbard alongside the rest. Doris placed his cloak over him for warmth, not realizing the deadly arsenal it held. She handed him his pouch as soon as he was settled.

Zack checked the contents after she walked away. Everything remained as he left it. He did not know who might have looked through it while he slept or been unconscious. Conclusions flashed through his mind: *These are good people. They not only trust me, they're willing to act for my well being as well as theirs.* Something stirred within him, and a knot of something loosened. It had been five years since he felt trust in anyone except Gaz and now Currat, but now he was also feeling it in these people as well.

He looked around the coach and saw every possible inch of space to store, place, or hang their belongings efficiently used. Rachel's and Doris' moist and red eyes again made regret well up inside him. Zack decided that anything he might say could easily be mistaken. He reached across and took Doris' hand. He felt she understood when their eyes met. She smiled bravely, squeezed his hand, and then she helped Rachel to settle in across from her.

Ursel and the driver came to the open door on Zack's side. Ursel said, "This is Darmon, our driver. I'll ride with him, and go on from Hagan's End to deliver your message. The men are going to stay behind and burn the house to the ground." Zack started to protest. The look from Doris and another squeeze of his hand stopped his words. "They will cover any tracks from the coach until they blend in at the village. I agree with your suspicion that they will come for you. We spread the word around that you came here and died in the fire with Doris and Rachel. Draw the curtains over the windows when we leave. I'll let you know when we're clear of the village." Ursel swung himself up onto the coach's top seat instead of waiting for an answer.

Darmon leaned into the coach. "It's my understanding that after I deliver you to the port city, the coach and horses are mine to keep." Zack nodded. "I assume you're in a hurry?" Zack nodded again. "We have four horses and a relatively light load for this coach. The springs and brakes are new. The horses are the four best from Master Donce's stable." Darmon grinned. "You should have seen the look on the old skinflint's face when we rode off with them in harness." His smile, certainly genuine, matched the smiles from inside the coach.

Spellbinder nickered, and then nudged his way to his master. Zack stroked his forehead. A man pulled him away and tethered him at the rear of the coach on a long lead.

They stopped at an unfamiliar inn when the sun surrendered to night. Zack sighed with relief at its presence. Ursel carried him to their room as if he weighed no more than a small boy. Zack's amazement at the gentleness the large man used carrying out his self-imposed duty dissolved into gratitude.

The inn boasted a laundry service and guaranteed the clothing's delivery, neatly folded, at first light. Zack ordered everyone to take advantage of it. His three sets of trousers and shirts, stored in his saddlepack, sorely needed cleaning. He also ordered a bath. The tub and hot water brought to his room called to him. Sore, cramped, muscles needed relief. Ursel helped him undress, carried him to the tub and helped him bathe those areas he couldn't reach without bending or straining his wound. Ursel spread a drying cloth before the fireplace and placed him upon it. Zack, still not able to stand without help, deplored his condition. Ursel gently lifted him, as he might a helpless kitten he favored, and placed him on the bed when the fire and drying cloth had done their job. Ursel stepped away and started to undress. Zack turned on his good side as much as he could to give the other man privacy.

Ursel finished washing and was drying dried his back when the innkeeper's wife knocked on the door to collect the laundry. He tied the cloth around him and carried their dirty clothes to the door. From the look on her face, the sight of the large man standing in a wet drying cloth provided the woman a pleasure she had not counted on. Ursel stepped back to shut the door and the drying cloth came loose from his bulging chest and back muscles and fell to the floor. Blushing furiously, he kicked the door closed and stooped to pick up the errant cloth. The door bounced open a crack and Zack could hardly keep from laughing at the woman's eyes and even wider smile. She gently closed the door while Ursel covered his, now redden, skin.

Zack gave Ursel time to compose himself, wondering about his shyness. "Ursel, you're a good-looking young man. Why is it that some good-looking young lady hasn't tied you to her instead of letting you wander all over Hamptor?"

Ursel clamped his mouth shut and his blush returned. "Zack, I need to talk to someone and I—trust you. This is hard for me."

Zack saw the pain and hurt show on the young man's face. He leaned forward and nodded for him to continue.

"I had a girl once, Naydene. She was quite beautiful, and I loved her. I knew she had had a hard time growing up. The town's gossip said her mother hated men, and her father gave her mother plenty of cause to hate. Do you know about the water that seeps to the surface and not from the rivers?"

Zack shook his head.

"We have some pools, but the water tastes foul. It doesn't smell and except for the taste, it's fine. After my Da and I finished felling trees to use in making our charcoal, I would bathe in a pool on the way home. It's hidden from the road, and I don't think a lot of people even know it's there. Of course, I bathed naked, as per usual. One day Naydene and a friend of hers climbed the hill overlooking the pool and watched me.

"Well . . . you know . . . at least for me." Ursel's face became flame red. "When I swim naked . . . well, you know . . ."

Zack took pity on the boy, almost a man. "You mean you got aroused."

Ursel gave a large sigh, "Well . . . yes!" By now the redness in his face had traveled over a good bit more of his body. "She screamed, 'You're a monster. You'll never put that thing in me.' I will never forget the look in her eye as she said that. She told the gossips in the village I was deformed and after that, none of the other girls would talk to me. The girl who watched with her told me she had tried to counter Naydene's charges, but Naydene kept telling everyone. I wanted to talk to my Da about it, but I didn't have time before Roland asked me to help you and Doris."

Zack spoke softly, "Ursel, you are a large man in statue

and also your member is . . . very large, but I've seen larger. Many women like a man who is large there, just as some women like men who have a smaller member. You are not a monster. In fact, many men would like to be as large."

Ursel sat on the bed with the drying cloth wrapped around him, his head pressed against his hands.

"Ursel," the young man looked up at the concern in Zack's voice, "the young lady did you a great disservice, and probably to several girls in your village, including her. The size of a man is usually unimportant to a woman and this Naydene must have issues you're unaware of to act in the manner that she did. I saw nothing that causes me to believe that there is anything wrong with you, and we have been physically closer than most men have due to my wound." *What would the poor lad have done with all the nudity between men in Ozlid?*

His words washed over Ursel like a healing balm. He nodded once with a shy smile, laid down on the pallet, pulling the blanket over him.

* * *

THEY stopped at a village the next day at midmeal. Zack sent Ursel to buy another set of trousers and shirt for himself, plus the personal things he and Darmon needed. He felt surprise and a little pleasure when Ursel returned with an outfit much like his own: its earth-toned colors blended easily with the local terrain, and the sturdy material gave it longevity and provided protection. He stood taller and walked with more confidence and that pleased Zack even more.

25

CURRAT rode into the village later than he'd hoped. He found the inn with little trouble and luck favored him. The innkeeper showed him to the only private room. He also surprised Currat in that he was one of the few innkeepers—or staff for that matter—which did not yell at him. He remembered Zack, and asked about him in yes and no questions. Currat nodded at the appropriate times letting the innkeeper know that he fared well. Currat prayed to the Great Creator that he was telling the truth.

He was getting ready to strip and bathe using the basin at the washstand—a far cry from his pool at the palace— when he heard fast footsteps coming down the hall. Currant grabbed his dagger, just in case, as urgent knocking rattled his door. Pulling his belt tight, he and raised the bar and opened it to find Robel, the groom, in a state of panic.

"Oh sir, please come at once, sir. We unknowingly put a horse in heat in the same stable as your stallion. He's a big one, and he's about to take the whole stable down! Please come, sir."

Currat chuckled and followed the lad down the rear stairway to the yard and paddock. He could hear the ruckus before even leaving the building. He and the big black stallion he'd named Snowflake now liked each other.

Currat had noticed the difference in the horse after being away from the messenger's influence a short while. His actions were more spirited now, where lethargy had reigned before. He pranced and responded to Currat's good care with nudges and nickers of pleasure.

He found the horse to be very well trained. He loved to run, and at times Currat gave him his head to gallop, and then reined him in after a while to let him cool down at a leisurely pace. Currat usually rubbed him down rather than let the groom do it if he had any doubt of the boy's competency. He soon learned that Snowflake would beg for apples, and bought them whenever he could.

Entering the stable, he found Snowflake enraged, outraged, and ready to mount any mare within five miles. He calmed in Currat's presence, and snorted a welcome. Currat stroked his damp hide and cooed at him, remembering not to speak. He reached up and scratched him behind the ears, another particular favorite. Robel calmed the mare that had seemed more than willing for the big black stallion of her dreams to mount her, then calmly walked her through the stable into the paddock. Snowflake's outrage diminished while Currat admired his fine stallion. With a chuckle, he promised the horse that he'd see if he could get him what he desired when they reached Hagan's End.

Robel thanked Currat for his effort as they walked toward the rear entrance to the inn. The boy looked up into his questioning eyes when they found the door barred from the inside. "Da locks the rear entrance about this time of night." He looked sheepish at requiring more of Currat. "We will have to go around, or I could run if you want to wait." Currat smiled and started around the building to the front entrance.

Upon entering the inn, he came face to face with a stringy, besotted man he had never seen before. Currat brushed by him quickly and headed to his room.

* * *

SOMETHING happened when Gusbarb saw Currat's face. His senses reeled from more than the ale he'd had that evening, and a flash of energy sobered him instantly. His eyes widened to their fullest, and he blinked until true vision reappeared as the light faded from the bright picture in his mind. His mouth gaped when Currat walked around him. He knew who the man was at once.

* * *

CURRAT left early the next morning, stepping over the snoring Gusbarb, lying next to a table a few feet from the front entrance to the inn. He gently closed the door, not wanting to wake the sleeping man he vaguely remembered from the night before, and headed to the stables. He saddled Snowflake and tied his saddlepacks in place as Robel came in, yawning.

The boy's surprise at seeing anyone up before the sunrise made Currat smile. He gave him two coppers, and got a large smile in return. "Thank you, sir and for last night, too."

Currat mounted Snowflake and headed south at a canter. The next inn's location, the farthest distance to travel in one day, required an early start.

* * *

THE innkeeper woke Gusbarb an hour later and shuttled him out the door. "No, do you not see? I have to wait for my good friend to come down. The one I described to you."

It took a moment for the innkeeper to make the connection. "Gusbarb, he left early this morning. He must be a really good friend; he let you sleep when he walked by on his way out." The snide remark looked completely lost on the sorry little man, and the innkeeper walked away in disgust, shaking his head.

Gusbarb's panic kept him from noticing; not that it would have really registered in the first place. He rushed around the inn to the stable. He tried to remember the groom's name and gave up in frustration.

Robel looked up with surprise when Gusbarb entered the stable; he had not had a horse for years. "Boy," he whined, "which way did he go?"

* * *

ROBEL didn't like Gusbarb, few people did. Actually, no one that he knew of did more than tolerate the man. "Who?"

"My friend, the one I met at the door last night. The one with you, remember?"

Robel knew exactly whom he meant, and he also knew Currat could not possibly be Gusbarb's friend. Robel believed the stories about Gusbarb. He had seen him drunk many times and drunks said things, often expressing their true feelings. Gusbarb was no different. "Oh, the one with the bay mare?"

Gusbarb didn't know what the man was riding. He hadn't seen him ride in from his vantage point in the tree, having somehow fallen asleep once or twice. "Yes, he's the one. Which way did he go?"

Robel knew whatever Gusbarb wanted with Currat, it promised nothing good. The bay mare pranced in the paddock, probably still dreaming of Currat's stallion, if Gusbarb took the time to notice. "He went north, heading toward the West road toward Arestead."

"He told you that?"

Gusbarb confirmed Robel's suspicions. "Well, yes, I cannot read minds." Gusbarb rushed out the door and stopped dead in his tracks. Robel shook his head and returned to his duties.

* * *

NOW what do I do? Gusbarb wondered. *I must wait for a man to come seeking me.* He did not like that answer; in fact, he feared it. Little cold shock waves crawled up his spine. He did not want one of the black form's men seeking him out. He did want the gold, though and that resigned him to wait. Pondering when he might be paid. He scurried to his hut on the outskirts of town.

26

ZACK laughed at the simple, direct message on the huge sign by the inn's door: *No one in this establishment knows anything about a black stone. We will throw anyone out that discusses a black stone. We will hold all weapons at the door.*

Zack went through the door in Ursel's arms. Derk or Kerk—he couldn't tell which—stood before him. The brawny young man started, first at having to look up to someone for a change, and again when he realized whom Ursel was carrying.

"Master Stand, are you ill?"

Zack felt gratified that the young man remembered him. "Tell your brother and father that I prefer my name not be mentioned on this visit. You might say that I've had a steel fever. We will need two rooms," Darmon had insisted on sleeping on the coach since the first night. "One for this fine lad and me, and one for the ladies." Derk looked past them as Doris and Rachel stepped through the doorway, glanced at the second warning sign, and looked around the common room."

Zack didn't notice a man's head jerk in his direction at the sound of his name. The man looked intently at Zack's face as he gulped his ale.

"KERK!" Derk's twin stuck his head out the kitchen door. "Bring the keys."

Escorting them upstairs, Kerk stood aside to let Ursel through the open door and watched him gently lay Zack on the bed. Zack saw concern and questions on Kerk's face. *You will have to wait a while for your answers,* he thought. *One of you will bring me my lastmeal, and there will be more than enough time to recount the story then.*

He was mistaken. Both brothers brought his food and a mug of ale to him. They sat in rapt attention while Zack explained that a little accident had resulted in a sword getting stuck in him, and declined to say more on the matter to their complete dissatisfaction.

Ursel left to insure that someone would take a trencher of food and some ale to Darmon. The twins looked a little discouraged at not getting more information from Zack when an idea formed. "Derk, I'm well enough now not to require Ursel's attention all the time. He's a good lad, and hasn't had much fun on this trip." *Or ever, most likely,* he thought "Do you lads think you might come up with a little entertainment for him tonight?" Zack gave them a sly wink.

Working and growing up at an inn brought a wealth of knowledge to the boys that most men did not receive until much later in life. Zack reached for his pouch and offered the boys a few silvers, but they waved his hand away.

Derk looked at Kerk and they both grinned. "Save your silver, Master Stand, we know someone that will give us an extremely pleasant time, and it won't cost us a copper. Do you think he has much experience, being entertained, I mean?"

Zack couldn't help chuckling. "No, sadly, I fear that's not the case."

Derk and Kerk's eyes sparkled and they nodded as one. "Send him down for lastmeal, and we'll do the rest." Their countenance said they would enjoy what they had planned. "Master Stand, I know Jace and Michael will want to see you as well. Do you object if we let them know you're here?"

Zack had wondered how that situation worked out. He agreed, and the twins left as Ursel returned. They both smiled at him on the way out. Ursel turned to Zack with a frown on his face. "Ursel, the twins are good lads, and

213

they're about your age. I asked if you might join them tonight for a little fun, and they agreed. You're more than welcome to take advantage of their offer if you like." The big man started to protest, but Zack raised his hand. "I'll have Doris check on me if it makes you happy, but I'll be fine. Now, you go and have a good time." Ursel looked unsure, but quickly warmed to the proposal.

He bathed at the stand, then got fresh water for Zack and placed the things he might need within reach. He looked quite happy when he left, locking the door behind him. Zack could hear him knocking on Doris' door, and then heard his footfalls trail off down the hall.

With a smile, Zack started undressing, and felt his recovery had progressed well when the completed chore caused no stab of pain. The wound looked and felt ready to remove the stitches. Cat's gut, cut away one stitch at a time without causing any rupture along the wound, collected on his side. Forward and backward movements did not pinch his muscles. At the end, Zack was quite happy as he settled in to relax and pulled the covers over his body, dropping discarded stitches to the floor.

Doris looked in on him an hour later. "Doris you must see this." Zack threw the covers further than he intended, exposing more than he'd wanted.

"Why?" she said, "I saw that before."

Zack felt the blush start in his toes and head at the same time as he scrambled to pull the covers over his more private areas. Very flustered and quite red in the face, he stammered, "No—of course not that... I—I mean, well—I know you bathed me once or twice. I meant this."

Afraid that he might reopen the wound if his hand slipped, Doris took it in hers and carefully inspected the wound. "It looks like Roland told me it should; I see none of the signs he warned me about." She looked up at Zack's face and smiled. "I can see you're fine. I'll return to my room and tuck Rachel in."

"Doris, I'm, uh, I'm sorry about, well, you know—"

"It's all right Zack. I know you get excited about some things." She instantly regretted the choice of words and blushed. Laughter soon ricocheted from the room's walls. Doris slipped to the door when she finally composed herself, wiping tears from her eyes. "Good night, Zack."

"Doris, thank . . . thank you." His face cracked, and they laughed again while she left the room and locked him in.

* * *

ZACK gingerly rolled onto his side when a key clicked in the lock. The door opened, and Michael and Jace's face peeked inside. Zack waved them in, and Doris left the men alone. They promised to tap on her door when they left so she could lock Zack in again.

Jace sat at the end of the bed, and Michael brought the straight chair over to bedside. "Is it true? You got stabbed?" Jace's voice was filled with awe

"Extenuating circumstances may conquer the best of us. Remember, I told you that chance always existed. Many things can happen in a fight that you cannot prepare for, even if you trained every day."

"Can we see?" Michael's face colored. He sheepishly looked from Zack to Jace without finding any support.

Zack chuckled at his discomfort. "Yes, you may look. I just took the stitches out tonight, so it may look a little red." He carefully folded the covers down to expose his lower abdomen. Fascination and repulsion fought for dominance on both boys' faces.

"Did it hurt?" Jace asked, and then realized what he had just said. "Of course, I know it must have hurt. I mean, did it hurt a lot?"

Obviously, neither boy had ever seen a sword wound before. Zack hoped they never saw one from his viewpoint and prepared for a long session of questions. "I need to know about your accomplishments before I start answering any questions."

They both started talking at once. Michael stopped and let the more exuberant Jace tell the tale. "Michael showed Da and me several things that helped at the cooperage, and Da explained a way to rebuild Michael's fences that made them sturdier. It worked out well. We both have learned many things. I never knew one did so much on a farm and for so many hours."

Michael cut in. "I never knew the frustration of getting to the step you had been working toward half the morning, only to have a customer walk into the shop, and losing another hour to get to the same point again after the interruption."

Zack smiled, satisfied that the boys—young men near the same age as the twins and Ursel—had formed a stronger friendship. The respect they gave each other now plainly showed. "Gentleman, what about the girl? That's what started all this."

Michael sat back and smiled, nodding to Jace, who started talking again.

"Well, I promised to meet her on a night that Da received a big order, and I couldn't go. Michael finished early, and I asked him to see her and explain."

Michael picked up the explanation. "I met her that night, and her surprise at seeing me instead of him took her breath away. She wanted to know why Jace hadn't come, and I explained everything. She stomped her foot and went off in a huff. We have not seen her since." Neither boy looked too perturbed over the outcome, but they also seemed quite puzzled over the girl's reaction.

Zack chuckled, "Well, I think you might want to let her know that you're still interested. Perhaps you could send her flowers or sweets, but I don't advise you to both send her the same thing at the same time."

Yes, Zack thought, *this might be a long night indeed.*

27

QUINON, the man who had taken an interest when Zack had entered the inn, sat at his table, deep in thought.

Everything fits. A man with the correct name and injured, traveling to Hagan's End, it must be him. Pure luck, that's all it is, pure, simple luck. Just think, I might have been at home listening to my dear, darling, bitch of a wife calling me every name she could think of and with all the sputtering that goes with it.

He laughed quietly at the memory. *Well, she did call me all the names she knew, and probably made up some of her own, too. Ah, well, she deserved what she got, and a good thing I shut her up, too. She'll be black and blue for quite a while, and perhaps I'll have some respect out of here for a change. I think I'll leave after I collect the gold. Besides, why should she share it? I'll be the one doing the work. Just think, if I hadn't beaten the old hag senseless, I might not have been here to hear his name. 'Master Stand, are you ill?' Well, good old Master Stand, you're going to be a lot more than ill when I get through with you. You'll be dead, is what you'll be.*

Frothy liquid spilled from the mug set before Quinon, alerting him to the common room's noise. The serving maid's hips swung invitingly as she sauntered away, leaving him watching and two coppers poorer. Two coppers remained. Quinon returned to his deliberations while watching the mountain of a man that had carried Zack into the inn eating at a table. *I still have all the silver that . . . that thing dumped on me. Pay me in gold for information, will you. How much will you pay me if I put a knife in him? Two, three times as much I imagine—perhaps more, much more.*

Quinon watched while the twins walked over to the big man's table. Barely-hidden glee filled him when the three left the inn together. He knew the inn's secrets as well as Kell, and he also knew the room Zack occupied. He had worked on the inn's construction three years ago, and felt it could not have worked out better than if he had planned the circumstances himself. He occupied the right room, and his bodyguard had left him alone. Quinon sipped his ale, a rarity from his usual guzzling and waited for the right time to strike.

* * *

KELL looked at Quinon staggering from the inn. Something didn't look right; his walk was different than his usual swagger. He dismissed it and returned to cleaning the common room. *My lads need a little pleasure and Adel will get a workout tonight,* he thought with a smile He didn't begrudge them an occasional extra night off, especially when they explained the reason. *Do they actually believe I don't know about Adel?*

* * *

TWO hours passed before Quinon worked his way behind the inn and looked up at Zack's room. The soft, glimmering light from inside made him smile. Callused hands reached for small handholds, hidden from all but a careful inspection. He had made the way possible with robbery in mind. The three bars across the window were not set deep into the plaster, nor anchored to stout crossbeams like on the adjacent windows. He had cut them short on purpose, and they were anchored to the wall in less than an inch of plaster. It would be a one-time thing; his careful preparations, discovered and corrected with the first robbery committed. But if there was any time, it was now.

He had started to rob another guest five months ago, but her amorous affairs with the twins had spoiled it. He had sat out in the cold throughout the night, waiting for the giggles and moans to stop. He remembered thinking the three of them were inhuman in their lovemaking, and visualized one twin following the other in cycles. *Tonight is my night,* he promised. *A man rich enough to travel in a fancy coach with all those people to feed and lodge is sure to have a large enough purse to tide me over until I receive the golds from that . . . that thing.*

Quinon almost burst with glee. He climbed the side of the wall without difficulty and peered through the window. Dark blankets covered the sleeping man. *Better and better,* he thought.

The bars pulled free from the wall with little effort or noise, and he tossed them to the ground, careful that they didn't fall on one another. He had just revmoved the last one when Zack stirred in his sleep, making Quinon freeze and held his breath. He waited, hardly breathing until the sleeping man settled again. Nearly silent scratches made the only unusual sounds while his pick found the trough he had made in the window edge. The latch gave him more of a problem than he'd expected, but with concentration, it finally worked free and he pushed the window inward.

Surprise blanched Quinon's face when he looked up. Zack sat up in his bed while bringing something out from under the pillow. Drawing a blade, the would-be thief braced his knees against the wall's corner and threw it.

The knife caught Zack in the left shoulder when he stood. He fell backward and thumped the wall with his head. His body lunged forward onto the bed.

* * *

THE new groom did not know how angry Kell could get from a minor infraction like leaving the pitchfork propped against the water trough with the tines pointed toward the sky. Quinon had planned well, and his plan succeeded, except for one minor detail. The force required to throw the knife loosened his grip on the building. He fell away from it with alarming force while desperately scrabbling for a grip. The shock of falling off the wall was so sudden he didn't make a sound.

Sudden pain drove into every fiber of his being, and he looked down at the pitchfork's middle tine sticking through his chest with bits of flesh and blood—actually, a lot of blood—adhered to it. Blackness surrounded him, and a pain he never imagined possible enveloped him. A single revelation burst into his mind, bringing with it even more pain many times greater.

"You are mine." A deep, dead voice whispered, *"Welcome to the void."*

* * *

SWIRLING darkness slowly cleared. Zack looked down on himself, bleeding from a knife stuck in his left shoulder. He felt no pain. He did feel calm, even with the awe that rushed through him. He looked toward the open window and suddenly he floated outside the building looking down on a dead man. *Ursel, where are you?* Pressure pulled at his back, and he felt himself soar in that direction. He saw a thin, silver cord when he looked around; it disappeared into darkness and generated a sensation of well being instead of the stark terror his intellect told him he should feel. Stars became a blur while he sped back to his room. He settled once more over his body, feeling an irresistible force drawing him upward the next second. He went through ceiling and roof faster than he could register the experience.

Golden light, comforting and warm, encased him. "Zack." He spun around, to see her floating there, just outside his gossamer, golden orb. He questioned his death for the first time since the strange experiences started.

The beautiful face of his wife smiled, and he heard a voice he had dreamed of for five long years. "My love, I'm dead only to your world. I'm at peace and happy, as is our daughter. Our deaths had nothing to do with your actions. Our time had come. You must release your bitterness and sorrow. You are a good man, my love. There are many good men and women in your world. Use the mirrors provided, they are there in front of you. Find the happiness you have denied yourself these last years. I feel your love constantly, as I did before I came to this plane. Love again; it will not hurt me. I wish it. Remember us fondly and fare thee well, my love."

Zack reached for her as the globe faded, seeming to dissolve into his most recent wound. Now he hovered over Jace and a pretty girl.

"Of course, I didn't mention I met with both of you," she said. "A fight might well have started long ago with your hot temper, and a sensible man with good judgment might not have been available to put your head straight. Now the two of you are like brothers. Next you will be comparing notes."

"No. I never . . . we never . . . such a thing is inconceivable."

The girl smiled. "Then I guess boys are different than girls in more than all the obvious ways."

"You mean that you talk about us with . . . who . . . who do you talk with concerning us?"

"No one that will breathe a word, silly."

"When are you going to make a choice?"

"I'll choose when I figure out which one of you is man enough to handle me." A coquettish smile played across her face.

Zack flew backward again and hovered over his still bleeding body. He had bled a lot; which concerned him, but before he could try to do anything about it, he suddenly found himself in Doris' dream.

Her happiness warmed him, and he could clearly hear her exuberant words. "I'm the happiest I have been since his death. I'll have a new life, and new choices to make. Education, yes, for Rachel and for me, I must make sure of that, and I think we'll like it, too. A fine new home built the way I want, and perhaps a business after I learn all I can."

Crashing darkness imploded on Zack's senses, and he felt nothing more.

28

DERK approached Ursel after he had finished his second trencher of mutton with various root vegetables and two glasses of ale. "Are you ready for a little fun?" A moment later Kerk joined them. The three stood at the same time, and it made quite an impression seeing all that muscle in one place. The boys hurried out the rear door. Derk stopped long enough to pull a small cask of wine from the cooling well. They started out at a brisk pace.

"Where are we going?" Ursel asked.

"To have fun," the twins answered in unison. Ursel chuckled and shook his head, following after them.

They soon reached the biggest home in the village. It was set apart on the crest of a small hill, and the only two-story house Ursel could see in the area. Derk pulled the chain next to the main entrance, and a bell sounded sweetly from within. An older woman opened the door and stood aside when she recognized the twins. Ursel followed them into the receiving hall and his mouth gaped open in astonishment. Reflections from crystal, something he had never seen, flooded the hall with light from a huge chandelier, causing bright colors to shimmer across the room. On one wall stood a low table where the largest mirror he could ever have imagined, much less seen, hung on the wall. It reflected an image of him whole and complete that he saw for the first time, and it rather pleased him.

Thick, dark blue rugs with a deep red border covered the pale, ash wood floor. Ursel felt like he was walking on thick moss in a forest. The soft cream color of the wall relaxed him. He started when he saw another reflection on the staircase behind him. He stared, and the only thought that came to mind was: *She's beautiful . . .*

"How nice to see you boys and . . . oh, you brought company. How wonderful, it's so nice of you to think of me." Ursel listened to the rich, velvet tones of her voice while her deep violet eyes superbly stood out in her reflection and dazzled him. He slowly turned to her and found that the mirror did not do her justice.

The twins met her on the second step and each kissed her cheek. "We brought wine, too."

"Now, you know you didn't have to do that." Her words trailed off when Ursel approached the staircase on her right. His head came even with hers. She leaned forward, over the banister and gently kissed him on the lips. "Welcome, stranger." Ursel felt a little limp in the knees.

Kerk made the introductions and Ursel faintly heard the name "Adel" while he followed her into a room with more rugs, pictures, candles, flowers, and even more books than he'd ever thought could be in one place. She wore a gown made of rich wormcloth the exact color of her eyes. Her sensuous sway of walking sent a chill up his spine. Her figure flowed, perfectly proportioned to her height that put the top of her head even with Ursel's breast.

They taught Ursel two board games, and cool wine kept the conversation light. Kerk stood to go to the privy, and reversed himself halfway to the door. "Adel, why not show Ursel your sculpture?" His eyes sparkled.

Adel held her hand out. "Come with me, dear Ursel." He rose and joined her. They walked upstairs hand in hand. Kerk returned from the privy and started a new game, confident that a much older one would soon play out upstairs.

At the top of the stairs, Adel abruptly spun to Ursel and pulled his lips down to hers. Ursel's universe became awash with color, softness, wetness, and a thousand sensations he never dreamed of, and sincerely hoped he may find again.

* * *

THE twins knew Adel's habit of noise making when she became, well, excited; and hearing it now caused smiles of mischievous glee. It started low and slowly raised three octaves in pitch and several times in strength. The twins looked impressed when they heard it a third time. It became unusually quiet over the next half-hour, and they grew curious. Removing their boots, they padded up to the second floor. They peeked in Adel's room to find her lying on the overlarge bed with Ursel spread out nude beside her. She stroked his hair and smiled when she saw them. She rose to stand beside the bed and donned a sheer robe the twins well knew.

Her perfect figure and creamy skin muted to a new softness under the robe enticed the twins and they smiled at her nod. Her long, black hair hung loose and cascaded down her back. She pulled the bedclothes and light blanket over Ursel, dubbing him, "My Stallion." Ursel did not wake when she followed the twins to a guest bedroom with an equally large bed.

Two hours later, Adel silently slid from between the twins and watched as they reached out for one another while half-asleep and wrapped their bodies together, legs and arms intertwining around one another. They both fell back asleep within the time of a few breaths.

She had witnessed the same actions many times before, and marveled at their symmetry. Adel knew they rarely stayed apart for any amount of time, and still slept together at the inn. She again questioned if sleep accounted for all they did. They had deeply kissed one another many times in her presence. Otherwise, they provided every manly caress and sated every desire she had. She blew them a silent kiss and walked back into her bedroom.

Ursel, sound asleep, breathed deeply and silently. He lay on his side and she snuggled next to him, sighing happily when his huge body conformed to hers. The twin's sweet remembrances came to her. She truly loved them. Neither Ursel nor the twins might ever believe her age unless someone told them and she held no intention of telling them she had lived nearly long enough to be their mother. In truth, her age counted fourteen years their senior.

Adel had heard all the gossip concerning the twin's adventures with the village girls: there must be two girls; they would all be together in the same room or at least close by, perhaps in a hayloft, and the twins never stayed the entire night. They obviously did not act toward one another as they did with her, or there would have been much more gossip. The twins kept their adventures clandestine, and that relieved her of many complications. She knew they went home to hold each other, and she would be quite happy to sleep on either side of them. *Might we ever formalize our relationship? I know they care deeply for me. They're beautiful men, not the rugged, handsome features of Ursel, but in no way less male, and they manifest a softer quality I adore.* Unfortunately, dawn was approaching, and the time to awaken her sleeping, gentle giants had come.

* * *

URSEL walked to the inn in a fog of bliss. The twins laughed and teased him with little reply. Their quiet companion proved difficult to rile, and after several mocking remarks, gave back as well as he received. They quietly slipped back into the inn. Ursel followed them to their room, where they could talk quietly without disturbing anyone.

The twins stripped with no embarrassment and washed themselves while asking Ursel how he had enjoyed the evening. Finally, somewhat embarrassed, he stated he did not have the words to describe how he felt, and thanked them profusely. They gave him a knowing look as they climbed into bed and pulled the covers over them, curling themselves around one another and, to Ursel's amazement, fell asleep within a few minutes.

He took the extra key they had given him, and quietly left them to their dreams. The stairway creaked with his weight that made the only sound while he returned to their room. He still felt in a dreamlike world from the night's activities and quietly entered the cold, dark room.

A chill breeze flowed around him while he closed the door, setting off alarms in his head. He shivered and searched in the darkness for the lamp and striker. He saw a large, dark shadow spread across Zack's bed the wrong way, and hurried his search. The lamp caught on the first try, and Ursel looked over his shoulder and groaned.

Doris looked annoyed until she saw Ursel's face. She went where he pointed while he raced down the hallway. The twins set up in bed as one, still intertwined as one. "Get your Da and a healer. Master Stand has been stabbed." Ursel did not wait to see if the twins complied, but raced back to the room.

Doris stood over Zack's still body. Rachel entered the room and the color drained from her face. She nearly screamed when she felt Ursel's strong arms lift and turn her toward him. The choked scream came out as a whimper, and Ursel carried her to her room. Darmon appeared in the hallway at the same time Derk came running from the opposite direction. Darmon arrived first. "Watch over Rachel." He handed her over to a puzzled Darmon and followed Derk into his room.

Kell and Kerk arrived moments later with a man in tow wearing a long nightshirt and carrying a large bag. He took one look at Zack, then shooed all but Doris from the room and closed the door. Doris reappeared, almost at once, requesting hot water. The twins ran down the hallway toward the common room in bare feet, wearing nothing but trousers.

Ursel sat in the hallway with his face buried in his hands. *I should have been here,* he thought for what seemed like the hundredth time.

* * *

URSEL looked in on Rachel, who lay on the bed across the room, finally asleep. Darmon had gone to ask about Zack an hour ago; Ursel said he would let him know when he might be seen after the healer finished his art. Darmon said he refused to believe that Zack could be killed by one little knife. He went back to the coach after asking Ursel to let him know the outcome. Several hot buckets of water later, Doris and the healer emerged from the room. Ursel followed Doris to her and Rachel's room and made sure she did not need anything. The question on Ursel's face took no words.

Doris turned toward him, her face lined and tired. "He will be fine. He lost a lot of blood, and will be weak for a while, but there is no permanent damage. He has more herbs to take tomorrow and he's asleep. He insists that we continue to Hagan's End tomorrow—" She glanced out the window at the graying sky, "today, rather. The healer said he could travel in the coach as he did before. We're to stop if any bleeding starts again, but he does not expect that to happen. Zack made me promise to leave before midday." Ursel only nodded and walked off toward the rear stairs leading to the stable yard to tell Darmon the plans.

Ursel estimated he slept no more than two hours. He washed with the unused water from the last bucket brought to the room and dressed. Zack lay still, three feet away while Ursel approached his bed, when Zack started awake, a knife blurred suddenly into his hand.

Ursel backed away with his hands held out. "I'm sorry, Master Stand, I didn't think."

* * *

ZACK looked at Ursel and turned away; awake for some time thinking about the previous night's strange occurrences, he had finally dozed off.

Pleasant memories made him smile. The terrible hurt and pain he had carried for five years lay dormant, drained of its power to hurt him anew. He missed his family and wanted their deaths not to have happened, but he felt at peace with the acceptance of their deaths for the first time. Puzzlement seeped into his expression. *Use the mirrors you are provided? What does that mean?*

He dwelt on the more pleasant scenes he had seen on that strange journey.

* * *

THE light smell of a woman's fragrance on his discarded shirt caused Ursel to smile. He would not voice his experiences until he was convinced that Zack felt fine and his wound wasn't going to bleed. Ursel sat across from him on his bed, staring at the bandaged shoulder. Zack set on the side of his bed with no apparent discomfort.

Zack's question took the matter out of his hands. "Tell me, Ursel, how did your night go?"

Ursel started blushing before the question finished. He stumbled over a few words, and then they tumbled out as if the floodgates of his experiences disintegrated. He told Zack everything that happened in somewhat more detail than Zack required.

"Ursel, you seem destined to find extraordinary women; and in this case, a couple of men, too. The twins that I have known don't act like Derk and Kerk do to my knowledge, but then, I never saw them in their beds. Although, I have known several wealthy women, I have not experienced their entertainment in quite the fashion your Adel provided. She sounds like a remarkable woman. I'm not saying that you should not have enjoyed yourself, so don't get that idea. I'm only commenting that your education included some unusual—er, aspects that one does not encounter in everyday life, and they should be regarded in the proper prospective."

Ursel considered for a moment. "I think I understand what you're saying. I don't believe any of the women in my village ever behaved like Adel. I can also see what you meant about Naydene, the girl I told you about, saying the things she did. Adel seemed quite happy with me as a partner, and I couldn't have been happier with her. Ursel reflected on the conversation between them and the blush returned to his cheeks, darker than before. He pulled the bedcover over his head and fell back laughing hard as Zack chuckled. Ursel loaded the coach with Zack safely tucked inside.

* * *

ZACK enjoyed watching Ursel that morning; he did not exactly walk; strutting might be a better description. Then, he saw Kell approach. The innkeeper looked sheepish on his way to the coach's open window. When they found Quinon's body, he had apologized to the point of groveling.

"Master Stand, I thank you for the referral of a good guest to my inn. I meant to mention it last night, but when I saw your condition, it went from my head. I wanted to let you know that we took good care of Master Duval. I questioned if he might be part of your family. The two of you look so much alike, except for your coloring, of course."

Zack pulled up to a sitting position. "I knew I could count on you." Kell grinned at the praise. "How long ago did he come through?"

"A week ago, today."

Zack started to respond when Darmon called out, "Brake is loosed and we're rolling." The reins snapped and the horses started out from the inn's stable yard.

Zack returned Kell's wave while they turned south onto the main road.

Zack felt confused to say the least. He suffered few aftereffects from the stabbing. His shoulder was slightly sore, and the bandages restricted his left arm, but there wasn't much pain to speak of, and he had much more energy than normal after losing that much blood. Earlier that morning, he had looked at the wound and found a scar forming to his astonishment. He leaned against the seatback, refusing to use the mattress.

Zack saw a golden light settle around him when he opened his eyes, slightly out of focus, from dozing. The effect dissolved when he focused clearly, only returning when he forced his eyes out of focus. He sighed, not knowing exactly what had happened to him, but he liked it.

He slowly settled on a more pressing matter. *Currat made good time, and is on schedule. Wathdure will not give up so easily. I expected him to make more efforts than he has done so far, although it would be nice if he stopped now. Obviously, Wathdure has spies in Hamptor and I don't doubt that he has more than one way of contacting them. We need to be more careful and so does Currat.* Along with these concerns, worry forced its way into his ruminations.

29

"GUSBARB!"

The shout startled him from his foggy morning hangover. He shuffled to the door of his hut and threw it open. The bright sun seared through his half-closed eyes and sent a surge of renewed pain to his head.

"What? And, do you have to yell?"

The man before him stared with contempt. "Did you see the men our Master described to you?"

Gusbarb had grown used to seeing contempt in the faces of those that knew him and some that he did not know. It no longer annoyed him, and he barely recognized its occurrence. *I'm my own master.* He did not like the inference. Then, as if his mental declaration called him, he saw Wathdure's image, and decided not to voice that particular response. "Yes, and I have been waiting for you to find me. He went north three miles to the West road and on to Arestead."

The man looked somewhat surprised. "Are you sure of this?"

"Of course I'm sure," Gusbarb lied. "What do you take me for?"

The man in front of him gave no name. He also did not answer Gusbarb's question. "They went west to Arestead?"

"They? No. Not they, he, the blond one went to Arestead. When will I get the gold promised me?"

"You received the silver our Master gave you. You will receive the gold the same way when we find the blond one on the road to Arestead."

"On the road? He left a week ago. He's probably there

by now. How the blazes are you going to catch him?"

Once more, Gusbarb called up the vision that appeared before him when the silvers popped from the air. He felt nausea that had nothing to do with the ale he had consumed the night before. He felt an oppressive weight cascade down his body and took a step back into his hut. He did not see the smirk on his visitor's face.

* * *

GUSBARB's visitor mounted a black stallion and rode toward the village without answering the fool's question. Brodder turned in his saddle and stared at his informant's shack with new interest. *Will I have to return and kill that man-sized piece of slime? I would enjoy that. Yes, indeed, I'll enjoy killing this one.*

He passed a closed coach on its way south, and admired the four matched black geldings pulling it. The horses made a good team. They worked well, with harmony and structure in their placement, obviously well cared for and well fed. That pleased Brodder. He forced recognition of more immediate things: *I'll stay at the inn tonight, and wait for the Master of Masters to contact me. I will report what Gusbarb said, and my reservations as to the information's accuracy.*

* * *

DARK clouds covered the moon a few minutes before midnight. Brodder felt his Master's presence in the room, and listened for his voice. It came almost immediately. *"Brodder, what did you find today?"*

Brodder knelt on the floor. He may not have been able to see his Master before him, but he had no doubt that the Master could see him. "Gusbarb reports that Currat stayed at the inn a week ago, then traveled north and west the next morning on the road leading to Arestead. Gusbarb stated this positively. I don't put much faith in his words, my Master. I have followed your orders, and

233

have not asked the Hamptorians."

"You are right to be suspicious. I will investigate this further. You are to continue south in the morning. There is only one place they will be safe for the time being, and that is the Seven Realms. They must be in Hagan's End at some point in order to get there. I have disbursed the raiding party, and five of their number will be joining you near Hagan's End.

"Zack Stand may well be dead. We must concentrate on locating Currat and the information he carries. His father's memories overflowed with many interesting things, and I learned much of what he gave to Zack Stand before their escape. I could have learned more if the arrow through his eye hadn't destroyed most of his brain." Wathdure said something Brodder didn't understand, but he was sure it a curse. *"Make sure none of those I send you speak until it is safe. They don't have your linguistic ability."*

Brodder rose to his feet when he felt the Master's presence fade. The mental visitations from his master usually made him hungry, and tonight the pattern held. He paid too much for inferior wine, brown bread, and cheese, but discarded any contemplation of complaining. His Master had many vouchers. He ate and drank his fill, and found sleep soon enough.

* * *

BRODDER awoke refreshed, as he always did after the Master's visits. He arrived with one guest before him in the common room where a decent firstmeal awaited him. Brodder noticed the innkeeper, or one of his get, keeping an eye on him. *I didn't slip up in speaking, but perhaps I best be on my way.*

The groom quickly brought his large black stallion out. Brodder could see the boy had done a good job in caring for his horse. The Master favored the stallions. Brodder much preferred a gelding, like the ones he had seen the previous day. The boy held the reins while he mounted. He flipped the boy a copper and started to ride, then, pulling in the reins and easing the horse back toward the stable he looked down at the boy. "Have you recently seen a horse like this one?"

The boy's eyes did not flinch. "No, sir. Not many horses as fine as yours come through here."

Brodder started to turn onto the road south and changed his intention midway. Instead, he rode across the road to that inn's stable. The innkeeper he queried might not have seen a guest's horse, but the groom must have. He made the same inquiry to Robel.

"Yes sir, about a week ago a man came through on his way to Arestead."

Brodder looked surprised at the answer, and left with a scowl on his face. He nearly started north at the entrance to the main road. However, the Master did not take it well when one took initiative and acted without new orders. His indecision lasted long enough for that notion to form and no longer. Brodder pulled the stallion's reins to the south.

$*$ $*$ $*$

ROBEL and Harle, the groom across the road, usually ate midmeal together. Today, Robel's turn to furnish their food meant they would eat on his side of the road that separated the two inns. The boys squatted in the grass, where they could see if anyone approached their respective stables.

Harle's recollection settled on the strange guest that had departed that morning. He disliked the man's arrogance as he remembered the encounter. Blackness covered him: his hair, eyes, gloves, horse, smile, and manner. Thin ugly lips had barely parted when he spoke, and the few yellow teeth he saw were disgusting. "Did you see that man all in black this morning? I saw him go back to your stable."

Robel giggled. "He was asking about a horse like his. I told him the man went to Arestead." He laughed. "The man that had a horse like his couldn't have been a friend like he claimed. He was nice." Robel had not presumed such a man might be Currat's friend, and had mentioned it to Harle after Gusbarb's inquiries. Harle nodded and told Robel of his encounter earlier and his answer. Both boys laughed at fooling the man, and enjoyed the rest of their midmeal.

30

WATHDURE wasted little time. He centered his presence over Hamptor, near the intersection of the South and West roads. He could not feel the nearness of some of his subjects and now knew why, since he raped Duval's memories finding the room he could not penetrate, and wondering what blocked his incursion into their minds. He would have to search out Currat with other senses. His pleasurable anticipation of the coming inquisition on those his mind had not recognized or controlled before would have to wait; stopping the information that Currat carried from reaching the Seven Realms held his highest priority.

He could not speed his senses westward while searching for Currat's signature as quickly as he wished. Wathdure's capabilities included great speed, but the faster he traveled, the greater the chance that he might miss something. Again he cursed his inability to instantly sense Currat's whereabouts. Still, he traveled several times faster than any horse could gallop, until he reached an inn that took time-consuming scrutiny. Searching the inns for Currat took time that would have been better spent elsewhere, accomplishing different things. It all made Wathdure seethe with impotent fury. He traveled beyond the point Currat could have possibly reached in a week by the next morning.

He sped north over one mountain range, across the length of Ozlid, and over the northern mountains to the rough, freezing hills at the northern most point of his land. He materialized in his true form; the one Zack Stand had met. Wathdure regretted not killing him after receiving his information.

He stood in human likeness, covered in a black cloak, his hands sheathed in black gloves and the cowl of his cloak completely hiding his facial features. Everyone here could see his true manifestation; all of them had previously met his special death. Black gloves touched the cowl and pulled it back, exposing his head's great beauty. His body reflected all light and produced the darkest black; his features moved like animated marble. Luminous eyes and teeth showed no white, but every feature glistened in perfect detail. Graceful strides that any dancer would have craved and envied carried him deep into the cave he used as workshop and storage facility.

Wathdure did not need sleep. Dark energies drawn from the evil committed in the world did not follow a clock, and those energies constantly fueled him. Delightful sensations from murders, mayhem, and rape thrilled him. There awaited so much for him to draw from, and he craved each violent act, although rape remained his favorite. Rage from a male taken against his nature, the pinnacle of his pleasure, soothed and excited him while he drew the life's force from the hapless victim. Female rape came next on his list, and was certainly more prevalent. Horrors of each crime lingered in his consciousness from both the perpetrator and the victim while their dark energies merged and flowed to a dark pool of power in the void. Enjoyment washed through him, and he savored each delicious morsel while he drew his fill from that heinous pool.

Wathdure looked upon his creations with fondness and pride. His necromantic army grew as he lured more and more men and women into his traps. He chose those in the army or without kin. White, naked bodies stared, unseeing, as he strode past. Dead flesh transported easily with his capabilities. Their physical alterations and animation took energy that he replaced with little effort.

He stopped at the first new arrival.

She had been a beautiful woman that he had raped to death in the form of a muscle-bound man with a hideous face. Muscles and tissues had ripped her until the loss of blood stopped her heart. Memories of her fear and pain flowed into him like ambrosia. Wathdure rarely took time for his pleasures; this one had been especially satisfying. Distorted facial features frozen in death's rigor mortis softened and partially exposed her former beauty with a pass of Wathdure's hand. Rounded breasts with large nipples had flattened to the appearance of a man. Her orifices curled inward and skin had folded over them. Tiny sparks flew where Wathdure's finger touched the center of her forehead.

Expressionless eyes followed the path of his hand. Commands entered a consciousness devoid of memories from its former life. It stepped forward in hesitant, jerky steps to follow the directions to find a black uniform in a nearby cavern filled with supplies. Motions smoothed into normality while it selected clothing and dressed.

Rows of Wathdure's necromantic army lay on gelid ground. Its latest addition lay in the last shallow grave of a row, crossed its arms over its chest and closed its eyes. Wathdure had performed as his name prophesied in ancient texts: "Wath," meaning death; and "dure," meaning master. Graves were filled, one by one, until the last row of twenty lay complete. Wathdure's beautiful face formed a smile, reflecting an outer beauty that would have melted many women's—and more than a few men's—hearts until the evil from within devoured them. At last, he reveled in his self-congratulating discourse. *I have ten thousand of my creatures ready to fight.* Wathdure looked out over his army resting in frozen, mindless slumber awaiting his call. Shadure, the spirit-master, one of immense powers exceeded only by the Dark One, and from whom he received his orders, would be pleased.

Emotionless eyes watched Wathdure enter his study

one level above his hellish army. Entries written into the accounts of his achievements flowed in a beautiful script across the pages of a journal by preternatural powers. He motioned for a messenger to step forward while another messenger entered the room. Wathdure noticed the shorter one's eyes, and his mental touch of hidden memory confirmed the identity of the being before him. He—when it had been a he—died in much the same manner as the creature Wathdure made a few moments before, except his screams had held indignation in addition to the usual emotions Wathdure savored. He smiled his beautiful smile while remembering the young man's agony and death. Memories and commands, quickly imprinted on their still usable minds, set them in motion. Wathdure summoned his powers, and the two creatures vanished.

They appeared in the dark shadows of a mausoleum overlooking the road seven miles from the outskirts of Hagan's End. Wathdure could see them there if he wished, and laughed a beautiful cascade of notes, too pure to be human, while he watched them fade into the dark. One more task to do, he remembered.

* * *

GUSBARB woke instantly. The blackness swirling around his room loomed greater than it ever had before. A pervasive depression of evil hung in the air. He might have been more afraid, and would have certainly released his body's waste once again if he knew what the new presence meant.

The blackness formed into a much more solid mass than Wathdure had previously created. Wathdure stood before the cowering man within a moment; his cowl fell onto his shoulders. His perception touched Gusbarb's frantic mind as lust filled Gusbarb. He felt the other's surprise and recognized the feelings of newness, as he had never considered actually being with a man. Gusbarb faltered; too stunned by his emotions to be scared. Wathdure smiled and partially withdrew from Gusbarb's consciousness.

Wathdure's melodious voice formed a notion and forced it into his victim's mind. *"You failed me, Gusbarb."* Wathdure felt the first delicious tinges of fear grip Gusbarb while his ragged clothes disintegrated from around him. Another emotion generated from the weak intellect before him flew to Wathdure's consciousness: *Lust.* Therefore, it shall be.

Gusbarb felt the hugeness that entered him tearing muscle and tissue. Wathdure alone heard expressionless screams of fear and unimaginable pain soar through the night. Wathdure stood motionless, not one foal of his cloak stirred while his mental forces shredded Gusbarb's body. He made sure Gusbarb knew his pain's every nuance, until his spirit finally departed his body. Gusbarb's screams magnified repeatedly while the Dark One embraced his spirit and they slowly faded from Wathdure's consciousness. The gore that spread across the hut disappeared with a wave of Wathdure's hand, and he and the empty shell of Gusbarb's existence faded from view. The creature Wathdure planned to make from Gusbarb's body might replace the messenger Zack Stand had destroyed, if he turned out well. The unlikely possibility that he might fail did not concern him.

Wathdure imbued his messengers with greater abilities than the simple killing machines he produced for his army. They could make rudimentary choices of action based on implanted circumstances. Such was the case with the messenger that had circled back when one of their numbers went missing. His messengers retained only one imperative when they found an imposter: Kill!

He gave the messengers he transported to the mausoleum outside Hagan's End several directives, and made more options available to them: They must seek their prey only at night, keeping to the shadows and avoiding humans. They must kill anyone who discovered their presence. They could recognize Currat or Zack's life force once they identified one or both of them and then be able to fix on that stimulus like a homing pigeon returning home.

Wathdure felt this last contingent involving his creatures might be unnecessary. His faith in Brodder and his men aside, events had not gone as planned, and his every fiber advised caution. He raged at the need to utilize so much of his forces for two men, not to mention wasting his precious time. He needed to concentrate his efforts elsewhere. His thoughts caused a beautiful smile. *My prey will not escape me. I have more seekers of death than they can possibly imagine.*

31

CURRAT stopped at the last inn described on Zack's map, glad to deliver the one remaining message to an innkeeper. Master Ballrand also remembered Zack, like most did where he had stopped. The innkeeper took him to a room and mentioned that Zack had previously used it as well.

Ballrand asked many of the same yes-and-no questions as the others. Currat answered with nods, headshakes, and shrugs, as he had throughout his trip. He had not spoken to anyone except Snowflake, and then only when they traveled alone; he constantly watched the roadside for anyone within hearing distance. He desperately wanted to converse with another human, and thought that if this charade lasted much longer, he might scream simply for the pure joy of hearing his own sounds.

He stripped to trousers and shirt, sat on the bed against the headboard, and tried to relax. He did not, however; he continued worrying about Zack, as he had ever since leaving him. Zack had saved his life more times than Currat had ever imagined the need. Besides that, he felt closer to him than he did to his lifelong friends.

A light rap on his door alerted him to company. He rose and opened the door a crack, and then all the way. Beautiful, green eyes and a bright smile greeted him.

"Master Currat, I have your lastmeal." The comely girl delivered a trencher loaded with food and two mugs of ale. She gave him an appraising look that he did not notice. "Will you want hot water for a bath, sir?" He nodded, and received a smile that conveyed more than he could puzzle out. The maid nodded and left quietly.

Currat barred the door and attacked the trencher of food with delight, his appetite greater than usual. He had eaten lightly throughout the trip. *Perhaps coming to my journey's end makes me hungry,* he thought. The knowledge of reaching Hagan's End the next day made him feel better. He finished the ale and relaxed a bit when a knock on the door tensed his muscles again.

Currat thought the serving maid had returned, and his surprise at finding the bright eyes of a boy struggling with a large pail of steaming water made him smile. Currat reached down and took it from him. "Thank you, sir."

The boy followed him into the room. "Master Currat, my name is Tym, and I spoke with Master Stand when he visited here. Please tell him that I shall take his advice when you see him. I don't know if he will stop here again." Currat nodded at the boy's solemn attitude, and ruminated when the boy left the room: *Let's hope that I see him again.*

Currat finished bathing and put on a fresh privatecloth when he heard a noise behind him. Leather grips on his sword felt moist when he drew it and swung around in one motion, berating himself for not barring the door when the boy left. Amused green eyes greeted him from across the room. He slid his sword home with a sheepish grin on his face.

"My name is Loyl." Her hips swayed gracefully as she came to him instead of the table holding the empty trencher and mugs. She slid her arms around his neck and pulled his head down. He kissed her gently on the lips, and subsequent kisses increased in time, passion, and depth. She released him and ran her fingers over the taut muscles of his chest. "I don't do this often, and I don't sell myself. I would like to stay with you tonight, if you find me to your liking." Currat answered with a long, passionate kiss.

Their lovemaking, both skillful and fulfilling, exhausted them. They slept the special sleep of young lovers.

*　*　*

EARLY the next morning, Loyl awoke first, and kissed him awake in the dark room. "I must leave. I hope to see you again." She lit a lamp to dress. Currat started to speak and caught himself; the words died in his throat producing a sound much like a moan.

"I must. I don't work the next two days and I must see about my mother in Hagan's End."

Currat fished around in his saddlepacks and found the small writing case containing Zack's messages. He wrote a brief note asking if she would like to ride with him as he journeyed to Hagan's End.

Loyl read the note and smiled warmly. "Yes, I would, if you don't object to traveling at first light?" Currat smiled and nodded, then realized she might think he was objecting to the proposed departure time. Hastily he scribbled that it was fine.

"Then I'll meet you at the stable at first light." Loyl scampered from the room when Currat nodded again.

He had enough time for firstmeal in an empty common room. He bought bread, cheese and a skin of wine for midmeal. Loyl awaited him when Currat reached the stable as the first rays of sunlight sparkled, reflecting off the dewdrops.

They rode out together and ventured south. Loyl chatted as they rode, telling Currat about her mother and home in Hagan's End. Her company gladdened him. Her mare did not have Snowflake's stamina, and he relaxed the ground-eating pace he had maintained so far. *How large* is *Hagan's End?*

The rolling hills of Ozlid had developed into one village or town after another, with few farms or ranches in between. The largest complex, centered on the palace, made up of several towns and villages that radiated outward from four cities. He remembered Zack telling him the city of Stonefire had a population of over four million people. He could not imagine one city that large.

Arestead, Hamptor, and to some extent, Ozlid, all limited the size of their families. Their reasons derived from different motives. Arestead and Hamptor did not have the agriculture to support more people after bartering away their foodstuffs for water. Ozlid kept their families in check due to the limitations of the land. The limiting of children born in a family became a decision made by family groups from matriarch down through cousins. The governments did not try to enforce or even suggest such a thing; nevertheless, a potion that kept its users infertile had become mysteriously available. Currat was ashamed at the deprivations his country—meaning Wathdure—had caused. He went over these sentiments and agonized over what the future might hold for Ozlid. He started when Loyl placed a hand on his arm.

"There is a place I often stop for midmeal." She pointed to a shaded spot near the river, and they headed to the secluded spot. Loyl surprised him by pulling a blanket from her saddlepacks and spreading it out under the tree. Currat took the horses to the water's edge to drink, and then tethered them to graze. The last of the grain and oaks would be a dessert, and then they could drink their fill after Loyl and he had finished eating.

Loyl laid her head in Currat's lap when they finished their food and wine. He relaxed for a few minutes, and then leaned down and kissed her gently on the lips. She stirred and began putting things away while he took the horses over for one last drink.

Back on the road, Currat's thoughts dwelled on how much he favored and enjoyed Loyl's company, and wished he might talk to her. That, he realized, may not be wise. He liked her forthright manner. That same forthrightness may result in a forthright death, and too many had already tried to accomplish that. He rode on, hopefully, not showing his musings.

They passed under the mausoleum in the late afternoon, a two story building with columns beside the two brass doors rising to its peaked roof and Light's Source symbol of the sun encased in a ribbon circle on each one. Currat rode to Loyl's left with her between him and the silent watchers above. Snowflake reared suddenly and broke into a full gallop. It took Currat several minutes to calm him while he waited for Loyl to catch up. Currat nervously looked over his shoulder but relaxed when he saw no one nearby except Loyl. *What spooked him? The horse is solid mentally and physically, except when near a messenger. There's no way one could be nearby—is there?*

Their horses walked over a rise, and Hagan's End stretched out before them. The port city had supported a population of some ten thousand families before Ozlid's interference; its present numbers reduced it to half its earlier prominence. Currat looked to the harbor. To his dismay, no ships nestled near the quay, and none were anchored in the harbor. He needed to contact Captain Briggs and continue his charade until Zack arrived, or until he sailed in a month. The idea of not having a conversation with anyone for another month did not make him happy.

Currat had used silver, for the most part, to supply his needs. He knew the vouchers he carried held less value to the people than hard currency. He also had the small cask of gems and gold from Dalward's camp that would more than meet any requirements to travel alone to the Seven Realms. That possibility depressed him. *I'll cross that bridge—or sea, in this case—when I get to it.*

They arrived at Loyl's home as the lamplighters began their work throughout Hagan's End. The bright glow of the glass-fronted streetlights mixed with the last, golden rays of sunshine and gave the city warmth Current hadn't expected.

He remained mounted while Loyl took her horse to a small stable at the rear of her mother's home. Wide, green eyes looked up at him when she returned. "Where will you go?" Currat pointed toward the harbor. She nodded and thought for a few moments; she had noticed the empty port, too. "There is an inn called the *Blue Sail* across from the seawall. They will have comfortable rooms, good food, and the best service." Only one other inn offered individual rooms in town, and she felt the *Blue Sail* was by far the best.

Currat nodded, then leaned down and kissed her lightly on the lips. Loyl watched him ride toward the sea until he disappeared behind buildings.

* * *

THE steps she took to the house became lonely ones. Currat had treated her well and with tenderness. He may not have been able to speak, but he said more than enough with his eyes. She had felt his great concern over something or someone. Loyl closed the door behind her, and met her mother's smile with one of her own.

"Does that handsome man have a name, dear?"

She still does not miss a thing, Loyl realized. "A nice and gentlemanly person Mother, and his name is Currat."

"And a rich one, too." She gave her mother a questioning look. "Dear, that horse cost a fortune, and his upkeep is much more than your mare. Moreover, there is a certain refinement lying underneath his cold exterior. You can see it in the concern he shows for you."

Loyl imagined her mother was probably correct, as usual. She had based her relations with Currat on momentary feelings, and not delved into her deeper levels. She realized that her mother had discerned more about Currat in a brief moment than she had over several hours. *Well, perhaps in some things*, she thought with a smile.

* * *

ZACK had also suggested the *Blue Sail* as Currat's best choice, and Loyl's endorsement settled the matter. He easily found the inn and wrote out a note for the innkeeper explaining his needs in much the same way Zack had worded his notes.

"I have two suites of rooms, one with a sitting room, and there are fireplaces in both," the innkeeper, Yasho, told him. "The smaller suite has a small fireplace in the bedroom and both have comfortable beds."

Currat did not know how long he might have to stay, and chose the larger suite. He brushed away a helper, threw his saddlepacks over his shoulder, and followed Yasho to his rooms. Currat looked them over and nodded his approval.

"The big black is your horse?" Yasho asked. Currat nodded again. "He looks to be a fine animal. I'll have him stabled at the Tarnished Anchor, They're only a block away, and have the best stable in town. They'll take good care of him." Currat hastily scribbled a note requesting extra grains and oats; he gave it to Yasho with two silvers. "I'll attend to everything, Master Duval." Currat smiled his thanks. "I'll send some food and wine up if you wish." He continued nodding and smiling until Yasho left. He barred the door and put the room's key in his pocket.

Currat questioned his choice of using his father's name. Ozlid's culture differed from Arestead and Hamptor in their use of names. Currat's legal name in Ozlid combined the names of his sire and grandsire: Currat of Duval of Crocus, and his title would have been Master Currat if he had not been in the army. Arestead and Hamptor's populations used a birth name among friends and a family name in formal circumstances. Ozlidians generally used their birth name, while only family and friends knew the formal name contained in documents. He knew Zack would be asking about a mute man, and not using any name at all. They had agreed on the strategy while making their plans during what seemed several months ago instead of several weeks ago.

A boy came to light the small fireplace in the sitting

room and the larger one in the bedroom. Odors of fine food suddenly filled the room. Currat found the source, seeing a serving maid with a trencher of food and a small cask of wine with a mug. She didn't look nearly as nice as Loyl, but performed her duties efficiently.

Currat finished his meal and opened the cask. The bouquet alone told him its quality soared above any wine he had found outside of Ozlid so far. He settled into a plush chair and regarded his surroundings. The whitewashed walls with moldings of dark blue were crisp and clean. The sitting room held two plush chairs covered in deep burgundy, a writing table with straight chair, woven rugs in blues and whites and a cloak rack. The sea green colors and lighter shades of blue in the bedroom presented a softer feeling. Thin white panels hung around the bed. Currat did not particularly like the color scheme, but that was the least of his worries. The bedroom contained one plush chair near a window looking out on the wharf, as did the sitting room, and an open closet with a single white cotton panel covering it. One other thing in the bedroom surprised Currat; a large oaken tub.

* * *

THE serving maid returned to collect the trencher. She hefted the cask, and found it more than half-full. It pleased her. *At least this man is not a drunk like the last two occupants,* she thought. Currat made a sound in his throat, and the serving maid came to see what he was pointing at. She smiled again; *he likes cleanliness, too.*

"The boys will bring the water up in half an hour, and will empty the tub tomorrow." He nodded, they both smiled, and she left.

* * *

CURRAT enjoyed another mug of wine while soaking in blissfully hot water. He finished his wine and bath, and then crawled into bed. His sword lay beside him and a knife rested under the pillow. As usual, he worried about Zack, but then drifted off to the second night of peaceful sleep in a row.

* * *

TWO silent figures, dressed in messenger blacks, melted through the shadows, and quickly entered Hagan's End. The lamplighters put out three-fourths of the street lamps after the tenth hour; the darkness lessened their chance of discovery. They passed unseen by Loyl's home and continued toward the sea.

Real problems surfaced for the creatures that close to the sea. The salt air irritated them, slowing their progress. Their eyes did not work as well either, and they perceived strange, burning sensations over their bodies that confused them; they usually felt nothing. Their cognitive processes did not know what to do with the painful stimuli, so they kept following the stallion's growing stimulus they first felt at the mausoleum and marked the stallion's life force. Stumbling steps sounded on a nearby street, and they stopped in a dark doorway.

The drunkard's weaves were not conducive to his life this evening. Out of nowhere, a knife cut his throat, pushing through to sever the spinal cord, cutting off his startled gasp. The blade would not come free until its wielder placed a black boot on the victim's head and twisted it out with preternatural force. A rare thought formed in the creatures' minds from Wathdure. *You did well killing the fool. I am pleased.*

They hurried on, and soon stood in front of the Tarnished Anchor. The light outside the inn confused them. Their orders to stay away from the light conflicted with the circumstances. The inn's door opened, flooding the street with brilliance. Startled, they looked away from the light and scurried down the street away from the sea. Snowflake's pull, nearly as strong at the corner as at the inn's entrance, confused them more. Disappearing back into the shadows, they eased along the side street to the stable.

The Tarnished Anchor did not need to be much of an inn. The inn's owner held title to the land behind the buildings on that block of businesses. Only one inn along the waterfront district had room for stables without a paddock. The Tarnished Anchor provided stables and a large paddock to fulfill those needs, allowing the horses to exercise freely. The inn held no interest for the owner, and its neglect became immediately evident to all that entered. The last building in the block housed a smithy that provided horseshoes and repaired or made the things needed for wagons and tack.

Snowflake, let out of his stall to exercise, fled to the paddock's opposite end when the dark messengers approached the fence. They searched for a hiding place without entering the paddock. Across the street, the dark, dirty windows of a deserted building faced the paddock. Metal screeched as the messenger twisted the lock from the rear door. Silently, they searched the ground floor. A broken rear window allowed a cool breeze to flow from the sea that made them want to turn away.

Snoring alerted them. The derelict's dreams came to an abrupt end halfway through the slitting of his throat. No additional sounds came from the building while two dark shadows slipped into the second-floor room overlooking the paddock. They only needed to wait until the man belonging to the stallion arrived, and provided another life force for their attachment. One stood on each side of the window in absolute stillness.

Wathdure appeared in the room with his creatures when the first deep shadows of night fell. They pointed to the stallion across the street. He considered taking the dead body he sensed downstairs, but likely, its diseased organs made it useless. He imprinted a directive to have the body dumped in a dark area at least two blocks away and faded from sight.

The messengers transported the body as ordered. Blood from the corpse stained the street, forming a trail behind them; but their master had said nothing about blood. Soon after midnight, they returned to their vigil.

32

MOSSTELL sat across from Calbris, talking quietly and sharing a small cask of wine. "They said they were looking for two men, and their orders directed them to mete out long and painful deaths. I feigned disinterest and let them talk. They made bets on catching them together or apart. Currat's name came up first, and I put no meaning to it." He looked questioningly at Calbris, who shook his head. "A minute later they mentioned Delan Stand." Calbris started, but recovered quickly into his persona. "They don't know anything about his location, and they believe that Currat is in Hagan's End. They're to meet a man named Brodder at an inn a day's ride outside Hagan's End. This Brodder will wait there until they arrive."

"What about Briggs?" Calbris asked. He sipped his wine and tried to relax.

"Somehow they knew his ship had docked for repairs at Wellsport."

Calbris looked surprised at that. Wellsport was the port city for the realm of Deepwells, located on the southern end of the continent, and far from Briggs' usual sea routes. His ship's condition precluded him from making the voyage even in good weather, and an experienced captain like Briggs took his ship—his livelihood—seriously enough not to risk either against the major spring storms that would threatened such a trip.

Mosstell continued in his quiet whisper. "They laughed about a small but strong storm that blew Briggs off course, ripped his sails apart, and caused some structural damage. I wanted to ask them how they knew all this.

How could they know about something that took place across the sea so soon? They must have seen the look on my face. They laughed and said their master used great powers, and I would be glad that I had helped him in the not too distant future. I couldn't get any more out of them."

Calbris took a large pull of wine, as if he wanted to get something unpleasant from his mouth. He slid a gold coin across the table covered by his hand. Mosstell looked at the coin when he pulled his hand away. Surprise crossed his face, followed by an indignant glare at Calbris. "I know you don't expect payment, but you risked more this time, and the information is worth it. Use it for escape preparations if you have nothing else to spend it on."

Mosstell considered that, nodded, and placed the coin inside his tunic. "I don't think any preparations will make any difference if their master finds me out." He watched Calbris rise and nearly run an uncharacteristic straight line to the garrison, disappearing through the gates without a fuss. Mosstell could not know it had been years since his last visit.

He walked back to the great hulk of rotting timbers that barely held the *Graceful Seal* together for her return trip to Arestead, and wished for another ship. Standing on the forward deck twenty minutes later, he saw three fast birds circle the garrison once, and then fly out on a southeastern course.

* * *

THE next morning, Deepwells' garrison commander pulled High Lord Wells from his bed before sunrise after a priest woke him with a bird's message from Elizabethville. They conferred for twenty minutes before the commander left for the docks.

The High Lord received another message of a different type moments later. He gave orders for the

Captain of his Guard, Ta-Cern, to prepare to leave with him for the Spires, The Zenith Lord's seat of power on the outskirts of Stonefire.

* * *

CAPTAIN Briggs was awakened by the thud of many boots on his deck. He dressed hurriedly and appeared on deck five minutes later, gaping at the bustling activity around him. Experienced shipwrights inspected his ship. Many yards of new canvas, hauled into place, ready for ascent and experienced men labored to rig his masts.

The harbormaster approached the Captain, wasting no time on pleasantries. "Captain Briggs, High Lord Wells has commissioned work to make your ship seaworthy for strong seas. He requests your assurance that you will return to Hagan's End with all due speed. You are to wait in port for up to one month and bring one 'Master Stand' and any companions he may have with him to Elizabethville. For this service the High Lord will bear the cost of your repairs and a purse of five golds."

Five golds easily bought a new ship, and Briggs said so.

The harbormaster pointed to a newly built brigantine, fitted out and ready for sea. "If you wish, the *Flying Dolphin* is for sale for four golds, and the papers are ready to be signed." Captain Briggs stuttered for the first time in his life, but finally nodded.

The *Flying Dolphin* cleared the harbor on the morning tide with an astonished captain and crew. Briggs' new ship handled like a dream come true. The master shipwright reported her breakout cruise yielded no surprises, and she could easily stand heavy seas. Seamen had run personal belongings to the new ship for what seemed like hours before they sailed, and they had barely made the tide.

The captain's concerns gravitated to Zack Stand. *Well son, I always liked you, and now I'm indeed ready to think of you as a son. Whoever you are, you will always have a berth on my ship.* Briggs did not want to think about how the High Lord of Deepwells might have learned of Zack Stand's circumstances, but it still nagged at him. He looked around his new vessel with its polished decks and brass. *A fine ship and by damn, I'll keep her so.*

The ship carried more sail than Briggs had ever experienced on a fine day with a strong wind. He ordered full sail unfurled and the *Flying Dolphin's* response of top speed brought a swell of pleasure beyond memory. Crewmen, ordered to shifts, prepared to sail through the night. He gave orders to call him at any sign of trouble that produced smiles from the first mate and crew alike and then Briggs left to further examine his new cabin.

Bright brass fittings gleamed everywhere he looked. A broad set of windows looked out to stern, something else Briggs had not experienced before. He laughed at the extra work needed to keep his new jewel polished brightly and its wood gleaming. He could make a fortune with this ship, and an extra hand or two to keep her in top condition would not matter. New leather creaked as he opened the logbook for the first time, causing moist eyes and a shaky hand. Some minutes passed before his calm returned and the great swelling of pride subsided. His precise, graceful script flowed across the first page, putting down words his crew would have found surprising coming from the gruff captain they knew.

That night, Briggs appeared on deck while the sky above sparkled with diamonds through clear skies. First Mate Bronson smiled in greeting. "Evening, Captain, I don't know how you did it, but you have a fine ship here. She's the best built of her class I ever saw. I went over her every square inch and found nothing to complain about."

"Thank you, Bronson. Pass the word that I'll be taking on additional crewmen to keep the *Flying Dolphin* as she is now. That means I expect to see no damage done to her brass and fine woods, and no carving of initials or date marks in the crewmen's quarters, or any place else for that matter."

The First Mate chuckled, "I think they're as proud of her as you are, Captain. I'll pass the word, though I doubt it'll come as a shock to any of them."

33

CURRAT finished dressing as his firstmeal arrived. Astounded by the price of food here at first, he realized that his country had caused the scarcity that drove prices up in the first place. Again he felt the shame of Wathdure's evil. The knowledge of, and then seeing the results of what his former ruler had wrought, made him want to disseminate all he knew to everyone he could find. Awareness focused the shame of an entire nation on him, and he found that most difficult to bear. *What will the Seven Realms' Zenith Lord do to fight Wathdure? What can anyone do?*

He finished his food and mead, rummaged in his saddlepacks, and withdrew several crisp, new vouchers. The time had come to save what hard currency he possessed for a new life in the Seven Realms.

What little smoke the common room suffered from its several fireplaces the night before had vanished, replaced with fresh, pine-scented air. Two oak and glass doors protected the dining area from the common room's noise and smells. Yasho greeted Currat as a long-lost brother when he pushed open the heavy oak door. Fresh flowers were set in small vases scattered around the dining area.

Currat followed the innkeeper to the back bar and proffered the vouchers. His eyes widened. "Master Duval, these are enough for a month's lodging and meals."

Currat took out the small writing case and wrote a note saying that he wished privacy and didn't want his presence identified to anyone but Master Zack Stand. The extra funds tendered should off set any additional efforts his requests caused. Currat considered that sounded much

259

better than a bribe and Yasho must have too, from the smile on his face.

"I know Master Stand. He has stayed for short times over the years, and I'll be glad to see him once more. I'll let you know the moment he arrives."

Currat wrote another note asking for directions to the Tarnished Anchor.

Yasho spoke the directions and added, "Master Duval, please don't be put off by the Tarnished Anchor's condition. It's true one man owns both, but he has no interest in the inn after his wife died. She ran the inn, and he the stables. He is a consummate horseman, but never had any interest in the inn or knew how to run it properly. He has a private entrance to the stables, and I think he hasn't even gone inside the inn in two years or more."

Currat nodded and left to see Snowflake.

The Tarnished Anchor lived up to the report of its low status. The dark common room's smell of sour ale and scraps of rotting food on the floor proved the point to anyone's satisfaction. Currat went through a door marked "Stables," and found a meticulously clean tack room. The stalls contained clean fresh straw and barrels of grains covered one wall. The stable master approached, and Currat started to take out his writing case. There could not have been two businesses more opposite in their appearance than the inn and the stables.

"You must be the guest from the Blue Sail." Currat nodded, thinking again how tired he was of nodding and shaking his head, and looked about for Snowflake.

"Your horse is Snowflake?" Currat nodded. "Now, however did you ever label that magnificent animal Snowflake?" The stable master's laugh was strong, solid, and heartily contagious. He became serious again as quickly as his laugh began. "He has been skittish all night. My man checked him several times, and he wouldn't stir from the paddock's south end. I'll get him for you. My name is Chrylsom, by the way."

Currat walked to the paddock entrance. Snowflake saw him and pranced over to him before Chrylsom reached him. "Well, there's no doubt that he's your horse. I like a man that earns the respect of his animal."

Snowflake's jumpiness surprised Currat. He kept looking over his shoulder, and tried to get as far away as he could from the entrance to the paddock. Currat stood on the opposite side of Snowflake than Chrylsom, and hummed gently in his ear. Snowflake calmed down a bit, his nervousness still apparent. Currat feared he knew what caused Snowflake's concern. He wrote a note asking Chrylsom to keep him inside and have him rubbed down and calmed several times that day. He pressed the note and two vouchers into Chrylsom's hand. The horse master's eyes widened as Yasho's did when he saw the voucher's denomination.

Currat waved off the objections and gave Chrylsom the same note he gave Yasho concerning Zack. The stable master read the note and shook his head. "I don't remember men's names. What is his horse's name?"

Currat had to think for a moment before the name Zack had mentioned came to him and he wrote it and gave the scrap of parchment to the waiting hand.

"Ah, Spellbinder, another fine horse and well cared for, too. Now I remember the man. I will send word if he arrives, and I'll not banter your name about." Currat gave Snowflake a soothing scratch behind the ears and left him in Chrylsom's capable hands. As he walked back through the filthy inn, he noticed several bleary eyes in the common room watching his passage to the street.

The only answer for Snowflake's uneasiness has to be a nearby messenger. None of the other horses showed his irritation or nervousness. Currat returned to the *Blue Sail* to retrieve his cloak and wait until the setting sun produced the shadows he needed.

* * *

CURRAT reached the street in front of the stables and pulled the cowl over his head to hide his features. He walked cautiously past the Tarnished Anchor to the next intersection and stood in the afternoon shadows, unknowingly copying his prey. Old, scarred, unpainted wood covered the eyesore across from the Tarnished Anchor's paddock in the middle of well-kept buildings. The rest of the buildings stood with quality windows and fixtures. The brass on the doors shown even in the low light, unlike the derelict structure sandwiched between them. Dirty windows that sunlight could barely penetrate faced the street on two floors and sagging dormers across the roofline suggested a third floor or storage space.

Currat studied the dirty windows on the ground and then the second floor. Something bothered him about the middle window on the second floor, and then, satisfaction came slowly. Dark, unmoving shadows haunted all three windows, but the darkness of the shadow in the middle window exceeded its brothers. Whatever stood near that window was, or wore, black. He knew how still a messenger could stand for hours at a time. *After all, they're dead.*

He found the alleyway next to the abandoned building and followed it to the rear. The area behind the other buildings showed the care given to them. The pathway was well swept, and clean of weeds or trash. The rusty-brown trail of dried blood stood out from the shadows. He decided to follow the trail rather than attempt facing one or more messengers alone.

The trail thinned out after a few blocks, and Currat nearly missed the broken fence where the blood disappeared through. He examined the dried-out, gray wood that barely kept the fence up, swung a loose plank aside, and saw the body lying at the rear of another deserted building. He retreated quickly and retraced his steps.

Currat followed the blood's trail from behind the building where it started to where it intersected with a perpendicular alley a few yards away. He carefully left various footprints in place and checked his efforts from different angles until he was satisfied.

He ran back down the alley to the Tarnished Anchor's street. A trio of Hamptor's Guardsmen walked slowly toward him a block from the inn's far side. Currat saw their bored expressions change to surprise when he approached them at a dead run.

Their leader, a sergeant, reacted with concern to the terror that Currat feigned. "Here, here, what is this?" Currat excitedly drew his right index finger across his neck and then made it plain that he couldn't speak. He grabbed the guardsman's arm and tugged him in the direction of the body.

"Well boys, I guess we should see why this fellow is all done up like a scalded cat."

Currat noticed the guardsmen's lack of interest. *They probably think I'm crazy. I might, too, in their place,* he thought. He stopped where the blood trail started at the intersecting alleys and pointed at it. He watched while the guardsmen's countenance changed, and then they followed him closely.

Next, Currat stopped at the fence and pointed at the plank he had left ajar. A guardsman tried coaxing him closer and Currat refused, miming disgust. It became a moot point when the sergeant's expression changed as he saw the body and let out a whistle.

Currat's eyes, wide with seeming horror, met the guardsmen's leader when he approached. "You saw the blood while you walked?"

Currat nodded enthusiastically.

"Who are you and where do you live?"

Currat took out his writing case and wrote three words: *Duval, Blue Sail.*

"I want to thank you for your civic duty. You may go."

"Sir, you're letting him go?" his subordinate asked.

"Did you see the damage to the throat? The bone is nearly dust. Master Duval looks strong, but not that strong, and he has no blood on him. Plus, why would a killer lead us to his victim? No, I don't know who is committing these murders, but it's not Master Duval."

Currat nodded, then turned and quickly walked toward the *Blue Sail* with a smile. Hours passed like days. He barely touched his midmeal, and had no wine. He gave a note requested a late lastmeal to Janice when she cleared his table. His thoughts depressed him: *My stomach will be growling by the time I return, if I return. I must do something; Zack is in no condition to fight a man, much less an undead creature.* He looked at the small map he had made from his travels earlier in the day. *The success of this night falls on Snowflake's broad back.*

* * *

CURRAT left the *Blue Sail* after the lights in the lampposts had burned for an hour. His dark, thick cloak helped hide his weapons, and he bristled with every weapon he owned. He had imitated Zack's habits, purchasing several throwing knives on his journey south and using what time he could find to reacquaint himself with their use and hone his skills.

Hamptorian swords, however, did not match the standards of Ozlid's weapons. He wore his army sword at his hip, and used his left hand to keep the scabbard pointed straight down beneath his cloak. Darkness obscured his view when he pulled the cowl forward. He may not see someone watching for him, but whoever lay in wait for him could not be sure, either.

Currat walked the short distance to the Tarnished Anchor without incident. Conversation died in the common room as he walked through. A few regulars noticed the workmanship and quality of his clothing.

Purposeful, long strides swept people out of his way before he reached them. Master of the Blue Currat walked with the dignity and strength of character his father had exhibited all his life. Men instinctively knew to avoid him, and none of them had reached a level of drunkenness to take offense at the character they envied. Those men that took particular interest in his material status quickly disregarded their capricious notions and looked away.

Currat identified himself to the stable's night man-in-charge and waited patiently, regarding the professional manner the man used as he eased on the tack and saddled Snowflake. He stayed back from sight of the paddock's limiting street and the ruined building where the messengers hid. *They will see me soon enough.*

Snowflake did not want to go toward the end of the paddock he had stubbornly avoided all day. Currat made sure to keep his face hidden under his cowl. Quick, jerky changes in certain shadows caught Currat's eye from the second floor's middle window, and he smiled. Currat calmed his mount, and signaled him to go right after passing through the gate held open for him. Snowflake eagerly followed his master's instructions to head toward the sea.

Men made their rounds, snuffing three-fourths of the lampposts on schedule.

* * *

CONFUSION hindered the messengers. They could not make the connection from Snowflake to the men they hunted, and they had not seen Currat's face to make a life source connection. Their senses, diminished by the nearby sea, affected what little reasoning powers Wathdure had left them. Silently, they sped after the retreating horse.

Currat and Snowflake waited in the darkness and watched while the specters eased through the shadows.

He marveled at their approach. They shifted with the wind and shadows and one not looking, or knowing what to look for, might pass in the night never even aware of the danger. Currat saw shadows approaching in precise movements, and his mountain of doubt rapidly disappeared. They glided toward him with cloaks hanging preternaturally straight. Snowflake responded to Currat's light touch of his knees against his side, wheeled about, and walked to Seawall Street.

The street, darker still in the direction he traveled, comforted Currat. The absence of lampposts in the warehouse district, the stars and moon hidden by clouds, and the buildings' dark hulking shapes setting quiescently across from the sea provided what he needed. Currat found what he searched for by the smell of rusted iron, barrel stays, and ship's metal parts stacked high enough to form a narrow isle between two buildings.

Currat had heard officers joking about the effect of iron on the messengers at times. He did not wish to joke about anything concerning the undead beings. At the time, he had believed that they were still men, and not creatures from his worst nightmare. He remembered their soulless, dead eyes that had raised his neck hairs every time he received a messenger's pouch.

He soothed Snowflake with gentle strokes along his neck while they waited, completely sympathizing with the stallion's nervousness. Suddenly, they stood ten yards in front of him. Snowflake reacted to Currat's quick signals and burst from between iron bails, accelerating into a full gallop. He drew his sword and watched as the messengers jumped apart to let the stallion pass.

They moved fast, but not fast enough, and they were slower the closer they got to the sea. Light from a break in the clouds sparkled off Currat's sword as it sliced downward in a graceful arc to bring peace to the dead. The head flew from its shoulders and rolled toward the seawall while Currat nearly gagged from the stench.

Snowflake came to a sudden stop and his right foreleg kicked the severed head over the seawall into the ebbing tide with a resounding splash. Currat's amazement grew as the water boiled and churned around the floating head until it had completely dissolved.

Snowflake reared when the remaining messenger threw a knife. Probably saving Currat's life. Thrown poorly or thrown at Snowflake, it missed both. Currat hoped the aim was typical.

He wheeled his horse around and charged the black within black creature that stood several yards away. The messenger stumbled aside, but not fast enough. Snowflake's shoulder pushed him backward, his feet fighting to gain purchase.

Reining Snowflake in again, Currat watched the messenger jab blindly in any direction it heard a noise come from. He noticed the messenger searching with its arm stretched out while its feet jerked uncertainly, as if not wanting to follow their brain's orders.

The sea! It has to be the sea. Its vision is impaired! Currat slipped off Snowflake and positioned the horse to face away from the seawall. He slipped underneath the horse and froze. Silent boots walked past him as Currat ignored his mount's breathing. He remained still and silent while the creature slowly circled Snowflake. As the messenger walked behind Snowflake, Currat put his fingers to his mouth and blew a long, shrill, note. The messenger jerked at the sound, and Snowflake lashed out. His powerful rear hooves connected with the messenger's midsection. Currat rolled out and to his feet before Snowflake's hind legs returned to the ground.

Flailing arms jerked in wide circles as the messenger it teetered on the seawall. *No.* Currat thought, *I'll destroy you.* A sound like gushing, rotten fruit filled the air as Currat's thrown knife struck before his idea had hardly formed. It provided the added force to topple the messenger into the sea.

Snowflake shied away from the seawall. Currat covered his nose and walked toward the roiling sea. Saltwater dissolved the entire body as it had the other creature's head. Its empty uniform slowly sunk beneath the surface. Currat dragged the remaining headless creature to the seawall and pushed it over, careful to keep the creature's gore off him and Snowflake. Writhing stomach muscles fought to keep its contents down to no avail, and he lost the small midmeal he'd eaten earlier.

The smell faded while they rode toward the stable aided by a sudden hard rain, washing the street's filth into the sea. Currat handed over the reins of a now amazingly calm Snowflake to the stable's man and watched while he rubbed him down. Currat stroked his face, then reached in his cloak's inner-pocket and found the apple he had placed there before they had started out for the night, surprised it had survived intact.

Snowflake took both the petting and the apple with delight. Savoring his accomplishment, Currat returned to the *Blue Sail*. I'm hungry, he realized. The barest whiff of the creature's stench on the night wind sent another spasm through his gut when he walked through the Blue Sail's front door. Nothing remained of his stomach's former contents to lose, and his appetite returned rapidly.

34

A dangerous backlash created by the destruction of Wathdure's two messengers mere minutes apart disrupted his precious current pleasantries. His rage exploded, breaking the link to his power source. Rage and the link's abrupt cessation left him disoriented, and muddled his conceptions for several moments. Force fields buffered most of the shock, or he may have suffered real damage; as it happened, he felt the equivalent of a massive hangover.

His projected consciousness hung over the sea that ate away the creatures he had so lovingly made. Immutable laws of nature had done their prescribed duties. The evil permeated into each cell of his creations created a catastrophic effect when they encountered any salty liquid.

Reorientation of his priorities took too long. The surrounding darkness revealed nothing that might lead him to who had caused his creatures' destruction. Emissions from even a drop of the creature's gore might have led him to its source. Erupting rage doubled, snapping Wathdure's consciousness back to its physical properties—what there was of them—that comprised his being, currently in his cave, hundreds of miles away from Hagen's End.

35

JANICE, the serving maid from the night before, brought Currat his firstmeal. She went on and on about the murder of a harmless drunk two nights ago. He paid little attention until she described the destruction to the man's throat and spinal column. That sort of great and unnecessary force disturbed him. *From Zack's account, the messengers might have that kind of brute strength.* Careful not to show any undo interest, he smiled politely when Janice finished making his bed and left.

Delicious sweet rolls, hot porridge with honey, eggs, and a slab of ham earned his favor, a pleasant surprise. Currat hadn't eaten so well since leaving the palace, and he had never tasted mead. He decided he liked the warm, sweet drink.

As he ate, he looked out his window at the vista below. Sunlight sparkled on the calm sea. Small fishing vessels returned; some with mounds of fish under drenched canvas to keep them wet, and some held tubs filled with fish and seawater. Cooks from the city waited while the boats tied up at the dock, and then the haggling began. Currat could not hear their words, but it did not matter; he could tell the exchange's verbosity by exaggerated motions until one or several fish, thrown into buckets of seawater belonging to the buyers, were hauled away. Some larger purchases went into handcarts, wheeled toward establishments, mostly inns. Currat watched while a rather large cart made its way toward the Blue Sail. A knock on the door jerked his attention away. He cracked the door to find a youngster with a slip of paper in his hand. The note was brief:

Master Duval,

A young woman giving the name of Loyl is asking if you are here. Should I send her to your room?

Yasho

Currat nodded to the boy and gave him a copper. He smiled as the youth rushed off.

Moments later, a light knock at the door broke his attention. He unbarred the door and opened it a crack to find Loyl's green eyes staring at him. He smiled with pleasure.

"Mother had visitors, and I felt in the way. I hoped you might like me in your way for a while."

Currat chuckled and opened the door wide. Caressing fingers gently massaged her back while he kissed her. He barred the door, and followed her to the bedroom. "I decided you might not have stayed here, but I mentioned a mute and here I am. You don't object, do you?" Currat's smile answered any doubts she might have had.

The afternoon went fast in contrast to their lovemaking, timed to be slow and gentle. They sponged themselves playfully, dressed, and sat in the plush chairs, looking at the fire and each other's smiles, when a polite knock broke their reverie. Loyl answered it and spoke quietly to the person outside for a moment before returning to Currat. "They have lobster. Shall I order one for you?"

Currat frowned in puzzlement, having no idea what a lobster might be.

Loyl correctly identified his confusion. "You must try one—they're delicious." He motioned between himself and her. "Yes, I can stay if that's what you mean, but I must leave immediately after we eat." Currat nodded, and Loyl headed back to the door to convey their orders.

She returned smiling, and settled back into the plush

chair. "You have a treat in store. I ordered a nice white wine to go with it and green vegetables. The food and wine will cost extra. Lobster is hard to come by, so I can catch her if you don't want to spend extra for it."

Currat shook his head with a frustrated smile. He thought again of how much he wanted and needed to have a conversation with her. As before, he concluded that he dared not place him and her in jeopardy. She might react violently if she found out his heritage and he had not been honest with her, but a secret shared by two was no longer a secret. Plus, the townspeople might react badly if they knew of her involvement with him.

Currat's first glance at a whole, boiled lobster brought tears of laughter to Loyl's eyes. She showed him how to get to the tender meat, then drizzled clarified butter over his prize and watched as he took his first bite. Warm eyes beamed at her with pleasure. No scrap of tender, white meat remained as evidence the crustaceans might have lived when they finished. They washed one another's hands and faces, laughing. She kissed him, and then made her departure, promising to visit again in a week.

Currat closed the door and barred it behind her. He planned paying Snowflake a visit, but the late hour, the wine, and the afternoon's festivities had made him drowsy, and no sooner had his head hit the pillow than he was fast asleep.

* * *

CURRAT woke early, sponged off, dressed and enjoyed a sumptuous firstmeal on the second day after killing the messengers. Afterward, he watched while Janice cleaned his rooms. As she passed the window, she looked out and stopped, staring openmouthed at something below. Currat came over to see what had caught her attention.

Surprise, then relief, then despair, surged through him as he watched a ship approach. Full sails billowed several hundred yards out to sea without a trace of blue or yellow jibs or a red forestaysail. Zack said few ships harbored at Hagan's End, and he had described none like the one running with all sails to harborage. Currat returned to his mead.

He ordered a bath in an attempt to distract himself. His thoughts, however, were scattered over several subjects. *Zack, lad, where are you? Damn, you had better be alive or I'll never forgive you. I must tell you about Loyl. Do you know about lobsters? You must arrive, you must.*

* * *

CAPTAIN Briggs and his crew remained in fine spirits while the *Flying Dolphin's* crew furled her sails, leaving the gallant as its source of power to enter the harbor and gracefully dock with the touch of a master's command. She pulled smoothly into her harborage without incident.

Briggs' heart soared when he saw the fishermen's faces putting out to sea. He reminded his men that they remained on duty, and were not granted shore leave, as such, since they might to leave port at a moment's notice. They started to argue until the good Captain announced that their pay directly reflected their readiness. First Mate Bronson received his third briefing on whom to look for and to sound the ship's bell if he saw him or made contact with another using the proper names. Briggs left the ship smiling.

First, he headed to the only sign painter in Hagan's End. The man balked at having the order ready that day until the captain cheerfully handed over double the payment. The printer cut off his tirade in mid-sentence and Briggs walked out the door, humming.

Next he hurried to his home, where he barely greeted his housekeeper, and made his way to the cellar. Under the light of a candle, he opened the false side of a barrel labeled *Rags and Canvas*. Well-oiled rods silently rotated inside their hinges, as the strongbox door opened. Briggs dropped the remaining gold coin in a pouch containing silver. He replaced the purse and retrieved several high-amount vouchers. With the safe-hold secured, and once more appearing as an innocuous, sealed barrel, he headed back upstairs.

Next, Briggs went to the Harbormaster's office, and paid up his fees to the somewhat befuddled man. Briggs read the Sailor's Request, and picked men's names he knew, and a cabin boy from a family he had known all his life. *Finding sailors poses no difficulty; finding dependable sailors poses great difficulty.*

He spent the rest of the afternoon rounding up the cabin boy and men he wanted, ordering them to report to First Mate Bronson and then to settle into their quarters. He ordered Bronson to keep two men on deck at all times. Briggs chuckled at the consternation on the men's faces at his order. They looked questioningly between themselves, probably wondering if protocol usually changed to that degree on fine, new ships. He was quite sure they had not the firsthand experience to question such decisions on how to run such a ship that they now, proudly, called home.

He picked up the posters from the signmaker's shop and made his rounds to the warehouses and better inns, lightening his load by one poster at each stop. His last stop was the Blue Sail, where Briggs personally exchanged his old poster with the new one proudly listing the *Flying Dolphin*'s nomenclature and numbers. He enjoyed an expensive and good lastmeal in the Blue Sail's dining room, fending off questions from curious friends and Yasho while he ate.

36

BRODDER was relinquishing his watch when he saw the matched blacks pulling the coach into Ballrand's inn down the street. He admired the vehicle and its horses for the second time. Black wormcloth covered the windows, allowing the passengers to see out, but none to see them. The rider next to the driver jumped down, stretching to limber his tall, muscular body, raising his arms in the air as he swayed. Brodder wished his men were more like the ones he was watching.

Black doors opened, and the muscular man reached in and gently carried a supine figure wrapped in blankets to the inn's entrance. Brodder could not ascertain the figure's gender. An attractive women and girl followed them inside. The coach doors closed, and the driver swung up to his perch and drove the team slowly around to the inn's backside.

Brodder admired the horses again. They remained in good shape to have covered the amount of ground they had since he last saw them. The driver obviously knew his business, and the passengers let him do his job. He envied the coach's owner; if only he could count on his men to do their duties so well.

His musings soured on the subject in general. *Wathdure said my men should arrive today, and no one fails to meet the Master's schedule more than once. Now, if they only treated their mounts as well as that coach's horses, we could ride for Hagan's End tonight.*

* * *

BALLRAND noticed black boots in front of the table he had just wiped down. Dark eyes stared at him when he straightened. A man stood before him, representing the exact type he hoped never required ejection from his inn. Harshness radiated from him, and the cruelty within him tripped Ballrand's subconscious, and set danger signals clearly ringing.

"Ballrand, is it?"

Ballrand nodded and set his rag down on the table.

"I'm looking for friends."

Ballrand listened as both Zack and Currat's description, in exacting detail, spewed from the man in a rehearsed diatribe.

This man is no friend to himself, much less Zack and Duval, Ballrand concluded. "I don't recall such men stopping here. Perhaps the first one you described came through here a month or so ago, but no one I've seen recently matches your description."

The dark man nodded, never taking his eyes from Ballrand's face. "I'll pay a hundred silvers for information about them and their whereabouts. It's very important that I find them."

Ballrand only nodded. The man watched him closely for several seconds, then turned and departed without further comment.

Sighing with relief, the innkeeper went upstairs to Zack's room.

* * *

ZACK's displeasure at Ballrand's information ate at him. It confirmed his fears that Wathdure's efforts to find him continued, and he might not give up until they reached the Seven Realms, and perhaps not even then.

Ursel and he sat in a darkened room, watching the inn across the road. Less than an hour went by before four horsemen stopped, briefly went inside, reappeared and led their horses to the inn's stables. Zack and Ursel focused on the men's faces. Zack knew none of them. The horses, however, posed no problem. Tall, black stallions that matched the horses Currat and he rode left no doubt as to their identity. A fifth horseman arrived an hour later. Then, near midnight, the dark man and his five cohorts saddled up and rode south at a ground-eating pace.

A knock sounded at the door, which Ursel cautiously answered. The serving maid entered while the two men kept talking. Zack's voice sounded tired, and that made Ursel nervous. "There is no need to hurry tomorrow. I think it best to arrive after dark, and start our hunt for Currat quietly."

"Excuse me, sir. A man that looks much like you recently stopped here. Is he the one you seek?" Loyl asked.

"He's a friend of ours. Do you know him?"

She nodded. "Master Ballrand says that you're good people, and helped Captain Briggs put down a mutiny. Is that true?"

Zack laughed. "I did help Captain Briggs, and I hope we're good people. I hate to think we went through all this trouble for the wrong reasons."

Loyl smiled shyly. "Duval is at the Blue Sail. He told Yasho that he was expecting someone, but I didn't hear who he's waiting for."

"We thank you for your help," Zack said. "Was Duval in good health when you saw him last?"

"Oh, yes sir, he was in extremely good health." Loyl's face turned several shades of pink when she heard what tumbled from her mouth.

"Shall I tell Duval who helped us?" Zack's smile told much.

She smiled back and nodded. "My name is Loyl, and I must admit that the two of you look enough alike to be brothers."

"We're quite similar in many respects." Zack watched the pink flare again on Loyl's face. She curtsied and hastened out, balancing empty trenchers and mugs as she went.

Zack looked circumspect. "Well, that simplifies things. Hopefully, Currat will remain indoors tomorrow. I still think we should arrive after dark. We will go directly to the *Blue Sail* and see if Captain Briggs is in port. Spellbinder may be mad at me again by this time tomorrow—he hates ships."

Zack watched while Ursel nervously danced around something he wanted to say. "Ursel, we have been through too much for you to fear speaking to me on any subject. What is on your mind?" He leaned back in his chair and waited for the big man to settle himself.

"I have been thinking that those of us in Hamptor and Arestead might be able to do more in the Seven Realms than in our own countries. Many of us expected Ozlid to invade before now. I think I know why Wathdure hasn't done so. He already has everything he needs from us without the expense of a war, not that there would be much resistance. Hamptor and Arestead are in much worse shape than it appears." Zack nodded. "I don't know what we can do in the Seven Realms, but I would like to go there and see."

Ursel paced back and forth in front of Zack. "Those of us located in the best of the remaining fertile ground have been lucky the last few years with the best crops that could be expected under the circumstances. We don't delude ourselves—we know that luck and the weather won't hold forever. Hamptor and Arestead may soon find themselves choosing between foods or water. Our people are dispirited, with no hope for their future."

Ursel paused, as if considering his next words carefully. He stopped in front of Zack. "I'm sure there are many men and women that think like I do. You saw for yourself how the village's men came to your aid. That made every one of them—and me—feel better that we did something to fight back." He hung his head for a moment before continuing.

"I know I should not have said anything to Darmon, but I asked if he would go to Hampton in my stead. I didn't say why. He said he would." The distress in Ursel's words faded when a smile formed on Zack's face.

"Do you—do you think your Zenith Lord will permit those of us that wish to come to the Seven Realms for training in martial skills?"

Zack watched Ursel sit down looking like the world's weight hung on his young shoulders. Zack took a few moments to puzzle out the possibilities: *The idea has merit, but I have no notion what the Zenith Lord may think. The kings would have to agree, and the issue of funding might arise, well, perhaps not. Gaz did say that the Zenith Lord and his Captain of the Guard were disturbed over the situation caused by Ozlid.* He saw Ursel sitting on the edge of his seat. *Damn,* he thought, *he's actually sweating.*

"Ursel, I have no objection to Darmon delivering the message, and I have no problem with you presenting your idea to my Zenith Lord. I'll not try to second-guess him, however. You will be heard, and that's about all I can promise."

The tension drained from Ursel upon hearing Zack's answer. *The boy has strong feelings and perhaps the impetus for a new force,* he thought. "Just remember, I'm not a diplomat, not a policy maker, and I don't have direct access to the Zenith Lord."

Zack watched the effect of his disclaimers, and the determination in Ursel's countenance pleased him. *Sometime in the past,* he considered, *I must have been that driven.* "Tell Darmon the content of your message to the king tomorrow when we're on the road, and if he still agrees, you may come with us." Ursel looked as if he might whoop for joy. Instead, he collapsed into his chair and to Zack's surprise, breathed deeply for a few minutes.

Zack slept in the chair for the rest of the night, and was happy to do so. He also felt determined to sit up in the coach the next day. *They will leave the mattress with Master Ballrand and good riddance to it.*

37

CURRAT ventured down to the common room to stretch his legs at mid-morning. Yasho rearranged ship's posters, first one way and then another, when he saw Currat approach. "It's a marvel, Master Duval."

Currat's expression prompted Yasho to continue.

"Captain Briggs has that fine new ship in port. He will be able to trade from further distances, and that will help Hamptor and us. We have little gold and silver due to those damn vouchers. I wish him great achievements in his travels." Currat barely heard the last of Yasho's words as he ran out the door.

Currat didn't stop running until he'd reached the ship. A pair of guards stopped him from going up the gangplank. He wrote a hasty note that he wished to see Captain Briggs. Neither of the guards could read, and a shoving match started and had almost progressed to near blows when a well-dressed man came to the quarterdeck's rail.

"Yield!" he bellowed, then came down the gangplank to find out what was going on.

Captain Briggs gasped when he first looked at Currat's face. He smiled, wondering if Briggs believed Zack stood there. Briggs brought him aboard. *One look at my eyes and he will know I'm not Zack. One can change their hair color, but not the color of their eyes.*

Thirty minutes later, they returned from Captain Briggs' cabin after much writing on Currat's part. Captain Briggs saw him off the ship, and returned to his cabin. Currat's brisk walk toward the *Blue Sail* came with some relief after making contact with the captain. *Now, if only Zack will show up, I'll be quite happy.*

38

BRODDER's second informed him on the way down to the common room that the inn's last guests had departed. He had just checked, and the innkeeper's wife remained safely tied-up in an upstairs room. *I must reinforce my instructions to the innkeeper to follow my orders if he wants to see her alive again.*

Brodder started when one of his men burst into the main room. "I saw him. I saw him." The man gasped for breath and doubled over from the run. Brodder's wish for men like those he had seen the day before crossed his mind, and he sighed.

"Lower your voice. We don't want the innkeeper to hear. Where and which one did you see?" *It's time our luck changed,* Brodder reasoned.

"Going on that ship we saw. It was Currat, and he went alone."

At last, I'll see my old friend, he thought with a smile. *It has been entirely too long. This will be touchy.* He needed two men watching the innkeeper and his daughter in the common room and one watching the innkeeper's wife upstairs. *Currat must be subdued with three men, in the open and in daylight. I don't think he'll go out at night.*

Brodder went to the stable in the rear with his two best men. He chose the Sailor's Quest for the separate stable. He could not risk the large stable behind the Tarnished Anchor after seeing a black stallion stabled there. Brodder realized Currat would go to ground if he saw more stallions like his suddenly appear. They needed to be able to leave at a moment's notice, and had left their horses saddled for that reason.

They had just turned onto Seawall Street when Brodder saw Currat heading the opposite direction. He dug his heels into the stallion's sides. His men followed, galloping down the adjoining street, and then turning left onto the street running parallel with Seawall Street, leaving a trail of Hamptorians cursing their backs. They cut up a side street that emptied into Seawall Street and reined in their horses. Brodder signaled for quiet and left one man holding the horses. He whispered his intent, and the brightest of his men nodded.

Currat heard a call from the wharf, stopped and turned to look at the ship. He started when he heard a step behind him. Brodder struck before he could react, and caught him under the arms as he slumped over, unconscious. Brodder mounted and ordered Currat thrown over his saddle in front of him. They rode out on Seawall Street at a trot to the Sailor's Quest, ignoring a few startled glances. Brodder noticed the saddle's pommel pounding into Currat's mid-section and smiled. He felt queasy about what lay ahead of them, but the victim being Currat almost made it right. *Currat and Zack Stand, the bastards who killed my baby brother at the palace, will feel pain, a lot of pain, before they die.*

One man stayed behind to unsaddle the horses while Brodder and his second—with Currat slung over his shoulder—burst into the common room, passing the wide-eyed innkeeper and his daughter. After waving the man carrying Currat upstairs, Brodder turned to the innkeeper. "We have one of the two men we came for. The remaining one will be along soon enough, and if you follow our instructions as we told you, your wife will live, and we'll be gone."

He headed upstairs before they could answer. *Give them a little hope,* he decided. *Always leave them with a little hope.* He chuckled while taking the steps two at a time.

Brodder went into the middle of the five rooms on the hallway's outer side. The innkeeper's wife—he'd never asked her name—glared at him, tied to a chair and gagged. Her eyes widened at seeing Currat's unconscious body. *They're going to get wider before this day is through,* he thought.

Brodder's men had removed the small bed from the room earlier, replacing it with a table from the common room. One started tying Currat to the table.

"Strip him first," Brodder hissed.

Moments later, Currat lay tied to the table, naked, with his feet toward the woman. She tried to look away and could not; her head, tightly positioned straight ahead could not look anywhere but on Currat. She gave up squeezing her eyes shut and saw with fear and horror seeping deeper into her being. Brodder chuckled louder this time.

He punched Currat in the lower abdomen, and was cocking his fist to deliver another blow when the door opened. "Please refrain from doing my job for me, Master of the Blue Brodder," a quiet voice said.

Brodder looked into the dead eyes of the man he feared the most next to Wathdure. He wondered if Master of the Blue Dalsom retained any human feelings, and what had happened to him since they left training. He had become Wathdure's torturer, although, rumors said that Wathdure could make Dalsom's administrations seem like the caress of a babe. Brodder wished never to test the accuracy of those rumors, or find out their truthfulness firsthand, even as an observer.

Dalsom's voice and style made Brodder as uncomfortable as it would most of those who encountered him. *Why can't I just beat it from him? Perhaps that's all I require.* A bad feeling about future events formed.

* * *

DALSOM watched Currat. *He's probably fighting dizziness and nausea while his cognizance floats from nothingness to sharp pain,* he thought. Currat's eyes stayed shut, and Dalsom knew he was trying to hide his awareness, but he was sure the bound man could not help feeling the pain of the ropes tied to his wrists.

Dalsom smiled and spoke in his flat, dead voice. "Loosen those bonds to allow his circulation to return." He glanced at Currat. "He's awake." One man held Currat down while another loosened the ropes until Dalsom's satisfied smile stopped them.

Currat opened his eyes and grimaced with pain. Dalsom rested against the table. He leaned over to look into Currat's eyes, and saw fear in the man he had not seen in years. Dalsom opened his senses, and felt Currat's fear and humiliation. Pleasure swept through him as those feelings flew over his psychic link to Wathdure.

Dalsom's words sounded dead and far away, but the pleasure remained as control seeped into his mind. "Master of the Blue Currat, I'm acting on specific orders from the Master of Masters. Do you understand me?" Dalsom waited patiently while Currat blinked several times, and finally nodded. "Good. I require all documents you took with you when you left the palace and the location of Zack Stand. Do you understand?"

The innkeeper's wife moaned and Dalsom felt the wave of fear escape from her. *Ah, she has identified our accents.* No one paid her the slightest attention.

Currat flinched as Dalsom's dead words came inches from his face. "Master of the Blue Currat, try moving a hand. Either one, it does not matter." He easily lifted his right hand a half-inch before the ropes restrained him.

"Good. We're getting along. Now, you know what I require. Are you going to provide those answers?"

Dalsom spoke to Brodder as if he read his earlier thoughts. "My methods have proven most effective, Master of the Blue Brodder. Mere beatings and the application of pain alone seldom work as we need." Dalsom pulled a leather pouch from the floor and removed a black cloth, precisely folded and tied with a black ribbon.

He placed a small table next to Currat's head. He held the folded cloth where the bound man could see it. Dalsom spoke calmly and enunciated every word exactly. "I am going to show you everything I will be working with, and explain in detail how it will affect you, Master of the Blue Currat. Do you understand?" Currat nodded. Dalsom placed the bundle on the small table out of Currat's line of vision. He gently untied the ribbon and painstakingly unpacked his instruments. Dalsom ceremoniously smoothed the cloth and arranged the contents in a specific order. He neither rushed his actions, nor wasted effort.

Brodder shuddered, bringing a thin smile to Dalsom's face. The ritual—the only way Dalsom described his actions—continued without interruption. Seven steel rods, each one the thickness of a small reed, were evenly spaced across the top portion of the cloth. Twenty razor-sharp slivers of extremely thin steel, lined up in two neat rows, covered the cloth's bottom half. They measured an inch long and a quarter of an inch wide at the blunted end, tapering to a needlepoint at the opposite end. Dalsom reached into his leather pouch and pulled out another bundle wrapped in the same black cloth and ribbon.

He gave Currat an appraising look. "I don't think we'll need these, but one never knows." He placed the bundle to the side of his instruments, away from Currat. "Master of the Blue Currat, you know that you can raise your hand or feet—and they're such nice feet—to signal your acquiescence at any time."

Currat nodded. Sweat beaded across his brow in the cool room.

Dalsom picked up a sliver of steel. He held it between the tips of his thumb and index finger over Currat's head. He asked, as slowly and as precisely as he had said everything else up to that moment, "Master of the Blue

Currat, can you see this?"

* * *

DALSOM's slow speech got on Brodder's nerves. He considered how it was affecting Currat and surprisingly, found himself glad he did not know. Brodder knew his brother was a raving lunatic and, with his temper rapidly cooling, also realized that Zack Stand and Currat had acted in their own defense. It seemed simple.

That notion began to weigh heavily on him. His thoughts came rapidly. *Why am I realizing this now? What is different? I'm further away from Ozlid. No, Wathdure. I'm further away from Wathdure.*

* * *

CURRAT nodded to confirm that he saw the shiny piece of metal. "Now, Master of the Blue Currat, anytime you want me to stop my loving care of your body, just signal with your hand or foot." Currat nodded again. "Good. Now, before I start, are you absolutely sure that you don't wish to comply with those two very simple requests?"

Currat opened his mouth and tried to speak, but coughed instead. Dalsom raised his head gently, almost tenderly and gave him a sip of water from a mug. He gently laid Currat's head on the table and asked, "Is that better, Master of the Blue Currat?"

"Yes, thank you."

"You are most welcome." He raised his eyes to Brodder's intense stare. "Master of the Blue Brodder, you never told me that I would be working on a gentleman. Never mind; it alters little, although it's nice to work on someone that's not a senseless beast from time to time."

Brodder's anger rose at Dalsom's slow exactness and formality. He watched while Dalsom faced Currat, still holding the sliver of steel. His reservations about Dalsom and their circumstances grew.

"Master of the Blue Currat, you may signal me at any time when you're ready to give me what I require of you and I'll stop my actions, as I have said. Now, you see this little piece of steel that I showed you before. It really would be in your best interest to speak."

* * *

CURRAT looked into eyes vacant of any emotion. "I don't know where Zack Stand is at the moment, nor do I know that he's coming to Hagan's End. He was badly wounded, he may have died." Currat sent a prayer to the Great Creator that that was not the case. "The documents you spoke of are locked away at the Blue Sail, and I don't think you will be able to get to them with the men you have."

"Will you please excuse me for a moment, Master of the Blue Currat?"

"I would be delighted."

"Now, now, Master of the Blue Currat, you must not jest with me so, I might think I'm mistaken about the gentlemanly part."

"I meant no offense."

"I'm so glad to hear that. I'll return shortly." Dalsom motioned Brodder outside.

* * *

BRODDER followed the torturer without speaking.

After closing the door to the room, Dalsom looked to insure that the hallway held no witnesses before speaking. "Master of the Blue Brodder, Master of the Blue Currat has just told us the truth. I may torture him until the hell we're all going to have fellowship in becomes a paradise, and the Dark One willingly bows to the Creator, but you won't get another answer more truthful than the one he gave. Master of the Blue Brodder, what do you wish me to do?" Dalsom acted as if he fought to get the words out.

Brodder answered with clenched teeth. "Dalsom, we have known one another for years, and you knew Currat. Don't you think we can do away with all the titles?"

"Formalities, Master of the Blue Brodder, are how we remain civilized, and I do insist that we remain civilized." Dalsom watched as his same, plodding cadence raked over Brodder.

"Master of the Blue Dalsom, we must be absolutely sure that we regain the information that left Ozlid with Master of the Blue Currat and Zack Stand." Brodder's awareness of Dalsom standing, patiently waiting, with his head cocked slightly to the side irritated him. A smile, which translated to a mockery of any emotion, played across Dalsom's lips. "Master of the Blue Dalsom, do what you must to be absolutely sure that his words are truly spoken and we'll proceed from there." Brodder let out the air he was involuntarily holding. *Will I regret those orders? Currat has always been a decent man. Wathdure decided the task should fall to me because of my brother. I would have forgiven Currat by now, especially when I learned what actually occurred. Where has all my anger gone? Was that from Wathdure's influence also?*

"As I said, Master of the Blue Brodder, I'm satisfied that he spoke truthfully. You're the one that must be convinced." Dalsom cocked his head to the opposite side and retained the same smile Brodder found so incensing. "I also agree with what Master of the Blue Currat said about you trying to get the papers at the inn. It would create more disturbance than the Master of Masters wants at this time, or so he just informed me."

Brodder sighed. He knew Wathdure could communicate with many of his men from a distance, but he never thought it could be this far. "Continue then, by all means, and let me know if there are any changes to his story, Master of the Blue Dalsom."

"As you command, Master of the Blue Brodder. Perhaps you should watch for a while to insure yourself that I'm working as you have ordered and in Ozlid's best interest."

Brodder made a sweep of his arm and slightly bowed. He followed Dalsom into the room, thinking, *he's still carrying that damn piece of metal between his fingers.*

Dalsom resumed his place at Currat's head. "I'm sorry, Master of the Blue Currat. I am afraid that Master of the Blue Brodder is not convinced of your words and therefore we must continue. I'm going to take this little sliver of metal and place it tenderly underneath the little fingernail of your left hand. I'm afraid that it will be quite painful and for that reason, we must gag you. It will go better for you if you don't try to fight me. That could make a real mess of your finger."

Dalsom took a thick, white cloth from his bag of misery and gently folded it under Currat's left hand, while Brodder and his underling filled his mouth with the privatecloth they had stripped from him.

Dalsom ordered Currat's little finger immobilized. Brodder watched; sweat glistened on their prisoner's upper body. Brodder could not think what the sliver of metal may do or the pain it would cause. *I know it'll hurt like hell,* he thought, *but how much will it weaken him?* Brodder's contemplation came into sharp focus when Dalsom placed the pointed end under the tip of Currat's fingernail. He held it there, brought the cloth up and over Currat's hand and transferred the pressure to the metal from outside of the cloth. He pushed slowly, with no trace of emotion showing.

Currat's body arced off the table while he tried to scream around the gag. Blood welled up into the white cloth. Brodder cringed and looked over his shoulder. The woman's eyes bulged before she squeezed them shut. The man holding Currat's hand looked away as well, disgust on his face.

Currat's body fell back on the table, his rapid breaths slowing as he fell unconscious. Dalsom patted the finger dry of blood and left a clean cloth in its place. His detachment to the stimuli in the room became paramount, and Brodder felt sick at what he knew was only the beginning.

* * *

PAIN seared throughout Currat, and vivid memories returned. He had never known such pain could be inflicted on another person, and a single realization flooded his consciousness: *I'll feel it again.*

He made the mistake of moving his left hand only once. The metal caught on the cloth, and he hoped he might pass out again. Somehow, he didn't scream, but felt someone stir beside him. *Damn, he knows. How long was I unconscious and can I fake it?*

* * *

DALSOM immediately noticed the change in Currat's breathing. He lifted the cloth off Currat's hand and the removal of the slight pressure brought tears to his subject's eyes. Dalsom gently pulled the privatecloth from Currat's mouth, lifted his head, and gave him a sip of water. "Now, Master of the Blue Currat, that was not too bad, was it?"

Currat looked into Dalsom's dead eyes and didn't answer. Dalsom laid his head back on the table with the same care he performed each task. "Now, do you see this?" the torturer held up one six-inch long metal rod.

Currat's teeth clenched in sudden agony. Dalsom looked down to see Brodder leaning against the table, his shirt rubbing against Currat's left hand. Brodder followed Dalsom's eyes and jumped as if scalded.

Dalsom continued. "Look closely. You will see barbs pointing down near the point and barbs pointing up above them." Currat looked away. His eyes slowly came to rest on what Dalsom was holding. "Those little tiny barbs are quite sharp. A superb craftsman, Aresteadian actually, makes them for us. The rod will go through your flesh, unfortunately, tearing little chunks from your muscle and bone. The result, should you live, is quite painful for an exceedingly long time. Now, I want you to rest your concern for your physical body. I have made quite a study of this, and I know the correct placement to keep from harming the major blood vessels. The object of this exercise is to position the rod's barbs next to a bone, in this case, your rib. The barbs will cause you no little amount of discomfort while I rub the rod against the bone. Be assured that the body usually does not sustain permanent damage. You will recover, or I should say, I have found it so in most cases."

* * *

BRODDER wanted to leave. He wanted to be anywhere except in this room. He knew he had made a serious error. Once started, under his orders, Dalsom would not stop this insanity. Even without Wathdure's directions, his continuance remained undoubted. *The only way to stop this insanity is for me to kill Dalsom and that means my death, probably by Dalsom's gentle endeavors.* Then it dawned on him that Dalsom wasn't following his orders; he followed Wathdure's commands! *If I had ordered Dalsom to stop, would I now be lying on a table next to Currat?*

Currat's death, encompassing the worst agony a man could bear, might last quite a long time until either Dalsom put an end to him, or his strength failed and released him. Brodder's conscience told him too late that he did not deserve what Dalsom was doing to him. Death, yes—he had committed treason against Ozlid and he should die for it. But not like this. Brodder's thoughts took a sudden turning. *Was the treason against Ozlid . . . or against Wathdure?* In the past, he had always considered the two as the same. Now, farther away from Wathdure's influence, his mind reacted differently, and many things he had previously taken for granted now raised questions he had rather leave unexplored.

Currat's scream, muted by the gag, ceased Brodder's deliberations and forced him to focus on what was going on nearby. Dalsom had inserted the rod into Currat's left side. Currat's feet and right hand banged on the table. Brodder heard a loud *thud* behind him.

The innkeeper's wife had fainted; she and the chair were lying on her right side. Brodder righted the woman, smelling the stench of vomit around the gag's edges. He leaned the chair against the wall. Bounding, quick pulses along her jugular told him she still lived. It made little difference; the deaths of the innkeeper and his family were certain—he would leave no witnesses behind. Still, no reason required that she watch Currat's struggle for the waiting arms of death now. Currat's renewed scream brought Brodder's attention again to Dalsom's deeds.

Dalsom spun the rod while moving it up and down in what looked like a gentle caress. Currat's body fell limply to the table once again. Dalsom stopped moving the rod, but left it in place. Brodder's hair threw drops of sweat when he shook his head, trying to wake from the all too real nightmare he was seeing. Finally, he could take no more, and made for the door.

Dalsom's voice stopped him. "Master of the Blue Brodder, he will be unconscious longer this time. Your men must stay here and keep watch while I go downstairs for lastmeal." Chills spiraled down Brodder's spine when he caught the glimmer of fire and passion in Dalsom's eyes. He projected a strange countenance, as if sated of all he desired. Brodder left the room, hardly aware of his journey to the common room below or the deepening shadows while evening flowed into night.

The innkeeper's words broke into the walled fortress of his mind. "My wife, Surelle, is she unhurt? We heard noises made in agony. You . . . you said she won't be harmed."

"Your wife is fine. She's bound to a chair, and hasn't

been harmed in any way, uh . . . uh." Brodder looked blankly at the innkeeper

"Jadel, sir, my name is Jadel."

"Jadel, have lastmeal prepared for us." Brodder said over his shoulder as he approached his men sitting in the corner. The two of you, go upstairs and relieve the man up there. If Currat comes around, give him some water as gently as you can and don't touch him or anything protruding from his body." Brodder slid warily into a chair at their table.

"Gently? Sir, he's a traitor. He should—" Brodder cut him off with a wave of a hand and leaned into the table, his face inches away from his subordinates.

"Currat has already told us the truth," he whispered. Both men looked startled. "He's going to die in unimaginable pain by Dalsom's loving embraces. Currat was a good soldier and officer; he served Ozlid well for many years. If he truly committed treason, he deserves to die. Nevertheless, no man deserves what is happening upstairs. Dalsom is under Wathdure's control. I strongly suggest that you don't talk with Master of the Blue Dalsom; you probably won't like the conversation. Now, go up there and see for yourselves."

The two men glanced uneasily at one another.

"*Now!*" Brodder barked.

39

NIGHT settled over Hagan's End. A black coach, pulled by black geldings, rounded onto Seawall Street and stopped in front of the Blue Sail. Ursel helped Zack out of the coach and walked with him to the entrance, supporting his wounded side.

Yasho rushed to greet his new guests. "Master Stand, you have been hurt." He blushed at stating the obvious.

Ursel led Zack to a plush chair, and looked down on the hovering innkeeper. Zack's voice was strong, and he did feel much better, considering that he had rode sitting up. Thankful for the coach's new springs, they still did not ease the roll and sway. "Yasho, I'll need a room for two ladies, another for this gentle giant beside you and myself, and one more for my driver. I'll just rest here for a few moments. Please ask Master Duval to come down and join me, and let me know the moment Captain Briggs docks." Zack savored the luxurious chair's softness, savoring anything that his body sat on that did not bounce and sway.

"The rooms will be ready shortly, Master Stand. Master Duval has been out since mid-morning and Captain Briggs is master of that splendid ship you must have seen in port."

Concern crept into Zack's voice. "Then send someone to fetch Captain Briggs at once and my driver, Darmon, will need instructions to the Tarnished Anchor's stables." Zack waved Darmon over to him when he came in with Zack's saddlepacks. "Darmon, Yasho—" he nodded to the innkeeper, "—will give you directions to the best stables in Hagan's End. Search for a large, black stallion, and ask if

295

it belongs to Master Duval. If there is more than one, find out each owner's whereabouts. Use the pretense that you are interested in a matched set of horses. I'll be fine here. Ursel, help Darmon unload the valuables and our traveling clothes. The rest will be safe enough in the coach. Then go with Darmon and take a good look at the stallion. Currat is missing, and the men that have him will be riding stallions like Currat's horse. Be quick. We may have little or no time to save Currat, and remember that he has done much for Hamptor and Arestead at a great cost to himself." Zack knew neither man needed the encouragement, nor did they need the warning of speed's importance, but his instructions did seem to build a fire under them.

Yasho sent a boy to find Captain Briggs, and then saw to Doris and Rachel's needs personally. Their impression of Hagan's End and the Blue Sail's quality plainly showed. Rachel had squealed in delight upon seeing the ship that lay at anchor, and the inn's fine furnishings left her quietly awed.

Finally, Ursel and Darmon returned from their information-gathering mission, right about the time that their rooms were ready. Taking one look at Zack, Ursel reached down and gently picked him up from the chair. Zack started to protest, but immediately reconsidered. Once in his room, he ordered food and wine for all of them and they sat around, solemnly sipping wine, waiting.

The knock at the door brought Ursel from his seat and racing across the room. Captain Briggs entered and Zack motioned for Yasho, who stood in the doorway, to join them.

"Yasho, I'm going to ask you to do something quite from the ordinary—well, several things, actually. I don't want anyone here to know our names or anything else about us. We're recluses, and our privacy is precious to us." Zack winked at Yasho, and he smiled happily in return. His smile didn't last long, however. "Captain

Briggs, did Master Duval visit you this morning?"

"That he did, Delan, and he wrote that he would await you here." Briggs looked distressed as well, and Zack realized his condition might have caused it. *Perhaps he does value my friendship,* he thought.

Zack grinned at the captain's concern and continued. "Yasho, you know that I come from the Seven Realms. I have found a great evil in Ozlid. Master Duval saved my life at the cost of his friends and father's lives to get valuable information out of Ozlid. He's Ozlidian, and that's why he didn't speak."

Yasho and Captain Briggs immediately nodded.

"I suffered my wound while escaping Ozlid, and he also suffered much there. Master Duval has that information in his room. We must get it aboard Captain Briggs' ship and to the garrison at Elizabethville, even if my men and I are killed." Briggs nodded. Zack looked directly into Yasho's eyes. "I know this betrays your trust to a guest of your inn, but you know Captain Briggs and me. Will you do it?" *What I ask could easily destroy the Blue Sail's reputation if made known,* Zack thought.

Captain Briggs cut in before Yasho could answer. "Deepwells' High Lord effectively paid for my new ship, and sent me here to be ready for Master Stand's departure to Elizabethville. I have faith that what he says is true." He sat back and folded his arms across his chest. He did not smile, even at the surprised look on Zack's face.

Yasho considered for only a moment. "Have you made arrangements for our king to be informed of this knowledge?"

Zack nodded. "Darmon has that task."

"Then I'll allow you to take only the documents. Captain Briggs and I will accompany you to search for them."

Zack continued. "Yasho, the men that have Master Duval rode in today on black stallions matching his. Ursel and Darmon tell me that Currat's is the only stallion at the Tarnished Anchor. Ursel reported men on black stallions nearly collided with people on the street at full gallop. We need to know what inns have stables, as well as any places that might afford them privacy, such as a large estate that they might easily take over. We believe Ozlid's agents will torture Currat . . . Master Duval, to death in order to find out what he knows about me. He does not deserve that. We don't know if we should trust— or perhaps *who* we should trust—in your army. We cannot have them killing Master Duval."

Yasho delayed a moment looking between Briggs and Zack. "I'll return shortly with all you will need. Also . . . I think I know where he may be held."

40

CURRAT's rise to consciousness grew into a stairway of pain that he could not deny. His first stratagem, to control his breathing and hope Dalsom would not notice the change, failed. The feeling of burning oil raced up his left hand in waves of intensity. The fire of live coals lodged into his side and he focused on the air for the putrid smell of burned flesh. He remembered slivers and rods of shiny metal and understood. He must play Dalsom's game—or insane fantasy—to remain alive. He did not know how long he might marshal his inner forces, but every minute the other man talked gained him time without additional pain. He prayed for unconsciousness to return quickly.

Dalsom shifted at a man's startled gasp after seeing Currat's right hand jerk. Finding the guard looking out the window, Dalsom turned to his prisoner. His suspicions soon bore fruit; he poked Currat's left breast with the sharp point of a rod. The involuntary jerk brought a little more fire to his eyes. The slight curl of his lips radiated no joy.

"Well, Master of the Blue Currat, you have returned to grace us. You have grown on us, and I'm most delighted to have your company again." Dalsom gently raised Currat's head and poured water around the privatecloth. The men in the room watched in repulsive fascination. Dalsom picked up another rod and twirled it above his prisoner's eyes.

Currat wanted to close his eyes, but his fear stopped him. The men turned away.

Dalsom's pleasure increased as he watched the internal

struggle. "My, my, Master of the Blue Currat, it's such a pleasure to work with a man who realizes the true position in which he finds himself. Tell me, Master of the Blue Currat, have you ever wished for children? I understand that you have not yet wed."

Currat nodded, the pain pulling the muscles of his face into a mask of horror.

"Why, that's wonderful, Master of the Blue Currat. After our next little amusement, it's still possible to have children. That avenue evaporates quickly while I continue, however." Dalsom did not bother to keep up the illusion that he was still trying to obtain information; a fact not lost on the guards.

He continued in his slow dead voice, his eyes blazing with interest. "Why, Master of the Blue Currat, you're such a handsome man, so well graced with masculine features. Quite well endowed, and, of course, your beautiful feet. It's a shame that we're not allowed a more comfortable respite but duty calls, as they say."

Dalsom splayed Currat's scrotum, immobilizing his testicles. He motioned the guards to hold him down. They hesitated a moment, but only a moment.

* * *

CURRAT tried to scream when the rod's sharp point punctured his scrotum. His eyes glazed over. He felt nothing; his thoughts swirled in a peaceful fog, and strange concepts of dreams came slowly.

He did not feel the rod cut through the bottom of his scrotum, and he could not see bits of various pieces of testicle caught in the rod's barbs. He did not see the various colors of human tissue that flew from underneath his arching body before the twirling rod stopped, imbedded into the table. Nor did he realize his hips tried to escape the table, or that the rod firmly held him in place.

* * *

CURRAT's unconscious condition visibly upset Dalsom. His face registered the first real emotion the guards saw, and both sweated from the first signs of acute nausea. Breath hissed out from his nose as Dalsom returned to his usual demeanor and the fire ebbed from his eyes.

"It seems that Master of the Blue Currat's stamina is not as strong as I first determined, or perhaps it's stronger than I believed. I'll watch him. You may tell Master of the Blue Brodder that we'll get nothing more from him tonight."

41

YASHO returned with three burly men at the same time Briggs returned with two of his guards. Both men had screened those they chose about their feelings concerning Ozlid and helping an Ozlidian that tried to help their country. Yasho spoke first. "This is Sondek Rus, Eckert Oldsi, and Byrn Daven." He introduced Zack's party except the women, who had returned to their rooms.

Briggs spoke next, "This is Rod Stemmer and Jafon Demlish." The new arrivals looked nervous and expectant. Byrn Daven looked around looked hesitantly, and then cleared his throat. The small amount of his remaining hair formed a horseshoe ring around his head. About Zack's age, he looked older, with broad, bushy, eyebrows expressively used as part of his speech patterns, full lips, and a flat nose. Muscles abounded in all the men, and Byrn definitely was no exception. "Master Stand, meaning no disrespect, sir, but why should we trust you?"

"Would you trust the words of one of your own?

Nods around the room signaled their acceptance.

"Ursel, would you like to comment?"

Ursel stood up, and the room got quiet from the look on his face that softened by the time he spoke. "I'm from the village of Creekwide, a hard day's ride from the border, the eastern market, and the fortress. When Master Stand first arrived among us, the village learned of him after he saved a woman and her daughter from two murderers. The lady and her daughter are across the hall if anyone wants to speak to them." The men looked on Zack with more respect and their expressions softened.

"When he next came to us, he was wounded and near death. The wound he received escaping Ozlid with one of

302

their officers."

Zack frowned when Ursel identified Currat as an officer in the army, but remained quiet.

"Zack discovered much information about Ozlid. So much, that Ozlid sent a large raiding party to kill them and recover the information." Several heads looked nervously at Zack for a moment. "Darmon here and I have received the information. Master Stand bought the coach we rode in to get here and paid for all our needs. I'm convinced that by helping Master Stand, I'm fighting Ozlid."

The general agreement among the men that Zack saw pleased him. "The officer that helped Master Stand escape is the man known here as Currat Duval. He's one of the few that knows the magnitude of the evil that rules Ozlid. It greatly surprised me to hear that the people living on this side of the mountain range are exiles from Ozlid for crimes they are accused of committed." A murmur went around the room. "The general population of Ozlid knows nothing of the crimes committed on Hamptor and Arestead."

The murmur got louder, and Ursel raised his hands for quiet. "Wait—if you think about it, it makes sense. How could a whole kingdom support the treatment that we received from its leader? I know I'm young, and that I have not seen much of this world, but a whole kingdom? Can you imagine mothers, grandparents, and children wanting to propagate such evil? I just don't believe that a kingdom could survive with that much evil contained in its borders. I always believed that Ozlid didn't permit us beyond the mountain range for fear we might do them harm. Now, I believe the reason is to keep knowledge of their affairs with us secret from their general populace, and it makes more sense when you look at the extraordinary steps they have taken to keep us out and their people in."

"I know Master Stand saved two of our people that he

didn't even know," Ursel said. "I know that he's fighting to get information to his ruler they call the Zenith Lord. I know he has treated Master Yasho and Captain Briggs fairly. And here is something you don't know: Master Stand is the one that put down the mutiny on Captain Briggs ship." Zack watched while several nods and a look of remembrance showed here and there.

Zack started to interrupt Ursel a couple of times and then decided against it. He never guessed the shy, quiet, young man's feelings, so thoroughly delineated, ran so deep. *It's amazing what a little confidence and self-esteem will do.*

"One more thing. There are Ozlidian agents in Hagan's End that are trying to find and kill one of their own, one who risked everything to help Zack. Is that not enough reason to provide help for Master Stand's cause?"

Ursel sat down while three men said, "Yes." as one.

"Master Stand, how can we help?" Byrn asked.

Zack's side hurt, but he stood anyway. Ursel jumped to his side and placed a strong arm for him to use as he willed. "Ursel, I never realized you're so gifted in oratory." Ursel blushed, and the ice broke. "Men, the Ozlidian agents will, and probably have, tortured Currat to the point of death. I saw the cruelty they're prepared to use, and I'm sure you have heard of it from the border, especially about the men who died, flayed alive, that reported they knew of the black stone. Would you men like to know about the black stone that's known in our lands as the Dark Stone?" The subject brought new alertness to the men.

"Two millennia ago, my lands, the Seven Realms, that you call Jewel, fought a war between the forces of good and evil. The Great Creator, which we call Light's Source, won the war. Some of our weapons included the Great Stones of Power. The one stone made and wielded by the forces of evil, is the Dark Stone that you seek. I went to the border and described the Dark Stone. I knew, the moment my description of the black stone passed their requirements and they sent me to see the ruler of Ozlid, that you and we fought the same evil we had encountered so long ago. Their leader confirmed it when he said, 'That is not the stone I search for. I know of that one.' How could he possibly know of an evil that old unless he was a part of it?" The men around the room looked startled, but they also nodded with Zack's conclusion.

"Currat is a brave man. He's not a traitor to the people of Ozlid, who are much the same as your people and mine. He's a traitor to the evil that infests that land. Now, you can see exactly what my interests are. I have discovered an old evil operating near my lands that I believe attacked us over two millennia ago. I need to take this information to my ruler, and I have made provision for the kings of Hamptor and Arestead to receive the same information. Now, will you help me?"

There was a resounding *"Yes."* from the men in the room. Zack took Ursel's arm and immediately felt his strong physical support. He had just heard his emotional support.

Zack remained standing, exhausted, but knowing they couldn't stop yet. "Yasho, you know your competition best. Have you the list I spoke of?" The innkeeper held up a piece of parchment. "I want your men to see the black stallion at the Tarnished Anchor's stables. The men we're looking for rode in on identical black stallions. They look enough alike that I doubt their trainer could tell them apart. Find the horses and the men we want cannot be far away. Don't approach them, and be careful not to be seen."

That caused a few grumbles. "You cannot approach them now," Zack said, raising his voice to be sure everyone heard him. "They are dangerous men, and I suspect they are holding some of your neighbors hostage. How else could they have a place to torture anyone if that's not the case? They may be in a deserted building, but they're looking for me, too. They have no idea I'm in

Hagan's End." *I hope,* Zack thought. "Our best bet is to look for an inn or large estate that would provide them with necessities and the space they need." Zack sat down before his legs failed him, but the strength of his words remained undiminished.

"Scout the horses and report back as soon as you can. I believe you can see the top of Captain Briggs mainmast from many places in the city. Captain Briggs, can you raise a lantern or pinion as a signal?" He nodded. "Come here as quickly as possible if you see the Captain's signal." Yasho's men filed from the room and tromped down the stairway.

Zack placed his attention on Captain Briggs and his men. "Gentlemen—" The honorific fitted Briggs, but the two men with him looked more the types that devoured large animals, like bears, with no hesitation. ". . . I want you to stand by as our attack force." The statement had the desired effect, as the men beamed with satisfaction. "Darmon will get the coach from the stables and have it out front. You will go with Ursel and me when we find their location. Get the weapons you're best with, and come back here as quickly as you can."

Ursel, Yasho, and Captain Briggs stayed behind. "Yasho, it's time we paid a visit to Currat's room," Zack said. They walked down the hall and Yasho opened the door.

Ursel assisted Zack while he walked directly to the saddlepack that had contained the documents when he last saw them. He fumbled in the pack and came up with the large roll of documents. The party retraced their steps, and Zack happily settled back into a plush chair in his room.

Yasho stared at the thick roll. "Master Stand, that's a lot of documentation. Are you telling me that Darmon knows all that's written there?"

Zack chuckled. "This is the general history of Ozlid over the last three hundred years. I'll have it copied in the

Seven Realms and send it to your king and the king of Arestead. The important facts are the ones that I told you. That's all we know about the current situation." Yasho and Captain Briggs nodded.

* * *

ECKERT Oldsi and Byrn Daven rode out to the outskirts of Hagan's End. Sondek Rus went on foot to search the area surrounding the waterfront. Dark obstacles offered no problem as he confidently and quietly covered ground he already well knew. Large, dark buildings surrounded him as he reached the warehouse district, located a hundred yards or so beyond the Sailor's Quest inn. Nose hairs bristled at the faint remains of a stench he had heard about earlier in the day. Nothing but oppressive gloom projected from the shadowed warehouse that he registered as nothing from the ordinary. The skies had cleared earlier that evening, and the large half-moon helped.

High walls seemed to tighten inward while he walked past large bales of rusty metal and on to the street running behind the buildings that narrowed to an alley one block before reaching the Sailor's Quest. Approaching the inn, he remembered the stable in the rear that no one used; most preferred the better stables four blocks away. The barred doors to the stable looked familiar to him from helping Jadel store the inn's old equipment. Barring the doors might be a natural thing to do, although, he had never noticed it before.

As he approached, the large, black eyes of a large, black stallion stared at him through the crack in the wall. Sounds increased when the horse's traveling companions recognized their neighbor's surprise. Heavy step falls alerted Sondek, and he sprinted to the stable's side. He dove between two barrels as the rear door to the inn opened and a square of light lit the area in front of the stable.

307

"Damn stallions. Why in the seven hells do they have to be so damn jumpy?"

"Yes, they're jumpy, but you don't complain when they outrun any horse that might be chasing you, do you?"

The light shining behind the two men kept them shadowed, and Sondek couldn't see their faces. However, he did not have to see them or the horses no matter how big and black; their thick Ozlidian accents told him all he needed to know. The raging impulse to kill these murdering tormentors and decimators of his kingdom slowly abated; the reasoning of Zack's words resonated through his hate. The stable doors creaked shut while the guards quieted the stallions, and Sondek silently retraced his steps. Purposeful, long strides quickly took him away from the stable. One dark block away, he started running the several blocks to the *Blue Sail* as fast his legs could go.

* * *

DARMON smiled when Sondek rounded the corner and burst through the double doors, usually locked at this time of night. He knew they had found the Ozlidian agents. Skittish horses rocked the coach. "Easy, my pretties, you will run soon."

* * *

THE pounding on Zack's door jerked his eyes open from a troubled sleep. Blurry legs carried Ursel to the door in the sitting room while he knuckled his vision to focus.

Panting breaths eased while Ursel helped Sondek to a chair. Rippling upper body muscles, used nearly every day as a warehouseman, did not entail running. Spent, Sondek labored to utter the sounds Zack prayed for: ". . . Sailor's Quest . . ." Yasho had followed Sondek to Zack's room with his kitchen boy. He flicked his hand, and the boy flew from the room, heading for the *Flying Dolphin*.

* * *

SWEAT and dust covered the last man to report to Zack's room as Yasho placed a large drawing of the interior and surroundings of the Sailor's Quest on the table in Zack's sitting room.

"It's owned and run by Jadel and his wife, Surelle, with his daughter, Risa, helping out with the cooking, serving and cleaning. The inn is in an 'L' shape. Four large rooms contain sleeping pallets and face the sea. Along the side street, there is an upstairs hallway with five rooms on each side. These are private rooms, with one or two small beds each."

The distaste on Yasho's face amply conveyed his feelings on the service Jadel provided. "The common room lies below the four large rooms, and the kitchen and Jadel's private quarters lie beneath the private rooms. The stable is separate, located on the side street with an alley between it and the inn. A staircase leads to the second floor, and a door in the alley to the ground floor. Oh and there is some storage space in the attic, but I don't know about access to it." Yasho stepped back.

Zack studied the inn's diagram and the streets, alley, and stables adjacent to the building. He looked up. "Thank you, Yasho. A good business man knows his competition." The innkeeper smiled.

"We know there are six of them in total. At least two will be in the common room to keep watch. I suspect that they have Surelle, and possibly Risa isolated from Jadel. One or more of them will be asleep. Rod, Jafon, and Darmon, you three will go and take their horses to the Tarnished Anchor's stables as quietly as possible. The horses are used to carrying different men, and you will be able to lead them without difficulty. Walk them in a staggered line. The Ozlidians will hopefully think it's normal traffic. Return as quickly as you can, and tie your horses a block away and out of sight. You three will keep anyone from leaving through the rear exits. Stay hidden as best you can. We don't want to tip our hand too soon. They will kill Currat if they get the chance when we're discovered." The three men nodded and gathered in a corner of the room, away from the table, quietly planning amongst themselves.

"Sondek, Eckert, and Byrn will play the part of friendly drunks. You three will stagger to a point just inside the door. The last one in will stumble back out and signal the number of men in the common room. That will also tell us how many are upstairs. Jadel may try to get you out of there as quickly as possible. Whatever happens, do not let on that you know the true circumstances until we strike. The Ozlidian agents will be watching Jadel closely. They'll know something is not right if he suddenly looks relieved. Is there any reason that Jadel might question your coming in to drink at his place?"

The men looked at one another and shook their heads with guilty grins. "The three of us have done just that on several occasions after drinking all night," Sondek said. "Without breaking the door, I mean."

Zack chuckled. "Better yet, raise more noise than you usually do, and get rowdy in a friendly manner. Have several mugs of ale and sip only small amounts. You'll have to spill most of it, just keep your wits about you. Remember, the Ozlidians will kill you if they suspect anything amiss. That should keep you sober and on your toes." Their expressions showed he had made his point.

Zack thought a moment before continuing. "Now, when the three return from sequestering the horses, the three friendly drunks will go in and start making noise. Then, when enough time has passed for the agents to settle down and become accustomed to the group, Ursel will go up the rear stairway and lure the guard out. If there is a guard downstairs, which I doubt, Darmon and his group will kill any that come out . . ." The three men looked over at hearing the name of one of their group, and Zack stared back at each of them in turn ". . . very quietly." Ursel looked a little surprised. "Remember, they may not be in the private rooms, but I believe they will be there for several reasons. Ursel's concern will be finding and eliminating the guard if any. If you don't kill the guard, make sure he's unconscious, tied securely and gagged and go to find the room where they're holding Currat. Signal the room's location if possible. Each room has one window. He'll hold up fingers to indicate how many rooms from the back of the building.

"Yasho, Captain Briggs, and I will be in the coach out of sight. If they're not in the upstairs rooms, Ursel will join us for new instructions. The rest of you will maintain your positions. Darmon's group will dispose of any guards and put them out of sight. This is most important; we must not raise the alarm until Ursel makes his move. You will swarm the inn when we hear the outcry that Ursel will cause. Noise and confusion is on our side at that point; use it. We will start after firstmeal, when the Ozlidians morning's activities are completed.

"Try to think of any holes in the plan, and report to me any concerns you have. Otherwise, I suggest that you get some rest until daybreak."

The men left quietly, talking to themselves. Zack signaled Captain Briggs and Yasho to stay behind. Yasho nodded and held up a finger and then left, returning a few minutes later with bread, cheese, and brandy. He ordered the kitchen staff to serve the same, minus the brandy, to the men downstairs. Zack figured dawn was no more than two hours away, and prayed Currat still lived. He and the remaining men needed a quiet place for a while.

* * *

URSEL watched Captain Briggs and Yasho leave the sitting room with more than a little trepidation. Zack's voice startled him. "Nervous?" Ursel nodded. "Scared?"

Ursel started to shake his head, and then nodded again. "Good. The lack of fear on any man's part in your situation is a cause for great concern. Ursel, have you ever butchered livestock in Creekwide?"

"Many times. The villagers called on me to help with the larger hogs and sheep."

Zack showed no emotion from what Ursel answered. "Did you cut their throats from behind?" the big man nodded. "Killing a man, even a man you despise, is a hard thing to do. He's not your enemy because he personally hates you. He's your enemy because someone has ordered it. I don't believe that you will fail to carry out your part in this. I do believe that it will be much harder than you think. Be ready for that and when it hits you, don't let it deter you. It does not get easier. Be ready for that, too. Come up from behind your target, and think of those swine at home. I don't think you will have a problem once you see what they have done to Currat. I trust you, Ursel, and I know your abilities. While I believe Yasho's and Briggs' men are on our side, I don't *know* them or their true capabilities. I know yours."

"I understand." Ursel became understandably pensive. "How do you know Currat is not dead?"

"That's simple; they're still at the Sailor's Quest, and they have made no attempt to reach me here." He let that sink in before he continued. Ursel's dark countenance convinced Zack that he understood some of what lay ahead of him.

"Ursel?" The young man looked up, appearing a little older. "The construction of that inn will be wattle and daub for the ceilings on the second floor. It's quite possible there is more than one access to the attic in a building of that size. You should be able to silently step along the supporting beams. Your weight will be unfelt and unheard, unless a real idiot built it. If that's the case, you can say they hired you to fix the roof." Ursel smiled with Zack, and the gloom left his face. "However, the wattle and daub will be fragile, and easily broken."

Ursel nodded, smiling anew as he saw Zack's plan form. "Don't try to jump through without something under you. The paste fragments and sticks are sharp, and might cut you badly. I watched you practice with my knives. You are quite good. I'll give you four throwing knives and a needle knife."

As Ursel started to ask, Zack pulled the object from his belt, where it lay carefully hidden on the inside of his trousers, and tossed it to him. Leather was wrapped securely on the small hilt, which gave way to a steel projection in the shape of a cross, with four razor-sharp edges that narrowed to a sharp, sturdy point. "That is definitely not a throwing knife, it's too unevenly balanced. It will slide easily between a man's ribs and into his heart, or through his nose to the brain. It has drawbacks, too. The four sides are quite sharp and it's easy to cut yourself if you're not careful. It's only a good tool for infighting." Ursel slid the scabbard inside his trousers and tied the holding strips to his belt in the same manner that Zack had worn it.

"Thank you, Zack," Ursel said a bit hesitantly.

"It will go well, and you'll do fine. Get some rest now—try to relax." Zack chuckled. "I always hated it when they told me that."

Ursel smiled as he stretched his long legs out in front of him, then leaned back and closed his eyes.

The lad is good; he has a chance, Zack surmised.

* * *

SUNRAYS danced across the black coach. Grim determination was etched on Zack's face as he looked out on the men gathered round the open door. The expressions of Yasho and Captain Briggs matched his own.

"Gentlemen, there is only one piece of advice that I can give you now from my own experience." Zack felt no need to explain how extensive that experience was. "The best-laid plans are only a jumping-off point, and they may well fall apart when you land. Keep the overall objectives in focus and flow with the river of events while they unfold, and you will do well and stay alive. Good luck." Zack sat back, pleased with the amount of seriousness balanced with just the right amount of bravado. The men separated off in twos and threes toward their objectives.

Darmon stopped the coach and set the brake out of sight from the Sailor Quest's front windows on Seawall Street. Yasho, Captain Briggs, and Zack said their farewells. Yasho left the coach to circle around and take care of people straying into harm's way. Zack had added that assignment when he'd learned that Yasho held the position of mayor in Hagan's End.

Yasho had tried to reject Zack's payment for the services he'd provided at his inn. Zack quietly explained that he wished Yasho to remain in business when he next came to Hagan's End. In the end, silver had changed hands, and left both men pleased.

Captain Briggs left to make the *Flying Dolphin* ready for sea. Zack sat in the empty coach. Doris and Rachel remained onboard the ship with their belongings safely stowed away. Zack had seen Doris briefly that morning. Worried lines settled her brow over dark eyes from the lack of sleep over the past day.

Rachel, oblivious to the danger surrounding the men about her, had become enthralled with the ship almost to the degree Captain Briggs was. He had brought the ship about during the night after Spellbinder, Snowflake, and other possessions were loaded without incident. His four longboats were tethered, and his men waited for the command to assist the ship into the prevailing currents, no matter the tide. The First Mate and the newly hired Second Mate waited in the rigging with most of the crewmen for orders to cast off and make sail.

All they needed now was to collect their last passenger.

42

"**MASTER** of the Blue Currat, I'm aware that you're awake."

Currat opened his eyes. "Good morning, Master of the Blue Dalsom." His voice had shriveled to a croak, and Dalsom listened hard to catch his words.

"Oh my, you have no idea the pleasure I receive when working with a gentleman of your quality. When one's father embodied protocol, it is expected. He will be greatly missed in Ozlid." Dalsom watched with pleasure while Currat's right fist tightened into a fist. His smile faded when the fist relaxed as quickly as it had formed. The one guard in the room grinned at Currat's style, but said nothing.

"Pardon me, Master of the Blue Dalsom, I must relieve myself. I'll return shortly." He left the room before Dalsom finished his curt nod and walked to the end of the hall, nodded to the guard at the door and went in the last bedroom on the hall's outer side to use the chamber pot. He stopped on the way out.

"Do you think we could get away with killing Currat without Dalsom catching on?" he whispered.

The guard sadly shook his head. The table of steel slivers and rods drew his eye when he returned to the room; he silently cursed the thing that wielded them.

"Master of the Blue Currat, see what I have here." Dalsom held up another sliver of steel. Currat managed to show none of the fear that tore through him.

* * *

SLOWLY, silently, the stable's doors swung opened.

315

Darmon smiled at the newly applied oil running from the old hinges. The men entered and immediately went to each horse, proffering apples and sweetstones. They stroked them and spoke softly to them. The horses had rarely heard soft voices, and had never received treats before, and reveled in the new experience. Bridles went on with a minimum of effort, and they walked out on their leads with only the sounds of crunching apples heard in the early morning silence. At the alleyway entrance, Ursel waited for the men to return.

The inn's backside facing the stable had no windows. A closed door at the wall's center on the second floor matched the one under the small balcony. All remained quiet. The spacious second floor platform, with an oversized door made to accommodate the storage for larger pieces of trader's wares, stood closed and silent. Ursel picked up several small stones and silently went up the stairway. He stood behind the door and threw a stone down to the stairway's bottom, then a couple further up, and finally he threw the largest stone to the stairway's middle steps. The men below slipped from sight underneath the staircase and landing.

The rear door cracked open a few inches, and then opened wide enough for a man to exit. The guard looked to his right in time to see Ursel's fist shooting toward his jaw. Being a large man did not keep him from rising a few inches off the floor from the punch's force. Ursel caught him under the arms and eased him to the floor. He knelt beside him, drew his needle knife, and waited. It did not take long for the man to come around. His eyes fluttered, and he said, "Great Creator..." No one could mistake the heavy Ozlidian accent.

Ursel shoved the thin knife through the right nostril and pounded it into the brain. He pushed his arms around his back and in one swift motion pulled him erect. The body, totally limp and quite dead weight, made no sound. Ursel bent to the corpse's waist and hoisted him over his shoulder. He saw no one in the hallway, but could hear voices coming from a room halfway down the hall. Another sound made him wince when a loud moan haunted the hallway.

After checking for any noise from within, Ursel went through the first door on the left and let the corpse's dead weight slide onto the floor. Catching the feet, he silently laid the body out. Looking down on the dead man, Zack's advice about killing came to him. He had been correct about the emotional strain and Ursel greatly valued his knowledge and advice. Stepping out onto the balcony, he held up three fingers and pointed to the outside rooms, then quickly returned inside. He eased the door open a crack and peered down the hall.

Voices came from the middle of the five rooms on the street side followed by a pounding on the floor from his target room. Heavy footfalls on the stairway at the hall's opposite end made him close the door, leaving barely enough space to see the middle room. He felt more alert and aware than ever in his life, even if his racing heart felt like it was about to pound out of his chest. A man from below went there and knocked once, then opened the door and entered. Ursel looked quickly while the door was open, but found no access to the attic space above.

He could hear parts of sentences from the people inside. The accent sounded as unmistakable as a bugle call; no wonder Zack had told Currat not to speak. Every sound, magnified many times in Ursel's mind, jarred his concentration while he slid out into the hallway. He silently crept—as much as anyone his size could creep—down the hall's length. Eight steps led down to a small landing. Additional steps continued down in the opposite direction, leading to the common room. The door at this end of the hall opened inward. Ursel eased it open and entered the room. He found saddlepacks for six horses piled on the floor and bed. Voices from two rooms away drifted through the partly open door.

The door opened, and louder voices increased Ursel's heart rate. Heavy footfalls came toward him down the hall. Ursel pulled the door open a few more inches and stood behind it.

The footsteps stopped in the hallway outside. It swung farther open, and a man entered the room. His eyes widened as his head jerked backward when he passed the door's edge. Ursel pulled his head back and cut his throat in one swift motion, silencing his scream before it passed the knife blade. The look of total surprise registered on the man's face, but not a sound came from him except soft gurgles. Ursel silently laid the twitching man out, pulling the bedclothes from the bed and placed it under the man's neck to catch the blood. He looked down and smiled weakly. Only a small drop of Ozlidian blood was on his boot, and his clothes remained clean. He rubbed the glistening, red blood off the polished boot while blood dripped down the splattered wall.

He stayed alert, anxious energy radiating throughout his body. These men, or men like them, had killed countless thousands of his people, even if it happened a hundred years ago. He also considered the many men and some women that never returned from the giant markets, their spirits had joined with the Creator through the deeds of these men or their cohorts. He held a single ambition: *two are dead and there are four more to kill.*

A door slammed open downstairs, and boisterous, out of key singing echoed up the stairway. Ursel smiled at the sound. About to head back into the hallway, he glanced around the room one last time, and stopped as his gaze fell upon a square hatch in the ceiling.

* * *

BRODDER sat at a table in the corner of the common room. He refused to stay in the room and watch the senseless torture of a man he'd come to respect for his courage any longer. Windows vibrated and sound exploded as three drunks broke through the door marked *Closed* to the world at large. A loud song, if it could be called that, filled the room as two of the men staggered toward the bar and a scowling Jadel, while one ran back through the door. A few seconds later, noisy vomiting could be heard outside.

"ALE, Jadel!" Eckert Oldsi slurred.

"Ssh, ssh . . ." Byrn Daven responded, pointing his finger at the frowning innkeeper.

Brodder sat back down. *It will be better to let the drunks have their ale than the trouble it'd cause to throw them outside*, he thought with a nod at Jadel, whose helpless expression he found comical. The innkeeper hurried to the door and closed it on barely functional hinges as one man stumbled back in.

* * *

THE bed's mattress crunched as Ursel climbed on it. He reached up and pushed at the square cover in the ceiling that had caught his eye. The loud commotion downstairs covered any sound he made. Or, anyone else, for that matter, he realized. Hinges squealed until it lay completely open and resting on the inside of the ceiling at an angle.

The hatch was definitely not built for someone his size. One shoulder had to go through first with his head tucked down until he could squeeze his other arm through the tight space. Skin tore along his right ribs. He dangled in mid-air for a few moments until his hands found enough purchase to push more of his body into the attic. Ursel sat for only a few seconds before rolling onto the small square of supported planks. Ventilation vents at both ends of the building gave him a small amount of light. He closed the cover, and made his way along the beams and around storage crates to the middle of the attic.

In between each beam, small, straight sticks stuck out from the outer branches used in the building's wattle and daub construction. Globs of hard, white plaster filled the space around the sticks. One man's voice sounded louder and deeper than the first voice. He could make his words out with little effort, ". . . and you will tell us when and where you're to meet Zack Stand. Tell me now, and you will have a quick death. You know how long we can make the pain last, Master of the Blue Currat." The voice's dead tones sent anger coursing through Ursel.

Ursel determined that the man might be directly under him, and judging by the ties to the beam, he must be standing with his back to the door. A quieter voice came from where he judged the room's middle to be. He could not make out the words, and each time they stopped, he heard a moan, and then silence.

A lid from an empty crate stubbornly gave way a few feet from the loudest voices. Each time Ursel moved it, his heart leaped into his throat. He guessed it was about four feet on each side, and it barely fit into the space where larger branches made a crosswork pattern connecting to the support beam over the door, with barely enough space to miss the door jam. *What if I land on Currat?* he thought.

At that moment, an agonizing moan filtered up through the ceiling. Ursel held his throwing knife in his right hand and the needle knife in his left. He jumped up from the crossbeam and pushed down from the ceiling with his clinched fists using all the leverage he gained to crash through the wooden square.

The wattle and daub below him collapsed, and he fell into the room below in a shower of broken sticks and chunks of plaster. Ursel's knee protested as he landed hard on his feet and thrust the needle-pointed spike into the closest man's chest. Death captured a look of total surprise on the shocked face.

Catching a flash of movement on his right, Ursel swung around and threw his other knife. The quiet-voiced man lunged forward as the knife caught him in the right shoulder. He screamed. Ursel pulled the spike from the chest of the first man and plunged it into the screaming man's chest as he stumbled on from the momentum of his lunge.

The dying man's last words were mixed with a soft gurgle. "I thank you . . . and may the Great Creator have mercy on me . . ." he whispered. "You have released me . . . from an evil . . . greater than you can imagine . . ." The supreme effort to say those words allowed his fading eyes to close after regaining a tinge of humanity. Dust from the shattered plaster floated in the air, making Ursel sneeze. He saw nothing else in the room to challenge him, only a woman tied to a chair in the corner, and a brutalized man in front of him.

* * *

BRODDER became more and more irritated with the loud men. Jadel looked worried, and stayed away from his customers. Risa sat in a corner away, from both groups. Sondek, Eckert, and Byrn played a hand game, placing bets on the number of fingers held out when each man pulled his arm from behind at a signal. It was a game enjoyed by children and drunks.

He wondered about what was going on upstairs: *I never dreamed a man like Dalsom could exist. He has changed into something inhuman. Currat killed my brother, and I made great noises about catching and killing him. My brother's actions might have caused his death at any time. He was crazy as a loon. How many sword and knife fights required his rescue? I know of ten or more, and there must be others. Currat does not deserve what is happening to him. Great Hells, no one deserves to die like that. I can see only one way to save Currat, and that's to kill Dalsom. What reaction will my men have—?*

A great noise sounded the second floor, like a ceiling might have collapsed. The three drunks straightened up and their arms flew from behind their backs. Brodder saw bright, sharp, steel flying toward him. He tried to dodge.

321

Four inches of warm steel imbedded into the middle of his chest with enough force to shatter his sternum, pierce his heart, and sever two major blood vessels. Brodder slumped to the floor staring at the knife's hilt sticking out of him. Everything around him slowed. *I feel no pain. Am I dead?*

With the last of his strength, Brodder focused on his remaining man, crouched behind an overturned table. His men moved slowly like his mental processes. *Am I dreaming?* He watched the man make a desperate run for the rear door. He looked over his shoulder as he yanked the door open. Brodder saw the look of pain mingled with surprise in crystal clarity as the point of a sword emerged from his lower right side dripping blood. A big man pulled his sword nearly all the way out, twisting it as he did so to cut the abdominal muscles, allowing the intestines to slide to the ground. The dying man reached down, trying to replace his organs into the cavity, until he jerked once and fell back after receiving a second thrust from the same sword through his chest.

Brodder's eyes fluttered and focused again as the dead man's legs were slowly pulled from view. Another big man carried a bloody bundle with limp left hand and foot showing, out to a familiar black coach.

The irony made a slight smile appear on Brodder until his eyes slowly closed and his muscles completely, and permanently, relaxed in death.

* * *

CURRAT lay face up and nude, his limbs spread wide and tied to the table. Rods protruded out of several places on his man's body. Ursel approached the woman tied to a chair and gagged. She motioned with her head toward Currat after he cut her ropes. He nodded and returned to Currat's side. Steeling himself, he reached down and extracted the closest rod. Tiny bits of flesh came with it, stuck to barbs carved into the metal. Currat did not make a sound when the rod slid free. Ursel removed six rods through Currat's body, learning from his first mistake, pushing the rod through from the top stopping the bards doing greater damage.

The last one remaining, impaling Currat's left testicle, made Ursel's stomach heave just looking at it. The speared testicle, sticky with blood and things he didn't want to think about, made a soft, popping sound when he dislodged it from the table and gently pulled it up the rod's shaft to leave enough space to free the barbed point from the table. Hard steel slid through the organ without further damage while Ursel fought to keep the contents of his stomach down. Currat moaned weakly. Then the sound of agony filled the room as the rod cleared its unnatural home.

Ursel cut the ropes holding Currat and watched while he curled up in a ball on his right side. He made no sound and his eyes remained closed. Small amounts of dried and fresh blood pooled on the table corresponding with the puncture wounds, except near the small of Currat's back. There, copious amounts of blood spread across the table, freed from the dam created by Currat's body. He expected Currat to bleed as if he had suffered a severed limb in more than that one place. Ursel gagged and finally lost the fight with his stomach.

After he'd finished, Ursel wiped his mouth, freed the woman, and held his finger to his lips while he removed the gag. She put her hands to her face and wept. Ursel took her hand and she looked up at him through tears. He whispered. "There are more of us downstairs and behind the inn; you're safe now."

She quietly said, "They have always left at least two downstairs with my husband and daughter. Who are you?"

"I'm called Ursel. I need to get this man out of here. He has gone through all this pain for our people. We cannot let him die. Can you walk?"

"Yes. They tied the ropes tight, but I never lost feeling in my legs or feet. I'm Surelle."

"Surelle, can you find a cloth big enough for me to wrap him in and bandage his wounds?

"Yes, I have a large bedcloth that should work."

"Go, the rear is clear. One is dead in the room closest to the back, and one in the room next to the stairwell. I'll tend him until you return." Ursel did not worry about sounds made up here any more. The downstairs had quieted within the past few minutes, and he knew it made no difference at this point. They had won! If they had lost, they would be dead by now.

Currat remained curled up in a ball, making no sound when Ursel gently took his shoulder. He just cringed, and tried to curl himself into a tighter space.

Ursel spoke softly into his hear. "Currat, I'm a friend. Delan sent me. I must get you away. Will you let me help you?" His hand gently massaged the battered man's shoulder.

"Delan sent you?" Currat croaked.

"Yes, Delan sent me." Ursel found water, and Currat drank it with small gasps of pain.

Surelle returned, her arms filled with a heavy bedcloth. Ursel gently rolled Currat to one side and placed the folded bedclothes next to him. Currat gritted his teeth when Ursel rolled him back onto the of cloth to his other side. Ursel pulled the bedclothes through, covered him, and stood back to let Currat recover from moving him. The battered man tightened into his ball of pain again and cried out, as Ursel felt his own tears of frustration against his cheeks.

Heavy footsteps sounded on the stairs, and a moment later Jafon Demlish came through the doorway. He stared at the table, color draining from his face when he saw the bloody rods and the dark patches on the bedclothes. Ursel could not help smiling grimly when the biggest and strongest man in the group, except for him, fainted.

Surelle went to Jafon's assistance as Jadel and Risa also rushed into the room.

* * *

CURRAT felt agony through every part of his body. He raged at the things done to him by men he had known for years. He curled tighter, trying to pull all of himself into a ball as tight as possible until he realized that effort was only causing more pain. Relaxation merely exchanged old pains for new while sounds faded and sweet darkness fell around him in the tightest ball yet.

* * *

URSEL folded the top of the bedclothes around Currat and picked him up as if holding a babe. They went down the inn's rear stairway to the waiting coach and rode slowly to the ship to make the ride smoother. Zack started to look at the damage done, and Ursel shook his head.

Zack sat back with a sigh and put his hand on Ursel's shoulder. "You did well." His voice carried almost as much pain as was on Currat's face.

Ursel carried Currat from the coach to the captain's cabin, where the healer waited for him. Briggs appeared at once with a question in his eyes.

"He lives," Ursel answered.

43

WATHDURE had suffered one of the worst days he could ever remember. He was two messengers short, and could not use any of his army for that purpose. They no longer retained mental capacity beyond simple directions like run and kill.

Pain seared him in molten streams of fire. His shields against such an attack shattered under the overwhelming force. He writhed in pain until he could build another shield against it, allowing only a small part through. An hour passed before he had drawn enough strength from the void to reinforce the shielding and cut the pain off completely.

Reaching out with his consciousness to the void, Wathdure pulled all he could from the dark pool. Absorbing that much power in so short a time generated severe pain. It did not hinder him. Another hour passed before he felt confident enough to lower his shields and investigate the backlash's signature. The familiar feel of Dalsom's manipulations had disappeared completely. Nothing remained on the ethers either, and he felt nothing on the higher planes he traveled. Wathdure initiated contact with the dark void again, and knew immediately Dalsom's spirit had escaped that world, too.

He cursed loudly. He didn't do that often, and was glad he had broken his contacts with all but the physical world of man. *Dalsom repented of his deeds, and now formed a part of the Creator,* Wathdure thought with disgust.

Too far from his nexus of power and weakened more than he had first thought, Wathdure did not have the power needed for both major works, and to keep control of the many things that depended on his power in Ozlid. He sighed and then cursed again.

If only I could work from the Gray Plane!

44

URSEL watched from the *Flying Dolphin's* stern as Darmon negotiated the coach from the quay toward the main road leading to Hampton and their king. He felt the longboats impact the deck. Brisk winds and a strong current pushed the brigantine faster than he'd ever imagined a ship could travel.

He stood beside Zack and shook from pent-up memories released into sharp focus. He looked down at his hand and watched it shake. Zack grasped it in both of his and turned Ursel toward him. "You did well. You destroyed an evil that held a death grip on men."

Ursel calmed after a bit, and gripping the railing tightly with both hands. "The man I killed, the one who did those things to Currat, thanked me for killing him. He invoked the name of the Great Creator before he died, and his insane eyes cleared. I have never imagined such evil as I felt there. Sondek told me another man also smiled briefly before he died."

Ursel started when a strong hand grasped his shoulder. Briggs said, "You're a brave man, Ursel, and you probably don't yet feel that confidence inside yet, but it is there."

Zack continued, "You saw more than any man should see. You are young, and it will follow you. See that you recognize it for what it is, and put it in its proper place. Otherwise, it can warp you beyond recovery. A man from across the seas, an Ozlidian and a Hamptorian, worked together to fight evil and won, for the moment. Now, go to the galley and get something to eat, and then get some rest. Captain Briggs and I'll still be available when you want to talk."

Ursel slowly walked to the forecastle ladder, but he stood taller as he went. He honestly did not know if the salty moisture he tasted formed from sea spray, tears, or both, and he did not care.

* * *

CAPTAIN Briggs watched the big man's retreating frame. "The healer said he never saw anything like it. He's amazed that Currat remained sane."

Zack looked out to sea, his expression grim. "He may not be. It's still too early to make that determination."

Briggs looked surprised. "You have seen this before?"

"I saw men who endured too much pain, and afterward, they became less than men. That involved evil too, the same evil that Wathdure used to plague Ozlid and its neighboring kingdoms; I fear that evil encompasses all evil, and it will again attack the Seven Realms as it did two millennia ago. Does not evil of all kinds come from the Dark's Source? I fear, too, that the human fodder Wathdure plans to use in war will come from the three kingdoms and who knows where else.

"As to your question, I saw the results of bandits and others that captured and mistreated or tortured their victims. Nothing compared with this. I saw men fight and sink into depression from the men they killed, like Ursel is going through now. I believe Currat will recover. He has the necessary strength to do so. If I can get him to High Healer Sternwood in Stonefire before his condition declines too much, I'm sure he'll recuperate. It will pain me deeply if he does not come from this whole and sane, although it will take time. My wounds, although not quite as bad as his, took a year to heal."

Zack stood silent and motionless, looking out to sea. Captain Briggs did not ask what was going through his mind. A few moments later, he spoke slowly, "Forgive me, Captain, but I think I'll take the same advice you gave Ursel. Wake me at any sign of trouble. Oh, and thank you for having the healer stay aboard for the trip. Good night," Zack looked up at the noonday sun, "or rather, good day."

Briggs nodded and watched Zack walk haltingly with the help of a cane toward the ladder leading below.

* * *

URSEL drew a rod from the scabbard of his long knife and handed it to the healer. Currat cringed involuntarily at the sight of it, but managed a weak smile at the concern in Ursel's voice. "Watch over him. He's a brave man and we owe him a great debt. All of Hamptor owes him a debt."

Ursel walked briskly down the companionway before the healer could ask any questions. He looked down at the steel rod, and Currat saw him recognize it as the implement that caused the damage to his patient. He quickly concealed it from his patient's sight.

Currat met the healer's gaze and nodded weakly as the healer shivered, as if ice dripped down his spine. The healer addressed him, modulated his voice into a gentle tone that differed from the usual, brusque way he spoke.

"Master Currat, there is no permanent damage to your muscles. You will bleed off and on for a day or two. I have seen such a wound to a testicle once before when a predator cat bit a farmer. The cat's fang didn't penetrate completely through and your injury might take a while longer to heal. Your wounds must be bathed twice a day, which won't be pleasant, but it's most necessary. Your fingernail will probably become black, and another may form. The nail lifted from its bed, but did not die, and if we're lucky, it may not be necessary for a new nail to form. I don't know which to expect yet. The man who did this to you must have kept the implements he used—" The healer looked at the rod still in his hand and shivered again. "—very clean. There is no sign of infection. While you were unconscious, I probed your wounds with herbs;

I don't believe that the procedure needs repeating. Master Stand informed me that there are excellent healers in Elizabethville, and no doubt he's correct."

"The small barbs from the rod rubbed against bone like you told me. It will take time to heal the bones and the adjoining muscles. In the meantime, the movement of your muscles against the sharp ridges cut into the bone will be painful. Your ribs and your finger will have to be wrapped tightly. There is a danger in this in that you must not cut off the blood circulation to those areas. You must loosen the wrappings if you feel any numbness, and you must see a healer if you see any sign of infection."

The healer cleared his throat. "I am afraid that your testicle won't heal. In the few cases that I have seen where one has been injured so, it shrivels up and is useless. It won't cause any harm if it remains within the sac. However, should it swell or discharge pus or blood, you must see a healer in all haste. You will still be able to have children, if that is your desire.

"There is not much more I can tell you. You have the paste for pain, and I have explained everything to Lady Doris. She has performed in a most competent way caring for Master Stand." The healer leaned against the doorway to the small cabin. "Are there any questions that you have?"

Currat's tongue still tasted the paste the healer used. He had drank all the diluted paste in the warm tea, and now felt numb and sleepy. "How is Zack?" he mumbled.

The healer's obvious experience with groggy patients allowed him to answer right away. "He's growing stronger every day. His recovery will be much faster than yours, and I feel you both have many good years ahead of you. I'm sure of that. I'll wrap your wounds and then leave you to rest and sleep. Oh, no, that's not quite right. I'll not wrap your testicle." His chuckle sounded forced and self-satisfying to Currat.

Currat settled into a soft place in his mind and sleep

reached up for him. He would not remember his last mental challenge: *Leave my balls alone, you old windbag.* His own chuckle quietly trailed off as the potion took effect and he slept.

* * *

DORIS periodically checked on Currat, Zack, and Ursel as they slept from mid afternoon until dawn the next morning. She tended to both injured men, continuing to tend Zack's side wound, which had healed to a thin, white scar. She felt for any swelling or pain from pressure that might indicate infection lurking about, but found none.

The knife wound in his shoulder had healed completely within two days, creating surprised comments from Zack's companions until he asked her not to discuss it any more. She had no problem following that request. *They scarcely believed me as it was,* she thought.

She added Currat to her list of wounded. He grew more and more embarrassed about the dressing changes and bathing; Doris ignored his various excuses not to let her attend him and went on with her work as if he hadn't said anything at all. Later, Zack told to her that Currat had said she'd a good job of not hurting him any further, and had made sure his wounds stayed clean.

A few days into their trip, she watched in surprise while Zack walked out on the deck with Ursel carrying Currat beside him. Zack and Ursel were dressed in clean clothes, compliments of Yasho. Currat was dressed in loose-fitting trousers and one of Ursel's large shirts. With a smile, she headed across the deck toward them. Her smile deepened when she saw the new color in Currat and Zack's faces. Ursel looked pleased to be helping.

"I understand that we'll have over a three-week coach ride from Elizabethville to the Spires," she said quietly. "I don't want to see one spot of false modesty from anyone who needs my attention on the trip." She eased her tone. "I bathed Master Zack after he suffered wounds." Zack blushed. "Master Currat, I bathed you last night while you remained unconscious." Currat gave her a happy smile, and did not blush. *After all,* she concluded, *if I saw Zack, I saw Currat.*

"Are you two sure you're not long lost twins?" Doris asked at the knowing smile on Currat's face.

Zack chuckled and shook his head.

"And young Master Ursel here probably does not know it, but I bathed him when he caught the fever a few years ago, and his mother needed to be away for a day." Ursel's face turned scarlet instantly, and he sputtered something undecipherable. "My point is that we will be fine, and Rachel and I are excited to seek out our new home," Doris concluded.

A moment later, a strong voice called down from the crow's nest, "Land, ho!"

Rachel raced to her mother's side and started recounting, for the tenth time, her experiences aboard ship. Doris had heard it all before, and smiled as her daughter lapsed into her own world, relating it to them again. A few crewmen and the captain had showed her a few things and told her how they navigated by the stars. Currat, Ursel and Zack smiled appropriately as she rattled on.

Doris felt pleased as Rachel became caught up in telling her story; it did not take long before amazement completely took its place. She also looked out over the port city of Elizabethville that indeed, was much larger than Hagan's End.

* * *

TRUE to his word, the captain had navigated the trip in excellent time, easily the fastest trip between the two lands Zack had ever made. He supposed the strong winds might have had something to do with their speedy crossing, although, he could not recall being on a better ship.

Captain Briggs approached when Zack pulled the small spyglass from his pocket and looked out at the horizon. "Here, use mine, it's bigger." Zack handed the Captain the small spyglass. Briggs put to his eye and started. "Great Creator!" He alternated looking through the large one and then the small one several times, before returning the small one to Zack.

"We shaved a full third off our time between Hagan's End and Elizabethville," he said. "This is the best ship I have ever sailed. Will you be seeing that High Lord Wells?"

"It's possible," Zack replied. "I'm sure I can get a message to him."

"Please give him my humble thanks."

"I'll do that, captain."

45

ZACK watched men polishing brass and washing the deck while they disembarked. Spellbinder and Snowflake both pranced off the ship and the crewman tethered them to the forward line; they looked relieved.

Zack walked down the gangplank with Doris on one side and Rachel on the other. He still used his cane, and Doris watched him closely. Ursel came next, carrying Currat. He gently placed him down on a crate and stood beside him, supporting his weight. Currat slumped in a reaction Zack had noticed before after he'd became a little groggy from his last mug of doctored tea.

Zack found a guardsman and spoke to him away from the others for several minutes. The guard ran off, and a half-hour later a coach pulled onto the pier. Doris and Rachel's belongings went first, with guardsmen tying them to the top of the coach with a case for their everyday needs strapped to the rear.

Zack and Currat received help aboard, and the coach headed toward the garrison gates. Doris smiled while she watched Rachel enjoying every minute of her adventure. Zack smiled at both women's delight. After arriving at the garrison, he arranged for midmeal, and watched as they all ate as if their appetites had returned in full force.

* * *

ZACK had been gone for nearly two hours to meet with the garrison's commander while a healer went over Currat's wounds. He watched in amazement while the man removed the splints and guards from his fingers without additional pain. Grasping a small, gray stone that

335

hung around his neck, he closed his eyes and appeared to concentrate deeply. Moments later, the throbbing pain ceased, and the healer replaced the splints and guards to his three wounded fingers.

"The pain will return if they're bumped or touched without the guards, but should fade over the next day or so. They will heal much faster if they're not disturbed. I suggest you wrap your hand in a soft cloth before you sleep. The nails will recover. I have sealed them in their beds again."

Currat's surprise left him speechless. The healer rested for a moment and started again, placing his hands over the puckered holes left by the rods. Currat felt strange sensations while the healer's hand went from one wound to another. His pain decreased at each wound's site, and completely disappeared from his testicle. He also felt calm for the first time in days, relieved from the tension and anxiety caused by the pain. "I . . . I don't know how to repay you . . ."

The healer only smiled and went to assist his fellow healer treating Zack while he made his requests in the commander's office.

* * *

CALBRIS had another unusual appearance at the garrison. He made detailed notes while Zack reported on his trip to the new garrison commander. He justified the need for the coach and that his visitors had a legitimate reason for being in the country, and assured the commander of reimbursement by the Spires for its use.

As the interrogation continued, Zack became tired and upset at the commander's stubborn, arrogant attitude. Finally, he looked at Calbris. The commander's questions stopped abruptly, and he was shocked when Zack wrote out code words that required the commander's complete cooperation by the order of the Zenith Lord, followed by Calbris writing a different set of codes with the highest level of importance. They disliked using the codes, and felt the commander should have cooperated without their use. Zack stared into the commander's eyes.

"Did not your predecessor advise you that I might need your cooperation?" Zack asked.

The commander looked startled. "Yes, but I need to reassure myself of your needs.

"*Rest assured,* Commander, I'll let the Zenith Lord know of your cooperation."

The commander left his office looking deflated.

A healer arrived, conferred a moment with his colleague, and then placed his hand over the scarred tissue on Zack's lower abdomen. He felt the graystone's weak power while the healer closed his eyes in deep concentration, then felt several twinges before the healer withdrew his hand.

The healer spoke quietly, his brow moist with sweat. "I have realigned the tissue into its proper location. You should have no further pain, but you should exercise slowly. Strenuous exercise could cause you to reinjure yourself. Take it slow, and you will completely recover in a few weeks. The bruise to your hipbone is deep, and will take longer. You should continue to use the cane until you can stand straight without pain." Zack thanked the healers and offered coins that they both refused.

The healers left at a nod from Zack, leaving him alone with Calbris. "Wathdure is part of the same evil we fought two millennia ago. He knew about the Dark Stone that Mountglen wears. I get chills when I think of the time I spent before Wathdure. There is great power there and he uses it."

Calbris reflected on what Zack said for a moment. "You may be right. Something is happening at the Spires. I received word it is sealed, and I've never heard of that happening before. The Zenith sends messages, and I'm sure he's safe. I'm at a loss to name an event of such importance that would close the Spires." Calbris appeared in deep concentration for the moment.

Possibly weighing the events, Zack thought while he watched Calbris shake himself loose from his musings. Calbris continued with crispness so removed from his befuddled drunk's persona that it still amazed Zack.

"I received a message last night from Gaz stating that upon your arrival I was to aid you in any way to speed your trip to the Spires. A troop of thirty will escort you. The officer in charge knows you outrank him, and he received the word to facilitate your speed and not his comfort." Calbris smiled. "He's a good man, you won't have any trouble. I'll send the messages that you're on your way, and that you carry information of the highest urgency. That ought to put a fire under Gaz."

Zack chuckled. "Calbris, you're going to give Gaz a death attack one of these days."

"How can I? The man is made of steel."

* * *

CURRAT arrived in Ursel's arms, dressed in lightweight, and oversized clothing. Ursel gently placed him in the largest coach he had ever seen. A strange-looking man in dirty clothes walked with Zack to the coach and they said their farewells to each other.

Currat noticed through the window that men added supplies to the coach. He admired the garrison's construction and the professionalism of their escort without comment.

* * *

THE escort's handsome officer instantly enthralled Rachel. She believed her mother might like an officer.

* * *

DORIS marveled at the grand coach they would be riding in. She watched Zack stride toward it, standing straighter, and with the confidence she remembered from

338

when they had first met. She knew he might still use the cane when tired, but not at that moment.

She felt his warmth and caring, buried deep inside him. She had considered him romantically once or twice, his attractive features and appealing personality plain to see. Not many men possessed the charm and caring attitude she found under his somewhat brusque façade. However, she had lost one husband already, and did not care to lose another. His occupation did not bode well for a long life, nor would she suffer through long absences without knowing his condition. She was sure there would be more suitable eligible men in Stonefire.

* * *

THE coach soon rolled through the garrison's gates onto the long road leading from Elizabethville. Only Zack noticed three large birds fly from the garrison's highest tower toward the northeast.

He kept his dire deliberations from showing on his face: *What could be serious enough to close the Spires? Wathdure is of the same evil that attacked us two millennia ago and according to Duval's documentation, his power is growing. Are we ready for another war? Is Mountglen involved?*

Zack left off his dark thoughts when Rachel squealed with joy while looking out the window. He looked at the seaport and smiled. The *Flying Dolphin* made for the open sea under full sail.

* * *

HOURS later, the coach's passengers all slept, except for Zack. Captain Briggs' words to Ursel kept running through his mind. *I did the exact thing Briggs warned him not to do. I let the evil that took my loved ones from my life eat away at me until my humanity became as much a victim as my family.* He looked at Currat, sleeping quietly. *Wathdure's evil is not all there is. Life continues. Currat found truth and a way to fight Wathdure at a tremendous cost.*

Ursel's voice filtered down as he talked with the driver. Zack's deliberations turned to the Hamptorians. *Ursel found confidence, valor, and renewed his feeling of manhood. He presses his cause to fight for his land. Will the war come before he can realize his goals? Briggs, Yasho and Durton fought against evil with men drawn into the common good. Will the Seven Realms fight as hard?*

Zack's thoughts flew back to the strange night when he'd received the knife wound and the subsequent miraculous healing. *My loves, I don't know if you can hear my thoughts, or not. I see now, the importance of your words and I feel the impact of being a whole man again. My companions have shown me the trust; friendship, courage and loyalty that I foolishly thought no longer existed.*

He looked over at Currat. *Yes, you have been my mirror, and it reflected my heart.* He remembered the twins back in town and looking at the other man now, he understood them. His love for Currat had deepened, and now he saw its full scope. Warmth and contentment flooded through him for the first time in years. A ray of sunshine sparkled on the coach's brass fittings, and for a brief second, Zack saw a golden orb form. He smiled, lay back his head again the seat, and found rest.

46

WATHDURE responded to Shadure's call and traveled to the Gray Plane. He reported the readiness of his necromantic army and nothing else. "They'll be ready in time to attack the Seven Realms."

"Keep them at the ready. Our powers grow, but so will all the Stones. We must discover how strong the Zenith has become, and if he has access to the powerful Stones. Until our power reaches higher levels, we will bide our time and I plan to make full use of the fool, Mountglen."

GLOSSARY OF TERMS

Pebble: Led by a Skimmer – ten men

Rock: Led by a Rocker, – thirty men (first level officer)

Trass: Led by a Lieutenant – ninety men

Scree: Led by a Thrower – two hundred and seventy men

Small Boulder: Led by Gal – six hundred men

Boulder: Led by a Gal – eight hundred and ten men plus forty support personnel

Tor: Led by a Looker – twenty-five hundred men plus fifty support personnel

Mount: Led by an Apex – fifty-one hundred men plus one hundred support personnel

ACKNOWLEDGEMENTS

I once wondered why an author acknowledged so many people. Now, I know! I'll start with my writer's group founded by Sam Barone who brought a talented group together, although to my dismay, the group is disbanded: Sharon Anderson, Deborah J. Ledford and Thelma Rea. These folks gave of their talent, friendship and time. Besides that, they are nice.

And then there are the editors. One thinks they have written a masterpiece until an editor gets their head wrapped around a manuscript. Nonetheless, they found the writing, character and plot flaws I never thought of while writing my first novel. Even with college training, this craft has a huge learning curve. I had a fine editor on this novel; John Helfers is a well-known editor and writer.

Fellow authors have given support, time and friendship. Chief among these is L. E. Modesitt, Jr. He has become a friend and good advisor of authorship over the years. Paul Genesse has been supportive and become another friend. Michael Stackpole gave me good advice and several tips about not only my novel but also the publishing industry.

Other friends in the industry have always been supportive and thoughtful in their counsel: Colleen Confit and Krista Wallace are but two of these. For several years I've attended the World Fantasy Conventions held in a different city each year. Nearly all of the authors, editors and other industry professionals are approachable and helpful.

I have been fortunate to know and learn from all these fine people. I wish them all the best in life and careers. Of course, the minute this manuscript goes to press, so to say, I'll remember someone who should have been included!

AUTHOR BIO

Born in Atlanta Georgia, Mr. Cox lived there until he joined the United States Air Force and served in Texas, France and Germany. Writing is his fourth career. He started in large mainframe computers, and then moved on to become a real estate broker. He returned to college to obtain a nursing degree and practiced as a Registered Nurse and also began writing his first novel, which he stated became his most rewarding work. He lives in Phoenix, Arizona with a large Great Dane that thinks he's a lap dog!

THE ZENITH LORD

Mid-Summer, 2014

Jarod Greatstone, the Zenith Lord of the Seven Realms, must face the Dark's Source in battle as the minions of the Dark gain power. Its existence confirmed by the Zenith's Spy as the same evil the first Zenith Lord defeated two millennia ago. Through the use of the Major Stones, Jarod starts to build his army and explores the Gray Plane while dealing with murder, treason and personal loss.

He brings others into the fight: Apex Kyle Byrne, Captain of the Guard; The Holy One; Segquo, Leader of the High Desert People; The Protector, The Lords and Angels of Death and Deathcats to name a few. Be ready for a great adventure in *The Zenith Lord!*

THE ZENITH'S WARRIOR

Fall, 2014

The Zenith's Warrior, Lenzel from the Clan of the Cat finds a cache of Stones used to fight the Dark's Source. He is trained by the Zenith Lord's men and fights the Dark's hideous minions before searching for other caches of Stones with his own Compressed Stone. He continues with the help of the Maidens of Desert's Ire, the Zenith's Guard and the Zenith's spies to complete his mission, facing creatures of the Dark, betrayal, hardship and murder.

SPECIAL PREVIEW OF

THE ZENITH LORD

BOOK 2 OF THE ZENITH SERIES
EPIC FANTASY by DAMEON COX

1

SECOND only to the Dark One, Shadure's presence floated near the ceiling of the opulent room, watching the lone occupant of an immense bed encased by canopy and drapes tied back at the four bedposts with gold inlay swirling around in a leaf pattern from floor to top. He had surveyed the space earlier, a large bedchamber in the grandest of keeps, with side rooms for both clothes and refreshment. A suite made for exhibition by the vain and pretentious, yet rarely seen by more than one person. Richly appointed furniture with more gold inlay, a walk-in fireplace high enough for a tall man and as deep, built-in bookcases filled to overflowing, overstuffed plush chairs, and a large, marble-topped table formed a study area and more than fulfilled its arrogant purpose. The few candles that burned increased its illusion of size.

* * *

THE giant bed swallowed Eric, High Lord Mountglen's towering, thin frame except for his overly-long feet that made peaks in the bedcloths. As he settled into large pillows waiting for sleep, his musings drifted to the coach ride earlier that day. He remembered the children waving from a field. The children always waved. He wondered

1

why; he never waved back. *The innocence of children, was I ever that innocent?*

No, his memory did not journey that far back. *My spirit belongs to Dark's Source, with all the pain and horror that entails, if indeed it exists.* He wished no Dark One or his Source existed. His long, slender fingers automatically grasped the Dark Stone hanging from his neck by a gold chain. Its power flowed, relaxing him, and a wave of pleasure seeped through him until it became ecstasy, and then ecstasy approached pain in the degree of its manifestation, pulling him into sleep and dreams of pleasure.

The dream started normally enough, except for his awareness that it was a dream. That sent fear through his mind; he had never experienced that phenomenon before. He floated in a void of dark shadows that churned in roiling currents around him. A single idea surged through his consciousness. *"You belong to the Dark One and to me!"*

Mountglen sat straight up in bed, awake and shaking with a burning sensation on his chest. He pulled the Dark Stone from his sleepcloth, made barely visible by the dim candlelight and clutched it for comfort. His hand burned with its unusual heat, but he did not let it go.

Darkness returned to his senses as a disembodied voice filled his mind. *"Your use of the Dark Stone called me. You have used the Dark Stone to pleasure yourself and to provide your success in many things."*

Mountglen's words, a barely audible, ragged whisper, came slowly. "I am Eric, High Lord Mountglen. I have not summoned anyone!" Fear surged through him.

Mountglen watched swirling shadows and currents coalesce into a tall, dark figure; the head, shrouded under a cowl, pulled in the little surrounding light and dissolved it in the blackness within. Shadure's presence gave the room the same feeling of Mountglen's dream: a void.

Shadure's deep, rumbling voice hissed with disdain *"High Lord? You are nothing without the Dark Stone! The*

2

Stone's influence has given you capabilities, and you have prospered by them."

Mountglen's reply projected equal disdain; "I am ruler of Mountglen, descendent of the Heroes of the Seven Realms, and I know you not!"

The dark robe's long sleeve barely stirred, but a searing pain gripped Mountglen's arm, traveling slowly through his chest to the rest of his limbs, and then exploded in his head. His back arched in spasm. He fought to scream, his mouth gaping open, but no sound came, and he had never felt such agony.

As quickly as it has come, the pain vanished, leaving him gasping for breath. He slumped back against the pillows, his body trembling and his strength gone.

Mountglen cringed and pushed himself farther back into the mountain of pillows. Words came to his mind and ears at the same time, creating a disturbing feeling of deep power. *"You hold the Dark Stone. You used its power to sow pain and ruin on your adversaries, and gained great benefit for yourself as well. You murmured your desires to the Dark Stone, and it heard you, and your avarice and lust for power became fulfilled.*

"I, too, heard your pathetic pleadings," the dark figure said. *"I control many forces in the void and have considerable power in your world. Through your dreams and desires, I know you for the true man you are. Your heart is as black as the Dark Stone you wear. You have murdered, raped, thieved, and borne false witness to achieve your own ends, and still that is not enough. You want what is not yours: the lands, titles, power, and wealth of your nephew, the Zenith Lord."* The twin voices of mind and hearing became softer but even more menacing. *"You summoned me through the Dark Stone's use as if you had called out my name! Did you think your deeds went without consequence? Your spirit belongs to Dark's Source, and to me!"*

Mountglen's mind raced. *How can this thing cause pain so great? Pain and ruin* . . . Agony spread through his body again, jerking him upright. He threw his arms up in a

3

useless attempt to defend against the indefensible and pleaded, "Please . . . no more! Just tell me what you desire." The pain left him with a soreness that racked his body. Mountglen's color faded from its normal whiteness into pallor.

"Desire? I desire your service to the Dark One and to me. I already have your spirit for all time. What else is there?" Mountglen whimpered as the eerie voice continued. *"What more can you offer except service? Your hate and loathing reached me through the Dark Stone, and I have felt it for a long time. The Dark Stone's power is increasing, and now I am able to come to you and make myself known."*

Mountglen's priorities fell into order, staying alive went to the top of the list. His voice became soft, calculating. "You wish to . . . make yourself known to me?"

"Do you acknowledge that your spirit belongs to the Dark One and me?"

Mountglen yielded a low moan of finality from Shadure's words. His mind shook off the thoughts generated in his head, and a single revelation took hold. *This is a negotiation!* Mountglen's reply was flat. "Yes."

"What do you know about the Dark Stone you wear?"

Mountglen forced confidence into his voice that he did not feel. "My father gave it to me. It has brought me pleasure."

"It has brought you much more than pleasure!" Shadure roared. *"It has given you the intuitive feelings that have made you successful in all your dealings!"*

Mountglen rebelled at the thought that his successes were not truly his own, but dared not interrupt.

"Now, through the Dark Stone and through me, you may earn even greater rewards. It will require much service to the Dark One and to me. Success and failure will provide appropriate rewards beyond your petty thinking. You will be the Zenith Lord in your world, and hold even more power in the void when you journey to me. It is your choice. But, you will not have the Dark Stone for your

comfort if you make the wrong choice. Do you remember when you last gave up the Stone?"

Mountglen knew he was defeated. He could no longer live without the Dark Stone's pleasures. He had tried, once, locking the stone away. He felt mounting despair for four days before hurriedly putting its chain back around his neck. His abject sigh accompanied his cluttered thoughts. *How can this Stone do so much?* He opened his hand and looked at his object of ruin. "It is the same since coming into my keeping; it feels no different."

"No!" The simulacrum shimmered beside Mountglen's bed. *"Fool, do you think the Stone physically changes while its power grows? The Dark Stone you wear is now strong enough for me to come into your world that I may help you obtain your dreams."*

Mountglen's voice grew incredulous. "What is your price? What is it you want in return?"

"I already have your spirit—it belongs to Dark's Source and will be mine to use in the void as I see fit." Mountglen struggled to keep from shouting obscenities. *"I can see into your world through the Dark Stone until that time. I will feed on the power of those you dispatch who do not belong to Light's Source. That and your soul are payments enough. I require nothing if you refuse my offer; the joy of your eternal pain will be mine soon enough. Your refusal means nothing to you if a future without the Dark Stone and your coming torment contents you. Believe me, the pain you felt is nothing more than a pinprick in the void."*

Shadure's voice changed to hold all the womanly enchantments in Mountglen's licentious dreams. *"But you need not feel any pain at all. You may feel great pleasure instead. It is your choice."*

Mountglen gained some bravado. "When will I receive what you promise?" He might have seen a smile form within the cowl, if he only knew how to channel the Dark Stone's power.

"You must be patient. There are few with the power I have

obtained under my Master. My supremacy will increase over time as yours will through me." The black form floated to the end of the bed, expanding to fill the space from the top of the mattress to the canopy, ten feet high. *"First, you must freely give me your oath. Your afterlife belongs to the Dark One. Service to the Dark One through me is your only chance of a reward in the void. Fail, and you will know torment you never imagined in both worlds. Your only hope now is through me."*

The form reduced itself to Mountglen's dimensions and floated over him at an angle: mere feet away from his head, and the hem of his cloak no more than an inch from the bedcloths over his feet. Its tone changed to a soft purring, its words now flowed like oily scum across a fetid pond. *"You may call me Shadure. Let my name fill your mind, think only of me. I will hear and come to you. I only offer this once. You must decide quickly."*

"You expect me to decide . . ." The Stone vanished from its gold frame. Dull aches came from Mountglen's joints; his vision blurred, and his head throbbed. Loneliness, despair, and grief filled him while his mind sunk into a black pool of horror. His breaths became short and shallow and stabs of fire lanced through his chest. *Is this to be my life without the Dark Stone?* Mountglen's mind settled on one imperative. *Rationalizations no longer matter! I must have it back!*

With his first contracted murder, Mountglen had resigned himself long ago that, if there truly was an afterlife, he belonged to the Dark One. Payment for his deeds was irreversible if the Dark One existed, or so he had believed. Now . . . perhaps not. "You have my oath."

Shadure's black form shimmered with satisfaction. *"And you have mine. I will aid you in your desires. I am pleased that you have joined with me in this effort to insure our mutual goals."*

Now his voice exuded command. *"There is something you must do quickly."* Enmity bathed both the tones of Shadure's words in Mountglen's mind and the sound that eerily floated to his ears. *"Soon, there will be another Greatstone born. You must stop this birth for both our interests. This child will be the undisputed heir to the Dais. You must do as I order if you ever wish to have the Seven Realms for yourself. You have agents in Stonefire. Use them for this. There must be no link back to you.*

"It may do great harm if my existence is known before we are ready. Remember the price of my displeasure. Remember also the sensual pleasure I bring you through the Dark Stone, and the great riches and power you have and will gain from fulfilling service to the Dark One and to me."

The voice slid to a low, throaty purr. *"You are a man of action—do not call me for unimportant reasons. Grasp the Stone when you need me and call the void with your mind. I will come."*

Mountglen started from the sudden emptiness he felt as Shadure relinquished his mind. The Dark Stone's mild heat again warmed his hand, and the maladies of age receded to nothing again.

He sat up in bed, wide-eyed and sweating. His sleepcloth clung to his damp, bony chest. He remembered the dream vividly and wondered *could it be other than a dream?* Terrible aches coursed throughout his muscles, the event's only evidence.

"Shadure is right," Mountglen whispered. "It will complicate the fulfillment of my desires if that fool Jarod Greatstone whelps a brat." He leaned back against his pillows. "I'd much rather be the tormentor than the tormented in the afterlife."

His only remaining question came from a lifetime of deceit. *Could it have been only a dream?* Sharp pain soared through his arm before the query completely formed, not as severe as before, but enough for him to cry out and gasp for air. Blackness swirled around him. He felt its presence in front of his face, and cringed in involuntary obeisance. The pain drained from his arm while he heard a sinister laugh echo in his mind.

The light knock at his door caused a frown. ". . .

Enter."

A guard ventured cautiously into the room. "High Lord, I passed by and heard a cry. Is something wrong?"

Mountglen's cold stare froze the guard in place. He strained to force words out. ". . . No trouble. Send Thord to me at once." The guard bowed himself from the room, and closed the door; he looked relieved.

Within minutes, the bedchamber door opened. Mountglen watched his man glide across the room. *How can someone so large glide with such stealth and grace?* Thord's scars over heavily muscled arms, face, and many more hidden beneath his leathers added to his already fierce countenance. The cruelest scar began at the corner of his mouth and ended at his right ear. His eyes held the promise of pain to anyone foolish enough to challenge him. His deep, grating voice reverberated around the room. "High Lord?"

Mountglen's throat suffered from his unuttered screams as if they had burst forth. His vocal cords felt like they might break with tension, and his first few words came out sounding like a cock's spur against slate. "Thord, I have an important task for you to fulfill."

He rose from the bed and walked past the table to the bookshelves behind. "Light candles for the table." Thord did his master's bidding without a change of expression or comment. Mountglen walked slower than usual, feeling hints of pain in every step. He selected a book and returned to the table where Thord lounged to the right of his chair.

Mountglen sat and carefully opened the book to reveal a hidden compartment. He removed its contents, a small, dark green bottle with a cork sealed in wax. Thord's face grimaced in recognition. His eyes stared with interest, and the left side of his mouth curled in a gruesome smile; he leaned forward with new alertness.

"Here is what you are to do . . .